THE TRUTH ABOUT DEATH AND DYING

THE TRUTH ABOUT DEATH

A NOVEL

AND DYING

RUI UMEZAWA

DOUBLEDAY CANADA

Doubleday Canada and colophon are trademarks.

National Library of Canada Cataloguing in Publication Data

Umezawa, Rui, 1959–

The truth about death and dying / Rui Umezawa.

ISBN 0-385-65908-3

I. Title.

PS8591.M49T78 2002   C813'.54   C2002-902057-3
PR9199.3.U535T78 2002

Jacket image: Christopher J. Boyle/Photonica
Jacket design: CS Richardson
Text design: Carla Kean
Printed and bound in the USA

Published in Canada by
Doubleday Canada, a division of
Random House of Canada Limited

Visit Random House of Canada Limited's website: www.randomhouse.ca

BVG 10 9 8 7 6 5 4 3 2 1

IN LOVING MEMORY OF HIROOMI UMEZAWA

SHOJI

TOSHI'S FATHER DIED WITH TUBES SPROUTING FROM his body. Shoji had always been thin, but now, he looked ready to break. He lay unmoving, but certainly not at peace. His chest rose and fell regularly, in time with the rubber-and-metal pump whooshing and shushing beside his head. From the bottom of his baby blue hospital robe, his bare legs protruded like bread sticks. They were terribly uneven because of some freakish accident during the war, a very long time ago. Too long to remember. The right leg was straight and unblemished, the left twisted and scarred. When Toshi pictured his father in his mind, Shoji was always limping.

Toshi let free a sigh as heavy as the world. A nurse hovered at the door. The staff had noticed that whenever the lumbering young Japanese fellow was left alone in a room for longer than a minute, every monitor would start making loud noises. They never knew that the commotion sounded to Toshi like a call to arms. It gave him fabulous goosebumps.

Rainwater was tapping on the windows. There were days in Milwaukee when it felt as though the rain had been falling forever. After the family doctor had told them about Shoji's cancer, the

1

remedies started coming from all directions: Chinese medicine, prayers, ads in tabloid newspapers and friends calling to say they knew someone who was cured just by eating lots of oranges. Or was it grapefruit? Oranges or grapefruit. Who knew which? Or was it all just baloney?

"But Toshi," Shoji said one night after a supper of beef kidneys braised with garlic and shallots, "I've been a scientist all my life. Even now, my dreams are of witnessing the glory of galaxies moving away from each other." He still had his appetite then, and other than his deformed leg, Shoji was perfectly proportioned, lean but not too lean, and he had square bones. Toshi had noticed long ago that women smiled a lot around his father. His mother was flinging dishes into the dishwasher. Mitsuyo was doing everything more forcefully now. It was a dark, empty nothing outside the window. Clouds masked any galaxies that might have blossomed overhead.

Shoji said something about Doppler shifts that Toshi didn't understand, but he squinted and nodded thoughtfully. He put a finger to the cleft of his chin. His father was smiling and crying at the same time.

"A scientist," Shoji said, shaking his head. "All my life, I wanted to be nothing else." Toshi sighed, his big shoulders wilting.

His father wasn't interested in much about anything after he found out he was dying a slow and horribly painful death. Most days, he read in his study and hardly said two words beyond what was absolutely necessary. He didn't even pardon himself when he went to the toilet to vomit. He never excused himself, and, even though he always closed the door, the bathroom wasn't soundproof, so Toshi and Mitsuyo weren't spared his suffering. Not completely. Never completely. Even when Toshi covered his ears and started singing "This Old Man" so loud his voice was hoarse the next day.

There was one instance when Shoji came to life, and that was to yell at his wife. He was sitting at breakfast. Mitsuyo was ladling him a bowl of clear broth brewed from bonito flakes because by then he couldn't ingest much else. She was wondering aloud why all these terrible things were happening to them.

"To us?" said Shoji, his voice hoarse and frostbitten. "*To us?* When did you catch a terminal illness? This is happening to me, *and has nothing to do with you.*"

This was hardly fair, and Toshi thought hard about telling his father so. Toshi recalled how one day, when he and his younger brother were still in elementary school, the wind was gusting, and they saw a baby robin fall from a tree in front of their house. As soon as it hit the ground, it began flailing its wings in that pathetic, hyper-panicked way that frightened animals have.

Before Toshi and Kei could get to it, a neighbour's dog, a huge black Rottweiler, materialized out of nowhere and took the baby bird in its mouth. They heard the muffled sounds of tiny bones being crushed. Kei screamed at the dog and threw a book at its face, which made it drop its prey and run off. But the baby robin was already dead. Whatever small flicker of light that had made it cry for food or its mother had flown from its tiny chest. Toshi felt a fragment of his heart break away and fall to the ground. His brother looked like he might never smile again.

"You crazy kids go inside!" yelled Old Man Garber in his thick Polish accent that sounded like gears grinding. He stood across the street on his porch, his thin, pale arms behind his back. What little hair covered the top of his head was neatly combed to one side, but his shirt-tails hung over his pants. His spine was petrified in an arc at his shoulders, making him hunch over. He had to look up in order to look ahead. An ugly grey cat named Mongoose sat by his ankles and licked its privates. "Big storm is brewing!"

The dimly lit foyer of their house was as quiet as an abandoned church when they returned with the dead bird. Mitsuyo had gone to the corner store on Oakland for some peanut oil. Shoji was home, though, in his study, behind the columns of paper, so they cried out for him. When there was no answer after a few tries, they went to find him.

"Why did you bring it back *here?*" was the first thing their father asked them when he saw it.

Kei's face was wet with tears, like grass in the morning. "I thought you could help us bury it."

Shoji looked at him as if he had just suggested they stuff it and put it on the mantel. "Bury it? Are you mad? It's dead. Put it in the garbage." And with that their father turned his gaze back down to the jumble of mathematical calculations that filled his note paper.

Kei wouldn't stop crying as they buried the bird in the flower garden out back. The daffodils were in bloom. Even though Kei was crying, Toshi could hear him swearing under his breath. "Fuck you," he said. "Fuck you." The words sounded funny coming from such a small kid. And it was odd that anger was burning so brightly behind a curtain of tears. Kei was angry and brooding as far back as Toshi could remember. Brooding, handsome and intelligent, like their father. Toshi had been always aware of life's unfairness in such matters.

Toshi couldn't blame his father for not understanding, though. Like Old Man Garber, Shoji hadn't seen. Kei and Toshi had been too close, and that's why death had affected them so.

Just like how Shoji's death was affecting them now because they were too close. So, in truth, the cancer wasn't just devouring Shoji. It was eating away at everybody around him. But this was hard for Shoji to see, because he was the main course.

"And one more thing: I'd most appreciate your not asking 'why this' or 'why that' any more, if you'd please," Shoji said. Mitsuyo didn't say a word as she dragged her feet upstairs, massaging her greying temples, looking as forlorn as a rotting piece of wood drifting aimlessly at sea. Despite her thin frame, frailty didn't suit her. Neither did the black-and-yellow sweater she'd thrown on that morning, but she was beyond caring. Her hair said she just didn't give a flying shit as thin, coarse wisps reached out in patches like weeds. "It's bound to drive all of us *mad!*" Shoji still kept yelling in the kitchen, to no one in particular.

But now that he was lying on a hospital bed, now that all he did was stare at the ceiling as if the emptiness fascinated him, Toshi could tell his father was ignoring his own advice. It was very apparent that Shoji was asking himself why, and that this was driving him crazy, just like he said it would. His eyes didn't move, and his breathing was regular, controlled by the cold, metallic pump by his head—his indifferent surrogate lung. But you could tell he was upset. He was thinking to himself, *Why? Why? Why?*

"Nothing heroic?" asked the thin nurse.

"Nothing heroic," confirmed the doctor.

What the hell does that mean? Toshi thought.

They had been referred to a surgeon who always made things better by winking and saying, "Let's do it." He was a big man. He must have played football in school, thought Toshi. His voice was as deep as the sea, even if his words were as shallow as a disposable diaper. But Mitsuyo and Toshi hung on to his words like they were precious jewels, as Shoji's skin turned yellow, and his belly swelled and became hard. The doctor kept saying not to worry, and he winked again when he said this, making it even harder to doubt him.

But on the day Kei flew in from Toronto, the football doctor came to them, shaking his head, as though a field-goal attempt had gone terribly wrong. "Mrs. Hayakawa," he said, "you have to understand that it's no longer a matter of whether or not we can save him." He sounded like he was explaining the play at fourth down. "We've got to address the issues of how much longer you want to keep him alive, and how comfortable we can make him. These are the only issues remaining. Do you understand what I'm saying?"

Mitsuyo bowed and thanked him for all he had done, which looked to Toshi like nothing. He wondered why the doctor still sounded so superior—how his voice could still be so deep and resonant. He also marvelled at his mother's unwavering courtesy. A diplomat's daughter, there was nothing she hated more than embarrassing moments. Toshi supposed having a family member die in someone's workplace without acknowledging the trouble this was causing was as embarrassing as it got. Even if the workplace was a hospital.

Shoji had not moved, not even blinked, since the morning. Toshi thought his father's eyes were probably drying out and becoming as brittle as eggshells. "His eyelids aren't moving. I don't think he can close his eyes," Toshi whispered to no one in particular.

"So tape them shut, then," Mitsuyo said, as though she was the only one with any courage left to propose a course of action.

And they waited.

It was like watching water spiral down the drain. The red numbers flickered. First the fever spiked, then everything descended gradually, as Mitsuyo kept thanking her husband repeatedly for something neither Kei nor Toshi understood. Toshi heard her whisper a couple of times that she was sorry. So sorry. The apologies sounded out of place, as puzzling as pennies dropping from her mouth. To Toshi's surprise, Kei spat on the floor, then turned away. Angie always said that Kei kept his upper lip too stiff, and, if that didn't work, he became offensive.

As the water of time kept turning, falling, falling, Toshi couldn't tell whether his father's spirit was enjoying the ride, like a reed passively flowing into oblivion, or if Shoji was clawing against the current, fighting desperately, going insane trying to keep from being sucked into the sewer. Fighting, screaming, shouting at them from inside his useless body to do something, anything, to keep him alive. Toshi wanted to run and ask him what he really wanted. Yell in his ear to make certain he heard, but he knew Mitsuyo or Kei would pull him aside before he had the chance. So he fidgeted on one spot for the two hours it took for everything to be over. Toshi learned that day that dying could take a terribly long time.

The red lights finally faded, and the machines hushed. Only

the pump still kept pushing and drawing air, making Shoji's dead lungs breathe. The nurse began unplugging the machines and turning off switches and yanking out tubes from cold skin, efficient beyond words, while everyone else watched. Nobody said anything for a long time, as though they had to learn how to talk to each other all over again.

"Let's give him a shave," Mitsuyo said finally. "The fool always liked to look his best." She tried to smile at her sons, but her face didn't know which way to go. It sort of went all over the place. Kei said he was going to call a few funeral homes, and the doctor and nurse went off to take care of people who were still alive and struggling. So Toshi was left to help his mother.

He lifted his father's head, which weighed as much as a large watermelon, so Mitsuyo could comb his hair. Toshi never realized a human head was so heavy.

At home later that same day, Mitsuyo, Toshi and Kei sat in the kitchen, drinking tea and eating rice crackers and talking into the night. They talked about some of the funny things Shoji used to do, and laughed. Like how his favourite phrase used to be, "Have you gone *mad?*" Like how he liked to pour fermented beans and tea on his rice. How, for a supposedly rational man, he could twist and turn logic to get what he wanted. And how this had always worked for him.

They had to talk about the funny things, because the funny things took them away from where they were. But when Kei said he was going to bed, Toshi remembered how tired he was. Kei went upstairs to his old room. Toshi could imagine his brother breathing in the memories. Toshi looked at the clock, and was surprised to see it was past two in the morning. Mitsuyo looked like she didn't want her eldest son to leave, but didn't bother to complain. Toshi went to his room, climbed into bed in his clothes and, as the boxspring groaned in pain, followed his father into the darkness.

But from far away, Toshi could still hear his mother crying in her room, free from the world and its embarrassing moments.

KITAGAWA

HOT OR COLD IMPLIED MOVEMENT, AND MOVEMENT implied time. Toshi imagined that when his father died, he stepped outside time, and therefore was in a place neither hot nor cold. Toshi imagined Shoji, after they'd taped his eyelids shut in the hospital, swimming in a vast, black ocean. Then as he tired, and eventually drowned in the murky waters, Toshi imagined his father saw, in an instant, the entire universe as it existed in every moment of time.

"Tell me, Toshi," Shoji asked, shortly after moving to Milwaukee, when Toshi was just nine years old. They were nibbling on doughnuts Mitsuyo had brought home from Kohl's. Kei was dipping his into chocolate milk. "Does space have an existence independent of the matter it contains?"

Toshi blinked.

"Can emptiness exist by itself?"

Toshi felt a fish hook prying his lips open, but he said, "Sure."

Shoji stroked his square chin, grinning. Toshi knew immediately that the answer would be nauseating. "Think about it for a moment," Shoji said, holding up a doughnut. "Doesn't the hole in the middle of this doughnut exist only due to what is around it?"

Toshi shrugged his round shoulders and picked his nose. He pouted. Anything he said was going to make Shoji laugh at him.

His father's laugh always sounded insincere, as though he dared not let it out freely and completely. Shoji arched an eyebrow to prod Toshi for a reply. Finally, Toshi said, "I guess so," and Shoji laughed. His laugh was held in his nose. "*Nyet-nyet-nyet,*" as though he was negating something in Russian. Kei, in a pair of Flintstones shorts held up by red suspenders, was finishing his milk. He had just turned eight, but looked like he'd already seen too many of life's trivial ironies.

Listening to his father's laughter falling like pearls around him, Toshi also could hear the walls tittering. The chairs were, too. So were Mitsuyo's favourite potted African violets sitting on the table. Toshi started eating the flowers to teach them all a lesson. Shoji's eyes widened, and he started yelling for Mitsuyo to come do something. She came in and grabbed Toshi and shook him until he spit the purple petals out. This made Toshi giggle hysterically, because his father wasn't laughing at him any more. Kei had disappeared.

Toshi imagined that when Shoji died, he realized he'd been wrong, because in death, you could see that space was defined by time as well as by matter. In death, you could see space existing separately in each moment of time, while you saw all moments of time spreading out before you. Outside time, you could see every teardrop that fell when people cried alone. You could see mountains rising, and in a separate space, watch them erode into the sea. You could see people scratching their asses, and picking their noses, sometimes in that order.

And Toshi imagined that all this information flooding his father's brain was not overwhelming at all—not because Shoji had been so smart but because this was simply the way it was when people died. It was like a wall of mirrors that trapped the soul within a labyrinth of reflections. Each reflection cast another in all the others, and every frame of reference presented a different perspective on a different moment in the past, present and future. And all these images simply were there without imposing.

When he was in high school, Toshi often stood in front of the bathroom mirror without a shirt and pretended he was Bruce Lee. He tightened his abs, pronounced his pecs and flexed his triceps and biceps. He made his arms into an O in front of him. In the mirror, his small muscles, usually docile under smooth layers of fat, took on godly proportions. This ritual was followed by short screams that sounded like castrated poodles, and a few flimsy side-kicks into the air.

But he found he couldn't do the same in the sterile air of clothing stores. There, he often enclosed himself among the folding mirrors, watching his naked upper body from every angle, each perspective layered on another, going on infinitely. There, the mirrors offered no shelter from the inescapable truth: he was not Bruce Lee. He was not even a stout Bruce Lee. Mitsuyo would look for him all over the store, yelling his name and waving underwear in the air. Toshi remained hidden among the mirrors, thinking this was what it must be like to be dead—able to observe life and all of its subtle nuances.

After he died, somewhere among all the perspectives laid out in front of him, Shoji might have seen himself growing up in Japan. He'd spent a number of years in a small village called Kitagawa. This was not Kitagawa as in "Northern River" but as in "River of Much Happiness." Either way, the name did not mirror life there. There was a river, but the town was to the southeast of Tokyo, not particularly northern, and it certainly wasn't a very happy place. Nothing much ever happened in Kitagawa, except this would have been wartime so people were constantly leaving to die. And there was never enough to eat.

People nonetheless mustered enough enthusiasm to send teenagers off on suicide missions. They gathered at the train station, waving banners and throwing their arms in the air, calling for a 10,000-year reign for the emperor, as if they might be sending the local softball team off to a regional tournament. The hills around Kitagawa and the summer sky above remained indifferent. The incessant calls of the cicadas were grating.

On one particularly sultry day, Shoji and his best friend, Shima, stood among a circle of boys beneath the trees lining the back fence of Kitagawa High School. A strong wind blew that day, scattering the dirt and blood from the courtyard, which earlier in the afternoon had been the stage of a sumo competition. The brutal enthusiasm of young men had broken a couple of noses and dislocated a few shoulders. It was puzzling how enemy soldiers could withstand such naked, youthful energy.

Only the teachers matched the students in fervour. They instilled "iron will" into those who lost with a thick rod known affectionately as "the spirit stick" on their backside. It was little wonder, then, with all this exuberance, that a few students would turn their excess energies toward exploiting the weak.

Shoji seemed very committed to being terrorized in a dignified manner. "Look," he said to the circle of indifferent faces and dead eyes. His words were hurried, exasperated. "You can't expect us to give you money *every* day."

"For heaven's sake, Sho," said Shima. "Just give it to them!" Shima was as thin as a willow branch.

The circle broke when one boy, heavier than the others, walked up to Shoji like a wall. Kono was younger than Shoji and Shima, but this was impossible to tell from his size, or from his eyes. He stood a full head above Shoji and was wide enough for four Shimas to hide behind. His eyes were set beneath thick, knotted brows, and never moved. When he looked to the side, his head moved with his eyes. His older brothers had already been killed in the war, and he was also ready to die at any time for his country and emperor. He shivered with excitement at the thought and fingered his acne.

"Listen to your skinny friend, Hayakawa," he said, holding out his huge hand. "Give it up."

Shoji looked at Kono, then at Shima, then sighed wearily. His shoulders wilted. He fished in his pocket for some change, then offered a closed fist to Kono, whose mouth curled into a cruel grin. The rest of his face remained impassive, lifeless. Shoji tried to crush his anger between clenched teeth. Anger was like a roach, hard to kill. It kept squirming, trying to break free. He looked into Kono's eyes for a long time, but this was like trying to stare down an approaching bull.

Kono knew he was going to be dead soon. He was afraid of nothing, least of all a bookworm who'd somehow avoided the draft. He didn't know the Japanese government didn't draft students who had excelled, as Shoji had, in science. They were needed to engineer better airplanes and bombs and guns. But in Kono's mind, Shoji should have volunteered. He should have been happy to fly a Zero full of fuel into an enemy aircraft carrier's hull. If it came to that, Kono would be right behind him in another plane. Being blown into tiny pieces in a glorious fireball seemed like a sensible life goal to Kono. If he had another life to live, he'd eagerly sacrifice it also for the emperor. Shoji knew this, and could not believe he and Kono shared the same number of chromosomes.

Finally, Shoji opened his fingers, but only the wind slipped through his hand. Kono's smile hovered momentarily, uncertain. Shoji spun and ran out from the circle before any of the others had time to react. As fast as his legs could carry him, he ran out the gate and down the road, angry voices in pursuit.

Running was about the only physical activity that brought him joy, even at times like this, in great part because he was good at it. He was fast, as he discovered the first time he ran from bullies in one of the countless towns and villages where he'd lived with his father and mother. Yasujiro worked for the national railway, which posted him all over Japan. Bullies were the same everywhere.

Decades later, at Lover's Bluff Elementary School in Milwaukee, his sons would have to endure all the schoolyard taunting that had to do with growing up as immigrant children. Shoji often took his sons aside to recount his own encounters with bullies and to share the philosophy that had emerged from the experience.

"Just remember that they're all monkeys," he said, his voice sour from a lifetime of bitterness. His eyelids fluttered, while he wallowed in memories that were neither misty nor watercoloured. "Left behind in the evolution from unicellular organisms to rational human beings," he muttered, then smiled. He patted his sons on the back and said he hoped this would be helpful in dealing with their own trials and tribulations.

"Did you ever fight back?" Kei asked excitedly.

His father looked at him, then at Toshi, then back again. "Are you mad? Why on earth would I do that?" He rubbed his stomach. Irrationality made his stomach hurt.

"Then they'd know they couldn't mess with you?" Toshi offered.

"And what would bring them to this conclusion? They were always in a group, and it would have taken only one of them to beat me to a bloody pulp with one hand while picking his nose with the other." Shoji sounded extremely proud of his logic. "No, I ran," he added, grinning. "I ran very, very fast."

"I would have fought back," said Kei.

"Then you are a fool," Shoji said. He frowned again, and rubbed his stomach harder.

"Even if it meant getting beat up," Kei said, "I would've fought back."

And at that, Shoji yelled at his son for being preposterously irrational, no more adept at suppressing his violent tendencies than the apes who had beat him up.

Kei listened mutely. The excitement faded from his eyes, as if he had opened a birthday present and discovered only socks. He watched his father pontificate endlessly. Shoji waved his arms and jabbed the air with his index finger. He was used to lecturing. He was a professor, after all. As Shoji lost himself further in the ideas he was spouting, he seemed oblivious to his own son's disappointments.

The odd thing about the way Shoji ran was how he did not use his arms to propel himself forward. They stayed rigidly at his sides, while, below, his legs were a blur. He looked like an ostrich. The wind brushed back his hair as he ran. The summer heat gathered on his forehead. The mountains and hills looked down at him, noticing his presence for the first time.

He ran past Mrs. Tanaka, whose only son had been drafted just yesterday. Her wrinkled face did not betray distress. Her dishevelled kimono was about the only thing out of the ordinary. She looked like a ghost, standing at her gate and staring at the sky. She smiled only briefly when Shoji ran by, his arms bony and stiff, his fingers extended fully and pointed downward.

He ran past the stores, most of which were closed because there was nothing to sell. The wooden shutters were dry and changing colour as the sun beat down on them daily. Shoji ran down the single path that cut Kitagawa in two, toward the Kaminohashi Shrine, beyond which was the Maruyama Chemical Plant. There, many of the town's women worked while their husbands were away. The winding road seemed to go on forever, but soon he heard the familiar rush of water that was the Kita River. The water was fast, and only a single, high wooden bridge led to the other side. When Shoji reached the middle of the bridge, he stopped and looked over the side. The minuscule needles of moisture stung his face. He closed his eyes and breathed deeply. The air was warm and luscious. He stood leaning on the railing for almost an hour before Shima finally found him.

Shima walked slowly, his steps uneven and uncertain. He looked like a bean sprout wobbling on its end. "Well! What were you thinking?" he cried, as soon as he was close enough.

Shoji wiped his brow. "What?"

"You left me alone with those assholes! Okay?"

"So? They weren't going to hurt you. They always come after me because they think I have money. That's why you were holding on to my wallet for me, remember?"

Shima didn't answer. He drew close to Shoji and joined him in staring at the hurried waters of the River of Much Happiness.

"Shima?" Shoji looked into his friend's face. "You didn't give it to them, did you? Are you *mad?*"

A pair of bony arms flailed the air. "Well! What was I supposed to do? They came back for me after they lost you. They were so angry they looked like they were going to beat me senseless just to let off steam. I had to do something. Okay! You know that they already broke my glasses once." Shima removed his wire-rimmed glasses. They were taped together by bandages ashen with dirt. He held them up to Shoji for inspection. Shima's glasses had been broken for as long as Shoji had known him.

Shoji waved it away. "What are we supposed to do now?"

There was no answer. Not that Shoji had expected one. They stood on the bridge for a long time, watching the river and the sky. Shoji longed for an escape from this life, this time in space. None was offered by the azure emptiness overhead, the silence of the mountains or the incessant whisper of the water.

"Well, come on," said Shima, finally, tugging at Shoji's sleeve. "There's no point in going to the bookstore now. Let's go home."

They walked back the way they came, toward town. Shoji tried hard to swallow the bitterness. He found he couldn't stay angry at Shima. Shoji knew better than anyone how it felt to be on the receiving side of a beating. He had been nearly killed one time, when everyone at Kitagawa High School was assigned the task of collecting mugworts to be processed into gunpowder at the Maruyama plant.

Shoji's father was a doctor. Yasujiro explained to his son that the white fuzz on the underside of the mugwort's jagged leaves was used for moxibustion in the treatment for rheumatoid arthritis. They had found other uses for it during wartime.

One day, instead of regular homework, each student at Kitagawa High School was given the quota of filling a basket the size of an oil drum overnight with mugworts. Shoji worked until close to midnight. His basket was just half full. He was on his way out of the woods, barely awake, when Kono and the others materialized from the shadows and jumped him. Shoji couldn't run with the basket. He wasn't even given a chance to cry out. They beat him unconscious, and by the time his mother found him the next morning, blood had caked dry on his hair and face. The basket of mugworts was gone. They'd been in Kitagawa less than half a year.

Shoji recalled that they'd loaded him onto a passing honey cart. When he came to, he found himself slumped in a heap, with his head on the driver's shoulder. He watched the blue sky, stupefied, clouds speeding by overhead. Then the smell made him vomit. There were voices all around him yelling "Faster!" and "This way is shorter!" and someone else pleading, "Will you slow down, you're spilling shit all over the place!" Everyone had different priorities. The docile old horse bridled uncharacteristically.

There was no one at Yasu's clinic except for a couple of nurses, who in fact weren't nurses at all. They were elderly farmers who couldn't tend to their crops because their sons were off at war.

Yasujiro had been called away to the next village on an emergency, so the old men did their best to stitch up Shoji's scalp. When Yasu returned that night, he looked at the scar on his son's forehead and scratched his five-day beard thoughtfully. Yasu hated to shave, but his handsome, weathered face wore his slovenliness well. He sat down beside Shoji's futon, lit a cigarette and said, "Sho, catastrophes happen all the time." Yasu's voice was like two pieces of sandpaper rubbing together. He was skinny, like everyone else in Kitagawa, but his muscles were pronounced and chiselled. Though his fingers were long—almost delicate—his wrists were thick and shoulders square.

"Shit, sometimes they're so subtle we don't even realize they're happening to us. But subtle or no, life can change in an instant— as you just found out for yourself. But what you have to remember is that there's nothing you can do about it. You can spend all your time avoiding shit on the ground, then wind up riding a honey cart bleeding like a virgin whore. All you can do is focus on what you're going to do afterwards. How you react, son, is who you are." Then he excused himself, because, he said, he needed to air out his balls. Shoji stared at the moth flying around the oil lamp, trying repeatedly to dive into the flame.

Mrs. Tanaka was still standing by her front gate when Shoji and Shima walked by, but she'd got a bucket and some water to settle the dust. Back bent, vaguely aware that she was wasting her time, she waved a bamboo dipper in a wide arc. All of them watched as the cascade fell like hope onto dirt.

Shoji wished he had money left to buy some cold tea. His stomach needed settling. Swallowing too much pride can make you sick. Shima kept prattling on about how Kono was too stupid to amount to anything, except divine wind—kamikaze. This was what they called the poor souls who enlisted on the suicide missions. It'll happen soon enough, Shoji thought. *Then Kono will be gone and we'll still be here.* Shoji looked at Shima, who'd also escaped the draft because he appeared too emaciated for the army. Shima even looked like he might have worms. His broken glasses kept sliding off his nose, and he pushed them back up every few minutes with his middle finger.

Even when he wasn't wearing glasses, he often would forget and slide his middle finger up the ridge of his nose. Sometimes he'd slip and jab himself in the eye. A couple of times, he'd drawn blood.

The railway supplied Yasujiro and his family with a house in Kitagawa—a mansion contained by high walls, its sloping, tiled roof barely visible behind ancient pine trees. Just down the road were the Fukanji, the local Buddhist temple, and its graveyard. "That's mighty convenient!" Yasu laughed when he first learned of this. "We'll either send them home or down the street!" His laughter sounded as though there were fragments of glass moving about in his throat. He would often choke on his own humour, causing fits of strangled coughing that made the earth move and made everyone around him quiver.

Shoji looked at the house through the half-open gate. It looked both inviting and imposing at the same time. He asked his friend in for a drink, but Shima shook his head. "You'll need a reason for not having the book with you. Tell your father you lent it to me." Yasu had given Shoji some money to buy an expensive book that he'd seen at Kitagawa's only remaining bookstore.

The sun was still high and blinding. Shoji looked at the vacant sky. He wanted to lick it and feel its heat dance on his tongue. He knew Shima was right. If he told the truth about what had happened, Yasu would charge like a mad cow over to Kono's house to demand the money back. Kono's father was a carpenter. He had tattoos on his back, and arms as thick as cottonwood trees. This would not matter to Yasu. He would face down a stable of sumo wrestlers if he felt an injustice had been committed.

Though no one had told him, Shoji knew his family had to move around so frequently because his father had angered another doctor when Yasu was still working in Tokyo. It had just been announced that this same doctor was to be chairman of the national hospital association. Yasu said aloud that this doctor's patients had mortality rates comparable to soldiers who fought in the Sino-Japanese War. Yasu laughed that this doctor was more effective in killing Japanese than any weapon the enemy could develop. "Are the Americans *paying* you to practise medicine in Japan?"

The doctor was not amused. His face, normally pallid, turned red like dusk. From that moment, Yasujiro could no longer obtain the reference he needed to work at any respectable hospital in

Tokyo. His brother managed to call in some favours to get him a job servicing railway staff posted around the country.

Shoji pictured Yasu marching to Kono's house, foaming at the mouth, screaming and brazenly flinging his cigarette in the senior Kono's eyes. "Do you know what *else* my son said about your son?" Yasujiro would yell. "He says your son's testicles are fermenting from this heat."

"Oh, yeah?"

"All right," Shoji said to Shima. "I'll tell my father that you begged me to let you have the book first."

Shima grinned, and with a wave of his hand, he walked off whistling, his thin frame billowing in the heat rising from the dirt. He seemed oblivious to being young during wartime. Shoji watched with affection, as well as a mild curiosity. Shima was truly an odd one. He had found Shoji on his first day at Kitagawa High School. Just before the lunch break, Shoji saw the thinnest boy in class approach him like a starving animal. "Hello! Do you have anything to eat?" was the first thing he said.

The lack of grace only mildly disturbed Shoji, who was desperate for some company. He gave Shima a rice ball, which disappeared in a gaping mouthful. He gave him another, then another. From then on, Shoji always brought an extra portion of lunch for his friend. Shima, in exchange, offered him faithful companionship that lasted through to adulthood. It helped that Shima was intelligent as well as hungry. When he wasn't talking about food, he was talking about magnetism and the g-factor, Einstein and Bohr. He and Shoji spent hours taking apart the wonders of ionized atoms.

Shoji was also impressed by how his friend would always feed his intellect before his starving body. He never had food, just books. Shima always managed to get hold of books. Oil was precious, so Shima read at night by the window. This explained his thick glasses, which could be also used as a paperweight. This was why, even as an adult, when anyone mentioned Maslow's hierarchy to Shoji, he'd remember his friend, and laugh, *"Nyet-nyet-nyet-nyet-nyet!"* He knew better. He'd seen otherwise.

Light spilled from the rear of the house into the dark hallway. The old floorboards immediately betrayed Shoji as he tried to sneak upstairs to his room.

"Shoji, is that you?" Yasujiro called out from the back room that looked out onto the garden. "Come and have something cold to drink!"

Shoji bit into his lip. "That's all right! I'm not thirsty!"

"Get your skinny little ass in here!" yelled Yasu.

Shade opened onto a large tatami room. There was a table at the centre, where Yasu sat cross-legged, beating the air with a stained paper fan. A cigarette lay cremated and forgotten in the ashtray.

Yasujiro was wearing only his underwear, although no one could blame him in Kitagawa in summertime. On the other hand, Yasu also liked to prance around nearly naked in spring and autumn. And not just at the rear of the house. Neighbours learned quickly not to come over unexpectedly, after being confronted several times by Yasu in his loincloth at the door. When he saw them, he turned around to call his wife, exposing his backside and the birthmark in the shape of Spain on his otherwise perfectly symmetrical rump. At least he kept to the house. That Yasujiro did not parade around the streets naked was a silver lining of sanity in the misty cloud of neurosis.

"Look at this," Yasu growled into the newspaper. "Reading this crap, you'd think all Americans do is drink, eat chocolate and chase women with straight teeth. This really explains why they're kicking our butts to Hell down along the Sanzu River. Right, Sho?" He looked up with sunken eyes. Still, Shoji knew, they were as sharp as a hawk's. "Eh, where's the book?" he asked.

The lies stumbled from his lips easily enough. "Shima wanted to see it first, so I lent it to him," Shoji said, hoarsely. "Er, *nyet-nyet*, maybe I'll have some tea after all."

Yasujiro arched a brow. "Mother! Ryoko! Bring Shoji some cold tea!" When there was no answer, he called out to Otama, the maid, who was shuffling about noisily in the next room. "He wanted to see it first? Whose goddamn book is it anyway?"

"Oh, leave him alone," Ryoko protested as she walked into the room. She was smiling, carrying a trayful of tea in tall glasses. Shoji saw how graceful his mother was, despite the restrictive kimono she wore under her immaculate white apron. There wasn't a single bead of sweat on her forehead, from which rivers of raven black hair were pulled back. Her thin eyebrows and red lips were like brush paintings on perfect rice paper. She sat like a flower petal floating slowly down onto the ground. "Sho-chan, here you are. My God! You're a mess. Put your clothes with the laundry after you've had your drink."

She passed a glass of tea to Shoji, then took a drink from her own. Beads of water collected on the glass and smeared under her thin, white fingertips. She regarded her son from the depths of her dark, brown eyes. "Although your father is right, I'm happy you're so generous with your friends who are . . . not so well off . . . but I wish you'd spend your time with someone more . . . appropriate . . . than Shima-san. Of course, most boys your age are now off serving."

As she said this, she crooked her head and stared thoughtfully into the garden. It was slowly dying. Weeds flourished among dry, brittle leaves and twigs. Still, the stones around the perimeter were majestic. The garden could have been salvaged, if not for the grotesque bomb shelter at its centre. The morning after it was installed, the gardener allowed himself a sigh that was heard around Kitagawa. Then he left and never came back. Yasujiro had said the bastard shouldn't be able simply to walk out on a job like that, but fell quiet when he discovered the gardener had just lost his son in an air raid the week before. The garden hadn't been tended to since.

Ryoko, for all her graces, came from a family not of nobles but of wealthy merchants. Her siblings and cousins owned and operated an immense pig farm in the Tohoku district. They kept the family supplied with ham and bacon during the war. Ryoko, though, had been always drawn to the mystique of Tokyo. Through *omiai,* an arranged meeting, she was introduced to Yasujiro. She was delighted when, five minutes after they sat across from each other, he let loose a stream of vulgarities because of an unfortunate accident involving a teapot and Yasu's freshly laundered slacks, the fly of which was open.

The farmhands she'd known had been simple, but not callous, especially around her. Yasu, with all his crass speech and habits, looked to her like some exotic foreigner. When he smoked, he reminded her of Clark Gable, although not when he drank until he fell onto the floor and passed out. Still, he was handsome, and a doctor. After a while, they married, and lived in a house of respectable size on the outskirts of Tokyo, until Yasu's forced exile. Now, letters from her brother-in-law's family, exquisitely written, reminded her that Yasu would still be out of a job if not for his intervention.

"Too much generosity can kill you," Yasu growled. Ryoko watched as dead leaves trembled in the faint breeze. "You've got to watch your backside, Shoji. There's no room for compassion when you're competing for university placements. One day, you're lending him books. The next day, he's pumping rat poison up your ass."

Ryoko laughed like chimes into the back of her hand. "As if Sho-chan isn't going to make it into university!" she said. "Besides, Shima-san wouldn't do anything to hurt Shoji. He's a good person."

"You can't take these things for granted," said Yasujiro, turning back to his paper. "Too many idiots running around in this country already. Look at all the goddamn lies they print. We're about to lose the biggest war in history, and all they can do is stick propaganda up our noses and call it information."

"Father, you should be careful what you say," Shoji said. The book now appeared forgotten, but Yasu was talking so loudly anyone walking by beyond the back fence could hear. Shoji wondered if there would ever come a time when his stomach didn't feel like a pitcher full of ice water. He began to rub his stomach.

Yasu laughed, then coughed heavily into his hand. "You wouldn't turn me over to the *kempeitai*, would you, Shoji?" he said. He was talking about the military police—swarthy men in black uniforms. A group of them, led by a man named Tamura who had a face shaped like a roofing tile, had come to town around the time the Maruyama Chemical Plant started producing gunpowder instead of fabric dyes. Tamura talked about the weather like taking note of it was a duty to the emperor. Everyone else was appropriately reverential.

"For heaven's sake, Shoji," Yasu continued, "you must get an enlightened education! You owe it to society! Look at the garbage they're printing here! We think we're doing the Manchurians a favour by raping their women and stomping on their men's testicles! Do you remember the letter from my friend in Korea? I was goddamn embarrassed to read it!"

He was no longer laughing. Neither was his wife. "Lower your voice!" Ryoko hissed.

The letter had been delivered the previous day, by a Japanese relative of the Korean doctor. It was a time, Shoji's father would often say, when friendships could kill, but there was little else worth dying for anyway. He fell quiet for now, though. Then all they could hear were the insects slowly coming to life in the twilight, and for the moment the world's troubles seemed very far away. Though, of course, they weren't. Fear and hatred were in the bomb shelters, the newspapers and the skies. It blazed in the maniacal look in Kono's eyes when he harassed Shoji for money. But all of this hid behind the silence.

"It's late," said Ryoko. "I have to go over to the Kaminohashi Shrine." She rose with the tray, now empty.

Yasujiro slammed his newspaper on the table. *"Why?"*

She glared at him. Shoji felt his scrotum shrink, but Yasu didn't waver until his wife said, *"Because,* I have to see if the priest would be willing to exchange some of our meat for fish and some rice. Or would you care for ham again for dinner tonight?"

"Oh." Yasu swallowed a breath. Suddenly, something else in the paper caught his eye. "Carry on, then," he said.

Just around the time Yasujiro went back to reading his paper, across town, Shima and his sister were dancing around in the kitchen of a dilapidated house, a shack not even a quarter of the size of Shoji's house. The floorboards threatened to give way, but their mother could do nothing but watch, in turns smiling and crying. She very rarely smiled these days. Her husband had been killed in Okinawa. She supported the family by removing the white fuzz from mugworts at the Maruyama Chemical Plant.

But this had been a good day—a rare day when the plant gave every worker a basket of fresh eggs. Where they came from, no one knew. She had just told her children that each of them could have one for dinner tonight to go with their rice and millet. And this was why they were dancing. Relativity, in the end, was everything.

THE FUNERAL

IN SCHOOL, TOSHI LEARNED THAT THE NAME MILWAUKEE came from an Indian word that meant gathering place. No Indians gathered there any more as far as he could see. He'd never even seen an Indian until his father drove them to northern Wisconsin, where they saw some Indians dancing on a football field. Other Indians went up and down the bleachers where Toshi sat with his family. The Indians sold corn on the cob, salty peanuts and Coke that was watered down by ice melting in the damp heat.

Down on the football field, the frantic dance told a story about a great hunter who'd wandered far from the river and got lost. Throughout, Mitsuyo kept telling her sons to eat their corn. She still looked reasonably happy, then. Meanwhile, Shoji made notes in his spiral notebook that were not about Indians. It was impossible for Toshi to tell what the series of Greek symbols, strings of numbers and countless x's and y's were about. He understood the significance neither of the dance nor of his father's work. He rarely understood anything, in fact.

Miss Steinky told him the place where they saw the dance was called a reservation. The Indians had packed all their things and moved there to maintain their "traditional" way of living. She made quotation marks in the air with her hands as she explained, which elevated the breasts under her pink wool sweater.

Breathing deeply, Toshi asked why the Indians had to move when they were here first. Come to think of it, he said, kids were always telling him to remember Pearl Harbor and to go home. "Maybe the Indians should have told the pilgrims to go home, instead of going to a place very far from where they were used to gathering," he wondered aloud.

"Who's telling you to go home?" Miss Steinky said, shoving her large nose in his face. She smelled like fresh-cut flowers but wore too much mascara.

Toshi felt his groin shrink like a frightened turtle when he realized he was a hair away from being a snitch. "No one," he replied, then inspected his frayed shoelaces. His chin folded over in layers whenever he looked down.

Miss Steinky looked at him suspiciously but didn't pursue it any further. All the teachers at Lover's Bluff Elementary School were trying their best to help Toshi and Kei adjust. Toshi appreciated this. He felt guilty about not telling Miss Steinky the truth. Then, a moment later, he forgot everything anyway and went out to recess. He decided to go to the baseball field, where he would talk with some grasshoppers before stepping on them.

For Toshi, coming to America was both liberating and stifling. Liberating, because Mitsuyo for the first time didn't seem overly embarrassed to be seen with him in public. Americans were amazingly tolerant about some things. If Toshi broke into a few cars in a parking lot, and blew their horns or turned the knobs on the radios, Americans just came forward and asked his mother what *the fuck* his problem was. Then they usually tried to find out more about his "peculiarities."

"Did you ever fall on your belly while you were pregnant with him?" they might ask Mitsuyo, or, if Shoji was there, look at his bad leg and wonder aloud about genetics. They were, after all, simply trying to help everyone make sense of things. Who could fault them for that? They usually concluded by blessing the family and driving off. Mitsuyo always thanked them. She smiled and waved goodbye and bowed, watching the car's rear lights disappear around a corner. Toshi hoped he might see some of them again someday.

In Japan, the cars' owners would look at the ground, set their lips painfully rigid, as if they were holding back a fart, and drive off without saying anything. By not making a fuss, the Japanese waved Mitsuyo's shame back in her face without forgiveness or closure. This was why she appreciated the relief offered by Americans and their frankness. She didn't like the loneliness, though. She had been lonely for a long time.

When Toshi was still in kindergarten in Tokyo, there was an expression in Japanese that said when something you ate tasted especially good, your cheeks fell off. His teacher, Miss Ito, unfortunately exploited this to stimulate her students' imagination. "Let's have some of this delicious-looking ice cream!" She would gleefully mime licking the tip of an enormous chocolate cone.

Miss Ito was as pretty as a tulip. She moved her hands to simulate flesh falling from her face, and motioned for the class to mimic her. As soon as they did, she exclaimed, "Uh-ohhhh!!" Her dark eyes bulged like rats abandoning a sinking ship. "It's soooooo good, our cheeks fell off!" She reached down to the floor, picked up an imaginary chunk of skin and muscle and slapped it back on her perfectly round jaw. Everyone laughed, except for Toshi.

"Let's do it again!"

Poor Toshi's knees were shaking below his shorts. He imagined his face in a bloody pool on the floor. He thought of ice cream seeping out of Miss Ito's gaping wound. She was oblivious. "How about this banana?" she said with joy as she peeled the invisible fruit.

Toshi stood up from his desk, screaming. His thick hands held on to his face, which was frightfully pale. As pale as someone whose cheeks have been sliced like ham. *"Hyaaaaaah!"* His scream abruptly stopped Miss Ito's miming game. When the girl sitting next to him tried to calm him down, he punched her in the nose.

When Miss Ito first told Toshi's parents that he perhaps should go to a "special" school, Mitsuyo complained so loudly that the walls shook. Toshi stayed in the public kindergarten. By the second time the Hayakawas were called into a meeting, when Toshi fell off the slide and split his scalp, Miss Ito had learned to have the principal present. Still, Mitsuyo brought up the proverb of the Zen monk who stayed loyal to his most troublesome acolyte, and they were silenced. Mitsuyo herself had been worn down by her son considerably, though, by the third meeting, when she was told Toshi had hit a girl in his class.

When Toshi was expelled from kindergarten, his parents also took this to mean he should not be taken out in the pubic. The Hayakawas had always taken pride in being different: but there was more than a fine line between rare and discordant, eccentric and freakish, eating sushi and swallowing live goldfish. Being proud people, their shame was acute. Poor Toshi spent almost all of the next five years locked in his own home, a small apartment in the Meguro district in Tokyo.

The only time he was allowed outside was when he and Mitsuyo went to the roof of their five-storey building. From there, they could see people rushing back and forth on the streets like worker ants, and trains crawling among the buildings like worms. If Toshi had been a political dissident, they'd call his confinement house arrest, but there was nothing so noble about his life. He spent his days turning every knob and dial in the apartment, learning how to dismantle doors, collecting vacuum tubes from inside the television set, feeding sugar to the anthill in the roof garden.

Experts in psychology may say he did this to silence the voices, but this would not be true. They were not so much voices, actually, but more of a constant presence. Toshi found he could eliminate all the noises around him, one by one, and still end up with something discernible. A hiss. A hum, perhaps. Toshi heard the hum in plants, animals and, most acutely, in machines. *If only I could raise the volume,* he often thought. *If only I could, maybe then it would be clear to everyone.* Then, perhaps, someone could explain to him why the hum also made the inside of his head vibrate, sometimes so much he feared it would crack open like a coconut under a machete. Or maybe the hum would drive everyone else crazy, too. Level the proverbial playing field, although what they were playing, he had no idea.

When Shoji learned his son was not what most people considered normal, he shrugged. "It's genetic," he muttered, then buried himself in work. Irrationality made his stomach hurt. He did what he did best when confronted with a complicated problem—he ignored it. Mitsuyo, on the other hand, did her best to cope with her eldest son and his eccentricities, trying a wide variety of strategies, from A to Z, from yin to yang. The flip-flop was abrupt, and wrenching.

"Toshi, oh, Toshi. Let's tighten our loincloths and wipe your runny, crusty nose. We're going to beat this together!"

Then, "Tighten your butthole! You hear me? Tighten your butthole!" Sometimes, she slapped the back of his head as she said this.

Then she hugged him, murmuring, "Oh, Toshi-chan, you know we're on your side. No matter what happens. Don't forget."

Then, "You wise up, or your father is going to irradiate your fat head with those gamma particles he goes on and on about!"

And so it went, every day for five childhood years—the length of ten adult lifetimes. Not exactly Helen Keller and Anne Sullivan. More like Norman and Mrs. Bates. Mitsuyo at first allowed Toshi to play with other children if any appeared on the roof. But their innocuous laughter soon turned to taunts, and the other parents' knowing smiles quickly became burdens. Mitsuyo was getting tired.

Freedom therefore was hope. It was glory. And this was what coming to America meant to Toshi. He was free (sort of) and so was she, although she never overcame the loneliness.

The principal at Lover's Bluff Elementary School, Mr. Strong, was an extremely friendly mountain of a man. He had a face so red Mitsuyo wondered if he wasn't choking on whatever gargantuan sandwich she knew Americans always had for lunch. Mr. Strong had a rolling paunch flooding over his wide leather belt, and a rumbling voice as ancient as the Great Lakes. He said Toshi was special, and smart enough to attend class with kids his own age, but only after he learned to speak English. Until then, Toshi, who was supposed to be in fourth grade, would be put back with Kei in third. Mr. Strong sounded like God proclaiming the fate of the human race.

When they arrived at their classroom, Miss Steinky, the pretty young teacher with yellow hair and jade green mascara-laden eyes, made Toshi and Kei sit together. "Miss Stinky?" said Mitsuyo, raising her head from a deep, reverent bow. Miss Steinky just smiled and shook her head.

Young Kei needed only three months to completely master English. Toshi took twice as long, partly because he enjoyed hearing people say things he didn't understand. If Miss Steinky said, "Turn to page twelve," Toshi heard, *"Trretpetwpe."* This made him clutch his stomach and fall, laughing, onto the floor in a heap. When people started yelling at him, he disassembled in tears, gut wrenching, knees turning to water. Then one day he heard one of his classmates say "Fuck you!" and this made him sit up and listen. And he listened ever since.

He was speaking English with native fluency after about a year, but they kept him back for one more year with Miss Steinky, while Kei skipped fourth grade and went on to fifth. It escaped no one's attention that Kei wound up where Toshi was supposed to be.

They always walked home together from Lover's Bluff Elementary School, because kids picked on them over Pearl Harbor, as if Kei and Toshi were personally responsible for the Second World War. When Kei first explained to his older brother what was being said to them, Toshi had been amazed that kids in the third grade could be holding a thirty-year-old grudge. They were picked on also because of Toshi's odd habit of frequently lying face down in the middle of the hallway after recess. He did this when the hum became too loud. After a while, Kei began to run home, alone.

This was how life in America was stifling. When you wake up in the morning, your body can feel as heavy as dead winter when you know you're going to be made fun of all day. In Japan, where they weren't foreigners, and where Toshi was locked in the apartment all day, this had not been a problem.

There was one student at Lover's Bluff Elementary School who was genuinely interested in learning more about where Toshi came from. "Teach me some swear words in Japanese," Scotty Taylor said.

Scotty was in Miss Steinky's class the year Toshi was held back. His was the appearance Toshi would associate, for the rest of his life, with growing up among Americans—short, cropped blond hair, translucent white skin and sapphire eyes. In fact, Toshi was surrounded by countless Jews, Italians and Irish (although virtually no blacks or Orientals), but somehow, Scotty's look was what impressed him most. Toshi always carried an oil portrait of Scotty in his mind, in a heavy gold frame. In it, Scotty always wore the kind of ornamented outfit with knee-high stockings worn by Gainsborough's *The Blue Boy*.

"Swear words?"

"Yeah. Y'know, like 'fuck.'"

"Oh. Fuck. Right." Toshi rolled his eyes and put a finger on the cleft of his chin. He didn't move for about a minute.

33

"Yeah. Or 'shit,'" Scotty prompted.

"Oh."

Now they were getting somewhere.

"*Kuso*," Toshi said.

"*Kuso?*"

"*Kuso.*"

Just then, a Ford station wagon with fake wood panelling drove by with high-school students hanging from its windows. "Heeeeeey, Chinky-chinky-chinky!" they yelled. Laughter fell away down the street.

"Hey!" yelled Scotty, running after them. "Eat my *kuso!*" Then he turned around and mooned the car that had already rounded a corner and disappeared.

Toshi paled. He had never before imagined that someone would pull his pants down willingly in public. Why would anyone do this? Toshi was just coming to terms with the undeniable idea that his parents saw his bare ass regularly when he was an infant. Perhaps, so did a select number of their friends. They never referred to this in Toshi's presence. What were they trying to hide?

By the time Toshi had made it to Whitefish High School, his eccentricities were no longer amusing anyone. The idiots who kicked him around, in body and spirit, became bored and turned their attention to Kei. They traumatized him practically every day, with the same pleasure children feel when tearing the legs off locusts. It didn't help that Kei never cried or asked for mercy, but simply stared at his tormentors with the contempt normally reserved for maggots on bad meat. Everyone knew he was the smartest kid in his grade, probably even the whole school. His silent gaze merely reminded them of this. The bullying went on for a long time, across the seasons and past many years, as shoulders on all the boys grew broader and their voices fell deeper.

They lived in a suburb of Milwaukee not far from the University of Wisconsin, where Shoji taught things Toshi never truly understood. Sometimes, Shoji's students came over, and they talked about event horizons and singularities. Toshi recognized that his father was handsome, with strong, youthful features, and that a stranger would have a difficult time discerning the students and the teacher. Other than the long hair and dirty clothes, Shoji's students did not look any younger than he.

When they weren't talking about subatomic particles, they talked about Northern Ireland or the West Bank. To Toshi, everything that was being talked about sounded very far away from where they sat. Milwaukee was pristine and orderly. The only bit of unruliness occurred in the spring, when tornadoes crept by, turning the sky yellow. Mitsuyo often pondered aloud whether she preferred Japanese earthquakes or American wind funnels. Her mother, Hanako, always said she preferred the earthquakes.

When it rained a lot, the mould infested the bread. The Hayakawas mostly ate rice, so a loaf of bread might sit in the hamper for days, growing old, untouched. Toshi threw away a lot of mouldy bread. Some days, the rain seemed to go on forever. Others were as pleasant and gentle as the waves on Lake Michigan. Aside from that, there really wasn't very much to be said about Milwaukee.

Toshi's stomach always imploded by supper—not that his round, protruding belly would have looked different to anyone. Some nights, he hovered about the kitchen, forlorn and silent. Other times, he made growly sounds like a castrated raccoon. But a few minutes before dinner one day, on the evening they received news about his paternal grandmother, Toshi was preoccupied with rigging the doorknob to his bedroom. Biting his lip, he connected the bolts with a car battery using strands of insulated wire.

His brother had been going through his collection of *Playboy*s again. Kei had thought Toshi wouldn't notice, because he didn't realize Toshi had sorted the magazines according to the Playmate of the Month's bra size. Now, everything was in chaos. Three weeks' work down the drain. Toshi was going to teach his brother a lesson about privacy. It was either this or tell their parents about the cigarettes he'd found in Kei's room, beneath the loose floorboards by the radiator. Seeing how Toshi himself pilfered from the stash of Marlboros from time to time, though, he didn't want to give it away.

This was more fun anyway. He hummed softly to himself and screwed the outer knob back onto the door, his large hands working as nimbly as elves. Kei and he were always taking things apart and putting them back together. They knew their doorknobs inside and out. Toshi also knew their televisions, radios and lawn mower intimately.

He just dearly wished he knew girls as well as he did appliances. He'd loved girls all his life. He thought they were as cute as those red-and-white polka-dot toadstools that were in every illustrated copy of *Alice in Wonderland*. But since Scotty Taylor was his trusted guide through all that was expected of American boys, Toshi did whatever Scotty did. They ran around like chickens on amphetamines, snapping rubber bands at girls' faces and screaming about diseases that no one had heard of. This was what it meant to be an American boy.

Toshi didn't mind. He only wished Scotty had warned him about the sudden shift in gears that occurred sometime in junior high. Even in his sophomore year at Whitefish High School, Toshi was still gleefully giving out onion-and-garlic gum to girls, putting plastic turds in their desks and lifting their skirts, while everyone else was making out in the booths at Marc's Big Boy.

Toshi carefully threaded the wires through the door and connected the copper leads to the battery. Just when he finished securing the connections, his mother called from downstairs. Mitsuyo was always making things that they'd never heard of in Japan. "What's for supper?" Toshi yelled back.

"Steak tartare!" said his mother.

"The French or German recipe?"

"German!" Which meant there would be no raw egg mixed into the uncooked beef. The mild musty flavour of the meat would be more prominent as it blended with the sharpness of onions and black pepper.

Downstairs, his grandmother, Hanako, who loved to suck on fresh sea urchin, made a face at the bowl of red ground meat in front of her. "This is raw," she said. Toshi thought Hanako must have been the tiniest woman in Milwaukee. She had on a shirt worn by Toshi when he was in the sixth grade. On her feet were bunny slippers that were once white but now looked like week-old snow. Hanako had come to live with Mitsuyo and her family two years after they'd moved to Milwaukee.

When they first moved to America, Mitsuyo had left her mother in Tokyo with her older sister, Tatsue. But on a hot, humid day in mid-August, Hanako and Tatsue fell into an argument over how to sweep the front steps of their house. Hanako believed in gentle, uniform strokes, while Tatsue—who was three times her mother's size—advocated letting the dust scatter. Neither of them were saints, on a summer day so uncomfortable even saints could be forgiven for losing their composure. Tatsue tried to yank the broom from her mother's tiny hands. She ended up throwing Hanako out the gate, where she seemed to float in the wind for a moment before falling in front of a noodle delivery boy on his bicycle. The noodles flew through the air, as did the poor delivery boy. The hot noodle soup falling on Hanako's head burned her scalp, and she received twelve stitches on her knees and hands.

"You could have at least ordered cold noodles," Mitsuyo said when she was back in Japan to fetch her mother. Tatsue's remarkably large hands fidgeted with her apron. "Don't worry," Mitsuyo added. "We'll take her. We'll get her shovelling our driveway in winter."

This turned out to be the last time Hanako would see Tatsue, her eldest, who for the rest of her life was haunted with nightmares of flying soup bowls attacking her as she ran naked through the streets of Tokyo in midsummer. As it turned out, Hanako would never set foot in Japan again.

Mitsuyo realized only after returning to America with her mother that the freedom she had enjoyed here was short-lived. Hanako replaced Toshi as her burden, the cross she would have to carry to Golgotha. But she wasn't embarrassed by her mother in public. It was only Shoji who made her feel ashamed.

Mitsuyo spooned the steak tartare onto pieces of rye bread, then topped them with pepper, all the while watching her mother. The open-faced sandwiches looked lonesome without the second slice of bread. Hanako sang softly to herself, as if no one else was in the room:

"The nursemaid doesn't want to return
After the Obon festival
The snow flickers
And the baby cries."

"Please don't put onions on my sandwich," Toshi said. Kei was about to take a Coke from the fridge. He was growing fast. He was in a phase when stoicism seemed to be the best defence against everything. Saying something clever all the time was too daunting, so he chose to say nothing. But his raven black hair flowed down past his shoulders, and his deep, brown eyes looked as though he saw your thoughts before you'd thought them.

Shoji was on the phone upstairs and looked like he wasn't coming down for a long time. They started eating without him. Toshi pretended to be a hyena and made giggling sounds while flinging rye bread and raw ground beef about the table. Mitsuyo hit him across the head with a wooden spoon.

By the time she started clearing the table to make room for dessert—shaved ice garnished with strawberry syrup—they'd almost forgotten about Shoji. The dishes clattered like they were talking to each other. Toshi shovelled enough shaved ice in his cavernous mouth to guarantee a delicious headache. He often crossed his eyes to intensify the pain.

They heard the uneven footfalls descending the stairs. When Shoji showed his face through the doorway, it was as pale as a spoonful of ice. His shirt, as always, was buttoned to the collar, but today he seemed to find this uncomfortable. He seemed to be having trouble deciding whether an electron decaying with two neutrinos would truly violate charge conservation. These kinds of things, funnily enough, bothered him even more than hemorrhoids. Mitsuyo soon realized, though, that whatever was distressing him this time did not involve ultimate truths behind the entire universe—just a small portion of it. They all waited for him to speak.

"Mitsuyo," he finally said. "My mother's dead."

Mitsuyo looked at him as if he'd just announced his conversion to Russian Orthodoxy.

"What?" she said.

"How?" Hanako asked. She hadn't touched her shaved ice that was melting quickly in her bowl.

"Apparently a heart attack. Last night."

Shoji sat, and dropped his face in his hands. Hanako started praying aloud. Mitsuyo stood unmoving. Kei finished his dessert, and placed his spoon in his empty bowl. Toshi could not read his brother's face. He wanted Kei to look at him. He felt he needed to make eye contact with someone. Anyone, really.

As if awakening from a reverie, Mitsuyo suddenly stirred, gathering more dishes and taking them to the kitchen. "You won't be going to the funeral, of course," she said as she walked out the door.

Shoji looked up, slowly. His eyes were both anguished and puzzled. His lips quivered.

"May I be excused?" Kei asked, pushing his chair back. His jeans were so tight they looked like they might break if he moved any faster. "I'd like to go to Telly's," he said.

Toshi suddenly felt very happy. He blurted, "Are you guys going to smoke pot?" and tried to get up and follow. He couldn't think of a better time for brotherly betrayal. But Kei shoved him back into his chair, still stone-faced, like Buster Keaton. "Hey!" Toshi fell back, laughing. "Cut that out!" No one seemed to notice, and this made Toshi breathe harder. His cheeks ripened to the colour of tomatoes.

"M-M-M-Mitsuyo," Shoji stammered. "Have you gone *mad?*"

"You're not going, Shoji," Mitsuyo called out from the kitchen. Her voice was hurt, bleeding all over the yellowing floor tiles with the outdated flower pattern.

Their house had been decorated in a way that defied sanity. On the living-room wall hung an original Harunobu woodblock print, an explicit depiction of prostitutes entertaining guests in a brothel. Beneath it was an antique Italian leather couch, on which Hello Kitty cushions were scattered. On the marble coffee table rested a vase of pink plastic flowers. On a side table stood a ceramic bonsai tree that almost looked real, though not quite.

The walls were lime, and the carpet orange. A mirror hung over the fireplace didn't do anything to make the room seem bigger, but gave everyone a feeling that they were constantly being watched. In the sitting room was a Bechstein upright, a plaid couch and a dead rubber tree. The rubber tree unfortunately had been real, not plastic.

In the kitchen, the light fixtures looked ready to fall. Above the sink hung the Japan Airlines "Beautiful Women of the World" calendar. In the dining room, Hanako stopped praying, and looked at her discarded bunny slippers on the floor. Her legs did not reach the floor from her seat, so she always sat on her heels. Toshi glanced at her. He could tell his grandmother was thinking about how her heart, too, might stop beating any time.

Hanako loved to talk about dying, and about the parts of her body that pained her. When Toshi asked her about her day, Hanako always gave him an inventory of everything that hurt, or was going to hurt tomorrow. He waited for her to say something now, but she only closed her eyes and went into one of her prune-faced Buddha meditative trances.

Shoji followed Mitsuyo into the kitchen, dragging his bad leg as if he was cleaning dog crap off his shoe. Toshi soon heard them arguing. The windows were open, and the trees whispered lazily, saying everything was as it should be on this balmy evening. Funny thing about the weather: sometimes it was completely oblivious. Kei said fuck this, pushed his hair back away from his face and left. He was starting to swear like an American.

"Remember, Sho," Mitsuyo shouted in the kitchen. "I'll leave you if you go to this goddamn funeral! Mark my words!"

"Mitsuyo, just think of the ramifications if I don't. . . ."

"What ramifications? Since when does your tail go between your legs over ramifications? You weren't too concerned about ramifications when you decided not to go to *my father's* funeral!"

"So is that what this is all about?"

"No, it's about the skid marks you leave in your underwear. *Are you a fool?*"

"Please, Mitsuyo, my stomach hurts when you shout. . . . Make me an open-faced sandwich, please."

Toshi rose and excused himself to no one in particular, because he was sure no one would hear. He bounded upstairs, taking two steps at a time, the stairwell groaning under his weight. He just wanted to escape, to flee the hellfire burning in the kitchen. To go to his room, just so he could look out the window and see the huge American cars rolling by like tall ships. Just to watch the girl across the street slapping tennis balls against their garage door in short-shorts. Just to forget he had any family at all.

He reached to open the door to his room and a million needles shot up his arm, through his shoulder to the top of his scalp. They hurled him backwards against the wall. From behind the half-open door, he heard the car battery fall on its side. His large mass crumpled to the floor. Slivers of dust drifted across his vision. He found himself laughing and crying at the same time. Kei appeared from his own room and looked at Toshi as if he was a giant dead skunk. In one hand he held a tattered guitar case.

"You all right?" Kei asked, after a pause. It sounded more like a statement than a question.

"Yeah." Toshi scratched his head vigorously. Nothing seemed to be falling from his scalp.

Kei thought for a while about helping his brother get up, but he turned and started down the stairs.

"See you later," said Toshi. "Say hi to Telly for me."

There was no reply. To Kei, getting close to Toshi was like going to Pearl Harbor as a tourist. Kei blamed the war and his brother for having to run home every day. They were the reason everyone beat on him. That he himself might have an abrasive personality never crossed Kei's mind.

Toshi looked up at the ceiling, marred by carroty water stains at the corners. He recalled what his mother told him about his grandfather. Taro had spent almost his entire life with Japan's Ministry of Foreign Affairs. He died at the start of the 1960s when Japan was tumbling toward modernity. Toshi used to wonder if his grandfather was killed because he'd been on some top-secret mission, keeping the evil SPECTRE from conquering the world. But, in fact, Taro had not been a "double-O" agent. He was merely a diplomat, posted in Lithuania for a time just before the war, then to London afterwards.

Kei's other grandfather, Yasujiro, had been a doctor. He had died violently during the war. Taro just faded away during peacetime. He smoked, drank and worked far too hard. One day, a stroke took him, just like the doctors had said it would. But no honourable Japanese worker would ever take a doctor's advice seriously. That would not be worthy of a samurai, and all Japanese workers at the time were samurai.

Mitsuyo had said that as long as she could remember, her father's breathing was laboured. The muscles in his square face always moved involuntarily, colliding when he smiled. His cheeks were flushed, engorged, ready to burst. Christmas depressed Mitsuyo, because Santa's red face always reminded her of Taro just before his stroke. "That Santa," she said to her sons, "doesn't have too many more sleigh rides ahead of him." This made Toshi sad.

Taro's funeral was held in a Buddhist temple, a sanctuary of peace in Tokyo. It was surrounded by construction on all sides, just beyond its walls. The war had been over for fifteen years. The Japanese were frantically rebuilding everything that had been razed, and adding more as they entered a decade in which they would host the Olympics for the first time.

The motto of one university's baseball team was "Dry sweat, bloody urine." One hundred and twenty hours of overtime was par for any samurai worker worth his wages. During the war, kamikaze pilots had hurled themselves against enemy ships with the passion of hungry lovers seeing each other naked for the first time. Now, every adult Japanese blindly dove into the task of regaining their notorious honour in the world's eyes. Because they were so blind, they had no idea their children and grandchildren would later take the wealth they'd built and eat it for lunch at McDonald's.

A priest with a shaved head and sagging face chanted to the closed casket containing Taro's remains. The priest's massive black robe looked ready to swallow him whole. In front of the casket was Taro's photograph, with strips of black ribbon cutting across the top corners of the frame. In the photo, Taro stared directly at the camera. His face looked like a square wooden sandal. He looked as if he was passing kidney stones. Sharp incense made the air heavy, as if there wasn't enough death around already.

Hanako sat impishly in a black kimono. It was the middle of August. Tiny beads of sweat clustered along her eyebrows. Someone gave her a letter from the Japanese foreign minister, which she gave to Tatsue, who in turn handed it to Mitsuyo. She handed it to someone else who handed it someone else who put it atop a pile of other condolence messages in the kitchen.

Mitsuyo sat next to her sister, shimmering with anger. Unlike Hanako and Tatsue, she had chosen to wear a dress instead of a kimono. The dress, as black as the bile in her heart, was wilting in the heat. Her hand was at her neck, fingering a large tiger opal set in a tear-shaped pendant. The stone was perfect except for a faint crack near the clasp. To Mitsuyo, the flaw made it unique. Shoji had bought the necklace for her in England. She had been shocked by his extravagance, knowing how little money he had, but she had not refused his gift either.

In front of her, friends and relatives shuffled about, looking lost. As their turn came, they dragged their feet up to the casket and lit thin rods of incense. Then they clasped their hands and prayed. Their feet stank. With Western-style democracy came stinky feet. Before shoes were common in Japan, people removed their sandals indoors without worry. When people's feet were engulfed in leather in the name of modernity, they began to sweat. By the time people noticed the smell in their houses, it was far too late for anyone to do anything.

After the guests had said their prayers, they went to Hanako and muttered things no one remembered. This went on forever, as Mitsuyo wilted away like week-old mountain lilies. Shoji was nowhere in sight. "He really isn't coming, is he?" Tatsue remarked for the fifth time that afternoon. You could see her broad shoulders heave, even under her layered kimono.

The priest gave a sermon, called a Buddha talk. He knelt with his hands clasped loosely on his lap. His face was appropriately solemn, but relaxed. He was as priestly as anyone had a right to be. The words came slowly and deliberately—like sand settling in a riverbed:

"The world in which we live is an intricate system of interaction and interdependence. Everything, living or inanimate, is derived from other things, and becomes other things when its existence is over. Rock dissolves into earth, which yields plants that we consume. And we ultimately return to the earth as well.

"Today, there is much talk of modernity in Japan, and of the wisdom of science. Even a planet in distant space will someday cease to exist. It may explode, or collide with a star. And its fragments, after many years travelling through darkness, eventually may reach our Earth. On the other hand, our Earth by that time may no longer be here also, and that fragment may pass through empty space while a piece of what was once Earth will be on its way to another part of the universe. Over infinite time, then, anything is possible.

"But within a system, a change in one component affects all others—a change such as death, for example. No one is feeling the effects of death today as much as the family of the deceased, but even the most distant planet in our solar system has been affected in some small way by the departure from this world of a single soul.

"Death is constantly with us in life, as is birth. They are as constant as changes in weather and erosion of riverbanks. Thus the universe, not just small parts of it but in its entirety, is constantly changing. But there is one thing that does not change, and we call this Truth. This Truth is not something we can describe in words, so we choose to symbolize it—as light, for example, emanating from the Buddha or a candle, a symbol so often used in Western religions. This Truth is timeless. It does not change. And as our loved ones leave this world, we might take comfort in knowing they are embraced by a greater Truth."

After the service, Mitsuyo directed the guests to the main dining hall with tatami mats. She thought the room was too vast and brightly lit. How can there be so much light when her mind was sinking into cold darkness? The question made her stomach growl. Small lacquer tables were lined along three walls, leaving the centre of the room as well as the entrance open. On each table were small portions of food: broiled freshwater fish, a clear broth, marinated cucumbers and a few pieces of raw tuna.

The fish was salted just enough to complement its plump, sweet flesh. The broth, though, had grown tepid. As people ate, more saké flowed than tears. A red-faced man in a dishevelled shirt stood up and dedicated a song to Taro. It was about a samurai playing a drinking game, of which a finely crafted and celebrated spear was the prize. The man sang terribly. People around him were embarrassed. They wondered why this asshole could not go singing in a bar somewhere after the funeral, just like they were going to.

It always amazed Mitsuyo to see how the Japanese could drink themselves to oblivion at the slightest opportunity. Her father used to tell her how, when he joined the foreign service and was getting by on a young civil servant's salary, he and his friends would share a bottle of cheap saké, then go ride the subway. They would walk, he said, from one end of the train to the other, making themselves sick. "We *wanted* to get sick! We were broke, but we didn't want that to keep us from getting drunk!"

"And did you?" asked Mitsuyo. "Get drunk?"

"No, but we *did* get sick!"

The drone in the dining room swelled. Mitsuyo crushed her handkerchief in her hand like a moth. Everyone had asked about Shoji. When her father died, Mitsuyo had suggested their wedding be postponed for a year, but Shoji was scheduled to go for a six-month fellowship to Milwaukee. This might eventually lead, he told Mitsuyo, to a tenured position in America. He reasoned aloud that Taro would not want to hinder their plans, and Mitsuyo found herself agreeing.

Hanako had also remained adamant about carrying through as planned. "You're not getting any younger, you know," she'd said, when they were going over the menu for Taro's funeral banquet. Mitsuyo had just turned twenty-five. Hanako could not afford for her to wait any longer. Tatsue had disappointed her enough already.

Then Shoji told Mitsuyo that he wouldn't be coming to Taro's funeral.

"I find the whole irrational ceremony deplorable, really," he said. He wrinkled his nose, as if the funeral entailed some blood ritual of the sacrificial virgin. "The man is dead. Let him rest in peace." Besides, he said, he had to attend a seminar on quarks and leptons that day. Then he put on his clothes and told Mitsuyo to put on hers. The apartment floor rumbled as a commuter train passed nearby. It always seemed to Mitsuyo that Shoji was getting everything he wanted, leaving nothing for her.

"Oh, my, he *really* isn't coming, is he?" Tatsue said again.

"Shut up," Mitsuyo replied.

Ryoko, Shoji's mother, sat in the corner, ignored by everyone. She raised a slice of cucumber to her nose and sniffed like a back-alley dog. There were bags under the old woman's eyes. Although she was about the same size as Hanako, she was much rounder. She looked like a slightly deflated soccer ball as she sat picking at her food suspiciously.

At first, Mitsuyo considered not acknowledging her future mother-in-law, but Taro invaded her thoughts. Despite making himself sick on the subway, he'd still been a diplomat, representing his country to foreign kings and queens. Mitsuyo closed her eyes and thought long about this before she stood up. The floor tipped precariously, and she realized she hadn't slept for days. She clenched her jaw, just like her favourite actor, Kirk Douglas, and found this gave her incredible strength.

Shuffling her feet across the tatami mats, Mitsuyo made her way over to Ryoko, who was now adjusting her dentures. The old woman pushed her spotted hand into her mouth, her cheeks expanding and shrinking like a poisonous blowfish. With everything in its place, she resumed picking up morsels of food with her chopsticks, then putting them down again. Mitsuyo sat down just behind Ryoko's hunched shoulders.

"Mother, thank you so much for taking the time to come today."

Ryoko turned and looked at her son's fiancée as though they'd just run into each other naked at a hot-springs resort. "Oh, my, Mitsuyo-chan. What a tragedy. But you seem to be holding up well."

"Thank you."

"I have to mention, however—and please take this as something for future reference—that the tuna is not as fresh as it could be."

"I beg your pardon?"

"The tuna, dear," Ryoko said. "It's not fresh." The look in her eyes said that her sagging cheeks wouldn't be falling off any time soon.

MUSIC

"MISS B." WAS SHORT FOR SOME UNREASONABLY LONG Ukrainian name that Toshi could never remember. Her hair was curly and stiff. Her cat's-eye glasses were thick, but the gentle green of her eyes still shone through. Her lipstick was always bright red. The colour reflected her passion for music, the passion that took priority over love of any man. At sixty-three, she had never married.

She had taught for thirty years at the conservatory, an ancient stone building not far from the university. Toshi and Kei were her first Japanese students. She had never met any Japanese before, but knew of their reputation for discipline and self-restraint. She certainly saw those qualities in the younger brother. She consoled herself that the older brother at least possessed a vivid imagination. Miss B. was a patient woman, but her patience was wearing so thin that both she and Toshi could see through it. Toshi had been taking lessons from Miss B. for two years. Mitsuyo and Shoji had enrolled him and Kei at the conservatory almost as soon as they moved to Milwaukee.

Toshi played piano like Godzilla walked. He crushed key signatures into dust. He chopped up quarter notes into unrecognizable pieces. *Andante* became *presto*. *Mezzo piano* became *fortissimo*.

At the end of each piece, he screamed at the ceiling victoriously like some ancient Celtic warrior.

Miss B. removed her glasses and rubbed her eyes. She considered retirement every week at around the same time. She looked at the door, as she did every week, knowing Kei was waiting just outside for his turn. It was always tempting to cut Toshi's lesson short and go right to Kei. Still, she prided herself on being a good teacher, and the test of a true teacher was not what she made of the talented students but how far she could carry the ones like Toshi. Only there were no others quite like Toshi.

"Toshi, do you like playing the piano?" she asked, as she did every lesson.

"Sure!" Toshi beamed. He fidgeted on his piano bench. He was ready to attack the Steinway's keyboard again.

"Is there anything you don't like about having to practise?"

"Well," he thought about it for just a moment, "all the Italian words make me hungry for pasta."

Miss B. scratched her head. Being unmarried was a hard life for such a passionate woman. She looked outside. The sun at dusk played with shadows and light in a funny way. She thought she might be dreaming.

"Toshi," she asked. "What's the title of the piece you just played?"

Toshi squinted at the music in front of him. "*The Dancing Bear*," he answered, with the confidence of a statesman.

"So, what do you think the piece should sound like?"

Toshi furrowed his brows. He looked at her as if he didn't trust the question. Slowly, he ventured, "Er . . . a dancing bear?"

"Very good!" Miss B. clapped. Toshi waved his fists in the air like a champion quiz-show contestant. "Do you think," Miss B. asked, "that how you played the piece sounded very much like a dancing bear?"

"Sure," Toshi replied, "but my bear gets sick of dancing. Then it gets hungry and it wants to kill, kill, kill!" He gnarled his hands like claws and snarled at Miss B., who blew her nose into her perfumed handkerchief.

The first song he ever wrote he wrote for her.

Listening to music while stoned was one of Kei's biggest joys. Every note, every phrase came alive, and he felt he knew exactly what the artists intended to convey when they composed the pieces. He considered the pleasure second only to sex. Or he would have if, at the painful age of fourteen, he had any first-hand knowledge of sex. The closest thing to sex that Kei had experienced at that stage in his life—other than relieving himself with his right hand—was sitting close to Jaime, who let their shoulders and knees touch. It was amazing how much warmth and tenderness he could feel through denim and wool.

She'd just returned from Paris, where her father had been transferred for four years by his corporation. She left Milwaukee a little girl and came back a teenager with all the goods.

For a long time, something about Paris popped out every time she opened her mouth. Like how she would go for walks along the banks of the Seine and visit Notre Dame Cathedral to take in the rose windows. Or sit on a bench, getting soaked while needles of rain hit the river's surface. Pressing his back against the wall in Telly's dark basement, Kei could imagine watching the murky water as it flowed past her, beads of moisture sparkling in her long hair. He could see this clearly, as she turned to him, offering him another toke with a slow smile. Telly's parents were away visiting cousins in Madison.

"Dig this, man." Telly was demonstrating the opening riffs of "You Really Got Me" by the Kinks, playing along with the record on his used Les Paul. Without fail, he would fall behind at the third bar. "Fuck!" he always said, and let the song run its course. Later he would get up, and the stylus would skate across vinyl as he fumbled with the turntable. Then "You Really Got Me" started again with him following until the third bar.

Music, like most things, came easily to Kei. It was after all just another language, with its tricks and turns of phrase. He had mastered English in three months, but music expressed more of what he really wanted to say—all his accusations, every one of his desires. After he learned the basic Hanon piano exercises, he started weaving them into evolving patterns of colour and texture, using dynamics and tempo.

Mitsuyo noticed immediately. She was convinced Kei was on his way to becoming another Arturo Benedetti Michelangeli, whom she'd seen in concert during one of his tours of Japan. She imagined Kei on his way to playing for the emperor in the Imperial Palace in Tokyo. She was going to push Kei along every step of the way. She staked a lot of herself on this dream. No one realized that she'd staked too much. Not Kei, not Shoji, and least of all herself.

"Are you still playing the piano, Kei?" Jaime asked. Some questions were too uncomfortable to answer. Kei let it fall to the floor. "I used to love how you played," she added. Maybe it was this presumption, or just the tone of her voice. He tossed a few more thoughts around his befuddled head, then got up and turned off the stereo.

"Hey!" Telly protested. "Why'd the fuck you do that?" They had listened to "You Really Got Me" straight through seven times. Stoned or not, this was getting to be too much. Telly, deep down, knew this also. He didn't resist when Kei took his guitar from him. Telly didn't resist much that Kei did anyway.

He'd thought about her a lot while she was away—just about every day, in fact. He would recall their friendship and be pleased by how it differed from how he related to Telly, and at the same time be saddened that there had been no one to replace her. He often wrote her letters but never sent them. Most of all, he wondered if he'd ever see her again.

But she'd come back, and how she'd looked when he first opened the door to find her standing there was something he would never forget. The leaves on the trees were still green, but the autumn chill sharpened the wind. The sun shimmered behind her, and this hurt his eyes. She wore a clean denim jacket over a red T-shirt and black pants. And she wore her new boots from the Champs Elysées. If there were movement in the street, Kei could not see it. He could not hear Mitsuyo calling from the dining room.

He'd written his first song shortly afterwards. Like any first song that anyone writes, it was a love song. While Telly swore under his breath, Kei adjusted the guitar on his knee and looked right at Jaime. The basement grew darker somehow as Kei began to strum. The chords were simple enough—switch between C major seven to A minor seven for the introduction, strumming like river water running, running, off to nowhere:

"When the sky opens and the rain's on fire, I'll see only your eyes
When angry voices call hope a liar, I'll hear only your whisper."

The words that he'd kept hidden for so long rode the melody's current. The verses rose and fell among passion, despair and hope. He repeated the chorus and let the chords fall away. He could see the surprise in her eyes. He was pleased, but at the same time could not think of anything to say to her. It did not cross his mind that this was why he wrote the song in the first place.

Telly sat on the bed, trying his best to be unimpressed, and obviously failing. His face was trapped between the irritated frown he wanted to wear and the smile that Kei's song was pulling to the surface. No one stayed angry for long when Kei sang, even when anger was what his song was about. Kei gave Telly's guitar back to him.

The ceiling creaked above their heads. A woman's voice was crying out, "Telly? Telly, we're home, sweetheart!"

"Oh, fuck." Telly bolted for the bag of dope on the floor. He stuffed it under the cushion. "They're fucking home early!" He picked up the few roaches in the ashtray and threw them in his mouth.

"Listen, I have to go anyway," said Jaime, who acted as though she had not understood the significance of Telly's mother wandering around upstairs while the basement reeked like an opium den. She grabbed her denim jacket by the collar and threw it over her shoulder. Everything looked like a performance to Kei when he was stoned. "God, look at the time," she said with a wink.

"Good, good," said Telly. "Fucking go upstairs, Jaime, and stall them."

"I've gotta go too, man," said Kei, rubbing his eyes.

"Right. Fucking go, man. Excuse me for not seeing you to the fucking door." As they climbed the stairs, Telly was picking at the rolling papers scattered on the floor like snow-covered leaves.

Telly's father always looked like his heart was going to stop at any moment. Roger's face was red because he started drinking at eleven in the morning. His eyes were wide and colourless, like those of a snake. His wife, Fran, wore so much makeup that it often fell off her face in chunks. They lived in a bungalow just north of Lover's Bluff Elementary School. It was a pocket of relative destitution in an otherwise affluent area of Milwaukee. Roger and Fran were not rich, but they owned their house and paid their alms at church every week.

They were hanging their coats in the front closet when Jaime and Kei appeared from the basement. They always had been ambivalent about Kei, and their smile showed it. He was such a little kid, and a gook, as Roger put it. Fran always pointed out to him that Telly's marks improved after he became friends with Kei, ever since Miss Steinky's class.

At Lover's Bluff Elementary School, the principal had taken a liking to the Japanese brothers. This was why his present task seemed so difficult. Kei fidgeted in his seat while Mr. Strong contemplated the trees outside his office window. Kei clicked the heels of his shiny leather shoes together. He looked at his fingertips as if they were the most interesting things in the room.

Telly wasn't sure why he liked this Jap shrimp wonton. He often wanted to wrap Kei up in a giant egg roll and deep-fry him. When Miss Steinky first assigned Kei to the seat next to his, Roger and Fran had been threatening Telly with remedial summer school. God had apparently answered his prayers with Kei, but it turned out to be a deal with the devil.

"I understand your grades have improved considerably, Telly," said Mr. Strong. He hadn't turned away from the window. The floor trembled.

Telly could neither speak nor move. His scalp itched under curly black locks, but he couldn't raise his hand to scratch it.

Mr. Strong turned around to face the silence. "Is it because you've been cheating off of Kei all this time?"

The devil's plans were always so simple, so alluring. Kei was short. It was nothing to look over his shoulder. Telly didn't even have to crane his neck. Kei also made things easier by leaning to one side. Who would've thought that Miss Steinky would be looking right at them as she read the bonus question? Who the hell cared about all those x's and y's anyway?

Mr. Strong held up their tests. "Did you know," he asked, "your answers are identical? Where is your originality, Telly?"

Kei suddenly looked up from inspecting his hand. "It's not Telly's fault, sir," he said, sort of like Oliver Twist. Mr. Strong and Telly arched an eyebrow each. Kei looked down and pouted his lips. "To tell you the truth, he wasn't cheating off of me. I was copying from him."

The words tinkled like broken glass in Telly's ears. Mr. Strong looked like he had just witnessed Kei turn into an angel. The hardened school principal beamed. Tears welled in his eyes. He knew he was witnessing a noble young samurai making what was the ultimate sacrifice for a selfish classmate.

"That is a very brave thing you're trying to do, Kei," he said, patting the unbelievably small Japanese boy on the head. Then he turned to Telly to see if he'd also understood.

In fact, Telly had understood all too well. It had to do with the sour taste in his mouth that had nothing to do with anything he'd eaten. Mr. Strong had let him go with a warning then, and although he kept on cheating, he never allowed himself to be caught after that.

Roger said that gook kids gave him the creeps. So quiet, he said, and they had eyes that judged you. Both had noticed how Kei was over more often since they bought Telly the guitar, and that Kei already played better than their own son. Nonetheless, they were always polite to Kei whenever Telly had him over.

When they appeared at the top of the basement stairs, Fran looked at Jaime and Kei like she could not be more glad if the pope had come to visit. "Hi, guys!" she said. "We didn't know you'd be here!"

Roger grunted his greeting. "Where's Telly?"

Jaime was wearing the perfume she'd brought back from Paris. She smelled like the flower garden at Versailles. Even Roger couldn't help smiling as she drew nearer. He seemed to forget all about Telly and Kei. "Telly's downstairs," Jaime said in a near whisper. Fran frowned. Kei said nothing as he and Jaime slipped outside into the grey afternoon.

They cut through the playground of Lover's Bluff Elementary School. A few kids were shooting baskets on the asphalt court, their small bodies losing balance every time they tossed the ball into the air. Usually Jaime's face fell into a smile whenever she saw little kids. Kei noticed she wasn't smiling now. She suddenly turned to him, her hair falling across her face like a soft curtain. Baby, thought Kei, you look like an angel.

"Why do you have to complicate everything, Kei?" she said.

He didn't understand the question. He wasn't complicating things. It's just that they were older, and things were changing. At the same time, they were still not old enough, especially him. He was never old enough.

Jaime looked flattered, sad and angry all at the same time. She tried her best to smile but wasn't quite succeeding. Reaching out slowly, as if Kei was a frightened animal, she caressed his cheek. A pause, a rest, the kids playing basketball stopped to look, and she drew him closer. When they kissed, Kei thought her lips tasted like Paris rain.

"Thank you," she said, as she drew her head back. "That was beautiful." It took a second for Kei to realize she meant the song and not the kiss.

Any musical note when held long enough—not just seconds, but several minutes—after a while stops being music and becomes noise. For Toshi, it was impossible to tell when this took place. He resisted the change in perception because he craved consistency. He was also disturbed, rather than charmed, by sudden changes in music, such as a presence of a dissonant chord. A variation in time signature was enough to send him spinning, crashing onto the floor.

Miss B.'s puffy cheeks caved in as she sucked on the end of her Virginia Slim. She exhaled through her nose. She could hardly bring herself to look at Mitsuyo and Shoji, who sat on two chairs placed next to the piano. Miss B. sat on her piano bench, fidgeting. She was not accustomed to having to explain herself.

"It's not as if I couldn't have married," she said to Shoji, who nodded and rubbed his stomach. "There were plenty of suitors," Miss B. said, staring into the ribbons of smoke she'd just exhaled. "It's just that none of them could satisfy the passion burning right here." She pointed to her ample left breast. "No one man could ever satisfy me. Only the piano. Only the piano could fill me the way I needed to be filled."

Across the room, Kei and Toshi sat on an antique couch, upholstered in gold fabric with floral patterns. Mitsuyo looked at them while Shoji listened to Miss B.'s explanations. It was so odd, the contrast between her sons. They were like Skinny and Fatty, characters from the Japanese movie with the same name. Just like in the movie, it was Mitsuyo's skinny son who wound up with the brains and talent.

She tried to remember when the differences started to become apparent. Toshi had been restless from the beginning, hardly sleeping for more than forty minutes at a time. He was talking by the time he was ten months old, but mainly to himself. Left alone, he waddled around their apartment in Tokyo turning on every lamp, radio and alarm clock he could reach. He was terribly upset that he was not tall enough to turn on the washer. He lay at its base, out on the concrete veranda where they kept it, rolling from side to side, holding his ears.

When Mitsuyo went into labour with Kei, on their way to the hospital Toshi tried to crawl out of the car window, insisting he would rather wait for his new brother at home. He could maybe tidy the place up. Besides, *Prince Planet* was on television. As Shoji drove through the narrow streets in the suburbs of Tokyo, Mitsuyo fought desperately to ignore the pain, and to keep her son in his seat. It was the first time she remembered hitting him.

The only time Toshi settled down was when Mitsuyo sang a Japanese lullaby. A traditional folk song from the north of Japan was Toshi's favourite, even though its words were unbearably sad.

"This child cries a lot
Touches the nursemaid
The nursemaid, too, seems to grow thinner
With each passing day."

Mitsuyo had always found it curious that many traditional lullabies had lyrics that were either sad or frightening or both.

It was only after Kei was about half a year old that Mitsuyo learned there was more to raising a child than extracting him from the closet or lowering him from the roof. Kei spoke at an early age also, and was reading by the time he was three. Instead of listening to Mitsuyo's lullabies, Kei often sang them himself to his brother, to settle Toshi down. Once, Mitsuyo walked into the living room to find Toshi curled under a blanket, while Kei caressed his back, singing like an angel.

"That Kei is quite a little boy," Mitsuyo told Shoji later that night as they both lay in bed. He was reading a dissertation by one of his students. "You may not know this, but he is extremely compassionate. If I can only show him how to express it through music."

"He's too intense," Shoji remarked without taking his eyes off the page. Mitsuyo knew her husband could see both the beauty and the flaws in the mathematical formulas, just as an English teacher might spot bad grammar or poetry in a piece of writing. Mitsuyo wondered what would make Shoji say what he had. What did this have to do with the music? Clearly, Shoji simply did not understand. He never could relate well to his sons.

"So you see, this whole situation may be more frustrating for me than it would be to another piano teacher who doesn't feel as passionate about her craft." Miss B. smiled. The tips of her fingers, nails neatly trimmed, drummed the closed lid of the piano. She held the cigarette high with her other hand in the classic manner. "Kei is a treasure," she muttered, looking at Mitsuyo, who somehow understood. "I could work with him all day. He learns everything I teach him like it was as natural as breathing."

She looked over at the couch, where Toshi was pulling at a strand of thread that had unfurled from the upholstery. There was now a hole in the fabric where there had been none before. Kei was reading his Schumann book as if it contained words rather than music, humming the melody softly to himself. "And Toshi has a heart of gold," said Miss B. Something shone behind her glasses like a dying star. "But I'm not getting any younger, you see."

Shoji translated for Mitsuyo in a hushed whisper, although Toshi was too preoccupied with the couch's stuffing to hear anyway. Kei was too engrossed in his music. Neither of them cared much for adult conversation. Mitsuyo glanced at Toshi and bit her lip.

"I'm truly sorry," said Miss B., butting her cigarette to mark the conclusion of an always unpleasant discussion. Letting go a student was never easy. "Of course, we can just extend Kei's lesson into an hour. He's ready for it." Might as well still collect the full fees. There was no one to take care of her.

On the way home in the car, Toshi burst into tears. Shoji drove. Mitsuyo again tried to keep her eldest son from climbing out the window. Kei looked at the streetscape passing by as if he was looking for someone on the sidewalk. "Why?" asked Toshi. "Why doesn't Miss B. want to see me any more?"

"It's not that she doesn't want to see you," Mitsuyo explained gently, but feeling exhaustion setting in like a fast tide. "Miss B. just feels that perhaps you're not ready to take on something as complex as the piano. Maybe when you get older we can sign you up for lessons again."

Toshi pointed an accusing finger at his brother, whose attention still seemed very far away. "Well, what about Kei? He's younger than I am!" Toshi's nose ran as freely as white water.

Mitsuyo looked at Shoji for support but found him squinting ahead at the road. Either he was pretending not to listen or he was too absorbed in thoughts surrounding superconductivity to hear his son howling in the back seat. She squirmed as if Toshi's cry was the tip of a pencil poking her spine in irregular rhythm. A part of her felt genuinely sorry for Toshi. A bigger part felt that by this time he should be getting used to failure. "That's enough, fool," she snapped. "Kei is special. He always has been."

And he always will be, Toshi thought to himself. He looked at his brother and could not understand why Kei seemed so weary as he continued to stare out the car window.

COURTSHIP

SHOJI DID, IN FACT, GO TO HIS MOTHER'S FUNERAL.

Mitsuyo made him pack for himself for the first time since they were married. Not that he felt he needed help. Very systematically, he gathered seven shirts for the week-long trip, plus one extra. He packed a pair of slacks for every two shirts. He packed seven undershirts, seven pairs of striped boxer shorts and seven pairs of socks. Toshi pretended to help, and sprayed Mitsuyo's Nair in one of the boxer shorts when Shoji wasn't looking.

Shoji noticed almost immediately. He made clear to Toshi that practical jokes were ultimately a waste of time, of which there was only a finite amount between birth and death. Time was a precious commodity, so don't waste it on a laugh. Toshi hung his head. Shoji dragged his foot down the stairs to throw his shorts into the laundry.

On the balmy afternoon when Shoji left, both his sons saw him off at the door. Mitsuyo was upstairs. She hadn't answered when Kei called to say Shoji was leaving. Toshi helped his father carry the suitcase out to the Yellow Cab. He grunted and scowled, pretending it was heavier than it actually was. The day was warm

61

but cloudy, as though someone had been lazy and forgotten to paint the sky.

As the taxi drove off, Shoji took a last look at his sons as they stood at the door. Standing side by side, they looked like the number ten.

Toshi waved. When the taxi rolled out of sight, he and Kei looked at each other. They knew their mother wasn't bluffing when she said she was leaving. They just weren't sure whether Shoji knew it. For all his university degrees and awards and scholarly publications, he could be quite obtuse. Kei shook his head, and went inside for his guitar. He was going over to Telly's house to practise. He was practising every day, either at Telly's or in his room, for hours, until his fingertips bled.

Shoji took the train to Chicago. It was about an hour-and-a-half ride from Milwaukee, most of it flat farmland and patches of brush. When there was sun, the fields glimmered in gold, as pure as childhood wonders. When it was cloudy, like today, they were the colour of rust. Shoji had plenty of time to think, as the cows and the barns and fences flew past his window. Thinking was, after all, what he did best.

He wasn't thinking about the farms or the fields—nor of quantum fields, which usually occupied his mind most of his waking hours. He was listening to the radio through his Koss "Made in Wisconsin" headphones. A commercial bridged Chopin to Bartók. A stentorian voice hawked an upcoming television movie about an American marine who suffers a nervous breakdown during the war. It was apparently based on a Pulitzer Prize–winning novel. Shoji knew that insanity was infectious during war.

His mind drifted over the rhythm of the rails. His thoughts turned to Vietnam. He remembered a president with jowls like a basset hound's. He'd told American soldiers in Vietnam to come home. The same president made the Chinese and Americans be friends again—all Chinese, not just people like Mr. Lee of the Pink

Phoenix where Shoji and his family ate once a month. Then every-one found out about Watergate and the president had to resign from telling people what to do and with whom they should be friends.

Watching the scenery speed by on the train to Chicago, Shoji saw farmhouses and gas stations on the horizon blur into water-colour. Shoji recalled how the Communist movement in Vietnam started near the end of the Second World War, around the time Yasujiro was killed, when Ho Chi Minh led the Viet Minh against the Japanese occupation.

Life had changed drastically for Shoji and his mother when Yasujiro died. Neighbours were sympathetic immediately after-wards. Many of them had already lost family to the war. Because Ryoko had always been generous with the ham and bacon, they came to help with chores and housework. They brought what lit-tle they themselves had to eat—mostly millet, potatoes and pick-les. Shoji was grateful, but every time someone brought something over, he could see a fragment of Ryoko's pride chip away and scat-ter with the breeze.

She ate nothing but pastries filled with sweet red beans. Her kimono wrinkled as the weeks passed. Hair fell out of place. Her eyes sunk into her face, which grew round and pallid.

"How I wish your father was here!" Ryoko often cried, tears floating on puffy cheeks. "He would know what to do!"

He'd take off his clothes and run singing down the street naked, thought Shoji. He chose not to say anything. Thoughts and mem-ories were still wrestling like bears in his otherwise hollow chest.

Shoji was lying unconscious in the clinic when his father was killed by the *kempeitai,* the paramilitary police. When Shoji awoke, not only had he lost a parent, he also discovered one of his legs was crushed. He would always remember it being a dark, grey after-noon. He was lying not in a ward in the clinic but on a gurney in his father's office. He could hear the rush of wind, though the window was closed. His head felt ready to burst. Rain was falling outside the window. A spider clutched its web, which billowed like fate. The pain from his lower torso came suddenly, and Shoji grabbed the sheets. A crack cut across the ceiling. He wailed, both in pain and shock.

Ryoko rushed in, as if on cue, with Otama the maid and a couple of old men. They held him down and stabbed a needle in his arm. Everything softened to a dull roar. He felt his head sinking further into the pillow, and the tears still streaming down the side of his face.

When he came to the second time, they told him that Yasu had been decapitated by an overzealous *kempeitai* with a sword. Shoji and his mother had always feared that Yasu's mouth would get him killed someday. Ryoko began blubbering as if it had been her leg that was crushed. "This war's taken everything!" she screamed. The nurses looked at each other. They asked with their eyes whether this one needed to be sedated as well. "I've lost everything! *Everything!*"

Yet it was so clear to Shoji. It wasn't the war. It was insanity. Insanity had started the war and kept it going. And insanity had killed Yasu, in more ways than one.

The war had been hard on everyone. When the Americans dropped the nuclear bombs and Japan lost, it was as though the colour of the sun had changed overnight. People awoke every morning to a strange, alien world, and they never believed that they would ever become accustomed to the change. Ryoko cried all the time, then. The tears didn't stop when they discovered Otama was leaving to get married. They also found they could not afford to hire anyone else. Otama never once offered to stay. Shortly afterwards, the national railroad brought a replacement for Yasu to Kitagawa, evicting Ryoko and Shoji from the house.

The afternoon sun hurt Shoji's eyes as he and Ryoko waited for the train that would take them out of Kitagawa forever. It had taken the railway two months to repair the tracks after the bombing. The clouds were immaculate and white, the colour of surrender. Shoji stood swaying on his crutches. One of his legs still remained in bandages, broken and badly burned. Still, there was surprisingly little pain. It was as if losing a parent and a limb at the same time deadened his senses to life's more trivial problems, like surviving in a country ravaged by war.

Practically half the town came to see them off—their one last act of grace. Summer was gone, along with everything else. The hilltops were a kaleidoscope of flaming colours. A *yakitori* vendor was yelling from across the street, hawking skewered chicken pieces, pretending they weren't actually dog meat.

Shima stood uncertain, adjusting his glasses on his nose, over and over. His black school uniform was torn at the shoulder. His mother had lost her job when the Maruyama Chemical Plant was blown away by American bombers. She still wore her work pants, because she owned little else. The women who wore kimono still retained a quiet strength. Those who wore blouses were unable to keep them clean or unwrinkled. The men who stayed home during the war were visibly weary. Those who served but survived to come home looked broken. They all seemed to wish Shoji and his mother well, but unconfident that even this modest prayer was realistic.

Shoji tried for a while to ignore his friend. What could he say to anyone when the world had just collapsed around him? Still, perhaps he should try to think of something. The train appeared in the distant valley, the black smoke resembling a billowing flag of mourning.

"You're going to try for Tokyo University, aren't you?" Shoji asked.

Shima nodded. The war had changed him as well. It had actually angered him, albeit belatedly. He stood staring coldly at Shoji for a long time. He didn't seem to remember the books he'd borrowed. Shoji didn't bother reminding him. Shoji was still under the impression he could afford to buy them again.

Ryoko looked toward the mountains, humming softly to herself.

"Why does the crow cry?
The crow has seven young hatchlings in the mountains
It cries, 'Adorable, adorable.' "

The train was nearing. "Well," Shoji said to Shima, "I guess we might see each other there, then." Shoji began to understand that the most profound goodbyes often involved not saying the word at all.

Yasujiro had owned a small house in Tokyo. It had been rented to boarders while the railroad moved his family around Japan like *pachinko* balls. When he died, Ryoko had intended to sell it, but Yasu's brother caught wind of this and intervened. He stopped Ryoko with the threat of embarrassment. He argued that the house should retain the Hayakawa name, or what would people think? That Shoji didn't leave enough to provide for his family. That she and Shoji were as poor as they in fact were.

Ryoko succumbed in no time. She watched her brother-in-law move into her house with his family. Ryoko was only a woman with a dead husband, with little will and even less influence. She considered going to live with her cousin, who'd sent her the ham and bacon during the war, but it had been too long since she left the farm. Besides, someone needed to keep an eye on the house.

She and Shoji lived like unwelcome guests. She spent most days sitting and staring at the weeds growing in the garden and eating a lot of red bean cake.

Shoji's cousins made him carry their things to school. They laughed at him and called him a cripple and a cretin and ordered him to clean their rooms. Shoji's only sanctuary was the public library, a brownstone building across the street from a train station between the school and his house.

He did, after all, make it in to Tokyo University. After he graduated from the science program at the top of his class, he surprised everyone by saying he was going to England for a post-doctoral fellowship. He was expected to take care of his mother, who'd over the years deteriorated to a mass of flesh and flatulent insensitivity.

At times, she attempted to regain her former elegance. Yet, the more she alluded to her former stature as a doctor's wife, the more her in-laws ridiculed her. When she displayed a valuable piece of calligraphy, an old family heirloom, on the wall in her room, there were constant reminders of how she was from a family of pig farmers after all. They laughed about how Yasujiro had lost his job in the city. They recalled how the family was exiled to towns like Kitagawa, how Yasu was able to work only by virtue of his brother's intervention and so on, until the calligraphy was quietly taken down.

Ryoko often recalled how Yasu would scream in a drunken rage that his brother had testicles smaller than grains of rice. After he died, she reminded Shoji of this remark whenever things became difficult. Over the years, between long visits to the university library, Shoji noticed his mother was chewing food with her mouth open. By the time he was ready to go to Cambridge, Ryoko could fart on demand, and often did so without any encouragement.

She didn't take news of him going to England well.

"You're not going to just leave me here, are you?" she asked, the night before he was to leave. "How will I ever face the neighbours? Please, Sho-chan, tell me you're not some selfish lout who leaves his mother among wolves. . . ." As tears welled in her eyes, floating on bags of skin, an unmistakable odour filled the room. Shoji looked at his mother, who, still crying, nonetheless smiled impishly. "Sorry," she said. "It's the beans."

Shoji did go to Cambridge. In England, he met Mitsuyo and took her virginity. He returned to Japan to marry her, but didn't attend her father's funeral. Ryoko went in his stead, then complained about the tuna. Such actions and inactions, some subtle, others blatant, left their marks on Mitsuyo's spirit.

For more than ten years after they were married, Shoji took repeated trips to Milwaukee, where a classmate from Cambridge was working in subatomic physics. Finally, in the same year Americans handed Okinawa back to Japan, the University of

Wisconsin finally offered Shoji a tenured position. He had to leave his mother behind again because by this time Mitsuyo didn't want her coming along. Even after Hanako fell in front of the noodle delivery boy and came to live with her daughter, Ryoko was still left with Shoji's cousins back in Japan.

The cousins didn't complain. The house, after all, still belonged to her. But no one thought much of such details anyway. Time had discarded a lot of dead leaves in its wake. Ryoko lay among them.

As the train to Chicago moved forth, the grey scenery sped by like a silent picture, intimate and vivid. The vibration of the floor and the seat was entrancing. Before long, Shoji was struggling to keep his eyes open. On the tide of darkness came dream images. And music. Always music.

Happy birthday to you, happy birthday to you, happy birthday Old Man Garber . . .

Seventy-five flames billowed above vanilla frosting. Wax dripped like limestone, falling, falling. Old Man Garber was jubilant, looking younger than Shoji had ever seen him. Shoji had always waved at his neighbour whenever he saw him in the street. Toshi and Kei had told him the old man was a Polish Jew. Old Man Garber usually acknowledged Shoji's greeting with a grunt.

In Shoji's dream, though, Old Man Garber was smiling like an infant tasting his first spoonful of ice cream. He walked upright for once, without a walker or a cane. His spine was as straight as a needle. Unfamiliar children kissed his sunken, mapped cheeks. A single birthday present, wrapped in shiny red paper, reflected the candlelight. Old Man Garber said sourly that he didn't want any cake, so they made him unwrap the gift: a gargantuan Colt .45 that was as black as a moon in eclipse.

Old Man Garber looked caught between clapping his hands in delight and crying out in pain. Grasping the gun's handle firmly with his knotted hands, he lifted the heavy metal to his head. Shoji flinched. The aria "O mio babbino caro" from Puccini's *Gianni Schicchi* played overhead. The bony finger pulled the trigger.

As abruptly as a gunshot, the scene shifted. Shoji saw Ryoko in the courtyard of a Siberian gulag. Black barbed-wire fences stood raging against the grey skies. All the prisoners were old, dressed in rags, emaciated to nothingness. Shoji hadn't seen such hunger since the war. Yet the expression on his mother's face was unmistakable. It screamed: *"I want to live!"*

In truth, Ryoko hadn't said a word. She simply shuffled about with the other prisoners, as silent as the snow falling around their feet. When the dinner bell rang, she smiled like a child, happier than Shoji had ever seen her.

When he opened his eyes, he recognized the streets of Chicago, which were a little harder, a bit grittier, than those of Milwaukee. The train was pulling into the station. Another cab ride would get him to the airport. He stretched and yawned. A smile moved across his face. He felt rested. His dream, like many before it, had been forgotten instantly. He noticed his headphones had gone crooked. An earpiece had slid over his nose.

Around the time Shoji was checking in at the JAL ticket counter at O'Hare, back in Milwaukee, Toshi was pulling weeds in the garden behind their house. The clouds still hadn't broken. The lifeless grey blanket overhead trapped the humidity and stagnant heat below.

The garden fascinated him with its neediness, always in want of attention and care. He was also taken by the weeds, which were amazingly resilient. He tore at their stems, dug up their roots, yet they still returned, week after week. When he lifted a piece of dirt from the ground and turned it over, he saw the complex network of roots. Among them crawled beetles and faceless earthworms. Toshi imagined the cells reproducing at the tips of roots and in limbs growing in larvae. Mechanical reproduction was occurring everywhere. He thought that at some unspecified time, a spark of light ignited and made its vessel—be it plant or animal—wholly alive. Any living thing—human or weed—was a bundle of cells, of bone and tissue, carrying a spirit that made it run, eat, sleep and crap. Life was nothing more than a point of light trapped in sickly skin, he thought.

Above him, in his parents' bedroom, Mitsuyo was packing. She stuffed a mountain of things with fervour into a worn suitcase, then took half of them out again. She looked out the window a few times, and each time wondered whether it was going to rain. Some things she found in her dresser, she ignored. Other things made her pause, like the opal necklace with the gold setting shaped like a teardrop and the faint crack near the clasp. She thought again of how little money Shoji had when he bought it for her.

When Mitsuyo and Shoji met, he was studying at Cambridge and she had just graduated from school. She was visiting England with Tatsue, who was on summer holidays. They were giddy with the knowledge they weren't supposed to be there. Mitsuyo in particular, having come of age a year ago, was ripe for marriage. Hanako had protested repeatedly that her daughters were too busy with *omiai*, formal meetings with prospective husbands, to think about travelling.

Unlike Tatsue, who already had carpenter's hands and a sumo wrestler's face, Mitsuyo's inborn elegance glowed. Her skin had remained immaculate through adolescence. She walked with the natural athletic grace of a ballerina. It was only her mouth that Hanako found unpredictable.

While Taro served as first secretary at the embassy in London, Hanako had remained in Japan to make certain that her daughters underwent the obligatory lessons in cooking, flower arranging, tea ceremony and calligraphy. She was remarkably strong willed, despite her size, when it came to finding husbands for her daughters. Sadly, except for the cooking classes, Mitsuyo had failed everything miserably. This had less to do with any lack of aptitude than her saucy personality, which wreaked havoc on any teacher–student relationship.

She especially loathed the lessons in traditional flower arranging. As a child, she had experienced *sokai*, evacuation, just as the bombings in Tokyo were getting fierce. Children, along with industries vital to the war effort, were ordered out of major cities. For Mitsuyo, it was a time defined by hunger, homesickness and the majestic mountains surrounding the rural village in which she was placed. She often spent her days by a riverbank, frolicking in the fresh fragrance of wildflowers growing freely in the moist earth. Poplar seeds floated lazily on the breeze around her head and shoulders.

When she lay on the grass and looked toward the rolling clouds over the mountain ridge, the war seemed far, far away. The hunger that usually roared in her belly would settle for a time. The air-raid sirens cried out from time to time, but the planes usually just flew by overhead, on their way to somewhere else.

In the country, the local children, especially the boys, delighted her by using language she'd never hear at home. Mud on their cheeks, their noses caked with dust and snot, they said things like "ass," "shit-dripper" and "booger." This made the hair on the back of her neck stand at attention. The sensation was delicious. Like any child immersed in a new language, it took her no time to learn.

Then Mitsuyo was told the war was over. She was returned to a Tokyo she didn't recognize. It was no longer a city but a litany of despair. Rubble lined the streets like cobblestones. Twisted metal reached up from slabs of concrete to the sky, petrified in time. Shadows of dead flames remained on walls that were still standing. The smoke lingered in the air weeks after the last air raid. People built fires in the open and cooked over them—potatoes, dog meat, anything they could find.

Among the ashen lives stood her house, which miraculously had survived the bombs and the ensuing fire. Hanako and Tatsue were busy giving out blankets and spare clothing. Taro had just returned to Japan from his posting at the embassy in Lithuania, but he spent most his time at the Ministry of Foreign Affairs. He left in the morning and didn't return home until late at night, unaware that this devotion to his job was killing him.

Even though Mitsuyo was home, she found there was still the hunger—still the homesickness for a place that no longer existed. And now there were no mountains or rivers or flowers to distract her—just charred skeletons of architecture, waiting to be razed. In a state of general helplessness, she bravely reclaimed control by using the exotic language she had learned in the country. She told Hanako that the toilet stank, the food tasted like crap and that she didn't "care a bit about poor people, you stupid shit-dripper."

When she spoke to people this way, the shock on their faces made her dizzy with power. She couldn't stop smiling, even through Taro's spankings. Anything was better than being passive like her fat sister, a model child. Anything was better than letting the river's current push her around like a reed.

When she became a teenager, she was taken to her first lesson in ikebana, held in one of the few neighbourhoods still standing after the bombs. At first she dutifully bowed and used honorific language. Her teacher smiled, and gave her the cut flowers she was to arrange along with fragments of twigs and some grasses. Placing the limp pile on the table, she decided she was bored. She feigned horror when told to stand the stems on flat pinned holders called *kenzan.* "How would you like it if I stuck steel spikes up *your* rump?" she asked.

Her teacher wore a kimono as tight as a steel vise. She was a fortyish woman with cheeks like glutinous rice cakes. She looked at Mitsuyo with tiny, unblinking *kokeshi* doll eyes and began arranging her flowers for her. Mitsuyo at first was unsure whether her teacher had heard her. Immediately after the arrangement was complete, she dismissed Mitsuyo for the day.

The teacher was too embarrassed to tell Mitsuyo's parents

what had happened. Mitsuyo told them herself. Then Hanako became embarrassed to take her daughters back for another lesson. A new teacher was found for Tatsue, and Mitsuyo was never subjected to ikebana lessons again.

She didn't fare any better at the tea ceremony. All movements involved in serving tea were prescribed, from the foot with which you entered the tearoom to how many mouthfuls it should take to finish the tea. Ladling the hot water into the bowls containing the powdered tea required the server to hold the dipper at just the proper height. No one knew why things needed to be this way, and the masters spoke in vague, esoteric terms, ensuring that their students returned for further enlightenment.

Within the vast web of rules and etiquette, though, the tea ceremony was as much about entertaining guests with witty conversation as it was about tea. Mitsuyo again made an honest attempt at showing some grace befitting a daughter of a diplomat. As she grew bored, though, her choice of topics for discussion became less conventional.

Just before she came of age, she asked one middle-aged, balding foreign ministry bureaucrat when he'd started to lose his hair. At his stuttered answer, all she could say was, "You must be joking. You were just a baby!" before declaring any man she married would be allowed to go grey but not bald. She then made a slight error in etiquette. It was an extra, unnecessary movement of a hand that no one would have noticed had she not loudly proclaimed, "Shit-dripper! I did it again!"

It was therefore understandable that she had looked forward to her trip to England with such overwhelming giddiness it almost made her sick. To her initial dismay, she found there were many things in common between the British and the Japanese. (She could tell this, even though she understood very little English. Her parents had cancelled her language lessons back when she was attending a prestigious middle school in Tokyo, where she insisted on asking her teacher how to say *kuso*. They weren't about to take chances with a tutor.)

On the streets of London, men walked around as if they had umbrellas up their rumps. She imagined one man remarking, "I say, I think it's going to rain, and here I forgot to pack an umbrella up my rump." She imagined hospitals receiving several cases a day of umbrellas opening accidentally in people's butts. Thoughts like this kept her warm at night.

Still, there were patches of vibrant colour in the grey city, like the soapbox orators at Speakers' Corner in Hyde Park, pontificating on everything from the Suez crisis to their still new young queen. When Mitsuyo walked the streets of the East End, in neighbourhoods like Aldgate and Whitechapel, there were still a few scars left from the heavy bombings during the war. There, she discovered she could easily tell how people felt as she passed them by. There, she encountered expressions of fear and disgust. She quickly realized these emotions were directed at her.

Here were people whose fathers, brothers and sons had been held captive or killed by the Japanese during the war. Those who had been captured were put to work in death camps. She knew immediately that there was nothing she could say to allay their hatred. Guilt by association. She deduced further that even Londoners in more polite parts of the city must feel the same way. It was then she understood that *she* was the umbrella up their rumps.

She had thought about not going to the party at all, but filling vacuums in time had become difficult. She'd already been in England a few weeks. Other than her father and the embassy staff, there were few Japanese in London, at a time when Japan didn't let its citizens travel freely beyond its borders. And since discovering how most people still felt about the Japanese, she was more and more inclined to stay within the compound. Trying to get by on her limited English had also become tiresome.

She knew there would be only old farts at this party, but they were nonetheless warm bodies. Most of them were, anyway. Under the circumstances, they would not ignore her or be rude. Some of them might even speak some Japanese. Despite Taro's suggestion to keep to her room for the evening, Mitsuyo dressed in her favourite kimono, with gold and green embroidery on a subdued cherry blossom pink silk fabric. She would be on her best behaviour. The ambassador had ordered that all female family members of embassy staff be dressed in traditional Japanese garb. It was implicitly understood they would be on display. Sort of like Indians doing their dances on the reservations.

The British minister for overseas affairs stood up at the start of supper. He raised a glass of champagne and boomed, "To the Emperor of Japan!"

The ambassador jumped up in response, yelling, "To the Queen of England!"

Everybody nodded. Their champagne glasses glimmered like jewellery under a gargantuan chandelier. A young Japanese man stood leaning against a spotless white pillar close to the entrance of the banquet hall. Mitsuyo noticed that when everyone else toasted the Japanese emperor and the English queen, he didn't raise his glass. His arrogance made her heartbeat quicken a bit and her nostrils flare. Tatsue saw her sister staring at the stranger, and shrugged her wide shoulders. Around them, people were parroting the same things over and over.

"Are you enjoying your stay?"

"Do you have much opportunity for travel?"

"Are you having a good time in our fair country?"

"I just adore those miniature trees."

"And those paper umbrellas."

"Do you have the chance to travel much, then?"

"What is your impression of England?"

"We both come from island nations, don't we?"

"Did I ask whether you have much opportunity to go overseas?"

The words fell like pennies around Mitsuyo's ears. To her, they sounded like sparrows trapped in a cage. Everyone smiled. She smiled back. Old and young white farts with umbrellas up their butts did not dare reveal their disdain for her. They hovered around her, hungry for something she could not understand nor care enough to try to imagine. She left them with very little pretense, and strolled up to Shoji, who was still leaning against the pillar looking painfully bored.

Mitsuyo hoped her kimono made her look like an elegant lady from Kyoto. She introduced herself a bit more loudly than she'd intended. Shoji seemed not to notice.

He was wearing a respectably clean shirt and a black tie under a wrinkled blazer. (Shoji felt dressing any more than what was required to keep from being arrested was an irrational waste of energy.) He was skinny, Mitsuyo decided, but handsome in a bookish sort of way. She had yet to notice his leg. When he told her he was a student, her eyes widened. "You're very lucky to be here," she said, impressed.

Shoji peered into his empty glass. "I don't know. I was hoping they'd serve some rice at this reception. It's been months since I've had decent rice. It's the only reason I came all the way to London."

"To be in England at all, I mean," said Mitsuyo. "Exit visas for students are hard to come by. You must have worked very hard."

Shoji shrugged indifferently, then lit a smoke. Mitsuyo bit her lip. She was fighting a craving that would be unbecoming at a reception in honour of the emperor. Especially if this young scholar found out.

"And you?" Shoji asked Mitsuyo. She was trying desperately to straighten the hems of her robe. "What brings you to England?"

"Oh, I'll get out of Japan any way I can."

To her surprise, he didn't seem shocked. All he did was nod, while staring at the burning tip of his cigarette.

It wasn't until their first date, walking along the Thames, that Mitsuyo noticed Shoji's limp. She immediately found it ironic that all he could afford to do was take her for walks. The sky threatened rain. It also, she knew, often bluffed.

He was wearing the same blazer he'd worn to the reception. "Air's always damp, everywhere you go in England," he said. He was staring at the river, but somehow, Mitsuyo knew he saw her smiling at the edge of his vision. She'd changed into a dress the same colour as the sky. Her red jacket was the only colour in his field of vision. A rose growing among ashes. "Maybe dampness affects people in certain ways. Maybe that's why the English and the Japanese are the way they are."

"Hmm," she said. She was more impressed by his observation than she felt she should be. She wanted to add something about umbrellas, but changed her mind quickly.

They went to the bed and breakfast where he was staying, run by an old woman who was not Japanese but smelled just like Ryoko. The woman had invited him down for tea the day before. They sat together, eating stale toast and sipping from pink china cups that were chipped and cracked. She told him of all her relatives who were killed or maimed in the war in the Pacific, searching his face at the same time. He betrayed nothing. She wasn't the only person who'd lost something in the war.

He told this to Mitsuyo, and she nodded, looking out onto the street through smoky glass. The surface of his narrow desk was concealed under books and scattered paper. The walls were discoloured, the floors mutilated. The room seemed to float in empty space, separate from the sidewalk and the pedestrians outside. They were alone together in the city. This was why she offered herself to him—to anyone—for the first time in her life.

He made love fiercely. It was the only time he did not guard his desires. His sorrow flowed freely from within him, as did his joy. She was the vessel that would contain them entirely, and he allowed himself the luxury of drowning in this discovery. Mitsuyo meanwhile concentrated on holding on to her sanity amidst the pain and confusion. They met somewhere in between their heightened senses and floated downward, onto the worn, uneven mattress on his cot, naked. They held each other, breathing in the moistness of the room, of the city and of each other. Afterwards, she smoked for the first time in front of him.

As he walked her home, they passed a jewellery store. Even as the afternoon faded, light shattered into fragments that danced freely among the gems on display. Through his own reflection, Shoji saw an opal necklace, set on a gold band shaped like a teardrop. The stone was not large, but to him it looked as if it contained the entire universe. He envisioned the curved space in which all matter, from leptons to planets, floated freely. The smooth, uncluttered surface of the opal and the clusters of coloured lights within reminded him of the orderly, rational universe in which he would have liked to live.

When he asked Mitsuyo whether she liked it, she just smiled and said nothing. When he asked the second time, she said only that it was nice. The Japanese and British were alike in so many ways.

This was the first and last time she was less than forthcoming with the man with whom she would spend the rest of her life. Ironically, they would both remember this moment as the one in which they fell in love. She was charmed by his disciplined intellect, which succumbed in the end to the uncontrollable, irrational need to please her. He was enticed by her candour, as well as by her apparent concurrence with his good taste. He didn't realize this concurrence wasn't sincere at all—but neither did she at the time.

Mitsuyo stepped away from the window and started down the boulevard ahead of him. She held down her hat in the rising wind. Shoji watched her from behind, and when she noticed he wasn't beside her, she turned around. She stood in clusters of shadows cast by moving tree branches. She looked at him with questioning brown eyes. He stood in front of the store window, scarred physically and emotionally from another time. His sharp eyes tried to make sense of this suddenly inexplicable and unsound world. He wanted to follow her, with all his heart, but to give in to such emotion was against everything that defined him.

Mitsuyo held this image behind her closed eyelids, delicately, like a scented handkerchief. When she opened them, she found that the anger lingered, dripping hot through her insides. The airy fondness she held for these memories withered.

She heard the back door open and close. Toshi was coming in from the yard. He was probably trying to inspire daffodils to be more than just yellow, or lying face down in a mud puddle. She sighed. Perhaps Toshi was to be her penance for embarrassing her own parents. Shocking people with unconventionality did not seem as fun after she witnessed her own son do it so much more easily.

Who could have known that marrying and having children would be so tough? Or that moving to America was less about adventure than about loneliness and the drudgery of keeping house, secluded among people who could not understand what you said? Who could have told her that all these things would affect her in ways she could not have imagined? She suddenly felt very tired. Her clothes burst forth like cumulus clouds from the open suitcase. She needed to take a break.

She hunted through her dresser and found the small box in which she had placed the opal necklace. Shoji had given it to her when he returned to Japan, months after they stood in front of the jewellery store in London. He'd come home just to see her, to propose. And a few weeks later, her father died of a stroke, and Shoji was nowhere to be seen. Mitsuyo put the box back in the dresser. She looked behind her to see her life extending out like a strip of scarlet ribbon. After a few minutes, she went downstairs and opened the hallway closet.

"Hi," said Toshi. He was sitting cross-legged among shoes, holding a dog-eared copy of *Pride and Prejudice*. There was mud all over his shoes, jeans and his sausage-like fingers.

"Sorry," Mitsuyo said, not looking sorry in the least, "but I need a smoke."

Toshi's eyes widened. He noticed then that she was still quite beautiful. Lines on her face carved by time gave her a knowing gentleness. This contradicted almost everything she said or did.

"Wha-wha-wha-wha-wha? Who-who-who-who-who?" was all he could say at first. Then he swallowed, hard. "What are you saying, Ma? You don't smoke. And even if you did, why ask me?" Toshi, a sophomore at Whitefish High School, fluttered his eyelids and smiled. His enormous butt had crushed the cardboard box on which he sat.

"Don't act stupid," she said. She squinted at him as if trying to turn him into stone.

He threw his dirty hands up as though she was a charging bull and almost fell backward among the coats and umbrellas. "No, Ma, really." *Think fast*, he thought. *Talk faster.* "Say, maybe Kei has some!"

She raised an eyebrow.

"Yeah! He has them hidden underneath the loose floorboards in his room. By the radiator."

She nodded. "Go back to reading," she said, but left the closet door open. She went upstairs.

Toshi sighed and shook his head. The incessant rush behind his ears grew into a roar in which he could feel his brain drowning. Jane Austen was not saying much to him any more so he dropped the book to the floor. The coats looked down on him knowingly. The shoes looked up at him expectantly. He stood up and ran out of the closet, through the front door and into the street. Rain was starting to fall like tiny angels, but the sun also shone through a crack among the clouds.

"*Jesus Fucking H. Christ!*" he screamed at passing cars. "*Ma's smoking!"* He felt vaguely guilty about something but couldn't recall what it was. Nothing made sense—nothing at all.

"Go back inside, crazy boy!" yelled Old Man Garber from across the street. "You spread crazy germs everywhere!" He was wearing the same coffee-stained plaid shirt he'd had on yesterday, and the day before. As always, the shirt-tails hung over his pants. He was looking at his feet, because it was too painful to look up.

The clothes and magazines in Kei's room formed rolling hills. The underwear reeked of sweat. Mitsuyo knew there were fossils of forgotten Fritos and Chee-tos among crusty socks and wrinkled Led Zeppelin T-shirts. She stifled a gag.

Looking at the radiator, she saw a pile of garbage that was more symmetrical than the others. She knew it concealed the loose floorboards Toshi had ratted to her about. For a long time she stood, mentally negotiating her way around the debris on the floor. Finally, she went and moved the mountain of clothes and paper to one side. She lifted the loose boards and peered in.

She found no cigarettes. Instead, there was some sheet music and some envelopes. One, she noticed, was perfumed. It was from someone named J-A-I-M-E. Mitsuyo was unsure how to pronounce the name. She did not connect the name to the girl who would sometimes come by, years ago, to invite Kei for walks or for bicycle rides. Her gaze went from the letter to the envelope, then back again. She flipped the paper over in her hands, then again and again. She even considered the possibility that the name was a derivative of James, which meant a man might be sending a perfumed letter to her son. She thought nothing at all about opening it. Like many Japanese, she was unable to speak English, but was more than adept in reading it. She moved on to the sheet music. There even seemed to be some poetry written on the back.

It was evening by the time Hanako found her daughter, still sitting on Kei's bed. The house was dark and quiet. Toshi had fallen asleep in front of the TV, and Kei was still over at Telly's. The grandfather clock in the hallway punctuated time, the only thing left moving in the house. The same clock told the old woman that she was right to be hungry. The lights were off in Kei's room. Hanako thought this was strange, as Mitsuyo looked as though she was reading something. Hanako stood in one place for a long time, her hands playing with the ties of her apron. Better not disturb anything, Hanako told herself. She didn't feel like being scolded again. But hunger won over fear in the end. "Mitsuyo?" she finally asked. "What about supper?"

"I'll be right down," Mitsuyo said, standing up as slowly as sand. After carefully returning everything she'd found into Kei's hiding place, she replaced the floorboards and moved the mess back in its place. She decided to leave the unpacking for later. She'd forgotten all about craving a smoke.

KANAKO

SHOJI ALWAYS LOOKED AT SOMETHING VERY FAR AWAY when his sons asked him about the war. Mitsuyo was too young to remember anything but the experience of evacuation—the hunger and the sun-drenched summer flowers by the crystal-clear mountain brook. It was no wonder, then, that Toshi and Kei believed for the longest time that the war had been fought on the Japanese side by soldiers with thick horn-rimmed glasses and bad teeth. They had no idea war could affect ordinary people. They had no idea that war affected everyone, because dying affected everyone.

Toshi couldn't comprehend why his schoolmates picked on him and Kei over the war. All he knew was that neither of them wore glasses. And he had worn braces to fix his teeth. What more could be expected of him?

Later, he and Kei began to read, and understand. Reading had been a terrible hardship for Toshi. Reading was his cross to bear, his crown of thorns. How could he read when his mind was like some nightmarish department store where weekend specials were constantly being announced over loudspeakers? Toshi sometimes tried calming himself by turning up the stereo—but the music collided in his skull with voices and ideas. They bounced around his cranium like popcorn. He couldn't discern the words camouflaged among all the letters strung together on the page. Which of the countless, identical links on a chain were supposed to be more relevant than the rest? Why was an *M* an *M*, and a *W* a *W* when they were both the same shape?

It was not until he started locking himself in the closet that he got any schoolwork done. There, confined by walls that touched him on all sides, he found he could read for short periods, with one flashlight on his lap in an otherwise dark coffin. Gradually, the time he spent in the closet grew longer. By high school he would hide there for a couple of hours at a time. In the closet, Toshi discovered both Dr. Seuss and Tolstoy.

Many of the books on the Second World War he read contained pictures. They made it easier for him when there were no closets nearby. He thought the ships and fighter planes looked intriguing. But one day, he found a book with photographs from Hiroshima and Nagasaki taken immediately after the atomic bombing. His round face turned green as he looked at people with half their skin turned to ash and the other half to jet-black cinder. Skin hung off their bones like tattered coats. A bright white light spread before his eyes, just like he imagined it did for everyone in Hiroshima the day the bomb fell. The people of Hiroshima had been burned to a crisp immediately afterward. He felt only a mild chill. He ran to the closet after all, just to sit in the warmth and darkness.

By the war's end, American planes stationed at the Marianas infested the skies around Japan, flying about like they owned the place. People in major cities like Tokyo and Osaka lived every day with bombings. There was no food, because everyone was too busy fighting to worry about the farms. The rails, the roads, the bridges—everything—had been bombed by planes that could fly unbelievably far without refuelling. This was why Ryoko wasn't getting as much ham and bacon from her cousins.

People didn't sleep well at night. They feared the air-raid siren. Its presence loomed larger in silence than it ever could in an actual emergency.

The people of Kitagawa were as prepared as anyone could be. Their village was just large enough to be a target, albeit an unlikely one. Nothing major had occurred, which meant a perpetual state of anticipation. Water was stored in whatever was handy in case of fire, mostly wooden barrels. Shelters, a fancy word for ditches, were everywhere. Exploding bombs hit their victims with a wall of air pressure. The experience was not unlike falling belly-first into a pool of water—except bombs tore your arms and legs from their sockets and snapped your neck from your spine. Fragments of steel as small as insects shredded your skin. The ditches, as crude as they were, shielded you against this. All there was between life and death was often just a hole in the ground.

Shoji's house also had a shelter, dug into the rear garden, but it was anything but crude. The gardener would not have quit had it simply been a ditch. Yasujiro had designed the shelter over a period of three weeks. It was huge and cavernous, and panelled with wood. There was even a set of steps leading into it. Ryoko and Otama, the maid whose arms were starting to resemble the ham she was pilfering from the kitchen, could stand upright in it easily. Six or seven people could fit inside comfortably, and even have a meal.

Yasujiro furnished the shelter with an old dining-room table and some cushions. When there were still some flowers left in the garden, Ryoko placed an ikebana flower arrangement on the table. Then Yasujiro brought a Laughing Buddha figurine out from storage, and everyone agreed that this was probably enough ornament for a bomb shelter.

They spent a lot of time there at first. Some nights, just by themselves, they ate in the shelter. Fresh flowers were arranged elegantly on the table. Yasu often became drunk on saké, and hiked his kimono up to do the "eel-scooping dance."

The weeks passed, though, and the novelty faded. The shelter started to feel like any other part of the house. They found it inconvenient because they could not get to it without their sandals. Without giving it much thought, everyone spent less time there. Otama cleaned it like she did the kitchen and the closets. The more the war appeared to last forever, the more the shelter resembled a permanent fixture.

By now they were trying hard to think about anything but the war. Most people tried to live their lives as normally as possible. They would have gone insane otherwise. They ate and slept at regular times. The stores did their best to open every day, even if there was little to sell.

As usual, Shoji was at the bookstore. Ghosts rose from the ground in the blistering sunlight. He browsed through an esoteric tome by a mathematician-astronomer named Johannes Kepler. The German edition of *Harmonice Mundi* was the book he would have bought the previous day had Shima not surrendered his money to Kono.

The yellowing soft cover and the inferior paper belied its value and rarity. It was a pirated edition imported from Shanghai. Kepler was a student of the sixteenth-century astronomer Tycho Brahe. He expanded upon Copernicus's theory that the earth orbited the sun rather than the other way around by proposing that the orbital path was an ellipse rather than a circle. This was the kind of book that Shoji read for pleasure. He was not so clever that he understood how this might be related to why he was frequently beaten up at school.

The bookstore owner, Honda, was missing a few teeth. He smiled widely nonetheless. He was proud of the gaping void scattered among kernels of corn sprouting from his gums. He wore thick round glasses, which were held firmly in place by an upturned nose. He looked up from his counter and saw Shoji flipping through the book like a starving animal. Shoji was in the bookstore every day. Honda allowed himself a chuckle, and picked his butt.

There wasn't much on the shelves, but the small shop was crowded with people killing time. People thought nothing of killing time. They never seemed to consider how killing time was as permanent an act as killing people. Time died every fraction of every moment. A moment in time wasted might as well be a lifetime. No air passed among the shelves. Although the storefront was wide open, inside it smelled of sweat and dust and mould growing on the stained pages. Time was dying all the time here. You could smell it in the air.

"Sho-chan, will you be buying that today?" Honda shouted. He was still smiling. A few loiterers hastily put down whatever they were reading and scurried away like roaches. Shoji stayed where he was, squinting into the book and moving his lips like a goldfish. Honda shook his head and went back to doing his inventory. He knew the bookworm was too hungry not to buy the book. It was also too esoteric to interest anyone else in Kitagawa.

Except for perhaps Shima, who just then walked into the store with Kanako, the daughter of the head priest at the Kaminohashi Shrine. She was as skinny as Shima, resembling nothing more than a chopstick whittled down to a sliver. Though her forehead was almost always furrowed, her facial features were elegant, with long, almond-shaped eyes and a straight, high nose. Her white cotton blouse stuck to her tiny breasts. Shima stole glances at them often. She pretended to look the other way when he did. He wiped his brow with a handkerchief that was already soaked. Dampness defined Japan in the summer. He tapped Shoji on the shoulder.

Startled, Shoji turned around quickly. "Oh, it's just you," he said, relieved. "I thought it was old Honda."

Kanako looked at the shelved books. "It stinks in here," she said loudly.

Shima looked at his friend. He raised his bony shoulders for effect. "Well? Okay! Are we going to get it? Did your father give you some more money?"

"Why would he? I told him I'd already bought the book and lent it to you, remember?"

"Hmm. Well, this is a problem."

"I'll buy you the book," Kanako said. The words seemed to appear out of nowhere.

"What?"

Shoji squinted at her. He wasn't used to things he didn't understand. He hated being confused. He was about to ask Kanako if she'd gone *mad,* but just at that moment, he noticed her blouse, too—the smelly, sweaty blouse sticking to Kanako's chest. And he truly didn't know what to say. Shima at first only blinked at her offer to buy the book. As if awakening from a fever dream, he then nodded quickly. He even smiled as he wiped more dirt and sweat from the base of his neck. "What's the book about, anyway?" Kanako asked, stealing a look over Shoji's shoulder into the stained pages.

He made a sour face. "Well, it's not like you're going to understand any of it. . . ."

"Fine," Kanako said. She grabbed the book from him and walked to the counter as though she owned the store. Shoji felt an unfamiliar sensation. He noticed his tongue was hanging from his mouth. Shima also watched the willowy young woman with wide-eyed fascination, fists clenched, arms as stiff as bamboo poles at his sides.

Honda didn't see Kanako until she slammed the book down in front of him. "Eh?" he said, noticing the title. He turned to Shoji and furrowed his brow.

Before Shoji could say anything, Shima took his arm and squeezed hard. He forced comprehension. *"Let her buy it for us!"* he hissed. "Shinto priests are rich! Okay? She probably gets a fat allowance anyway!" A fly buzzed around Shima's head, making loops in the humidity and the stench.

Honda sniffed. He looked like an old sewer mouse who had just climbed out of the gutter and was perplexed by the sun. He leafed through the pages. He said, without looking at her, "Kanako-chan, does your father know you're spending so much money on such a difficult book?"

"Oh, this is just a loan to Hayakawa-san and Shima-san anyway," replied Kanako. She stared out onto the street. Old Mrs. Tanaka walked by, looking up at the sky in search of rain. Kanako couldn't remember the last time it rained. She only turned to face Honda when he didn't say anything. "Besides, they're such promising students," she added, smiling. "Father's always liked them. He always says education is the most inexpensive investment with the greatest return. Wouldn't you agree?" There was nothing in her voice that said she cared whether Honda agreed with her or not.

"Of course." He smiled. There weren't many who could afford or would even want the book anyway. "I'd be the last to get in the way of academic pursuits. Our country needs young scientists right now, don't we? We have to get these young men going on a secret weapon that will finally defeat the Americans."

He stopped himself from saying more. He was suddenly afraid people might hear him saying the war was taking too long. He scribbled a receipt on onion skin paper and tucked it between the pages. Kanako walked back to Shoji. She offered him the prize. He didn't move, and Shima eagerly snatched it away in the moment's hesitation. "Come on," he said. "Let's go."

Shoji allowed himself to be led out into the midday sun. A group of young boys buzzed around them like insects. Faces covered with blotches of dirt, wearing only shorts and tank tops, they made noises like Zeros shooting down American planes. They could not know that, according to American myth, they were supposed to look like Honda and wear horn-rimmed glasses and have buckteeth. Just as American children could not know that, according to Japanese myth, they were all supposed to be pale and blond and have bulging blue eyes and big noses.

Old women standing around barren vegetable stalls glared at the children. The noise made the day feel hotter. Shoji saw the women looking at him just as he was sneaking another peek at Kanako's breasts. He averted his eyes. Shima had his face in the book. He would have stepped in dog shit had Kanako not pulled him to one side. She looked at the kids playing war as though they were strange mushrooms growing on the side of the road. Shoji looked at her looking at the kids.

Finally, he said, "I still can't believe you just spent so much money on us. Aren't you going to get in trouble with your father?"

"Don't worry," she said. She seemed surprised that he might be concerned. Shoji even thought her thin lips had smiled, very faintly. "My father'll be too proud to deny his benevolence if Honda ever tried to check with him," she said.

"I'm not worried about Honda. Frankly, I think he's glad to be rid of that thing. I'm thinking more about your father's reaction."

"Well, if Honda doesn't do anything, it'll never get back to my father, will it?"

"Doesn't he ever ask what you do with your allowance?"

"He pays me to keep out of his hair." Kanako smiled. Her teeth were white and perfect. Shoji held his breath. "Discussing where the money goes would defeat its purpose."

The children scattered. The noise lifted. Shoji was surprised to find that Kanako was making him laugh. Shima was still absorbed in the book that had seemed so elusive before today. This made Shoji laugh some more. Sparrows sang overhead. Shoji even began to whistle, wondering what might be for supper.

A few shadows crossed their path. So did the wind. Kanako and Shoji stopped. Shima didn't see anything until he almost walked into Kono's wide chest. Then he scurried back so fast, he fell at Kanako's feet. He turned even paler than his normal pallid self.

Kono extracted a few strands of hair from his nose with his fingers. Then he spat on the ground. "Hot again, eh?" he said, scratching his armpit. "Eh? What do you have there, Shima-chan?"

"He has one of those foreign books," said one of the others. The boy tried his best to appear tough, but his shirt hung open, exposing the ribs pushing against his skin. "We should report them to the *kempeitai*. Reading things in the enemy's language is a serious offence."

"This book isn't in English, you fool," Shoji said.

Kono's eyes bulged. He stepped up to Shoji and looked down onto the top of his head. "You've got a mouth, Hayakawa," Kono said to Shoji's scalp. "Must run in the family."

Shoji winced. Being associated at all with his father was physically painful.

"That's *enough*," Kanako spoke up suddenly. They all looked at her as if they'd suddenly forgotten who she was. She wasn't smiling any more, but didn't look particularly worried either. Her face was as expressionless as it had been when she went to pay Honda for the book. "Leave them alone, Kono-chan."

"What are you doing with these bookworms, Kanako?" Kono's voice cracked like a brittle piece of wood.

This made Kanako look at her shoes. "They're okay," she muttered.

Kono gazed at the sky. He looked as though he was standing at the bottom of a glass bottle, looking for a way out. Shoji could hear his own heartbeat. Fear scurried like insects in his shirt. Kono spat again and strode up to Shima, who held the book to his chest. "Let's see what you're reading, bookworm."

Shima cowered and looked ready to surrender the book.

Shoji could not stop himself. "You wouldn't know which side was up," he said bitterly.

"What did you say?"

No cloud blossomed in the sky. No shadows rippled on the ground. Shoji felt naked in the light. Kono came toward him, hands curled into fists. Shoji took a step backwards. Kono smiled, and in a blur his arm shot out. Shoji doubled over, gasping. He imagined what he might see if he allowed himself to be sick. The ham he had for supper last night would be digested by now, but the pickled cabbage from breakfast might still be swimming in his otherwise empty belly.

The dirt slammed against his face, hard. All he saw was Kono's dirty feet and stubby toes, wedged in his sandals. Shoji sucked air like a fish out of water. He barely managed to keep himself from vomiting.

"I *said* leave them alone," Kanako's voice came from very far away.

Kono hesitated, then turned to her. She was suddenly pale. Somehow, though, she still managed to outshine the sun. Her dark eyes swallowed the day.

Kono took a deep breath. "Kanako, if this has something to do with what happened the other day . . ."

She laughed into her hand. "Don't worry, Kono-chan, I don't even think about it any more." But as quickly as it had blossomed into a smile, her face looked tired and lifeless. "Just leave these boys alone. They've got better things to do than put up with your rants. They've got important things to think about." She looked at Shoji. "At least they're thinking about *something.*"

It was the war, and being young. There should have been so much more to live for.

Kono grinned sourly. "They're free to go if you come with me," he said to her.

"Where?"

"We'll go for a walk. Just you and I." Kono looked down at Shoji struggling to get up. Everything about Kono's face was smiling except for his eyes. They made Shoji shiver in a spiral of dust. The wind was rising.

"Kanako-san! *No!*" Shima shrieked. He even took a half step forward.

Kanako tilted her head. "It's okay, Shima-san. Go on home." Then she turned away. Whether this was from Shima's gaze or the wind, Shoji couldn't tell. "Call off your dogs, Kono-chan. I'll come with you."

The group of boys dispersed like dust. Kanako started down the road to who knew where with Kono. Suddenly the day wasn't quite so hot any more. The summer was starting to die already. Shoji and Shima were left standing in the crosswind. A cloud appeared out of nowhere and cast a shadow.

"*Bastard!*" Shima screamed. Tears were flowing down his unusually flushed cheeks.

Shoji looked at his friend. The day was full of so many things that had caught him by surprise.

Aside from being a fast runner, Shoji had never been much of an athlete. He always dreaded physical education at school. It was worst during the war, around the time when he moved to Kitagawa. Day after day, he was forced to lift, jump and fight with the other boys in his class. He was a hindrance as Japan strove for greatness, Shoji was told by Tabuchi, the physical education teacher at Kitagawa First High School. Tabuchi often punctuated his lectures with "the spirit stick" across the backside.

Bayonet training was especially punishing. Mock wooden rifles, buffered only by a ball of canvas, were jabbed into Shoji's face, chest and throat. He fell, time and again, only to be pulled to his feet by Tabuchi. "What the hell's the matter with you?" Tabuchi screamed in Shoji's ear. "How do you expect to kill Americans with these rubbery arms?" Tabuchi's nose was so wide his nostrils flared directly under his eyes.

Shoji dropped his rifle. The ground tipped. Laughter sprang like a mountain brook all around him and faded into the brisk autumn sky. Even Tabuchi was smiling. Shoji could hardly keep his eyes open. He nonetheless noticed that Shima was the only one who wasn't laughing. His face revealed no expression, as if there was nothing remarkable about the situation at all. Then Shoji fell. His face landed on his rifle.

The laughter swelled. Tabuchi shook his head and muttered something familiar about shame and disgrace. Kono was laughing so hard he was crying. Idiots who had to cheat off Shoji during math and chemistry were behaving as though they'd won the war already.

Shoji stood up slowly. Something hot grew bigger inside him. Anger became incandescent. He screamed that none of them was any good for the country except as cannon fodder. That it was he who would discover how Japan could win the war. Then he and others like him will be running the country. The rest of them will be scrounging around for work as day labourers. Shoji stole glances at Shima, because everyone knew his mother was a factory worker at the Maruyama plant. Shima sat there, stoic, as though he didn't understand why his best friend was screaming at all.

As Kono and Kanako disappeared down the road, Shima fell to his knees and struck the ground with his small fists. "Bastards!" Shima kept yelling, over and over. Shoji watched with peculiar fascination. It was his turn to be struck mute in the face of brittle emotions shattering against the hardness of reality. It was the war. That's all. Just the war.

Shima turned to him and made a vain attempt at smiling through the tears and mucus. "I'm sorry, Sho-chan," he said. "Pretty pathetic, isn't it?"

Shoji shook his head. "No," he said. "No, I understand." He felt the air turning colder. The sky looked ready to fall. Shima didn't seem to notice. Shima stood up and dusted off his pants, while Shoji watched, helpless, wishing that this moment would simply go away.

TOKYO

SHOJI HAD ALWAYS KNOWN TOKYO TO BE CROWDED, but when he returned for his mother's funeral, it looked to him like the city was ready to burst. It looked like it might have one big coronary and keel over, bleeding an exodus of people fleeing from Gamera or some other urban madness. Cars buried the streets. Houses crowded each other in one indiscernible mass so that every street looked the same, even though, upon closer inspection, each was unique.

Shoji stood in front of a department store in the Ginza. The sun had fallen long ago behind the high-rises, but a pale watercolour rose still bled across the sky. The name of the department store was Wako. It reminded Shoji of the English word "wacko."

There weren't many people at the service. It was held at their old house, the one that had been taken over by Shoji's uncle after the war. Ryoko's family had all but forgotten about her a long time ago. Shoji's cousins mostly wanted to know how to bill him for the expenses. They had grown old, too, over the years. They were visibly relieved that the burden of taking care of an elderly aunt had lifted. None of them had even once thanked her for allowing them to live in her house.

Strangely enough, even Shoji felt indebted to them for living in his mother's house, and for arranging the sparse funeral for which he was now being billed. If Ryoko had lost any sleep pondering her lot in life, none of them could know about it now.

Those who came to light rods of incense for Ryoko were mostly from the neighbourhood and the hospital where she died. Everyone remarked on how she didn't have many friends. She must have been very lonely, they muttered, throwing glances at Shoji. It was like casting stones and trying to look the other way. They talked about their own elderly parents, and about taking them to the latest McDonald's to open in Tokyo. One woman had just bought her mother a Sony Walkman. Had Shoji ever heard of Sony Walkmans?

Just as everyone was leaving, the priest approached him. The priest's eyebrows were thick enough to compensate for the lack of hair on his shaved scalp. With a voice as deep as the ocean, he said only, "It's good that you came. Hmm. Hmm. Yes, very, very good." Without a trace of cynicism, he made it sound as if Shoji had rushed home to offer his mother an organ. Then the old priest, looking weary to the bone, looked at Shoji and smiled a smile of perfection. His eyes were so clear, his words could be nothing but sincere. Shoji didn't notice his own lips were quivering.

He knew his sons had only vague recollections of his mother, and what little remained was gradually fading away. Memories were as transitory as a dandelion seed floating on the breeze. Certainly Kei wouldn't remember anything beyond the touch of Ryoko's frail hands, the feel of her kimono as she held him to her chest, the mildly sweet smell of incense.

But Toshi had grown quite close to his grandmother in the first five years of his life, spent mostly confined at home by his parents. Ryoko's ability to break wind on demand had filled her grandson with an intense glee. Giggling at the triumphant sounds blaring from under Ryoko's robe, Toshi followed her around the house like a dog. All he ever wanted was another performance. Ryoko always capitulated. She sighed, made her cheeks tremble and let one fly. This made Toshi collapse, laughing as tears welled in his rolling eyes. If Ryoko treated him to a series of farts, he counted each discharge, reciting the numbers he'd learned at kindergarten.

When Ryoko tired of her grandson, she removed her wig, revealing a scalp of thin, greying matted spindles of hair. This always left Toshi screaming and running for cover.

Now, all Toshi remembered of his grandmother was her ability to manipulate her sphincter muscles and to remove her hair. If the dead remained alive only in the memories of their loved ones, Shoji's decision to move his family out of Japan killed Ryoko dead, utterly and completely. What remained of her was less than the collective human memory accorded to pieces of petrified dinosaur dung.

In the Ginza, people walked as though they'd rather be running. Aside from Shoji, everyone loitering in front of the Wako was young. Some faces were painted, others mottled. A school of papier-mâché fish swam across the shop window behind them. Wako was a popular meeting place.

Shoji looked around. He still couldn't reconcile this Tokyo with the one he'd left behind so many years ago. In the new Tokyo, lights flashed everywhere. They said he could have anything he wanted—cameras, stereos, naked girls. A wall of sound surrounded him constantly. Vending machines hummed like insects. Electronic voices thanked subway riders for using the automatic ticket dispenser. A million *pachinko* balls cascaded through a forest of nails. Almost every door opened by itself.

There wasn't much garbage. Herds of people, but no garbage. Just a bum sitting on the corner in tattered clothes. His face was streaked with dirt. He held his blackened hand out for change. He looked like a bomb had fallen on him just yesterday. To Shoji, he looked like a dream. Or maybe this new, pristine Tokyo was the dream. Perhaps the war had never ended, and the bum on the corner was just a bit of the real world trying to sneak in.

Shoji saw a thin shadow of a man stumbling toward him, wearing a wrinkled shirt and tie. The crowd pushed the scrawny figure back and forth on the sidewalk, like a feather in a storm. The man wiped sweat from his neck with a soiled handkerchief. He carried a tattered briefcase that he held from the bottom rather than the handle. His arms looked like toothpicks. He was breathing heavily.

Shoji wondered why he wasn't happier to see his friend. He forced a smile. "Shima," he said softly to the thin man, and extended his hand. "It's marvellous to see you."

Shima stuffed his handkerchief in his pants. His whole face transformed into a broad grin. They shook hands. His voice quivered like a leaf under spring rain. Each noticed in the other details inconsistent with their respective memories—sagging cheeks, creases around the eyes, streaks of white in their hair. "You haven't changed," Shima said.

"Really? Well, you're also looking very well."

"Well! You're a good liar." Shima laughed, pushing his glasses up the ridge of his nose.

Shoji quickly inspected his friend, from the receding hairline down to the worn-out shoes. Though Shima was leaner than most men half his age, he was neither robust nor healthy. He was a bit heavier than he'd been in his youth, but all of the weight had gathered around his waist. He looked like a worm that had swallowed a basketball.

When they began to walk, Shoji immediately realized his friend moved with the same speed as the rest of Tokyo. Neither he nor the city yielded much to someone with a limp. When Shima stopped—as he did frequently, in order for Shoji to catch up—he marched on the spot as though maintaining some sort of inertia. They walked into a side street that was less crowded, and Shima began to walk even faster. Shoji at first tried his best to keep up. Soon, he decided his friend could wait. Shima pointed to a pale yellow sign down the street and told Shoji that's where they'd be eating.

The Tori-gin was a *yakitori* diner. Men in pristine white uniforms and paper caps skewered pieces of chicken and cooked them over an open grill. The kitchen was behind a counter, in the middle of the restaurant where everyone could watch. People yelled their orders across the room, which were repeated by waitresses, which in turn were repeated by the men standing around the stove. There was a fan above the grill that siphoned off most of the smoke, but just enough lingered to leave no doubt that their specialty was barbecue. The smoke mingled with cigarettes and the overwhelming humidity. It all smelled exquisite to Shoji. There was no place like this in Milwaukee.

They sat on benches at a wooden table. Shima ordered two steins of beer. "Well! Okay! Sapporo may not be as good as Milwaukee beer," he said. "Sorry."

Shoji waved away the apology and smiled. Apprehension gave way to familiarity, which had survived after all.

"So, how's the family?" Shima asked.

"Fine. Really fine. And you? Have you found anyone yet?"

"Ah, you know me. I can't relate to women. Our department chair had arranged a few meetings for me, but none of them panned out in the end. And, to be honest, these women looked desperate enough to take just anyone. It's pretty pathetic when you're not good enough for the bottom of the barrel." Shima laughed again. Each laugh was less enthusiastic than the last. "Well! I wasn't seriously pursuing them anyway. I have some standards too, you know."

"That's hard to believe," Shoji said. "Come on. You have tenure at one of the most prestigious universities in the country."

"It's not like during the war, Sho. People have everything they could want now, and they want even more. Women aren't giving themselves any more to men who provide only security. They want all the love and understanding they see in American romance movies. Most of them make themselves up and behave like whores anyway. There isn't anyone around like Mitsuyo-san any more."

Shima lit a cigarette. He and Shoji both looked at the same time at the menu posted on the wall. Each item and its price were written in black brushstrokes on a small wooden tile. There must have been nearly a hundred tiles, hanging side by side. The restaurant barbecued not just chicken but onions, mushrooms, ginkgo nuts, asparagus and rice balls. And just about every part of the chicken was on the menu: wings, thighs, the skin by itself, the gizzard, the liver, the heart, the testicles. Shoji was particularly fond of what were affectionately called lanterns—eggs extracted from chickens before the shell had formed. A yolk contained in a transparent membrane hung by a wrinkled strand of pedicle off a skewer. There weren't many places that served lanterns, even in Tokyo.

"Did you ever think during the war that one day we'd have so much to eat?" Shima shook his head in mock disbelief.

"No," Shoji said, although Shima didn't look like he was eating any more now than in wartime. "No, never."

"I suppose you never get back to Kitagawa." Shima suddenly butted his smoke. "Wait! Well! I forgot to tell you! A while ago, I saw Kono!"

Shoji caught his breath. He stopped himself from standing up. He didn't expect the name to still affect him. "Really," he said, pushing his voice to calmness.

"Really," said Shima. "And you'll never guess what. Well! He's running a pantyless coffee shop!"

Every time Shoji went home to Japan, there was always something new and different. The pantyless coffee shop was the product of the same fertile imagination that had produced transistor radios, energy-efficient automobiles and Walkmans. Waitresses wore very short skirts, and when they bent over to serve the absurdly expensive drinks, the customers got a full view of that for which they were in truth paying. Most of these places did not serve liquor. They did not need to.

"I'd gone to Kitagawa to visit my sister," Shima explained. "She'd just got her appendix removed. Well! When I left the hospital, I realized I was early for my next appointment. I looked for a *pachinko* parlour to kill time, but the only thing nearby was one of those new Space Invader arcades. I've never got the hang of those video games. So I ducked into what looks to me like a regular coffee shop, but it turned out to be pantyless. Imagine my surprise! Okay! So I'm too embarrassed to stay, and too embarrassed to leave. And since I was trying to look at anything but the waitresses, I noticed this guy looking at me from behind the bar. Took me a moment to realize it was Kono. He'd lost some weight and had grown a very uneven moustache."

Shoji chewed on a grilled chicken heart. "Did you say anything?"

"No. What could I say?"

"Did he recognize you?"

"I think so."

"He didn't acknowledge you at all?"

"He ducked into the kitchen as quickly as he could. What would you have him do, Sho-chan? What would you have done in his place?"

Shoji knew he'd have done absolutely nothing differently. If the place had caught fire, they would have tried to escape from separate doors. "What was he doing there?"

"Well, since the war ended before he could kill himself, he had nowhere to go. I even heard he had joined the yakuza for a while. Might have entered the pantyless business that way, come to think of it. I think he's washed his hands of the gangs now, though." Shima waved at a waitress and ordered more beer. Shima chuckled. "You should go see him. Just to see him in his coffee shop would be worth a trip to Kitagawa."

Shoji shook his head. He asked what his friend had planned for the future.

Shima was shoving skewered chicken liver in his mouth. He looked up at Shoji. An awkward smile spread across his face. "Well! I suppose this would be the time to ask you," he said. He coughed into his hand, stalling for time. Someone yelled for another order of chicken testicles. He looked at a stain on the ceiling, then said, "I'm due for a sabbatical next year, Sho-chan. To tell you the truth, lately I've been reading papers on the application of thermal field dynamics on condensed fields, written by a colleague of yours at the University of Wisconsin."

He glanced at Shoji to gauge his reaction. Shoji was smiling. Shima sighed, relieved. "Well!" said Shima. "I was hoping you could arrange a visiting fellowship."

Shoji laughed loudly. *"Nyet-nyet,"* he said. "Of course. *Nyet!* That's the paper by Chet Wilkins. He's a good friend. He'd consider himself very lucky to be able to work with you. I'll arrange it right away. You'll stay with us, of course."

"No, no," said Shima. "I couldn't impose."

Shoji took Shima's hand. He raised both eyebrows, and said, "Are you *mad?* I insist. We'll take you around the sights."

By this, they both knew that Shoji was referring to perhaps a trip down to Illinois to see the particle accelerators at Fermi labs. If they had time to spare, they might possibly visit the Science and Industry Museum in Chicago. They giggled like schoolgirls.

"This is marvellous," said Shoji. "We're going to have a wonderful time."

But the past was not something to be toyed with.

That night, Shoji tossed on the bed in his air-conditioned hotel room. He dreamt of the poor bum he saw in the Ginza, lying on the sidewalk while a school of papier-mâché fish swam in the sky.

Shoji's dream images were always scattered. One portion of the picture changed place with another like Lego blocks, usually with no rhyme or reason. He often marvelled at how some people seemed to dream in coherent narratives. When he slept, disjointed images popped up together without warning. It was as though he worked too hard when he was awake at keeping his conscious mind orderly. He couldn't afford the same energy for his subconscious.

He dreamt of Kono wearing his old school uniform, making an espresso not in his coffee shop but at the faculty lounge at the University of Wisconsin. The papier-mâché fish had moved to the goldfish tank by the window. Mitsuyo and Kanako went around pantyless, slinging Sapporo beer. As Shoji stood in the corner of the room, bewildered, the rotund president of the university waddled over and put a hand on his shoulder. "Sorry we have to let you go like this," he said, "but you can't deny we've found someone better."

At that moment, Shoji noticed Shima sitting by himself in the middle of the dining hall. Suddenly his mother appeared also as a waitress, carrying a plate of skewered chicken. She and Mitsuyo, who held a stein of Sapporo, walked over to Shima's table, wearing stiff, eager smiles. Ryoko was about to bend over to put down her plate of chicken when Shoji bolted upright in bed. He clutched the sheets like a drowning man reaching for straw.

He took a desperate moment to remember where he was. The neon outside his window flashed from blue to red—cold to warm, then back to cold.

ANGIE

ANGIE'S FLAMING HAIR SETTLED AROUND HER SHOULDERS. In the familiar basement bar, waves of smoke rode the air like dragons. She'd come to the Twisted Neon with Alex, the big, swarthy owner of the furniture warehouse where she worked. Alex managed his sales staff as well as the drivers and movers with his wide, square jaw. But he was always nice to Angie. When Angie complained about how the washroom was never clean, he hired a new janitor and now it was always spotless. Even now, as she put a cigarette to her lips, he was all ready with his gold lighter. Alex wore a Toronto Maple Leafs tie every day during hockey season.

The Twisted Neon was a bar in Toronto where people went to be alone together. Everyone wore either blue jeans or leather, drank either beer or whisky and smoked. No one ever ordered a daiquiri. There was just enough light to keep you from walking into a table on the way to the bathroom. And it was always warm, even in winter.

Alex hadn't taken off his parka since sitting down—how long ago was that? Angie only knew there were empty pint glasses in front of her. Alex was always good for buying her a few beers after work. And for taking her anywhere she wanted to go. She told him that for the past few weeks she'd been following a band called Head around town, and its lead singer with his angry, faraway eyes. Alex had laughed at that, but not in a way that Angie might find offensive. Alex was never offensive, nothing like the singer with the angry eyes.

Shoji looked as if he'd swallowed a duck when Kei announced he was going to be a musician. He looked as if the duck he'd swallowed was still alive when Kei said he was moving to Canada. He visited Kei in Toronto only once. He never made that mistake again. It wasn't so much the city, which he thought was quite lovely and clean. But Mr. Man proved too much for his delicate constitution.

"Lorelei!" Mr. Man screamed into Shoji's face when he first walked into Kei's apartment. "Her name is Lorelei! Say it! *Saaaaay iiiiiiiit (tweet)!*"

Shoji looked as if dog shit was being waved in his face. He also saw that he and Mr. Man were about the same age, although Mr. Man looked like he'd been mummified and buried. Shoji spent half the time at Kei's apartment in the bathroom, hiding from Mr. Man.

Mr. Man's front teeth were chipped. He whistled through the gap when he talked. The only thing more wrinkled than his shirt was his face.

Before Head started getting some local attention, Kei and Telly had shared a couple of dilapidated apartments in downtown Toronto. They lived for a couple of years in the first, but moved when the building was condemned. Mr. Man came with the first place, along with the peeling paint and cardboard on the windows. When Kei and Telly moved into their second apartment, they moved Mr. Man with the furniture.

Mr. Man loved Toshi. They played together whenever Toshi and Mitsuyo visited Kei. Mr. Man would stick his face in Toshi's and scream, "I love my *fucking* girlfriend. Her name is Lorelei! Say it! Lorelei! *Loooreeeleeeeiiiii! (tweet!)*"

Toshi giggled and yelled "Lorelei! Lorelei!" while running through all the rooms. He stopped only when Mitsuyo hit him over the head with a saucepan. Toshi couldn't help liking Mr. Man. They were too much alike.

It had been Telly who persuaded Kei to put together a music career in Toronto. Many Canadian acts, from Paul Anka to Bryan Adams, had been making it onto the U.S. charts. It would be easier getting noticed by someone in Toronto than in Milwaukee, where they would have to drive to Chicago to kiss any worthwhile ass. Telly had a Canadian cousin starting up a band.

Telly and Mildred found each other when he and Kei first drifted into town. Telly had gone to her to buy some speed. She was flat-chested, had long salt-and-pepper hair. Her shoulders were jagged. She had a big mole on the tip of her nose. She talked end-lessly on the phone, complaining in her nasal voice about shaving her legs and how Telly wasn't making any money as a musician. He was thin but had a beer belly, she said. Her sunken cheeks made it apparent she'd not eaten a decent meal in years.

Kei never knew what Telly saw in Mildred, aside from a thin waist that fit well inside his arm. And Mildred could always be counted on for some stash. That was good.

Though Shoji was no longer willing to visit his younger son, he nonetheless kept sending Kei money. And even though Kei had not asked for it, he never returned it either. Late at night, after Mitsuyo had gone to bed, Shoji listed, in painfully meticulous detail, Kei's possible living expenses. After he felt the list was more or less com-plete, he estimated the cost of each item. When he arrived at a total, he wrote a cheque. So that Kei would understand that he was not receiving an arbitrary sum, Shoji always included a copy of his cal-culations. He never knew how accurate his estimates were.

He often enclosed a short letter with the cheque. Kei was too busy trying to forge a career to write back, but he enjoyed his father's letters. Shoji, who was so precise in so many things, had very bad handwriting. Kei grudgingly had to admit to himself that Shoji's letters brought him more pleasure than anger in his cold apartment.

Just before he got the call from Mitsuyo telling him his father was dying, Kei received the letter he would remember forever. Shoji usually wrote about the latest, incomprehensible ideas surrounding antimatters and other such things. But this one was different. This one, Kei could understand.

Shoji wrote about periods of mass extinction in Earth's history—when 75 to over 90 per cent of animal species existing before these periods disappeared. The first among them, the Ordovician extinction, occurred 505 million years ago when there weren't any animals on land. The Cretaceous extinction, which wiped out the dinosaurs, ended about 60 million years ago. Scientists estimate that about 10 million years must pass before the diversity of life is replenished, he said.

"My point is not that there are those who feel man is causing another such period of mass extinction, although from all the evidence this seems to be true," Shoji wrote. "Rather, when I think of such immense units of time, I find religion, or any other belief system in which humans are at the centre, to be absolutely absurd. Surely nothing—no words, no symbols, no vestiges of human spirit—can hold meaning over eternity, when even mountains erode and the seas evaporate."

After Shoji announced he could no longer tolerate the presence of Mr. Man, subsequent visits were left to Mitsuyo and Toshi. Once every few months, they took a plane to Toronto and stayed for about a week at the Holiday Inn. Mitsuyo went every day to the market for groceries and cooked for Kei and his roommates in their apartment. Whatever she cooked disappeared in the time it took an eye to flutter. (This was the other aspect of Kei's life that Shoji could not comprehend: why anyone should go hungry when there wasn't even a war going on. Time had changed the world in ways that made no sense at all.)

Kei met Angie shortly after he moved to the second apartment, which was almost as run down as the first, though not quite. She never moved in, but was always over, helping out. Unless Mitsuyo was in town, Angie did most of the cooking. She had fiery red hair down to her waist. Her eyes were dreamy, sleepy and green. She wore peasant dresses with long skirts. Toshi caught glimpses of her long, slender legs whenever she sat on the couch and crossed her creamy white knees. When she saw him looking at her, she smiled a smile as forgiving as a summer breeze. Then Kei would walk over and kiss Angie fully on the lips, and this always made Toshi look away.

Angie was a vegetarian. Mitsuyo thought vegetarianism was as insane as going through life blindfolded. Each visit, she stormed into Kei's apartment like a Canadian peacekeeping mission delivering goods to dislocated refugees. Madagascar curry, goose liver and truffle pâté, lobster sashimi tossed with salmon roe, store-made farmer's sausage and sauerkraut. As she crowded Angie out of the tiny, roach-infested kitchen, she said, "Angie, I'm old, and been enough places to recognize a gentle soul when I see one. Yours is a gentle soul. But believe me, my son would rather gnaw on one of his smelly socks than eat the mush you call tofu spaghetti."

She asked Toshi to translate. When he stammered, she hit him with a soup ladle. She was as polite as a diplomat's daughter should be to all of Kei's friends, except Angie.

"Yes, Mrs. Hayakawa," Angie said, nodding. She didn't dare call Mitsuyo by her first name. A part of Mitsuyo wanted to approve of Angie's subservience. A bigger part of her could not understand it.

"I'm leaving!" she yelled as she approached the newly painted grey front door. Angie was not sure anyone heard in the kitchen. Her mother's stew of dead animal flesh still hung in the air, as heavy as guilt. "Don't wait up!"

"Did you have enough to eat?" Her mother appeared, holding a washcloth to her face. "You didn't finish your bean curd salad."

"That's tofu, Mom."

"Bean toffee salad. Whatever." She looked at Angie's clothes. "Got a date with that boss of yours again?"

"It's not a date, Mom."

"Anyone else coming?"

"No."

"Is he gay?"

"Alex?"

Angie's mother sighed. "I tell you, it's a date," she said.

Angie looked up toward the second floor. "Bye, Dad!" There was no answer.

"He's probably on the phone with his new clients, dear."

Angie nodded. It was always something with Dad, wasn't it? He was either quiet or screaming.

Her mother smiled sadly. "Alex looks like he has a lot of hair. I don't want to know if he's hairy all over. Do you hear me? If you find out, please don't tell me."

"Not much chance of that happening, Ma."

"Why? What's wrong?"

"Well," Angie paused. "He's a nice guy, but . . ."

"Nothing wrong with nice." Her mother squeezed the wash-cloth tighter onto her left eye.

"You'd better have that looked at," Angie said.

The sidewalk was covered in snow. They lived at the end of a suburban cul-de-sac where there were no trees. The snow stretched from one lawn to the next, reflecting the streetlights, illuminating everything as if it was day. The houses were lined in neat rows on both sides of the street. There was not one blemish on the scenery. She knew the imperfection lay inside the houses.

That there were even a winter and summer at all in Canada had surprised Kei when he arrived. He'd imagined the country to be perpetually covered in unadulterated white snow. He later looked at a map and saw Toronto was only a few degrees north

relative to Milwaukee. It was no wonder life here wasn't dis-
cernibly different, aside from unfamiliar hamburger chains and
beer labels.

Other than singing and gyrating around the stage with a guitar strapped across his thin shoulders, Kei did nothing even
remotely resembling exercise. Nonetheless, he never gained weight.
This was probably because he smoked and drank coffee and hardly ever ate. On stage, he always looked like he might fade away,
until he started singing. Then everyone else faded away.

Had it always been this way? He recalled being secretly pleased
when Mitsuyo signed him up for classes with Miss B. He had
always been in the choir, starting back at Lover's Bluff Elementary
School. Even before then, though, music had been his sanctuary in
a strange world. He had no recollections of Japan, so his earliest
memories were of growing up in Milwaukee with Toshi—Toshi,
whose lumbering presence and insane antics did nothing but
alienate Kei further from his friends. Music had been his sanctuary
against all that was absurd.

Preference for music that was intense and visceral was something he shared with his father. They both loved to sit alone in the
dark and be immersed in their favourite recordings. For Shoji, it was
the noble, courageous strings of Grieg; for Kei, the tension between
despair and hope woven into the voice of Ella Fitzgerald. It took a
long time before he could play his guitar in a way that produced
almost the same feeling. It might not have taken so long had he been
given lessons, but Mitsuyo had given up on him after the piano. As
far as he could tell, Mitsuyo had given up on a lot of things.

A few bikers waddled to the can during the break, shaking
their heads. "Man, that Chink faggot can sure fucking kick ass!"
one of them said.

Hawke stepped in front of them and grinned, his eyes hidden
behind mirror shades. "Damn straight," he said, and laughed,
rubbing his enormous belly. Hawke was as tall as an oak tree, and

as immovable. His forearms were the size of Telly's thighs. He had a thick moustache that was curled at the tips, like longhorns. He drove a pickup truck. He was someone who defined drinking, smoking and learning how to spit as acts of heroism. His fondest childhood memories included filling a rabbit with buckshot at twenty feet on a bright summer morning.

The bikers looked at each other, unsure what Hawke wanted. They decided to laugh and walk around him, which he allowed them to do. He was always pleased when people liked the band's music. In all the years he'd been bouncing at the Twisted Neon, he'd never come across a band like Head. He always looked forward to when they played at the club, and usually had a drink or more with them afterwards. The biker had been right. Kei could sure kick ass. Hawke's ponytail bobbed in time with the music.

The band always moved in slow motion after a gig. They wrapped cables around their forearms, snapped the instrument cases closed and heaved the load on their backs. They moved even slower once they were outside. Trudging through snowbanks, no one cared that their shoes and socks were quickly soaked. Water wedged between their toes. Their van was in the alley, buried and helpless.

Hawke always gave them a hand. He was never paid for it, and he never helped anyone but Head. "You going to Dave's, Telly?" he said, carrying a monitor under one arm and an amp on the other shoulder. He spent his days lifting weights in the gym and practising martial-arts moves in front of the mirror.

"For sure."

"How about you, Kei?"

"Yeah. I'll just follow in the car, though, man. Just leave me a reef, Telly."

"Fuck you, squirt. I left the stash back at the apartment," Telly mumbled through a lit cigarette. "Go back and get it. I'll meet you at Dave's."

"What about Millie?" Kei asked.

"Bring her if she wants. Otherwise, just bring the dope."

Kei made a face. Everyone else stumbled over each other into the van. Telly flipped on the ignition. The engine choked on bad gas. Hawke hauled himself in through the rear. Wheels spun noisily in the snow before taking hold. Then they were gone.

Kei walked through the alley with wet feet. He tried to remember where he'd parked his Plymouth. It wasn't too cold. It never was when it snowed, as long as there was no wind. Snowflakes in Toronto were big and lumpy, just like in Milwaukee. The snow masked not just the cracks in the concrete, the jagged edges of broken Export bottles, dog shit and dead rats. It also muted the car engines, the sirens, the drunks and the pimps. And the silence wasn't hollow. It was rich and warm. Kei took a deep breath and let go. He saw the Plymouth's cracked taillights peeking from behind a Dumpster and laughed softly to himself. The exhaust pipe was falling apart into flakes of rust.

They walked out into the brisk air. Angie breathed deeply. Taillights on passing cars left lazy trails of red and yellow through the falling snow. The metallic jingle of keys as Alex fumbled with his pockets sounded like sleigh bells. He hopped on one leg, digging deep into a pocket that had twisted from hours of sitting.

"So," he said, struggling. "Where do you want to go? Want something to eat?"

Angie knew Alex would take her anywhere she wanted. He always had. He always opened doors for her, even though this unnerved her. Not enough attention paid to her needs made her miserable, but too much care also made her uneasy. He'd finally fished the keys from his pocket and was looking at her, perplexed by her silence.

"I had a nice time tonight, Alex," she said, touching his face. "But I've gotta go."

"Where are you going?"

She walked away, waving without turning around. As she walked past the entrance to the alley, she could see the band carrying their instruments out of the club. She could make out the tiny form of the singer. He seemed so young, even from the distance. She wrapped a lock of hair around her finger, contemplating her next move. Then she stepped into the alley.

The snow muted footsteps, too. Kei spun around, lost his balance and fell against the trunk. It took a moment for him to regain his balance and to see her. She looked like a tree in a clearing, standing ankle deep in snow. A thick poncho was wrapped around her thin shoulders. The snow was still fresh and clean. It shimmered in the light under the naked bulb that hung overhead.

Her hair was long, a red mass that burned in the darkness. Her skin was the colour of vanilla ice cream. Her large eyes were green and deep and looked at Kei as if he was walking on air. As if there was no ground beneath his feet. She looked at him for a long time. Kei never knew it, but she looked at him this way all the time, even after years of living together. She looked at him this way because Angie listened—*really* listened—to his songs. She had always wondered where they came from.

Kei met her gaze for a while, then opened the car door. He turned to her. "You coming or going?"

She thought about it. The faint flutter of guilt was still there in her belly. She decided to ignore it and gingerly stepped across the loose snow to climb into the Plymouth. Kei gunned the gas, and the car wobbled out onto the lane. As it shot out into the street, Kei swerved just in time to miss a bewildered Alex waddling about aimlessly in his parka. The car skidded out onto the street, swinging its tail like an ecstatic dog.

Alex saw who was in the car, and the bile coming up his throat made him loosen his Maple Leafs tie. He gave the car disappearing into the distance not one but both his middle fingers.

"That was close," Kei said. He laughed softly to himself as he lit a cigarette with one hand and steered with the other. Angie looked out the window without saying anything.

Once they were away from the cluster of tall buildings in downtown Toronto, the rooftops of identical low-rises became the horizon. Everywhere you went, you could see the CN Tower, the monstrous space needle pointing toward the heavens like a heroin addict's dream.

Kei shivered and gripped the wheel tighter. The wind was high. The snow drifted about like lost children. The sky beyond the aimlessly wavering searchlights was a dark mass of nothing. They drove to his apartment, a brown, ramshackle walk-up that stained the streetscape. Angie got out of the car first. She looked up, squinting.

The building smelled of mildew and disinfectant. They climbed past the stains on the torn wallpaper to his apartment, which he shared with Mildred, Telly and Mr. Man. It was cold, and the beige walls made the apartment seem darker than it was. Mr. Man sat in the shadows of the living room, mumbling secrets to himself and whistling. In the kitchen, Mildred took a drag off the cigarette tucked between her fish-like fingers. She blew smoke rings. She threw back her long, greying hair and kept talking into the phone.

"No, really, Rose. It ain't so bad here. Smells a little bit. But it ain't so bad. Mr. Man came with us. He hasn't shut up for a New York minute since we got here."

Mr. Man sat upright on a chair by the closet. His hands lay folded on his lap. "Lorelei, my princess. I love her so. . . . (*tweet!*)" When he noticed Angie coming in, he gave her a timid wave.

"Shut up, Mr. Man," Mildred yelled. She didn't bother covering the receiver. Mr. Man's mouth continued to move, but he stopped talking. "I don't know what the fuck he's saying, Rosanne," Mildred said into the phone. "Kei said we couldn't just leave him.

He can be such a snotty prick sometimes, but then he won't throw a bum like Mr. Man out on his butt. And how can such an asshole write such beautiful music? When I tell him how much I love how he does that, he looks at me as if I'm a moron.

"But I like the serious stuff you were working on, too. They're nice. Telly, he ain't even writing no more. Listen, you think I can come by and hear your new stuff? Your stuff, you know, makes me feel something inside. Almost like Kei's stuff." Millie smiled and butted her cigarette. She saw Kei's shadow on the wall, and wondered what he was doing home.

Kei motioned Angie over to his bedroom. She obliged after only a moment of uncertainty. There were fingerprints all over the window glass. Beyond, she could see the warm glow of lights scattered on the skyline, silent in the frozen mist. Just below the window, the warm neon flickered above a tattoo parlour across the street.

She sat down on Kei's bed. "You're a lot shorter than you look on stage," she said.

Jesus Fucking Christ, thought Kei.

A web of cracks ran across a corner of the ceiling. He pulled a nickel bag from his dresser and sat next to Angie. Kei always took his time rolling a reefer. He enjoyed the ritual. It helped calm him, maybe even more than the joint did. He lit it and took a long, deep toke, and blew blue smoke up toward the ceiling. *The stuff dreams are made of,* he thought. "Was that your boyfriend we almost ran over back there?" he asked.

"No," Angie answered quickly. "He's . . . *was* my boss."

"Oh."

They could hear Millie in the other room.

"You're not from around here, are you?" Angie asked.

Kei coughed into his hand.

"Where're you from?"

And this was the question that was always the hardest. Where was he from?

"Can I have some?"

She took the joint and turned it between her fingers. Kei wondered if she was going to take off her coat. Mildred was still on the phone. Her voice suddenly seemed very far away.

"I love your music," Angie said.

He slipped another paper from its pack and started rolling the second joint. He pretended this required all his attention.

"Yeah, you know which one I really like?" She began to sing.

"Falling through starlight down to a sea of mist,
You take me under to a colder place."

And for the next couple of hours, she sang all his songs. Only they weren't his when she sang them. Her voice was tender, easy and forgiving, unlike his, which was confused, angry, desperate. And as she told him what the words meant to her, he realized for the first time that his songs were alive. Not just alive, but free. Free to be a rant, a wish, a prayer, a dream, a memory. It wasn't even that she had a better voice. It was just different. He listened for hours while she sang his songs back to him.

THE ENEMY

SHOJI'S HOUSE IN KITAGAWA HAD A LOT OF EMPTY SPACE. As Yasujiro was transferred from one town to another, they never took much of themselves. The Hayakawas were not about to become attached to any one place by filling it, only to be torn away when the winds changed. They also never became too close to the neighbours, or to the domestic help. Still, Shoji felt sorry for Otama, the maid. She had to endure his father's endless rants, which he often conducted in the nude. She was obviously a simple girl, more than slightly awed by the sophistication, not to mention eccentricities, of her current employers.

Ryoko had taught her the rudiments of proper *kaiseki* cuisine, trained her in the art of ink-brush calligraphy as well as flower arranging and the tea ceremony. Otama was grateful for the training, but not the condescension that accompanied Ryoko's teachings.

"Of course, in a place like Kitagawa, you'll probably never use half the things I'm showing you, but knowing how to properly serve grilled lobster can't hurt," Ryoko once said at the start of a typical cooking lesson.

Otama's name in Japanese conjured images of pearls or rare gems, but her face resembled nothing more than worn leather. Her plain features were almost invisible on her dark skin. Her habit of eating any food that was in reach while working for the Hayakawas made her one of the rare people who actually gained weight during the war.

She was born out of wedlock to the senior maid at the Harada farmhouse a few miles outside Kitagawa. Otama was never told who her father was, and for a long time didn't even realize she had one. Everyone else recognized her resemblance to the eldest Harada boy. He grew up to head the farm until he was conscripted and killed somewhere in the South Pacific.

Aside from her mother being promoted to senior maid, which could simply have been a reward for hard work, Otama never received any special attention from the Haradas. Everyone around her knew, though, that simply tolerating her presence was more generosity than anyone could expect. The entire household was relieved when the railroad hired her to help the Hayakawas keep house.

In Otama, Shoji saw for the first time how some people were not allowed to belong anywhere, or to anyone. He saw Otama drifting, like a solitary firefly on a summer breeze. He had no doubt she would remain a maid for the rest of her life. She would go from the service of one family to another, living in their homes and eating their food, never making enough money to plan a different life. She might be married, Shoji imagined, to someone like a seasonal worker or a travelling merchant. Otherwise, though, she would never have a place in the world to call her own, in body or spirit.

(When he grew older, Shoji would realize that there were varying degrees to belonging. He would see that belonging was also a relatively rare commodity among himself, his wife and his sons.)

Kitagawa lay among mountains, and like everywhere else in

Japan, humidity permeated everything, especially in summer. Beads of sweat fell like flower petals. Mould grew on everything—cookies, rice cakes, underwear. The bathroom was especially bad. Black mildew grew between cedar panels, and when left alone evolved into mushrooms.

Yasujiro discovered some mushrooms growing in the darkest corner of their bathroom. He had been all ready to step into the steaming water. It was the middle of the day, and he was home from the clinic, taking a bath. This was partly because bathing in daylight meant not having to burn precious oil for lighting. It was also because Yasu took off his clothes at the slightest opportunity. When he saw the mushrooms, he immediately crouched and picked a few to show Otama when he reprimanded her for the shoddy job she did cleaning the bathroom.

He rolled a few of the fungi between his fingers. More steam from the bath collected on the ceiling, gathering into droplets and falling back down onto his head and into the tub. The mushrooms were grotesque and strangely curious. The long, skinny stems were soft, flimsy—even pathetic. They were obviously reaching out toward something, but what? Unlike plants, they disliked sunlight. What would they be yearning for in the darkness? The question occupied Yasujiro's mind so much he forgot to dress before leaving the bathroom. But when he saw Otama, his anger returned like summer rain.

"Otama!" he yelled, not stopping to wonder why her eyes would widen in horror before he even started the scolding. He waved the mushrooms in front of his face as he walked closer. "Please take a look at this! Heaven knows what else is growing in the bathroom because you're not more careful! You know, my feet have been itching lately, and . . ."

Otama was not looking at the mushrooms. Her eyes remained fixed on Yasu's manhood, which looked to her like an enormous silkworm. Its peculiarity at once disgusted and fascinated her. She had seen young boys on the Harada farm, running about naked outside the bathhouse with the same strange appendage between their legs, but this was the first time she had seen one on an adult. This was the first time she saw the silkworm emerging from a bush.

Otama had no idea that a penis was for anything but pissing. She had seen farm animals spraying urine from the same appendage. As to why the same animals mounted each other from time to time, she had no clue. No one had educated her about how children were made, except to say that an *oni* demon had delivered her to her mother one rainy night in spring. She had seen enough pregnant women and witnessed enough childbirths to know this was not true. But she could only assume babies simply materialized in women's bellies, like a kidney stone or the wart between her toes.

Otama's guileless interest in Yasu's cock was in stark contrast to Shoji's thoughts as he sat at that same moment in his room, thinking about Kanako's blouse, with his pants around his ankles. Images flashed across his dark mind, one after another, each putting Kanako, as well as himself, in increasingly lewd positions. These thoughts were delicious. So was the sensation of his fingers around his erection.

Unlike Otama, Shoji knew exactly how babies were produced, right down to the cellular level. He had known, in fact, before puberty. The erections and wet dreams only confirmed what he'd read. He didn't find his physical needs repugnant. Why argue with your own body? He didn't feel conflicted over his desire to masturbate any more than his occasional need to piss.

He was, on the other hand, unused to the emotions that accompanied his visions of Kanako naked—the violent desires, the tenderness, the yearning, the hunger. These feelings were something with which he would never come to terms, even after he grew and married and had children. All his knowledge and familiarity with the physical world, in the end, left him as helpless as a deaf,

124

blind mute when confronted with intimacy. In the end, there was little difference between his learned perspective on sex and Otama's utter ignorance of it.

There was no breeze, but the clouds outside his window were moving, changing. Air was moving faster on a higher stratosphere. He felt the desired tightness around his loins, then clouds of semen burst forth from the eye of his penis. There was a moment of rapture, when the universe seemed to settle slowly around his shoulders, like sand falling in water.

He wiped himself clean with a piece of newsprint. On it was a cartoon of big-nosed Americans cowering in fear before Japanese pilots and sailors wielding samurai swords. "They lie to us about everything," Yasu had once told him. "So when they tell us we're winning, that's the time to start worrying."

Shoji was buttoning his slacks when he heard the commotion downstairs. At first he thought it was his father still fussing with Otama. Then he recognized Shima's thin voice. His member was still hard and erect, so he shoved his fists in his pockets. He walked gingerly down the stairs to the front entrance, where Shima was talking with Yasujiro, both of them clearly agitated.

Yasu was still naked, save for a towel he held in front of his groin. Otama cowered by herself in the corner. When she saw Shoji, she pleaded with her eyes to be dismissed. Shoji normally would have allowed her to retreat back into the shadows, but he was too distracted by Shima. Shoji saw his emaciated friend had brought back the book that Kanako had bought them. His erection, which had receded a bit at the sight of his naked father, stood anew at attention at the thought of Kanako. Young men were always horny, even during a war.

"Well! They've ordered every man in town to gather at the Fukanji temple," Shima said, shaking his head.

Shoji forgot immediately about Kanako. Shima didn't have to say who "they" were. There were men in Kitagawa who walked around in crisp black uniforms and polished leather shoes. They clenched their jaws as if they were locked in place. They seemed to believe they were more important than the soldiers who were actually fighting the enemy. You never wanted to argue with them, the *kempeitai*.

"You go on ahead." Yasu spat onto the dirt in the foyer. "I have to take my bath."

Shima looked at Shoji, uncertain. A cold fist gripped Shoji's stomach as he watched his father's bare ass going back into the house. But there was nothing to be done. "Just leave him," Shoji said, stepping into his sandals. "And leave the book here if you're finished with it." He tried to sound as if it didn't matter to him one way or another.

The cedar trees surrounding the main hall of the Fukanji temple towered over the crowd. They looked like elderly gods passing judgment. Men too old for battle, or too young or crippled, milled about in the courtyard talking about nothing. Some smoked, holding thick cylinders of tobacco up to their mouths between their knotted fingers. One old farmer picked at scabs on his bony chest, which his loose-fitting cotton jacket could not hide. Hunger and fatigue in his eyes, he gazed at the highest branches of the trees, and looked as if he might start crying.

This was only the second time Shoji had set foot in the temple grounds. The first time he'd come alone, through the deserted woods, enjoying the seclusion. The air smelled of incense, and the silence, he found, was not silent at all. There were distant noises of everything that made up life in Kitagawa. There were the cries of birds and insects, the occasional distant train whistle and the sound of rolling river water. Shoji could also discern a distinct hiss, or a hum. A presence of some sort. He also heard it now, somewhere high above the grumbling men around him.

The abbot was a frail old man who looked like he could drift away at any moment. Dwarfed by a voluminous cotton robe, he surveyed the crowd sadly. Five men, dressed identically in black uniforms vaguely resembling those of Imperial Navy officers, stepped around him. They wore captain's caps with rigid brims. Collars dug into their stiff necks. They seemed to enjoy the pain. Everyone knew the *kempeitai*'s rigidity was an expression of their brittle minds, which did not bend to compassion.

When the skinniest among them screamed for the crowd to be quiet, the abbot looked down and sighed. An acolyte with the face of a young Buddha walked up to him and pointed to something a short distance away. At the foot of an enormous cedar tree that was almost as old as the mountains, a cat toyed with a mouse. The cat picked up its prey in its mouth repeatedly, only to let go every time. When the mouse tried to scurry away, it was batted about by the cat's paws like a ball of yarn. The abbot and his acolyte watched for a while. At precisely the same time, as if on cue, they clasped their hands together and closed their eyes in prayer.

The skinny *kempeitai* stood aside, and a burly captain stepped forward. Everyone in Kitagawa knew Tamura, whose jaw was as square as roofing tiles and whose eyes burned like hellfire. Shoji saw Kono in the crowd. He was watching Tamura with his mouth open, as if the captain of the *kempeitai* in this small rural village was the most charismatic leader Japan had ever produced. Kono wore a torn shirt, shorts and sandals. His knees were covered in dirt, but he stood at attention—as straight as chopsticks impaled in a mound of rice.

Tamura's voice boomed like rolling thunder. "You are all dirt!" he shouted. "Miserable parasites who cannot even defend your own country! But the time has come for you cretins to be of some use to our beloved emperor!"

Kono swallowed hard. He looked like he was resisting the temptation to applaud.

"We just received word that an American patrol plane was shot down last night just beyond the Takami Ridge." Tamura fingered the wart on his nose as he spoke. "When the local *kempeitai* squad reached the wreckage, they found the pilot gone."

Confused whispers rippled across the crowd. Many claimed to have heard a loud noise the previous night coming from the mountain, certain to have been the crash. Others wondered aloud why the Americans would bother flying a plane over their village. Kono smiled. Shima turned white. Shoji held his knees together to keep them from trembling.

"It is highly probable that the enemy has followed the river to this area. You will pair off and start combing the woods according to our instructions." Tamura motioned with his jaw, and his officers dispersed among the crowd.

They issued each pair of men just one rifle with a bayonet. Many argued as to who should carry the weapon. Many wanted to, just to feel secure. Others smartly figured that the enemy would probably try to shoot the one holding the rifle first. Shima wanted to carry the weapon but found it too heavy. He handed it to Shoji, who cradled it awkwardly in his arms. The sun was still high, although it had tilted slightly to the west. The heat had not abated any.

"Hayakawa!" Tamura's booming voice slammed into Shoji, who struggled to hang on to his rifle. All the *kempeitai* came over to him and Shima, like a flock of ducks, each afraid of being separated from the others. Tamura looked into Shoji's face. His eyes were engorged with blood and fury. He smelled like stale tobacco. "Where is your father?"

Tamura had no way of knowing that at that very moment, Yasujiro sat, naked except for a loincloth, lounging in the main dining room of their house, where he always took his tea. He was looking toward the garden and his bomb shelter, sucking on a pipe, listening to the cicadas. He reminded himself that Ryoko was off bartering food again. Shoji and his friend were out taking orders from the same idiots who were running the country into the ground.

Yasu sighed. He wondered how much longer the war would last, and how much longer they'd stay in Kitagawa. It wasn't such a bad place, really. He certainly could not take his clothes off so often in Tokyo. And the town deserved a better doctor than anyone else the railroad would send. At least he was confident of his own skills.

But didn't Ryoko deserve better than this? Sadness had turned to grey the hair on his wife's head. Frowning had left creases around her thin lips. She hardly ever said anything to him any more. He knew, secretly, that the reason she married him was to escape from places like Kitagawa.

And Yasu knew his son was at an impressionable age. Shoji was like a feather riding the winds of change. What was living in a place like this doing to him? What about the war? How would they come out of this all in the end? And were those mushrooms he found in the bathroom edible? Too many questions weighed heavily in his mind. He scratched his naked belly and drew some more smoke from the pipe.

At first he thought it was some animal that had moved into the shelter. The noise and movement came from the shadows beyond the stairs leading underground. Yasu slipped on his sandals and stepped out into the garden. He didn't mind animals, just the crap they left behind. And if they marked their territory with their piss, well, there'd be no getting rid of whatever it was.

He'd walked only a few feet when a figure, too large to be a dog or a badger, jumped out into the light. The soldier's face was badly bruised and cut. The hand that aimed the gun at Yasujiro was trembling. Yasu marvelled at how the young American could see through those eyes that were as blue as the sky. His skin, so pale, made the dried blood look like islands in an ocean of rice. He was incredibly beautiful, like a porcelain figurine.

The injured pilot wore bulky overalls, a cap and thick boots. He was perspiring so much he looked like he'd just stepped out of a bath. Yasu sympathized and wished he could tell the young man to take all his clothes off. He hesitated, because Yasu was unfortunately more comfortable with German than English. And he knew that German was the last thing this American wanted to hear.

Instead, he made do with pointing to the pilot's various injuries. The American's gaze, and his aim, didn't waver. Yasu placed both his hands on his own chest. "Doctor," he said in English. This much he knew, and he thought he saw the young man's cold blue eyes soften. Using gentle waves of his arms, he motioned for the pilot to follow him into the house. Yasu mimed that he would bandage the pilot's wounds. The barrel of the gun lowered, just slightly.

Life is timing.

Otama chose that exact moment to bring Yasujiro his afternoon glass of cold tea. She'd been so upset with Yasu for scolding her in the nude earlier that day, she'd chopped the mushrooms he had collected and mixed it with the tea to brew. For this, she felt more guilt than she should have and was walking with her head down. She did not see the young American holding a gun in the garden until she placed the glass on the table and looked up to see what Yasu was doing in the yard.

Her knees gave away before she found her voice. She could only stammer and crawl about on the floor before the American, reacting to the sudden movement, fired a few rounds over her head. She screamed, and the young pilot realized what he'd fired at. He looked at Yasu, took a few steps backwards, then turned and ran. He scaled the farthest wall in the garden, crying.

His name was James McArthur—Jimmy to everyone who knew him. He was just twenty years old. He had a sweetheart back home named Isabel. She would be saddened to know he'd been crying, but the tears would not stop.

Waves of fear swept across his chest. He thought about his parents, who ran a small shoe store on a typical suburban street in the Midwest. Across the street was the bakery where Jimmy bought their bread. He thought about his brother, who had lived for playing baseball before he was run over by a suicidal milk truck driver. They both went to a suburban public school, and Jimmy liked to dance to the jukebox in the five-and-dime. He liked to smoke Marlboros. His favourite beer was Schlitz.

As he tried desperately to find his way back to the river, he wondered whether he'd enjoy any of these things ever again.

In fact, Jimmy would live to have as many more beers as he wished. He would go home to America at the end of the war and take over his father's shoe business. He would question the validity of a life that involved handling other people's feet much of the time. But this would not bother Isabel at all. She would marry him not too long after he took over the shoe store. They would have five children, and in years to come, each of them would have to hear about the time when Dad's plane fell into the mountains of Japan during the war. They would talk about it at Christmas and at Thanksgiving, in front of the mantel in the living room of their house, which was on the outskirts of Chicago, Illinois, just ninety miles south of Milwaukee, Wisconsin.

Yasu turned to Otama. His eyes were like a fighting bull's. "What in heaven's name are you doing?" he screamed. She was sitting on the floor, her legs spread wide, her robe open, revealing her virgin bush. She had wet herself. She looked at Yasu as if she realized for the first time that he was crazy.

The shadows of the trees were growing longer as the sun fell into the afternoon. Shoji and Shima were about to enter the forest.

Shoji's left ear was still ringing. Tamura had screamed on and on about how Yasujiro was a coward of the most inexcusable kind and that he would not be so bold as to offend the *kempeitai* if he wasn't the town's only doctor. If his father was a coward, thought Shoji, it must be in the genes. He felt his stomach bounce as he walked. He wanted nothing more than to get away, from this mission, from Kitagawa. He wanted to run to somewhere deep in the mountains where the war would not bother him. What did *not* being a coward get anybody during wartime? What sense did it make that he, with this rusty rifle, was hunting in the woods for an enemy soldier who was undoubtedly armed and well trained? Shima looked ready to collapse from hunger and heat exhaustion.

No, his father was not a coward. Yasu was simply crazy. But no crazier than the rest of the war.

The sound of Shima's shoes dragging against the dirt made the gun seem even heavier to Shoji. His right shoulder was pinched. He doubted he would even be able to raise his weapon if they ever ran into the enemy. The sky was without clouds, though, and the woods provided welcome shelter from the unforgiving sun. Shoji heard his friend cough dryly, clearing his throat to speak.

"I wonder what he looks like" was all Shima said.

The wind carried hurried voices from town. Soon, the whole forest was afire with barked orders and whispers. The enemy was spotted in town, someone said. He was hiding in a bomb shelter. He had gunned down a man. He had gunned down a woman.

Shadows ran in every direction. Kono came up behind Shoji and Shima and pointed toward the river with his gun. "New orders!" he screamed. He was breathing like an overheated workhorse. Sweat fell from his jaw onto the dirt. "Tamura-san suspects the enemy is running for the river! We're to redirect the search along the shore!"

They ran for the Kitagawa river. They ran as fast as they could. They earnestly wanted to catch this enemy pilot, if for no other reason than to break the monotony of the day. They ran like the wind, hurtling over stones and fallen tree branches. But Shoji knew they were too late.

BIG BOY

THE LINOLEUM FLOOR FELT COOL AGAINST TOSHI'S forehead. The crowd murmured around him on their way to third period. Second period had been particularly dreadful. Miss Herndorff, his social studies teacher, who also coached the girls' basketball team and was a member of the community club string quartet, would not stop talking about her plight.

"My sister only told us she was bringing home someone for dinner. We were delighted, of course, because she hadn't really been seeing anyone since the divorce," she said. This was in reply to Billy Bogosian's question, Did the confrontational views of Louis Farrakhan and the Nation of Islam really enable blacks to establish a cultural identity, or did it simply encourage continued segregation? "Well," she said, holding on to her desk in case she fainted just remembering the ordeal. "Imagine my surprise when I opened the door and saw nothing in the dark but a pair of bloodshot eyes and a set of grotesquely big teeth."

She added that even in the light, their dinner guest did not look nor speak anything like Sidney Poitier or Harry Belafonte. "It was Woodstock," she concluded. "My sister's never been the same."

The name of the high school was Whitefish, not Black Cod or Yellowtail. There were no black students in Miss Herndorff's class at the time.

The two black students at Whitefish appeared as bewildered as the two Orientals, Toshi and Kei. All of them were trying to cope with their environment, in which people listened to Bob Marley and watched Bruce Lee movies but didn't know how to deal with people with different eyes or skin.

Toshi often noticed the black students staring at him. He assumed they were as mystified by fortune-cookie wisdom as he was by the elliptic speech and hip rituals he saw on *The Jeffersons*. Not once did it cross his mind that his habit of lying face down on the floor in the hallway between classes would be perplexing to anyone of any race.

He looked like a beached walrus. He could hear the loud swearing and hushed giggles as everyone made their way around him. Just when he thought he might get up, he recognized his brother's voice. Then a hard kick caved in his ribs. Gasping, he looked up just in time to see Kei and Telly walking away without breaking stride. From behind, Telly's long, curly hair looked like black sheep's wool.

Toshi struggled to his feet. He could hear them talking just above the drone of the crowd. The river of people flowed in all directions.

"So what the fuck did Jaime say in her fucking letter?" Telly said in between drags on his cigarette. "Did she write anything about your sorry song? Come on, don't fuck with me, Kei, or I'll tear your goddamn head off!"

Toshi's eyes widened at hearing Jaime's name. He tried to call out to Kei, but his ribs ached where they'd been kicked.

Like most boys at Lover's Bluff Elementary School, Toshi had hardly noticed Jaime Saunders's presence. When she appeared again, though, after being away in Paris, she was an exquisite young woman who pained him just by being in his field of vision. Thin, with jade green eyes and auburn hair down to her waist, she pained all young men.

Jaime led the cheerleading squad, and she was the president of the ski team. This alone would only have been a source of mild repugnance. This alone might make those who hovered on the periphery of school life, like Toshi and Kei, harden and ignore her exuberance. It certainly would not bring them to the brink of bursting with the white, incandescent desire of acne-infested love.

Everyone, though, loved Jaime, because she played "Cowgirl in the Sand" on the guitar, and sang with a voice as gentle as rain. Toshi loved her because she spoke French. He loved her because she wore riding boots over her skintight jeans, *and she actually owned horses.* He loved her because she hated discos and disco music. He loved her because she smiled without pity. She was the only person who ever asked him why he liked to lie face down in the hallway.

"The floor feels cool against my forehead," he told her. "And I can hear the earth rumbling."

"What?"

"I hear the earth rumbling. You've never noticed? There's this fu— There's this noise that always comes from the ground. A rumble. No, no. More like a rush. Like the rush of water flowing over waterfalls, never stopping. And above that, you hear people's footsteps. Yours and mine. The earth is alive and can feel our feet fall onto its skin."

Jaime tilted her head.

He added, "It makes me feel less alone."

Toshi had expected her to start laughing. He imagined her gnawing on a piece of his heart and spitting it out into the water fountain. Then Jaime did something no other captain of the cheerleading squad had ever done in the entire history of Whitefish High School. She lay down on the floor in the middle of the rotunda at the front entrance and put her face on the linoleum.

Toshi collapsed into laughter. He'd never realized how stupid he looked. Guffaws also gushed forth from the crowd around them.

Jaime was smiling, too, when she stood up. Then, without a touch of condescension, she said, simply, "Cool."

Toshi watched her as she faded from view, merging with the flow of the crowd. He would never recall later how long he stood there, or whether his mouth was closed or hanging open.

Kei and Jaime had known each other since Kei was moved into the fifth grade at Lover's Bluff Elementary School. They lived on the same street, and Jaime often came by to invite Kei for walks or bike rides in the summer. Together, they used to speed down the sidewalks on Stingrays with banana seats and sissy bars. Jaime always carried more money than Kei, so treated him to sour gumballs at the store at the corner of Kensington and Oakland.

He accepted her offerings with few words and even less expression. Once she reached for his hand as they walked out to their bikes, expecting him to pull away, like all boys did. He surprised her by not resisting. It was only when he saw other boys from Lover's Bluff Elementary School down the street that he drew his hand back as if she was on fire.

They sometimes walked home from school together. In winter, the snow actually stayed white on their street, even though it turned a scummy brown everywhere else. Jaime threw snow in Kei's face. She loved the way he calmly removed his hat and used it to brush the snow from his eyes, saying nothing. Then he would see her clearly again, and he could look at her forever.

Chinatown in Toronto recreated the streets of Hong Kong perfectly, even the smells. The only difference was that the streets in Toronto were wider. Vendors sat on the sidewalks hawking wilted greens. Water everywhere did nothing to settle the dust.

Angie and Toshi came often for dim sum to the second-best restaurant in the area. They used to go to the very best restaurant, but at its entrance was a tank full of live crabs and lobsters. Whenever Toshi was left alone, he would set them free. Waiters then tripped over crustaceans on the carpet as they wheeled their carts of steamed dumplings and chicken feet. The second-best restaurant in Chinatown kept its seafood in the kitchen until it was safely dead and on a plate.

"That's when Jaime lay down on the floor to see what I was talking about," Toshi said, chewing on curried squid. "She tried it, and heard for herself how the earth is always breathing."

Angie nodded and sipped her jasmine tea. It was lukewarm.

Toshi and Mitsuyo had moved to Toronto to live with Kei and Angie. Mitsuyo was always on Kei's back about something, but gigs out of town and recording sessions kept him away a lot of time, which meant they fought less often.

The Victorian rowhouse was bigger than the apartment they used to live in, but it was just as rundown. And there still wasn't enough room for everyone. It was bursting now with furniture Mitsuyo had brought from Milwaukee. On sunny days, Mr. Man sat on the front porch, listening to the traffic on Queen Street and mumbling. Millie came in often from the suburbs, where she now lived, to take him for walks around the neighbourhood. Mitsuyo was always running into Angie in the house, pointing out rooms that needed cleaning. Angie dutifully cleaned as she was told, but steered clear of Mitsuyo.

"I think she's really lonely," Angie once told Kei. She'd just bought him a new capo because the old one was so threadbare. Kei didn't seem displeased when she surprised him with it. He just didn't seem as pleased as Angie would have liked. She sighed and put it back into its box. It would be put with all the instruments and music books that cluttered the living room. She often thought of how Kei was so different from Toshi.

Kei lay on the bed and grunted. He was leaving on tour again the next day. The queen-size mattress and box spring lay directly on the hardwood floor because they ran out of money before they could buy the bed frame and the headboard. Kei liked it this way anyway. He said this was like sleeping on a futon in Japan.

"Just leave her be," he said.

"It's difficult, though, Kei. It's not as if I seek her out. She comes looking for me."

"Ignore her, then."

"That makes her angry. You don't know what it's like."

"Jesus Christ, Angie!"

Something in his voice told her she shouldn't say any more. Muttering something about going out for a while, Kei stood up and pulled on his worn leather jacket. She saw him less and less since Mitsuyo came to live with them. He was either on tour or out drinking.

To avoid Mitsuyo, Angie took to wandering the city. She usually took Toshi with her. They walked the streets of downtown endlessly. She hummed the songs that Kei wrote. Toshi either listened in silence or sang something by someone else at the top of his lungs. People stared, but Angie soon realized that she didn't care. She found Toshi's company comforting, precisely because it was so distracting.

On their way to Chinatown, they had passed an army surplus store. Behind the bars on the window was an old air force bomber jacket that looked brand new. Angie remarked that Kei might like it if she bought it for him. Toshi snorted. He thought Angie was being too generous and wondered aloud what Kei ever did for her. Angie looked at him curiously.

"He gave me a place to live, for starters," she said. She started humming one of his songs again. Toshi shoved his fists in his pockets and lagged behind.

Customers shouted at waiters in Cantonese. The waiters shouted back. Chopsticks hit porcelain. Cups and plates were noisily cleared off tables. Children cried over something they didn't like but had to eat. It was a strain to talk over the din.

"If you ignore all this noise, you can hear the earth breathing," Toshi said again, looking around. He said this softly, almost to himself. "Jaime was the only one who ever believed me."

The floor was a mess of dirt and grease and spilled tea. Angie looked at Toshi, and a mischievous smile crept across her mouth. She was wearing her usual peasant's dress, sheer and adorned with a pattern of summer flowers. Without a word, she slid off her chair and knelt on the stained tiles. Toshi watched, his mouth falling open, half-eaten squid ready to fall out, as Angie pulled back her hair and put her ear to the floor.

Her eyes widened when she heard the rush. She lay there, listening, for a long time. A few customers stopped eating and pointed. The waiters crowded around her, while kids laughed. Suddenly she stood up, as if no one else was around. She looked at Toshi, smiling. "I always believed you," she said. "Now, I know for sure."

It was only after she started drinking her tea again that Toshi remembered to keep chewing.

When he overheard Kei and Telly talking about Jaime in the corridor of Whitefish High School, Toshi needed to know, with all his hormone-saturated gonads, what they were saying. He caught up to them just as they reached their lockers. He saw Kei hand Telly a pink envelope.

"Hey, look the fuck over there!" It was O'Connor's voice behind him. The Whitefish Gumbos' star quarterback began to laugh. "The Chink faggot's passing a love letter to one of his ass-fuckers!"

O'Connor had led the Gumbos to the state championships every year since he was a freshman. He was at the centre of everything Whitefish. He was just eighteen but looked like he could be living in a trailer with a wife and four kids. His teeth were stained by tobacco, but the coaches pretended not to notice. Contempt and despair flourished inside him like acne on his oily skin. O'Connor's face looked like the blistered side of the moon.

The crowd around them abruptly stopped moving.

"Jesus Christ, Kei," Telly hissed. He went to hide the envelope in his jacket but then, wondering if this might not somehow look suspicious, he pulled it out again. He looked like he might start to cry.

Kei looked long and hard at O'Connor. He then glared at the rest of the Whitefish Gumbos. "Fuck you," he hissed.

Toshi winced. Here it came—a tidal wave, a tsunami. Masses of brick-hard muscle, honed by red meat and rabid coaches, pushing Kei and Telly against the wall. All the cues were there for the carnage that was supposed to follow, but nothing happened. Laughter disappeared down the corridor with the backs of their lettermen jackets.

"Jesus Christ," Telly said again. "What the hell was that?"

Kei carefully turned the combination to his locker. "Just don't tell anyone who it's from," he said.

"Yeah, yeah." Telly was still breathing fast. He turned the envelope over and over in his hand, as if he needed to see it from every angle before he was convinced it was real. "I still can't fucking believe this, Kei. You gotta understand it'd take a whole shit-load for someone like Jaime to go out with anyone who wasn't American."

Kei saw Toshi looking at him sadly. "Fuck you, Telly" was all Kei said.

Telly drew the letter from the envelope. Toshi leaned over to have a closer look, and the strong scent of lilacs made his head spin. The stationery was pink, a colour too soft for such a hard world. The paper whispered as it unfolded.

To Toshi, the words appeared surprisingly vacuous. They asked Kei his opinion on the Gumbos' chances of taking the championship again this year. They ran on here and there, expressing opinions on the merits of Steven Spielberg, how everyone hated the cheerleading coach and why pistachio was the best flavour of ice cream. A whole paragraph of such drivel.

I think about you all the time, it finally said. *Can we talk? I'll meet you behind the bleachers tomorrow at noon.*

"She doesn't fucking mention your song," said Telly.

Kei scowled.

"Well, she fucking doesn't. And why is this shit typed? On pink paper? It's fucking weird, man."

"Look, she likes to be fucking neat, okay?" Kei was sorry he'd ever mentioned the letter to Telly. Still, his mouth betrayed a fleeting grin as he took the letter back.

Telly never noticed, but Toshi saw his brother's ephemeral smile and understood it completely. Telly could not know how right he had been when he remarked on who usually got to go out with someone like Jaime Saunders. Kei and Toshi both knew their lives, like those of the black students, were inconsequential to most everyone at Whitefish. This was why the letter made Kei so happy he could not conceal his happiness completely. He even allowed his gaze to linger over the words a moment longer.

Toshi, who had been looking over his shoulder, spat into the pink stationery and turned around.

"Hey!" Kei called out as Toshi walked away. The crowd was hurrying to get to class. "What the fuck did you do that for?" Toshi heard the words falling behind him. Everything seemed to be falling, fading away. "You fucking moron!"

Toshi ignored him. Life around him was turning into a dark muck. This was his youth. Days in high school were fragmented and confusing. Homework took longer. Hunger burned all the time, but so did thoughts about acne. The thought of sex flowered every thirty seconds and lingered for twenty minutes. There was little comfort anywhere—certainly none at home. Toshi tried not to think of how his parents had been in a cold war since Shoji's trip to Japan. How they spoke only when absolutely necessary. How they avoided each other in the house.

Engagement was rare, and was usually initiated by Mitsuyo. "Would it ruin one of your scientific experiments if I put the cap back on the tube of toothpaste?" she yelled from the bathroom. "I'm just never sure if you're leaving it off on purpose, or if the washcloth soaking in the sink is also a part of the plan." She still seemed to find control in belligerence.

Whenever they were caught in the same room at the same time, Shoji moved around her, as close to the walls as he could get. He retrieved whatever he needed and got away as quickly as he could limp.

Not that he was helpless. All the household chores were tacitly understood by everyone to be Mitsuyo's responsibility. When she was late in doing the ironing, he put on the most wrinkled shirt to wear to work. He hobbled around the breakfast table with it on for a while. Mitsuyo's hands trembled as she grilled the salmon. Shoji always asked for a Japanese breakfast—some sort of fish, rice, pickles and miso soup.

Because Hanako's mind was turning to ash, Mitsuyo decided never to ask for her mother's help around the house. A minor catastrophe like Hanako burning toast could upset the delicate cold war balance of power. Mitsuyo could just imagine what Shoji might say. "Why do you have your mother make toast for me? Do I have *my* father helping me at *my* job?"

Toshi found his house was no longer a sanctuary in a world that was cruel and made little sense. He had always felt like a cartoon penguin, floating on a piece of ice that had broken off Antarctica. When he was taken from his familiar surroundings in Japan—as stifling as his house arrest had been—he may as well have been cast off to sea. His home and family became the fragment of ice on which he floated.

But nothing ever stayed the same. In the cartoons, the penguin's ice floe always melted or began to crack. Toshi felt the crack spreading like webs of lightning through his house. The cartoon penguin always ran about crazily as the ice floe grew smaller. Toshi sat perfectly still in the closet. He read *Cyrano*, thought about Jaime Saunders and jerked off.

Mitsuyo knocked on the door. "Hurry it up in there! After you're finished, take the trash outside. And don't leave any tissue on the floor!"

Toshi could never escape the darkness. The only thing to be done, if he dared, was to succumb to its allure. This was why teenagers were nocturnal. The night hid their pimples. The night hid the scratches on their cars. And when it became too cold, they could always escape to Marc's Big Boy.

The Big Boy served food for the gods: spaghetti with chili sauce and a slice of melted process cheese, strawberry pie with whipped cream, banana splits with steam rising like ghosts off hot fudge. The booths offered enough privacy to debate the Packers' last game, or to neck, or to pass tabs of acid. The jukebox was full, with a collection varied enough to please most everyone.

Marc of Marc's Big Boy was never around. Scotty Taylor told Toshi this was because the restaurant was only a front for a drug and prostitution ring. Marc disappeared one day, and no one had seen him since. Toshi looked into every Dumpster he passed on the chance he might find Marc's body.

"You know why those motherfucking Japs make everything so small?" Scotty asked. He was drowning a french fry in ketchup and pepper. He furrowed his brows under stringy strands of blond hair. Toshi and Darren shook their heads. They passed cigarettes back and forth, blew paper packages off straws and poured whisky into their Cokes from a mickey. Toshi wondered why the bulky, cylindrical sugar dispenser looked like a miniature fire hydrant. He shook it while making gurgling sounds, as if it might at any moment burst forth with water.

Scotty just kept talking. "Because they got tiny, fucking micro dicks," he said. "Right, Tosh?" His grin was mocking, challenging.

Toshi belched an explosion. He raised the dispenser high in the air, then brought it upside down to just above his coffee cup. The sugar cascaded into the thick sludge that reflected his face. He was not Bruce Lee. That much was clear, unlike most things in his muddled life.

"Fuck you," Toshi said to Scotty. He was feeling foolhardy. Scotty Taylor could turn mean, especially at night. Just like the Wolf Man. Toshi was running with the Wolf Man. *"Aoooooooooo!"* he wailed.

"Jesus fuck, man!" Darren pushed Toshi's shoulder. "What the fucking-shit-for-brains is the matter with you?"

Toshi looked across the room through the blue veneer of smoke. He saw Kei and Telly at the counter, nursing a couple of coffees. They'd just finished jamming over at Telly's. Both of them wore torn, stained T-shirts and tight, faded jeans. Their high-tops were scuffed. Their hair made their heads look twice their size, but they still looked like two skinny, horny, pizza-faced high-school kids without dates on a Friday night.

Telly's parents gave him his first acoustic guitar for his tenth birthday, but Kei, who was there for the party, played it first. The next day, he came over again, with some music books he'd found in the library. Kei played the first chords ever played on Telly's guitar. Later, Telly got his first electric, a used Les Paul for which he had to save for a year. Kei immediately picked it up and played the opening to the Beatles' "Ticket to Ride." It was Kei who eventually had to show Telly how to play the guitar riffs on "You Really Got Me."

The same fall that they entered Whitefish High School, they took in their first concert together. Lower bleachers at the performance of Led Zeppelin at Country Stadium. They both knew somehow that the night would change their lives. The sweet smell of marijuana had permeated everything. Telly whooped and screamed at the pyrotechnics, but when he looked, Kei was wearing only a mildly amused expression. But at least he was bobbing his head to the music.

More than anything, though, Kei seemed fascinated by the crowd, the mass of enraptured faces and waving arms. Telly saw that Kei was watching a group of university jocks, standing on their seats in their lettermen jackets, under the band's spell like everyone else. One particularly large, swarthy jock who had no neck was screaming his approval when an unusually loud fireball exploded on stage, sending him reeling. He fell again as he struggled to get up, but his willowy, blond girlfriend seemed oblivious. She never took her eyes off the stage. Kei laughed.

Shortly afterwards, Kei persuaded Shoji to buy him his own guitar—another Les Paul almost identical to Telly's—just before they formed their own band. Everyone wanted Kei to play lead. Telly could back him up on rhythm, if he wanted. Telly wasn't sure he would be in the band at all if he and Kei weren't best friends.

Toshi was making a lot of noise with Scotty and the others. Kei pretended not to notice their voices bouncing around the entire restaurant. Pretending not to notice things was something everyone at Whitefish High School did with a passion. Noticing things might make people think you were eager to do something. Kei stirred his coffee slowly, just like Elvis might have as he overdosed on Hostess Ding-Dongs. Even fat, though, Elvis never looked overly eager to do anything. He never stirred his coffee too fast. Of this, Kei was certain. He was not so certain whether the mushrooms he'd dropped that night were clean. Everything around him looked flat. Toshi was a cardboard cutout.

Even in this state, Kei found his thoughts kept coming back to Jaime. He'd waited at the bleachers that day for two hours, missing his first class in the afternoon. The sun had been bright, and the wind irregular, coming in gasps, raising sudden walls of dust on the baseball diamond. He kept looking at the letter, which wasn't making him smile any more.

She walked into the Big Boy with the football team's first string, with the autumn night air following. Jaime was hanging on to O'Connor's arm. The Whitefish Gumbos were hooting and snorting loud enough to let everyone know they'd won the game. They crowded into a booth by the window, while O'Connor walked up to the jukebox and flipped a quarter into the slot. A few seconds later, Donna Summer was singing "Bad Girls." Talking about sad girls. Uh-huh. O'Connor gyrated his hips as he walked back to their table like a drunken hula dancer.

Scotty and Darren snickered. Toshi had understood a long time ago that jocks had no edge. They thought they did, but all they had was bulk. Punks like Scotty secretly laughed at all of them. Jaime knew this, too. Toshi wondered why this didn't seem to bother her. She looked like a precious jewel made into a hood ornament. Toshi suddenly found breathing very difficult. Jaime caught him staring at her. She spared him a smile.

Kei looked over at Jaime from his seat at the counter. He tried to look at her like Bruce Lee might, with the same hawklike, passionate sideways gaze. He was as intense as Bruce Lee, as short as Bruce Lee, so incredibly beautiful and remarkably stupid. He strode like a cat over to the booth where they were all sitting. He stood over Jaime as if no one else was in the restaurant. He might even have been imposing if his hair didn't make him look like a Charlie's Angel.

Telly looked like he'd swallowed a bedpan. O'Connor looked up at Kei and grinned. His acne-infested face looked like a smiling pomegranate.

At Toshi's table, Scotty suddenly became animated. "So how about them fucking Packers, huh?" he asked no one in particular, and no one heard. Toshi swallowed. His throat was suddenly very dry.

"Jaime, I have to talk to you," Kei said.

Jaime smiled, but looked as though she might start crying at any time. "Hi, Kei," she said, barely above a whisper. "Listen, maybe this really isn't a good time, okay?"

"Aww, Chinky!" moaned O'Connor. He puckered his chapped lips. "You didn't take that letter from sweet Jaime here seriously now, did you? Are you that fucking stupid, you yellow piece of shit?" He snorted. Coke started dripping from his nose. "Lookit here, you assholes! Chinky thinks he's some fucking wherefore art thou Romeo!"

Kei felt the moment stretching and shrinking like an earthworm. A single thought surfaced in his mind, which was turning brittle. *How did he know about the letter?*

O'Connor rose above the crowd and kept yelling at Kei, spreading his arms with the poise of a messiah. His sermon filled the room. "You are really some fucking brilliant smart-boy."

There were words on the twisted surface of the mirror. Kei tried to remember what they were.

Why is this shit typed? On pink paper? It's fucking weird . . .

"Jaime fucking told me you had a thing for her, so goddamn, didn't my piece-of-shit buddies and my stupid ass decide to have a little fun with a typewriter. You didn't think Jaime would ever write anything like that for a fuck like you, did you?" Donna Summer had stopped singing a while ago, so all anyone could hear was O'Connor shouting above the laughter.

Years later, thinking back to this moment, Kei would wonder why he stood there for so long, listening to the laughter. Sometimes, he seemed to remember sixteen thousand years had passed before he could move again. He never knew how many people had laughed at him.

The entire restaurant? No, Toshi hadn't laughed. Neither had Jaime. "Kei, I'm sorry," she had said, looking . . . what? Remorseful? Fearful? Kei wasn't sure what he'd seen in her dreamy green eyes. "I didn't know. I mean, he didn't tell me until yesterday. I wanted to call you right away, but I had so many things I had to do, and he said . . ." Kei never heard the end of the sentence. Her voice faded behind the noise—the laughter, and some ringing that had grown to an unbearable volume in his skull. And in the end he understood that what he saw in her eyes was confusion. Nothing more.

She'd never understood, though, that the fake letter, or the humiliation in Marc's Big Boy, wasn't important. He had been used to things like that, and he knew as well as anyone else how anyone, even Jaime, can get caught up in a current so strong you're tossed like a feather in a windstorm. He would have thought she knew that.

What she couldn't have known, though, was how he'd gone to look for her when she didn't come meet him at the bleachers. He had found her in her English class with Mr. Epstein. The sky had clouded over, and a light rain was falling, but there was enough light streaming into the hallway through the half-open door. He hesitated from making his presence known, because even Mr. Epstein would not understand why Kei was not in class.

Mr. Epstein was the exact opposite of Miss Herndorff. She was blond and skinny and only wore dresses. He was dark and always wore jeans. She thought Woodstock was the worst thing to ever happen to America. He thought Woodstock was the best thing to ever happen to him. She liked everyone to sit still during class. He asked his students who studied music to bring in their instruments and play. Kei once told Toshi that if Mr. Epstein and Miss Herndorff ever shook hands, it would be like positive and negative matter colliding and the whole universe would disappear.

Shadows flickered inside the door. Kei saw Mr. Epstein leaning against the blackboard as strands of guitar chords shimmered in the air. It was only when he recognized the chords that Kei drew closer. He could see it was Jaime strumming, first C seven, then A minor seven. River water running, running, off to nowhere. She opened her mouth, and the words of a song Kei would never sing again came fluttering out like moths:

"When the sky opens and the rain's on fire, I'll see only your eyes
When angry voices call hope a liar, I'll hear only your whisper."

Between verses, Jaime looked up, toward someone or something that was out of Kei's line of vision. He clenched his fists, hard, and leaned into the room, not caring whether anyone saw him. No one did. Everyone was too enraptured by the love ballad Jaime Saunders was singing so wistfully to O'Connor.

The first song anyone writes is a love song. This had been Kei's first. It was a song full of every tender feeling he ever felt toward another. Jaime went on singing, unaware that he was there, and it was then that Kei realized you can only write your first song once.

Laughter filled the Big Boy restaurant, pushing at its walls. Even the busboys were laughing. Kei suddenly leapt at O'Connor, hands flailing. He felt his fists collapse as they hit the jock's smiling face. O'Connor blinked. Kei hit him again, then again. O'Connor rubbed his cheek, as if he felt an insect strolling among his whiskers.

They were on him in a breath. The Whitefish Gumbos fell onto Kei like he was a fumbled ball. Toshi rushed over to help his brother, but they quickly pinned him down as well. Telly didn't know what to do, so he lit a cigarette. Darren ate another forkful of apple pie. Scotty Taylor was trying to figure out whether to look away or bear witness to yet another memorable moment in the darkness that was their youth.

Kei would never be able to recall later how long he lay there. They showered him with their fists. The storm felt strangely distant. He tried striking back but hit nothing but air. He would never forget, though, the thought that went through his mind as he was beaten to oblivion. Falling into darkness, he thought of his father. Kei shouted loudly in his mind: *Look at me, Pa! I'm fighting back! I'm fighting back! I'm better than you! I'm fighting back!* As the words echoed in his hollow, splintering mind, he never stopped swinging.

Meanwhile, his face pushed into the cold linoleum floor, watching his brother being beaten to a bloody heap of denim and hair, listening to the unconcerned, indifferent hum of the earth underneath the racket, as knees pinned his arms and back, all Toshi could think was: *Fuck you! Fuck you! Fuck you! Fuck you!*

MERV

ONCE UPON A TIME, THERE WAS A TALK-SHOW HOST
on television named Merv Griffin. He came on air just as Toshi and
Kei got home from Whitefish High School. They had been told
that Merv used to interview intellectuals like Bertrand Russell and
Norman Mailer, but ever since he went into syndication he stuck
mostly to voluptuous actresses and models. He asked them psy-
chologically probing questions like, "So, how does it *feel,* to be so
beautiful?" He squinted at his guests, piercing their souls with his
fiery gaze, capturing every nuance of what they said, verbally or
through body language.

The women probably knew it would be futile to try to fool
Merv, because he once used to ask the real hard questions about
things like Vietnam. So they always gave painfully earnest answers:
"Well, I try not to think about it all the time," or "I'm just a regular person like the people in the audience." They tried to sound
humble and always failed miserably.

Every now and then, Toshi liked to imagine he was a guest on
Merv's show. He would sit on one of the plush white seats and look
Merv right in the eyes. "You mean your parents whisked you away

from your native homeland, just like *that?*" Merv would ask Toshi rhetorically, snapping his fingers in the air. He wished to illustrate to the audience the sheer callousness with which Shoji and Mitsuyo had detached their sons from Japan.

"It was similar," Toshi mused aloud, "to white people exiling Indians to reservations." Moisture shimmered in his pensive brown eyes.

"How do you *feel* about that?" Merv added. Toshi pondered the question for a while, looking at the floor. He formed a steeple with his fingers and put the tip to his lips. He averted his eyes from the camera. He sighed, keeping his shoulders deliberately tense and hunched right up until he exhaled. Then he let them drop fully and slumped in his chair.

"And your new so-called friends in America would *abuse* you?" Merv asked, with a passion he hadn't shown since his show was on late-night TV, when Abbie Hoffman once walked on stage wearing a T-shirt that was the American flag.

Toshi felt at this point he could afford to start sobbing.

"How did they abuse you?"

"They'd . . . they'd . . . *moon* me, in broad daylight!"

Toshi fell off his chair, howling in despair. The crowd began to chant, "To-shi, To-shi." Merv shivered, as though the cold November wind was blowing through a gaping hole in his chest.

Suddenly, Toshi was standing in front of a massive roulette table. "Life is a game, Merv," he said, steadying his voice. "You never know where the wheel will stop."

Janet, the *Price Is Right* girl, stood next to a life-time supply of wealth and happiness. They were all Toshi's for the taking if he played it smartly. The audience was hushed. Toshi knew they were rooting for him. He spun the roulette wheel and tossed in a marble, which jiggled and danced like hot oil on a frying pan.

"Will you cut it out, for crying out loud!"

Mitsuyo slapped him across the head, and Toshi's chopsticks went flying. Shoji shook his head. He drew a handkerchief from his pocket and blew his nose, hard. The lazy Susan was spinning wildly in the centre of the table. The porcelain soup bowls rattled impatiently, as if they were ready to fly free from the confines of gravity. Toshi saw that everyone in the restaurant was looking at him. The waitress stood transfixed, mouth open and cavernous, holding on to a large serving bowl full of winter melon soup.

Mr. Lee walked over, smiling easily, gently placing one hand on the lazy Susan to bring it to a stop. He waved at the waitress to bring the soup. He looked at Toshi knowingly. "You hungry, eh?" he said. "Sorry everything take so long. You get bored. Cause trouble. You have some soup now. Be good boy for Mom and Dad. You big now, right?"

"I'm sorry, Mr. Lee," said Mitsuyo, and bowed. Apologizing was something she did very well in English, because of all the embarrassing moments.

Despite Mr. Lee's thick accent, his deep voice and a hardness in his dark eyes commanded attention and obedience. Toshi settled in his seat for the time being. He liked watching the waitress ladle soup anyway. The tiny girl, as cute as a tadpole, never spilled a drop, but she did jump back when Toshi reached for his spoon. Shoji sighed, and dipped into the soup.

Years later, after Shoji died, Toshi often entertained the thought that his father could understand him much better in death than he ever did when he was alive. Shoji would then realize his son wasn't nearly as insane as he thought. Or as anyone thought. Toshi thought perhaps Mitsuyo might have suspected. Perhaps this was why she seemed even more ashamed of Toshi's demented antics than Shoji was.

Toshi often wondered if Mitsuyo blamed herself. Maybe she believed that her son might somehow have better control over his quicksilver thoughts and erratic behaviour had she done something differently. Guilt did not agree with Mitsuyo. It held a mirror in front of her own belligerence, and she found it grating. This made her even more antagonistic. And since there had been plenty of guilt in raising her sons, and in dealing with Shima during his visit, the effect was like a snowball from hell. Toshi found talking to her to be like raking his hand across broken glass, particularly after Shima had gone back to Japan.

Toshi suspected there were differences in the ways Kei and he were raised, causing his younger brother to be whipper-snapper smart and himself a hopeless lunatic. Yet, all of Kei's intelligence couldn't do much for him in the end, could it?

Listening to people was especially difficult for Toshi. When a teacher said something even remotely interesting, his mind scattered like roaches in light. The sky outside the window, the clouds, his desk, the floor, the HB pencil, all offered their own opinions on the matter. Ideas tossed and turned, shifting in shape. He would be too preoccupied to hear whatever was said afterwards. This was why his teachers and parents and even his brother were always yelling at him for not listening "harder," as if one could quantify the act of listening.

In fact, Toshi was trying to listen harder than anyone else. When someone spoke to him, he gritted his teeth. He furrowed his brows until his scalp hurt. *It's just that life around him was too fucking loud.* He liked to think his father understood all of this, after he died and went to a better place.

For now, Shoji was very much alive, and he was concerned about Kei. Kei had just disturbed the general cosmic balance surrounding the state of Wisconsin by announcing he was moving to Canada. *To Canada!* Where people ate baby seals raw, and you couldn't piss outside in winter without it freezing before it hit the ground.

Shoji had taken his family out for dinner at the Pink Phoenix to talk about this. They ate out often. Shoji always said, "Well, no matter how much life lets you down, at least there's food and drink to live for," as though the sublime joy of watching his children grow did not do anything for him any more.

The Hayakawas ate out so frequently that they received Christmas cards from restaurants around town. They ate almost anything, and the Chinese cooked most anything, which made the Pink Phoenix their favourite restaurant. Toshi and Kei were disgusted only once, when Mr. Lee offered their father fresh snake blood mixed with a shot of mao-tai, and Shoji accepted.

Mr. Lee was Shoji's age. He was from Hong Kong, the Pearl of the Orient. Kei told Toshi that Mr. Lee probably came to America to get away from the Japanese occupation, but neither Mr. Lee nor Shoji made any mention of the war in each other's presence. They were always very cordial to one another. Shoji ordered the most expensive items on the menu, and Mr. Lee always helped him with his chair on account of his bad leg.

"Don't let him fucking fool you," Kei once whispered to his brother. "Mr. Lee hates our fucking guts. I'll bet he's going to lace our goddamn Peking duck with fucking cyanide or some other shit one day. Could hardly blame him, either. Pay careful attention to the fucking dessert. Maybe someone will try to warn us by sneaking a fucking message in our fucking fortune cookies." This always made Toshi leap at the waitress whenever she brought the cookies with the bill.

Their grandmother usually came along too, even though Hanako considered it insane to pay someone to cook for her. She always pondered the prices on the menu for a while. She could read nothing but the prices. After a few minutes, she'd say, every time, "How much is this in yen?" which infuriated Shoji. He asked Hanako, in a very loud voice, why this information would matter. Mitsuyo then always told her mother to shut up. That was usually the end of it, except for some inaudible mumbling all around.

Toshi often wondered if this was why Hanako kept asking the same questions repeatedly—because no one ever answered her. She had been brought to Milwaukee to be properly taken care of. But shortly after she moved in with them, it became apparent that she could not do anything right, at least from Mitsuyo's point of view. Mitsuyo screamed at her mother for most of the day, every day. If Hanako did anything but breathe, it was as though Hiroshima and Nagasaki were blowing up all over again.

When Hanako kept the bathroom door closed when it wasn't being used—which was common practice in Japan—Mitsuyo yelled at her for making it unclear whether the toilet was occupied or not. If Hanako made her own lunch, Mitsuyo complained that she left the kitchen unbearably disorganized. If Hanako waited for Mitsuyo to cook for her, she was scolded for being lazy.

Mitsuyo's sister might have tossed their mother in front of the noodle delivery boy's bicycle, but Hanako seemed no happier in Milwaukee. Only Toshi considered this bizarre. He could not understand why his mother abused his grandmother. Perhaps insanity ran in the genes. Maybe he was normal, and she was crazy. Maybe it was all a wonderfully weird dream.

One morning, he overheard his parents arguing in their bedroom. "Just tell her to stay away from my things!" Shoji screamed. He was wearing only his underwear. He apparently had found his briefs in the drawer intended for pressed shirts. "Just have her keep out of my closet! Is that too much to ask?" He sounded as if he was asking that dead rats be kept out of his clothes.

"Why don't you tell her, for shit's sake?" Mitsuyo said. "You're not scared of her, are you?"

Perhaps his father *was* afraid of Hanako, thought Toshi. Afraid of his own shadow. She embodied all his fears of growing old, of his own mortality. She was a symbol of all his existential hang-ups. Until she came along, he was in cheerful denial of how, one day, he might be hunched over just like she was now—pathetic, smelly, unable to control his bladder or his bowels. Waiting to fall into that vast, empty nothingness without any warning or explanation.

When Shoji sat by himself in his den, turned out the lights and listened to *The Sea* by Debussy, he would see only a dark void above the waves. To see anything else would make his nose run and stomach ache. But the darkness also scared him. So he screamed at Mitsuyo with false bravado that fooled everyone but himself.

Mitsuyo, for her part, did not know why she yelled at her mother, either. She never considered whether she might feel guilty about burdening her husband with taking care of Hanako. She just felt compelled to make sure Hanako did nothing to displease her husband, even as she made him feel awkward when he complained about her.

Mitsuyo also noticed her mother never once asked why her sons were the way they were—Toshi's insanity, Kei's brooding—but she didn't stop to think whether this, too, might have something to do with her compulsion to scream at her. She felt the guilt, but never noticed it. She just tried to keep her frail mother in line with a heavy, iron fist that came down hard on Hanako's head of wispy grey hair. It was like cracking open a lychee fruit with a jackhammer.

Kei wore his hair short now, and spiked. (Telly had come over a week ago, and they cut each other's hair in the bathroom, plugging the sink, the tub and the toilet.) Kei kept staring at the Pink Phoenix's menu as though it was the sole reason why he was so miserable. Everything, in fact, made him miserable now. Life's small pleasures—like listening to music stoned—no longer allowed him to forget the cold, dark pit in his belly.

Shoji said, "So, how about sea cucumber tonight, then?" with nauseating gaiety. Kei and Toshi grunted in unison.

Mr. Lee, in his usual, impeccably efficient manner, disappeared with their order. Shoji then dropped the facade. Unlike Kei, Shoji was not the kind of person who was beautiful when angry.

Passion did not agree with him. His eyes bulged, then squinted, then bulged again. Some of his hair stood on end. "You can't hope for a long-term career in entertainment," he hissed at Kei. "And right now you've nothing to fall back on." He blew his nose again. "Why are you being so unreasonable?"

"It'll never last," Mitsuyo added. "I guarantee you he won't be able to take the pressure. He quit his goddamn piano lessons, didn't he? Dropped it like a hot bag of baked yams the moment things got too tough."

Mitsuyo respected Miss B., but wasn't sure if she took Kei's talents seriously enough. Miss B. seemed far too soft on her students, even the exceptionally talented ones like Kei, so Mitsuyo made certain she supervised his practising at home, employing the "what-doesn't-kill-you-makes-you-stronger" school of music. She had read Beethoven's biography. She was impressed by how Ludwig's father gave him a fierce rap over the knuckles with a rod whenever he made a mistake during practice. Miss B. was convinced Kei studied kung fu or karate or some other mysterious Asian martial art because of all the bruises on his hands.

The Bechstein upright was in the living room, next to the pot-ted rubber tree that had died years ago. On it was a plastic bust of Ultraman. In the afternoons, sunlight poured through the finger-prints on the picture windows and cast a shadow of whoever was playing onto the far wall. Usually there was also a silhouette of Mitsuyo, holding a large stick.

Kei's feet barely reached the floor when he sat on the stool. He often played by himself, when no one was home. When he was given assignments that pleased him, like a Chopin nocturne, he could barely resist mastering the piece as soon as he could, which was usually not long. He naturally understood the dynamics, the changes in tempo, the emotions that must have moved the com-poser's pen. Still, he always tried not to play when Mitsuyo was home and had time on her hands. Most days, though, there was no getting away from her.

She tapped her shoulder with the yardstick she was holding. Her chest swelled with the thought of how much Kei was going to appreciate all this when he was invited to play at Carnegie Hall. Her nostrils flared into wind tunnels as her smile stretched to its limit.

"When are you going to sign me up for piano lessons again?" Toshi asked from the kitchen.

"Just take out the garbage like I told you to!" Mitsuyo called back. The interruption irritated her. One son had failed. She was determined the other would live up to her expectations.

"You said you'd sign me up again when I got older!" yelled Toshi. "Well, I'm getting older every day, as you can see."

"Take out that garbage, or I'll make you eat it!" Mitsuyo replied. There was no more noise from the kitchen.

Kei sighed and rubbed his small hands. The welts were still fresh. Playing had been so pleasant the day before when Mitsuyo was away. Now, the notes he'd played smoothly and without trouble time and again bunched and stumbled under his fingertips. He started hesitatingly with the left hand's arpeggios. When he tried to layer melody over them with the right hand, the keys betrayed him.

"Again," said Mitsuyo.

Closing his eyelids to hear the melody more clearly—or to hold back tears, he didn't know—Kei placed his hands on the keys again. Magic wove sound into the air. A slight twist of the finger turned music into noise.

"Again!"

Now the tears were freely flowing down his cheeks. The white and black keys blurred into a mess of ivory and ink spots. His hands didn't know any more which way to go. Lost in space, they collapsed. There was a flash, the sound of flat wood on skin, and Kei pulled his hand back from the piano as if it was on fire.

"Now, try again," said Mitsuyo, raising the yardstick back up to her shoulder. "Concentrate."

Hanako was sitting on a couch in the corner, nodding. "Practise, practise, practise," she said. "You have to keep on practising."

Mitsuyo was shocked when Kei announced he was quitting piano. *Why?* she asked herself, which was precisely the question she should have asked. In looking for an answer, though, she turned her gaze outward and not within. A couple of years later, when Kei took up the guitar, Mitsuyo was convinced this would never last either. Now, she was convinced all of Kei's musical pursuits were motivated purely by spite.

"I can't live like you, Dad," said Kei.

Shoji scowled, and put down his spoon. "You mean sensibly."

"I mean dying all the time."

Shoji snorted. They ate the soup in silence. The empty bowls were cleared away quickly and with little decorum. Mitsuyo told Kei to stop looking at the waitress's butt. He sneered. He said he always found Chinese women had nice round butts. Mitsuyo called him a pig. They always said these kinds of things in Japanese, so no one around them understood. There were times, though, when they complained about the food, that Toshi noticed Mr. Lee looking at them with obvious, grave concern. But Mr. Lee never said anything. He always smiled when he knew they were looking at him.

"You can at least finish your education," Shoji said between sips of oolong tea, which wasn't settling his stomach at all.

Kei lit a cigarette. "I'm finishing high school, Dad."

"High school! Are you *mad*? What kind of secure job is that going to get you?"

"And what kind of Japanese woman is going to marry a high-school graduate?" Mitsuyo asked. Hanako nodded.

"I might not marry a Japanese woman," Kei said. Mitsuyo choked on her tea. "Besides," he added, offering Toshi a smoke, which he declined. Toshi hated smoking during a meal. Shoji and

Mitsuyo looked at each other. "I'm sure a lot of high-school graduates in Japan manage to get married."

"Not to anyone from a respectable family," Mitsuyo said. She didn't seem too worried about whom her other son was going to marry. Toshi often noticed that no one ever discussed this—at least not in his presence.

"I might not marry at all, Ma," said Kei.

"At least get a college degree," said Shoji. "Then you'll have more options if the sound of small animals being mutilated that you call music doesn't provide enough for food and shelter."

"I'm not waiting four years to do this, Dad."

"Are you *mad?*" Shoji slammed his fist on the table. Tea cups jumped. Waitresses flinched.

Mr. Lee brought the main dishes. Shoji complained in Japanese that the abalone slices looked smaller and thinner. When Mr. Lee asked if everything was okay, though, Shoji smiled and said, "Oh, yes! *Nyet-nyet-nyet.*" Toshi thought the best food in the world couldn't impress if there were too many angry people around the table. Relativity once again. Hanako said nothing once the food arrived. She stared straight ahead with tiny eyes hiding behind folds of skin, and chewed slowly, as if this small act required all her feeble concentration. At least she wasn't being yelled at. Life wasn't without its small favours.

Two weeks later, Kei left for Canada.

At around the same time, Toshi started working for Allied Partners in Moving Limited. Scotty Taylor had introduced him to the company president, a stolid man named Horace who was as round as a weather balloon. Horace was always half-shaven and had one glass eye. The glass eye always looked straight ahead, while his real eye wandered all over the place. Toshi could feel the glass eye's cold stare piercing the very depths of his soul, sort of like Merv Griffin's gaze. It seemed to know all about the wretched sores that festered there.

But when he was being interviewed for the job, Toshi realized Horace couldn't see anything clearly. His one good eye did not stay still long enough to focus on anything. Toshi sympathized, a little. He himself had trouble focusing on most things through the day. Then Horace said, "I had a Chink working for me once." His good eye drifted away into a distant, delicious memory. "Damned good worker."

It was always "Chink," rather than "Jap" or "Nip," even when some reference to Pearl Harbor followed. Perhaps this was because there were more Chinese in Milwaukee than Japanese. There were more Chinese in most places, except maybe Japan. The Chinese were more visible. Since there were more frequent occasions for disdain, the word rolled off people's tongues easier. And no one cared, since they all looked the same anyway.

Toshi knew he owed his job to Scotty Taylor and this Chinese fellow who'd worked for Horace before and impressed him so much he assumed all Orientals were equally upright. Whoever this anonymous Chinese was, whatever he may be doing now, Toshi was grateful. He even thought about rising at sunrise and saying a prayer for this person but never did.

Toshi was placed in a team with Scotty and Horace Junior, who hadn't yet developed quite his father's girth. But otherwise, Horace Junior looked just like Senior. Junior always kept one Baby Ruth bar in his back pocket, which he ate and replaced several times a day.

They moved families around Milwaukee, with an occasional trip out of town. Toshi rarely went on long excursions because he never learned how to drive. He was the only one in the company who was good for hauling and nothing else. He was also paid considerably less.

On Toshi's first day out, moving a German family to the west side of the city, he was overcome with an irresistible urge to shower while on the job. It was an exceptionally muggy day in mid-July. He had just carried the dresser into the master bedroom of the new house when he found some open crates in the bathroom containing clean towels. In the same way that foods often communicated spiritually with him that they *wanted* to be eaten, the soft, neatly folded towels told Toshi they wanted—no, *needed*—to be used.

He gingerly unlaced his boots. The smell of sweat pinched his nose as he removed his shirt and jeans. Naked, he opened a few more crates until he found some soap. It was pink, and smelled of strawberries—perfect for the summer. He turned on the shower and stepped into the bathtub, careful not to slip. He lathered the soap on his round belly, kneading it like dough. The shower curtains were not up yet, and water flew everywhere. He started singing softly to himself, thinking work wasn't so bad after all.

The family consisted of the mother, the father and their three girls. The mother, whose arms and legs looked like jelly rolls, said she'd mix a pitcher of lemonade, and asked Scotty if his partners would like some as well.

Scotty went looking for Toshi and found him drying himself off. Toshi was just about to look for some toothpaste and a toothbrush. Scotty shoved him into his clothes and mopped up the floor with the used towels before stuffing them back in the boxes. Then they went downstairs for some lemonade, trying their best not to laugh. Horace Junior was perplexed by their childish giggles.

When Toshi moved families who were from the neighbourhood, his grandmother casually made comments like, "Hope you were careful with the Meissen figurine the wife got for Christmas," or, "Don't take responsibility for the crack in the crystal table lamp. That's been there since Halloween." No one ever paid attention to Hanako, so they didn't realize she'd been peering into neighbours' windows for years, on her seemingly endless walks.

Concealed by the bushes, she'd watched Old Man Garber swing his cane at the aging, arthritic tabby named Mongoose.

Hanako pushed her dentures partway out of her mouth with her tongue and sucked on them, while the old man fell into his recliner, exhausted, and drank cheap red wine from a spotted wine glass until he fell asleep. When Scotty Taylor came to sleep over at the Hayakawas, Hanako went to his house and stood in the darkness among the lilies on their flowerbed, unmoving, watching Mr. Taylor take Mrs. Taylor on the dining-room table. Mrs. Taylor made squeaking sounds of pleasure Hanako had forgotten a long time ago. Hanako went on her walks every day, rain or shine.

After Shoji died, Toshi found his compulsion to turn knobs and dials starting to wane. Because of his work, he was always surrounded by appliances. When he started, Scotty and Horace had to make certain he worked mainly in rooms where everything was already packed. Toshi managed nonetheless to sneak an occasional encounter with stereo equipment, dishwashers, ovens—anything that had knobs to turn. After they moved one retired couple to the north side, the husband plugged in his stereo. The volume blew out the entire living-room picture window.

But a few weeks after Shoji's funeral, Toshi was moving some crates from a neighbour's garage when he came across a snow blower decorated with a bumper sticker that read "Up, Up, Up Yours And Away!" He turned on the switch. Nothing happened. It wasn't plugged in. It lay there as if it were dead, like Shoji. He drew his hand back quickly, as if he'd just touched decaying meat.

The epiphany, if it could be called that, was slow and drawn out. Months later, there were times when he still felt, and could not resist, the urge to turn knobs and throw switches. Other times, though, he felt nothing at all. Gradually, days characterized by the latter began to outnumber those dominated by the former. But the beast was only caged, not dead. Occasionally, Toshi still felt it pacing in his chest. When he saw the fire alarm in an art gallery, for example, the beast was very hard to contain.

By the time Head began touring around Ontario and the northeastern United States, Merv Griffin was off the air. Still, Toshi enjoyed his fantasies. "No, it's not true that Kei slept with three black men on a recent trip to Buffalo," he would tell Merv. "It was two black men and a Hispanic. And no, my mother is not devastated. She is much too enraptured with her lesbian horse trainer to care. That's a trainer of lesbian horses, rather than a lesbian trainer of horses, you understand."

MOVING

"TOSHI!"

The empty hallways swallowed her voice. Mitsuyo realized there was no one home. She was left alone a lot now, and she had even more unfilled hours in which to miss Shoji. On good days she remembered the times she or one of the boys had made him smile. On bad days, she remembered the expression on his face on the day she'd hurt him the most. Today was not a good day. On days like this, she could not bear to look at the bed they shared. She couldn't even stand to be in the bedroom.

She needed someone to drive her to Kohl's for some bread-crumbs. *Tonkatsu*, a Japanese-style breaded pork cutlet, was one of Toshi's favourites, so it irritated her even more that he was not here. Probably out drinking with his buddies again after a move. She peered into his room, made a face at the mess, then closed the door.

The first step down on the staircase hadn't moved. It was where it had always been, and she'd climbed up and down the same stairs countless times in all the years they lived in Milwaukee. Yet somehow she missed it. There was a bubble of a moment when everything seemed to be still and quiet—except her thoughts, which mainly consisted of "Oh, shit." Then the stairs rushed up to meet her face.

Toshi found her two hours later, when he came home. She'd broken her ankle and dislocated her shoulder, but miraculously, her hips were intact. This was around the same time that a left-wing entertainment tabloid in Toronto ran an article on Head, a lengthy piece about how the emerging band's lead singer was running a prostitution ring in the Amazon. The piece was based on the magazine's interview with his family, who lived in Milwaukee—the mother and his brother. The brother also had translated for the mother, who didn't speak English.

All things considered, Kei decided he wanted Toshi and Mitsuyo close by, where he could keep them out of trouble. He told rather than asked them to move into the rowhouse he'd bought on Toronto's south side, near the lake. Mitsuyo grumbled about having to pack and sell the house when she was on crutches. She hired people to take care of everything except the grumbling.

Moving from Milwaukee was difficult for Toshi. He never had any friends in Japan, but things were different in America. There were Scotty and a few others from Whitefish High School. He'd even grown close to Horace Senior and Junior. And now he was leaving them all for Canada. He thought about Toronto, Mr. Man and Angie, which cheered him up a little but not completely.

Since it was easiest, Mitsuyo hired Allied Partners in Moving and asked for the deluxe package. This meant linens were wrapped in plastic before they were crated. Toshi had quit his job by this time, and insurance rules said he couldn't help his friends move his own things. He did anyway, angering Mitsuyo, who muttered all day in Japanese.

When the house was emptied of furniture and boxes, Mitsuyo hobbled from room to room, pleased with how skilled she was becoming with her crutches. She wanted to make sure nothing was forgotten, or would be forgotten when she looked back. A cold draft came from nowhere. It blew right through her as she stood among piles of nothing. In the living room, she gazed at the walls that Shoji had painted just before he died. He hardly ever did anything handy around the house, but he had tried painting just that once. It didn't seem so long ago, but the walls were already covered in handprints and scuff marks.

In Kei's old room, she used one crutch to touch the floorboards by the radiator. She wondered whether cigarettes and the letter from Jaime were still concealed there, with all the letters he'd written to Jamie in Paris but never sent. And the sheet music and lyrics. They all seemed to be about Jaime. Mitsuyo still did not know who Jaime was and had resigned herself long ago to the likelihood that she never would. She shut her eyes for a while. Struggling to keep her balance, she leaned down and opened the space, but it, too, was now empty.

In Toshi's room, she placed her hand on the windowsill he'd once decorated with the colour transfers of superheroes that came in cereal boxes. She'd washed most of it off, but if she looked very carefully she could still recognize the tiny speckles that remained like pieces of a dream. A few flies lay dead on the windowsill like raisins.

When she went through the room that had been Hanako's, Mitsuyo didn't remember the rec room they'd installed after her mother died. She didn't remember the karaoke set they'd bought three weeks after the funeral. She didn't recall the big-screen television set, nor the Japanese chess and *go* set that her sister, Tatsue, had sent from Japan one Christmas. Instead, she saw the room as it would have appeared to Hanako when she was alive, sparse, with only a small bookshelf, a dresser and bed.

And Mitsuyo saw the impish woman sitting by the window, no matter the weather, staring at the emptiness of the back alley. As she pictured Hanako's face, looking out at her life in America, Mitsuyo tried hard to find even a trace of happiness in her mother's expression.

The beach where Capitol Drive met Lake Michigan became a favourite place to walk in the short time Shoji and Mitsuyo had with each other after Hanako died. The funeral had been modest. Hanako had no friends other than Old Man Garber, who came and sat alone in the back pew, occasionally wiping away a tear. Shoulders painfully hunched, he spent most of his time looking at his feet. The casket was closed, as Hanako's burnt remains were barely recognizable. Tatsue came from Japan to take her mother back for burial in the same cemetery as her husband, Taro, in a Tokyo that had changed so much since she fell in front of the noodle delivery boy.

Shoji and Mitsuyo started taking walks on this beach a few days after the funeral, usually at dusk. Shoji often complained that his limp was starting to affect his good leg. The knee was starting to hurt on days before a rain. He laughed and complained at how terrible it was to grow old. He still did not know he never would.

The air was often cold, but this refreshed their muddled brains. When they spoke, they talked of everything inconsequential that had occurred that day. They usually held hands, and neither admitted to spending most of the silence thinking back to those days in London, walking on the banks of the Thames. They had not talked to each other like that for a long, long time. And once, while looking at the darkening sky above, watching the moon rising over the water, Shoji told Mitsuyo that when he died, one day, he wished not to be taken back to Japan.

In the empty house, Mitsuyo spent the longest time in the bedroom she and Shoji had shared. The windows were open, and the branches outside moved lazily, while a million leaves whispered and sighed like the ocean. Their window looked down onto the street, where she could see Toshi and the others playing with the funnelator they'd found in the attic.

The funnelator was one of Toshi's favourite toys. When he was in the sixth grade, one of Shoji's graduate students had shown Toshi how he could make a giant slingshot by poking two holes across from each other on the sides of a plastic funnel and threading rubber surgical tubing through them, looped at the ends. Two of his friends would grab the loops and stand apart. Toshi would stand in between, pulling the funnel back, stretching the surgical tubings to their limit, with a water balloon chambered inside the funnel. When Toshi let go, the balloon catapulted about half a block.

Toshi found the funnelator with a bag of balloons when he was packing. On the day of the move, he and his friends weren't aiming for anything in particular, although they came precariously close to shooting a woman off her bicycle. She swore at them, then pedalled away as fast as she could. Mitsuyo watched without expression as Toshi whooped and hollered and another water balloon shot into the trees. Then she turned away. After they ran out of balloons, Toshi came upstairs and saw that his mother was quietly crying, perched on her crutches in the sunbeams spilling through the dusty window. He stood in one spot, not knowing what to say yet not wanting to leave her alone. He lit a cigarette. She glanced at him and scowled.

"Is Angie meeting us at the airport in Toronto?" he asked, blowing a stream of blue smoke through his nostrils. Mitsuyo simply grunted, but he'd made her stop crying.

They went outside, stepping through their front door for the last time. Scotty and Horace presented Toshi with a bottle of bourbon and a copy of *Playboy*. Mitsuyo laughed and poked them in the ribs and thanked them while Toshi scratched his head. She rolled her eyes to the sky when they weren't looking. They said their goodbyes, slapped each other on the shoulder and helped Mitsuyo into the taxi that was taking them to Mitchell Airport. Scotty and Horace assured her they would take good care of their things. The truck was scheduled to arrive in Toronto three days after Mitsuyo and Toshi.

In the cab, Toshi had to try hard not to peek at his magazine. The ride wasn't a short one, gliding through the verdant streetscapes out onto the desolate concrete of the freeway watching the fare rise on the meter. Toshi asked his mother why she'd never learned to drive.

"You remember that godforsaken ugly Rottweiler in the neighbourhood you and Kei used to play with when you were little?" she asked.

"We never played with it, Ma. We hated that dog."

"Really? I used to look out the window and see it chasing you two around the front yard. You sure looked like you were having fun."

"We weren't having fun. We were running for our lives."

"Remember how it disappeared just around the time your father was trying to teach me how to drive?"

He looked at her. She looked like she wanted to smile but didn't have the strength. Instead, she turned and looked out the window. "Besides, why did I need to drive? I had your father and Kei to depend on."

Toshi waited for her to say more, but the scenery was apparently fascinating that day. He thought maybe Mitsuyo was just saying goodbye to the city.

A little later, he noticed her looking into her purse like the secrets of the world were hidden there. She bit her lip.

"What are you looking at, Ma?" he asked, and she drew out a worn bankbook. It took a moment for the question to blossom in his brain, and another for him to get up the nerve to ask. "So what are going to do with the money you made off our house?"

She placed the bankbook back in her purse and snapped it shut, as if that solved everything. Closing her eyes, she tried not to think of how the only family she had left were a sister in Japan, a son who was crazy and another who seemed to despise her with all his heart. She tried not to think of why. Most of all, she tried not to think of how Hanako first came to live with them because she, too, had fallen.

Instead of looking at his magazine, Toshi looked out the window, wondering if, from the plane, he'd see his father sitting on a cloud with wings on his shoulders.

"That's sad," said Angie. "Isn't it?" They were walking past the French Impressionists in the Art Gallery of Ontario. Toshi wondered why it felt cold in museums and galleries. As cold as Shoji's skin felt after he died in the hospital. Their footfalls echoed off the high ceilings. "It must have been hard on you."

"Not really," Toshi replied. "I was used to moving."

"Do you think you'll be going back someday?"

The question surprised Toshi. He'd never considered it before. The thought of going back to Milwaukee struck him as odd. Sort of like opening a trunk full of old clothes that didn't fit you any more. He thought about Scotty Taylor. About Darren and Horace Junior. Even Jaime. He imagined a long hallway somewhere in the gallery where their portraits hung. At the end of the hallway was a doorway back to Milwaukee. Toshi opened it, and saw that there was nothing behind it but a dark emptiness filled with incredible sorrow.

Toshi gasped. Old men with stoic faces stared at him over their bifocals. Women with fur around their necks whispered. Angie took Toshi by the hand, concerned. He leaned his huge round shoulders against a pillar, breathing hard. She rubbed his back.

"Are you okay?"

He nodded.

"What happened?"

He shook his head, as if to clear it.

Angie had first brought Toshi to the gallery after she noticed how much the covers of *The New Yorker* fascinated him. As she expected, his reaction to the works in the gallery was infinitely stronger. This pleased her.

In Guido Reni's depiction of Christ, His eyes silently pleaded to Heaven beneath a crown of thorns. So vulnerable for the Son of God. His eyes told the story of countless sorrows scattered across all time and space. The painting made Toshi giggle. "He's just pulling our leg," he explained, pointing with his chin. "He's just thinking how surprised everybody's going to be when He rises from the dead in a couple of days. Inside, He's laughing like a naughty girl."

A Dutch still life of fruit and cheese nearly brought Toshi to tears. "The fruit didn't have a chance! *It didn't have a chance!*" His legs collapsed, and he fell to his knees in front of the massive wall of conflicting images, like the wall of mirrors he'd seen so many times in his dream. Standing behind him, Angie thought it peculiar that his anguish, his broad hunched shoulders, his blistered hands hanging limp at his sides, seemed in their own way very beautiful. This kind of beauty appealed to her, but she couldn't say why.

Soon, they were in front of the permanent exhibit of Henry Moore sculptures. Curved forms on concrete. The room was full of white light, making the shapes appear cold. Toshi's breathing became shallow. Angie noticed his fists were clenched, but she waited. He was going to say something soon, and she didn't want to rush him. When he opened his mouth, an anguished cry came out dry, like dust on ivory. Slowly his hand took hers. He brought it to his mouth gently and kissed it.

Her perfume brushed past his face. She considered his offer for a brief moment. She remembered her parents. She thought of Kei, and the ways in which he in turn comforted and tormented her. She even remembered the kindness of Alex, whom she hadn't called since that night at the Twisted Neon. Then she shook her head. Careful not to move too quickly, she retracted her hand from his. He steadied himself and began walking toward the Matisse exhibit. She followed quietly. They both pretended nothing was out of the ordinary. And Toshi supposed it wasn't.

The third floor of the Victorian rowhouse was formerly an attic but had been renovated into an extra bedroom. Left alone in the empty house, Mitsuyo walked up the two flights of stairs to the top floor and back down again several times a day once her ankle had healed. There were two more bedrooms on the second floor. Kei and Angie shared the master bedroom, Mitsuyo and Toshi took the other, while Telly and Mr. Man slept on the third floor. None of them ever thanked Mitsuyo for allowing them to use the furniture she'd brought from Milwaukee. She did not think Kei even told anyone the furniture was hers.

Kei and Telly in fact could barely afford the house. They had found the place shortly after Head released its first CD, with an independent label, which had done reasonably well in Toronto but had received only a minuscule bit of attention in the States. This was also soon after Millie's discovery that she was a lesbian. She and Rosanne, a square-jawed songwriter who often jammed with Kei and Telly, had just bought a house in the suburbs. This was also when Angie found she could never keep enough beer in the refrigerator for Telly, who drank himself to sleep while Mr. Man mumbled in the dark on the bed across from him.

On nights when Telly became especially drunk and abrasive, Mr. Man came down to the bedroom where Mitsuyo and Toshi slept. He stood at the doorway for a while, muttering under his breath, and if they ignored him, he walked in and stood at the foot of Mitsuyo's bed. She could hear Telly shouting and crying upstairs. Mr. Man stood perfectly still, except for his mouth, which was constantly moving. She inevitably got up, shook Toshi awake and told him to go quiet Telly. As soon as Toshi left the room, Mr. Man crawled into Toshi's bed and fell asleep.

Toshi thought nothing of accommodating Mr. Man, but Mitsuyo felt one crazy person in the house was enough. She asked Kei to get rid of Mr. Man.

He refused. "I don't have much family left any more," he said.

Mitsuyo complained endlessly to Kei about how her ankle still ached. She did the same to Angie when Kei was away, except that with Angie she also complained about her back. She hated herself for it. She remembered how Hanako talked constantly about her aches and ills when she moved to Milwaukee. Mitsuyo recalled how she'd reacted to her mother's muttering. Still, she still could not contain herself.

She also griped about the mess, of which there was very little, as well as the ancient ventilation system—it was either too stuffy or too drafty. The complaints spilled from her mouth like jagged glass. Angie took it all passively, like some ascetic saint. This infuriated Mitsuyo.

She'd met Angie's parents shortly after she and Toshi moved in. Mitsuyo thought them odd. Angie's father was a large man, and gruff. He looked as if he could not wait to leave and return to the familiarity of their home in the suburbs. Her mother was frail, like Angie. She rarely ventured to say anything, and when she did, she always glanced at her husband, who was usually ignoring her anyway. Mitsuyo never understood a word either of them said to her, but she knew oddity when she saw it. She was, after all, Toshi's mother.

Aside from an occasional streetcar ride to a sushi restaurant or the Japanese grocer on Queen Street, Mitsuyo spent most of her time at home. She was always very friendly with the neighbours. She always said hello to everyone, though she couldn't communicate anything further. The loneliness and fatigue never left her. They seemed to intensify after moving to Canada. Still, she kept smiling and waving to the mailman and the garbage collectors.

She was also surprisingly kind to Mr. Man, though she never stopped asking Kei to throw him out of the house. She even cooked Mr. Man the odd meal. She was equally cordial to Millie and Rosie when they would visit. They sat around the kitchen, Mitsuyo never understanding what Millie and Rosie would be laughing about, but smiling politely anyway. She was at first shocked when they kissed in front of her, but a part of her was also delighted by their unconventional love affair.

The television was usually on in the living room. The daytime soap operas were punctuated with five-minute newscasts, usually showing American military operations during Desert Storm. Millie's cousin was a pilot with the Canadian air force. He had been on exchange with the American forces at a base in Florida when the war broke out and was now flying with the Americans in the Persian Gulf. Millie explained all this with a face stretched to its limits by the tension between pride and concern.

Not comprehending a word, Mitsuyo nodded politely as Rosie smoked and swore about imperialistic American interests in oil. Mitsuyo understood Millie's concerned face for the first time when she produced a photograph from her wallet of a young man in military uniform and pointed to the television screen bursting with gunfire and explosions. Taking the photograph in her hand, Mitsuyo touched Millie's bony shoulder. It had been decades since Mitsuyo met someone who had a loved one actually away, fighting someone else's fight. It was always someone else's fight.

She cursed the TV and the orderly way in which it presented war. She knew it wasn't as neat and tidy as it looked. It wasn't as far away as it seemed to them in Toronto, either. Mitsuyo knew better, and now so did Millie's cousin. Mitsuyo recognized the familiar fatigue in Millie's face.

So Mitsuyo allowed herself to be a bother only to her sons, and to Angie. When complaining about anything to Angie, Mitsuyo spoke through Toshi. He took lines in Japanese like "We could give the soy milk soufflé to the neighbourhood cats but I don't want them to get sick" and changed them to "We have to be careful or your fabulous soufflé will drive the cats insane with pleasure." Angie usually just smiled at him, sadly.

Toshi and Angie never fooled Mitsuyo either. When they started going to the art galleries together, Mitsuyo noticed immediately. When they came home later in the day, she noticed this, too. Even when there was nothing out of the ordinary, she noticed. She knew when the most ordinary of things were deceiving.

She recalled how when Shima came to visit them in Milwaukee, he would drive her to the supermarket on days when Shoji was too busy in his den, scribbling his lambdas and sigmas onto scrap paper. Shima was a theoretical physicist also, but did not seem nearly as intent on spending his entire day at his desk or in front of a blackboard. He came over often, to help Kei with his science homework, or to shovel snow off the driveway if Toshi had not got around to it. He sometimes even went out for walks with Hanako.

But most often, he drove Mitsuyo to the store. There was a Kohl's down on Oakland Avenue that looked like a futuristic dome full of food. When Mitsuyo first walked into an American supermarket, she couldn't believe she did not have to walk to five different stores to get the day's meals. And the size of the American refrigerators meant she could even shop for the whole week at once. The only drawback was that she needed to ask Shoji to drive. Since his trip back to Japan to attend his mother's funeral, Mitsuyo never liked to ask Shoji for anything. When Shima offered to take Mitsuyo the first time, shortly after coming to Milwaukee, it was so that she could advise him what to buy. But he kept driving her, week after week.

Against the backdrop of mountains of food stood Shima's thin frame, close to disappearing among the cracks between cereal boxes. It was Christmas time. Mitsuyo remembered it well, because the first time their hands touched was when she tried to pick up a Butterball turkey. The frozen bird slipped and began to fall to the floor. She reached for it as the same time as Shima, and his head crashed into hers. The turkey hit the floor with a thud. Mitsuyo fell backward. *"Kuso,"* she said, sitting up, rubbing her head.

She saw Shima crouched on the floor, still fumbling with the Butterball. Mitsuyo quickly covered her mouth, looking into his face to see if he'd heard. He seemed too distracted. Still, she said quickly, "I mean, er, *uso.*" *Uso* meant lie or untruth and was often uttered when one was incredulous, as if it was incredible to Mitsuyo that she had fallen over and not Shima, whom she obviously outweighed.

Shima finally got hold of the turkey and threw it angrily into the cart. Then he noticed for the first time that Mitsuyo was on the floor. "Well!" he said. "That was something! Yes, sir. I never thought a dead bird could be so elusive." He tried to smile but looked like he might start crying.

Something stopped, though, when he took hold of her arm to help her to her feet. Their eyes met, about three feet above the floor. A moment later, he realized he wasn't strong enough to hold her weight, and he fell on top of her.

"*Kuso!*" she spat, not caring any more.

Shadows fell on Shima's glasses, and for the first time Mitsuyo saw his inquisitive brown pupils unclouded by reflection. They were on fire. Their passion burned into her skin. The sensation made her feel more alive than she had in months. It would never be clear to her whether she fell in love with him or with the feeling of being wanted again. In any case, the floor didn't feel so cold any more.

He helped her to her feet. She knew from the way he held her arm that he knew that she knew. Slowly, she pulled away.

"All Shoji cares about is his work, you know," he said, as an announcement came over the speakers saying that there was a special on chicken wings that day. "His work, and how he can get his way."

She began to take inventory of the things in the cart.

"I remember how he didn't come to your father's funeral. Well! You must have been infuriated when he insisted on going back to Japan for his mother's."

"He always gets what he wants," Mitsuyo said, without looking at Shima.

Shima, his nostrils flaring, his glasses clouding over, took her arm again. "I'm not like that," he said. People walking by looked at them with mild curiosity. Mitsuyo wasn't making enough of a fuss for them to be alarmed. They left well enough alone. It was the polite thing. They were in the Midwest, after all. Slowly, she pulled her arm free again, and shook her head.

"I never ate such a big bird," Shima said, staring at the turkey as they wheeled the cart toward the checkout. "This is how Americans eat. They were eating like this during the war, when most of us in Japan were starving."

Mitsuyo couldn't think of an answer. She recalled evacuation, and the return afterwards to the burnt remnants of Tokyo. The images were always accompanied with memories of hunger. These memories she shared with Shima more than with Shoji, whose mother always obtained ham and bacon from her relatives and bartered them for rice and vegetables.

"I remember a neighbour whose son came home from the war crippled," said Shima as the clerk keyed in the prices of cereal and beef and milk. "His name was Yukio. He was just a few years older than Shoji and me, but had stepped on a mine in China and lost his legs. He was also blinded."

Images in broken mirrors hung before Mitsuyo like a bad dream, deformed and twisted. The bells on the cash register jingled merrily. It was Christmastime, after all.

Shima kept muttering, looking over the aisles of food. "Well! There was no compensation, nothing to help the family pay for his medicine. Most of the time we were helpless, but there were a couple of times when my mother sent me over with a sweet potato. She had to tell me several times not to eat it myself. Then Yukio joked that the one good thing about the pain in his legs was that it took his mind off the hunger. He was lying on a thin futon in a dark room, the only other furnishing an oil lamp that was never lit. I couldn't see his eyes through the bandages, so it was very hard to tell whether he was kidding."

Shima looked at Mitsuyo. His eyes and mouth were going in all directions, like he might start crying and laughing at once. "So I told him, in that case you won't mind giving me the potato to eat, and ate it myself, right there in front of him. He started laughing, and was still laughing when I left."

Something melted in Mitsuyo's heart, though the December wind blew cold on their way out to the car parked in the snowy lot. Flakes flew about in the fading twilight like locusts.

Shima opened the passenger door for her and insisted she wait inside while he loaded the groceries in the trunk. Afterwards, he brushed the snow from the windshield and the hood. Mitsuyo watched as Shima parted the darkness and allowed more light in the car. The engine was not yet warm, so the heater was blowing cold air onto her face.

Finally, Shima climbed in, removing his glasses to clean them. "I'm not like Shoji," he said again, looking into her eyes. She looked away. "He takes everything he likes for himself. Leaving nothing for anyone else."

Memories like dreams. Dreams like memories. A sea churning with love and hate spread before Mitsuyo's closed eyelids. Leaning against the kitchen counter, she recalled how Shima seemed ready to float away in the storm that day. Angie and Toshi still weren't back from the art gallery, and no one was doing anything about dinner. She could start on it herself, but it angered her that Angie wasn't here to run the household. Mitsuyo's loneliness weighed her down, suffocating her.

Mitsuyo sat on the couch, fumbling with the Hello Kitty cushion. Empty spaces in time. There was nothing left for her. Nothing was ever left for her. Mitsuyo had known exactly how Shima felt.

XMAS

WHEN SHIMA FIRST WALKED THROUGH THE FRONT DOOR, Hanako and Toshi thought some starving Vietnamese had come to visit them. Toshi had seen enough photographs in *Life* magazine to recognize a victim of war when he saw one. Hanako had become accustomed to seeing fat people in America, which made this poor excuse for a human body all the more pathetic in her eyes.

Shima pulled himself and his luggage through the front door and muttered a weak hello before collapsing onto the couch. The only thing heavy about him was his breathing. He was breathing like a typhoon. He looked as if he might puncture the cushions with his elbows. His shirt was wet from perspiration and stuck to his rib cage. Kei was dispatched by Mitsuyo to get Shoji from the den, while she went to pour Shima a beer. "Milwaukee beer," Shima said, grinning, in the same way some people said, "Swedish stewardesses."

Hanako and Toshi stared at the stranger with their mouths open. Shima noticed Toshi's stupefied face and laughed. Shima's bones looked like they might not survive the strain of laughter.

"Well! You must be Toshi! Do you know who I am?"

"Pol Pot?" Toshi had no idea what the real Pol Pot might look like, but this skinny man whose glasses kept slipping down his nose seemed like he might be capable of slaughtering two million Cambodians for a plate of food. Shima's smile froze on his face.

Shoji hobbled in, leaning on one hand against the wall, laughing. "Shima! You made it!" Toshi saw the thin man exhale. There seemed to be hardly any air in his small lungs. When he stood up from the couch, Shima's joints cracked like thawing ice. He extended a hand to Shoji. "Are you *mad?*" Shoji asked. "You should have sent us your plane schedule with the telegram. We would have come to get you at the airport."

Shima waved the absurd thought away. "It was no trouble taking a cab. I wanted to ride in one of those yellow taxis anyway."

"So, you've finally made it."

"A year and a half felt like forever when we were young, but now it seems like just yesterday that we met in Tokyo."

Mitsuyo came back with Shima's beer. She told Shoji there was another one in the refrigerator.

Shima blinked. The usual platitudes about the house immediately began falling from his mouth. He picked up one of the knit Astroboy cushions from the leather couch and tossed it in the air a few times. "A wonderful, lovely home," said Shima, sincerely. He'd never seen anything like it in Japan. The antique coffee table with the water stains looked ready to collapse. Vaguely remembering what he'd seen on imported American TV shows like *My Three Sons,* he added, "A truly American house. Yes, indeed."

When they first arrived in Milwaukee, the Hayakawas served steak to whoever visited from Japan. Big slabs of meat so large you could write out all Ten Commandments on one side were broiled over a charcoal barbecue in the backyard. This was something most Japanese would have seen only in Hollywood movies. But white people didn't splash soy sauce on their barbecued corn, or serve miso soup and rice on the side.

"You can take the boy out of Japan, but you can't take Japan out of the boy. *Nyet-nyet-nyet!*" Shoji snorted at least once every summer.

Later, fish stocks around Japan became scarce. Raw fish was getting to be, if not completely prohibitive, an extravagance. Soon, good, fatty tuna cost more than sirloin, so the Hayakawas started serving their guests enormous plates of sashimi. Mitsuyo arranged thin rose-petal-pink slices of tuna alongside sea urchin, salmon roe, yellowtail, snapper and shrimp, all uncooked.

Mitsuyo had organized the thin strips of tuna in rows of increasing fattiness. She expertly cut every piece the same size and thickness, just right for sliding over the tongue and down the throat with no resistance. Roughly grabbing his chopsticks, eyes bulging from behind his glasses, Shima scooped the entire row of the fattiest pieces and piled them onto his plate. He didn't seem to care that this wasn't a truly American meal. Toshi and Kei looked at each other. Shoji's lips twitched, as if he'd just seen his friend blow his nose into his hands.

Hanako seemed oblivious. In a typical act of martyrdom, she didn't take any sashimi, but tried to look content eating rice and pickles. No one noticed.

Shima inhaled a few pieces of tuna, as well as some steamed okra and stewed daikon radish. He threw back his glass of beer and smacked his lips loudly. Mitsuyo wrinkled her nose. But when she reached over to take his soup bowl to refill it, Shima grabbed her hand. Containing it among his knotty fingers, he looked into her surprised face, pleading, as if he badly needed to go pee.

"The sashimi melts in my mouth." The compliments bubbled from his pouting lips. "And the okra and the daikon are exquisite. Well! You are as skilled in the culinary arts as you are beautiful," he murmured. Toshi and Kei could not have been more surprised had their guest thrown up on his plate.

Shoji always seemed happiest when there was another physicist sitting with him at the table. It was not every day that he could bounce his thoughts off someone who understood his abstruse logic. With Shima, Shoji talked about Higgs and superstrings, dark matter like axions and photinos and the ever-present lambda, sigma and x's and y's. (Toshi had noticed as a child that any talk on physics was not complete without lambdas, sigmas and x's and y's.) He also knew he would not have to talk to his wife as long as he was talking about his work.

All the while, Shima kept casting compliments toward Mitsuyo, about her cooking, her slim waist, her youthful complexion. Mitsuyo at first shrugged off the praise, replying when necessary by saying Shima was too kind, or that he was cruel to be teasing an old woman. But by the time Shima was asking for his fifth bowl of rice, and commenting on Mitsuyo's pale, slender fingers, she had fallen silent. Shoji seemed oblivious. He was just happy thinking of new ways to rearrange the lambdas, sigmas and x's and y's.

Holidays were confounding to Toshi and his family when they first moved to Milwaukee, especially the noisy ones, like Halloween. Sometime in early autumn, ghosts and witches and ugly rubber masks suddenly appeared in store windows, on TV and at school, all without much explanation. Shoji looked up the word in the dictionary. He explained that "Halloween" was a derivative of a pagan European festival called All Hallow's Eve. This, for Toshi, clarified nothing.

"And what does that have to do with vampires and Egyptian mummies?" asked Mitsuyo.

To everyone's utter amazement, children dressed as these horrible creatures, as well as fairies, Batman, Donald Duck and bumblebees, came knocking on the door one night. Most of them were screaming gibberish. Toshi and Kei listened to what they had to say, then explained to Shoji and Mitsuyo that they were expected to give each kid some candy. The children clucked their tongues and let loose a stream of swear words when they learned there was none.

Shoji and Mitsuyo woke up the next morning to find their windows caked with raw egg, and toilet paper hanging from the trees and bushes. They went straight to the police, and Mitsuyo couldn't close her mouth for hours after the desk sergeant laughed in their faces. He told them to be better prepared next year.

"Good thing it wasn't anything really serious," Mitsuyo said. "Like rape. What if I had been raped?"

"This is why Americans own guns," Shoji rationalized.

Other holidays were just as perplexing. Turkey was the most bland bird they'd ever tasted, and the cranberry sauce on the side made them wonder what they should be giving thanks for. Rabbits apparently went around dropping eggs to commemorate the resurrection of Christ. And no one they asked seemed to have a clear explanation of why these things were happening.

At least Shoji and Mitsuyo had heard of Christmas, even if they were unprepared for the overwhelming frenzy. As the end of the year approached, Toshi and Kei saw countless men and women, who otherwise seemed to possess irreproachable characters and nerves made of steel, melt like butter on a hot skillet. Many slobbered like it was the end of the world. Others accused their own family of deceit or betrayal. All this in the midst of a lot of hugging and smiling and kissing. It was truly an enigma.

Being Japanese, they were used to being called inscrutable. "These Americans really have balls," Mitsuyo said. "They call *us* inscrutable when they spend each December laughing and crying at the same time."

But they were eager to fit in. Shoji and Mitsuyo were especially concerned that by not celebrating Christmas in a truly American way, they would alienate their sons from their friends. This was like worrying about giving just one more cigarette to a terminally ill cancer patient. Toshi and Kei said nothing, though, and the entire family groped for all the right touches to make their holidays perfect.

The year Shima visited from Japan, Chet Wilkins, Shoji's colleague, invited them to cut their Christmas tree from his family's
tree farm instead of buying one from a neighbourhood lot. Chet,
like Shima, specialized in thermal field dynamics. He was born and
raised in rural Wisconsin. He looked more at home on a farm than
he ever did in a lecture hall. He had a big nose and no neck. His
wrists were as thick as Shoji's thighs. Chet was used to cutting his
own Christmas tree. He'd been doing it since he was three, he said.

Mitsuyo stayed home, because she didn't like the cold, and
Hanako was never really invited. Shoji, Toshi, Kei and Shima eagerly climbed into Chet's white van. There were only two seats, with
space for cargo at the rear. Chet and Shoji insisted that Shima ride
up front, where he could take in the scenery. Moose, Chet's basset
hound, was along for the ride. It drooled all over Toshi and Kei,
who were sitting on the floor, eating dried squid and chasing it
with Coke.

"Do dogs like squid?" Toshi asked.

Moose answered by snatching a strand of yellow, stringy flesh
from Kei's hand. It chewed with sad eyes, choking as it swallowed,
but its tail was wagging. Kei smiled and gave the dog a gentle pat
on the head. They opened another bag. When that was gone, Toshi
grabbed a sack of shrimp crackers. Moose could have been
Japanese in a previous life. They feasted like ancient emperors.

While Chet drove, he debated with Shoji and Shima about
whether Stephen Hawking had a better mind than Paul Dirac.
They sounded like men arguing about who was going to win the
Super Bowl. Chet even swore a few times. Those fucking quarks!

The tree farm was just beyond the city, among islands of bush
floating in a sea of unblemished snow. Chet pulled onto a dirt road
and drove through the gates of a rusting barbed-wire fence. Trees
surrounded them as they parked the van, then walked along a trail
marked by deer droppings. Moose wagged his tail and made
growling sounds. Chet insisted on picking the trees. When he

found one that was perfect, he yipped like a cowboy. He gleefully pulled the cord to start his chainsaw. To him, this moment was the sole reason for living.

"Gotta be careful," Chet shouted over the racket. "Luckily, I started chopping down trees as a kid with my old man, so I know what I'm doing. Why, I'll bet I could even do this with my eyes closed." He grinned. He looked like Paul Bunyan. He buried the saw into the trunk of the Scotch pine. "Just needs even, constant pressure!" he yelled to Shoji and Shima.

It was then that Moose vomited on his leg. Fragments of shrimp chips and strands of squid tumbled onto Chet's jeans. Maybe it was the buzz of the saw, maybe it was Chet's big boots, or the thermal underwear he was wearing, but he didn't notice at first. When he did look down, he cried out, "What the fuck—?" then swung the chainsaw wildly and sliced off his own foot. Blood scattered across the snow, transforming the ground into the old Imperial Japanese flag. "*Yeeeeeeaaaaaaaaarrrrrrrrrrgh!*"

Shima turned as white as the winter air. He wobbled, waving his arms, grasping for balance. Chet hopped around on one foot for a while before he fell face first into Moose's vomit.

Shoji kept screaming, "Don't panic! Don't panic!"

Toshi and Kei looked at each other. Toshi thought about kindergarten, and having to pretend his cheeks fell off. He thought telling the story to Chet might take his mind off his foot, but no one was paying Toshi any attention anyway. Ignoring Chet's pleas for God's mercy, Shoji made a tourniquet out of Toshi's scarf. Toshi didn't mind. He wished, though, his father hadn't ordered him to lift Chet by the legs. Toshi had to place his hand on the bloody stump. His glove immediately soaked through with blood.

Kei and Shima took Chet by the waist. Soon they were walking him out of the woods, Moose following close behind, still choking and coughing. Toshi could see his father moving awkwardly with his lame leg through the snow. Shoji was breathing hard, blowing swirling mists that disappeared in an instant like mischievous sprites. The night sky was clear, but the clusters of stars were only faintly visible above the distant city lights. The air was crisp, just like in that Robert Frost poem. Chet was no longer screaming, just shivering like a third-rate motel vibrator. Someone had placed his foot on his chest.

"Miles to go before I sleep," Toshi whispered to himself.

The next day, Shoji said they were buying a fake tree from Sears. It took two days for him to assemble it, even with Shima's help. (Because of his bad leg, Shoji for the most part just translated the instruction sheet into Japanese for his friend.) Kei explained to Toshi that they took so long because they were theoretical physicists. This meant they were good at thinking about how things were put together in the universe, but not so good at actually putting things together themselves.

By the afternoon of the second day, they were ready to trim the tree, just like the families on all the television specials. Shoji asked whether it was more logical to wrap the garlands around the tree first, or hang the ornaments. And what of the lights? He and Shima passionately debated various theories of tree trimming, spitting and pointing to the ceiling, for about twenty minutes. Mitsuyo slapped Shima playfully on the butt and told them to finish sometime before the New Year. Shoji laughed.

When things were nearly finished, Shima was given the honour of placing the five-pointed star at the top of the tree. "Here," said Mitsuyo, handing it to him as he waited on the ladder. "Here's the Star of David."

"Who's David?" Hanako asked. She was picking empty ornament boxes off the floor and stacking them neatly to the side.

"He killed Goliath with a slingshot," Kei replied.

"Yes! Well! We sure could have used something like that when we were growing up, eh, Shoji?" Shima said, then sang "Jingle Bells" in Japanese as he reached over and put the star on the tree.

To Toshi, this seemed like a Christmas right out of a Hallmark card: a father, a mother, a brother, a grandma and a skinny guy from Japan.

With Chet Wilkins in the hospital, there was no one left at the university to talk to Shima about thermal field dynamics. This left Shima with days full of empty hours. It was around this time that he started driving Mitsuyo to the grocery store. It took them longer and longer to shop for food. By Christmas, he was coming over to visit her every day. He usually stayed for dinner and ate like his stomach was left back in World War Two. Mitsuyo rarely complained. Everyone except Shoji noticed that she even started offering Shima seconds before he asked for some. There were also times when Kei heard Mitsuyo talking with Shima in the kitchen, and she was giggling like a teenager.

"We've gotta fucking do something," said Kei.

Toshi sat with one foot in the closet. He was holding a large hardcover book from the library, Cyrano de Bergerac's *A Voyage to the Moon; With Some Account of the Solar World*. Hidden inside was a copy of *Penthouse Letters*. His hard dick was bent out of shape in his jeans. He wanted badly to get into that closet. He certainly didn't want to go into a long discussion with Kei right now, so he decided to be agreeable. "You got that motherfucking right, man."

They were in Hanako's room, which always smelled like incense. She was boiling water in an electric kettle for tea. They used her room when they needed to discuss something in secret, because their parents were not likely to walk in unexpectedly. She brought out some powdered tea and a bowl, then started slicing a red bean cake, preparing a ceremony for her grandsons.

Kei made a face. He never understood what his ancestors saw in that bitter green swill they called tea, or in the red bean cake, a dark slab of gelatinous sugar that smelled faintly of flowers. Toshi, on the other hand, loved the tea ceremony. He found the hot and the cold, the bitterness of the tea and the sweetness of the bean cake, harmonious. When he felt the warmth of the tea bowl against his palms, it seemed for a fleeting few seconds that the incessant hum of the world fell silent.

At the moment, though, the restless pull of *Penthouse Letters* overwhelmed any subtle charms of the tea ceremony. Hanako was oblivious to her grandsons' discomfort. Nor could she understand what Toshi and Kei said to each other, because they were speaking in English.

"This whole thing's pretty fucked up, Kei," Toshi offered. "Ma and Pa may as well have the Great Fucking Wall of China between them for all the communi-fucking-cating they do with each other, ever since Pa fucking went to Grandma's goddamn funeral." He sniffed. "Why the fuck did he have to do that?"

Suddenly the kettle whistled sharply. The pressure eased in Toshi's erection.

"He just gets his way every fucking time, twisting what he fucking calls goddamn fucking logic to serve whatever fucking purpose he may fucking have at the time," said Kei. He sat down, looking weary beyond his years.

"We gotta start getting them the fuck back together," said Toshi. "I don't want them getting no fucking divorce. Ma says she'd go back to motherfucking Japan if it came to that. I sure as fucking hell don't want to go back there, for fuck's sake." Kei looked at his brother sadly, and, for once, didn't say anything.

Toshi noticed his dick had gone limp. He considered *Penthouse Letters* for a while, and this made him think of Jaime Saunders. Then an idea arose in his scattered mind like a wayward erection. For a fleeting moment, he thought he might share his idea with Kei, who always got straight A's on his report cards. This bit of trust came and went like a gust of wind passing through a corridor. "When is that tea going to be ready, Grandma?" Toshi asked in Japanese, with molasses-sweet gaiety.

"Never mind the fucking tea," said Kei.

"But I'm fucking thirsty," Toshi answered. "I can't fucking think straight when I'm fucking thirsty."

"You can't fucking think straight ever."

"That's not fucking nice, Kei."

"Would you like some tea, Kei?" Hanako asked, although she knew the answer.

Kei left the room, swearing.

"Grandma," Toshi said in a hushed voice. She was spooning powdered tea the colour of moss into a raku bowl. Toshi made her put everything down and took her wrists. "Stop that. We've got something more important to do. We've got to go into your closet."

Hanako sighed and nodded. She hadn't understood what her grandsons said to each other. She didn't understand a lot of things. She certainly didn't comprehend why Mitsuyo was always yelling at her. A long time ago, she realized she understood Toshi no less than she understood anyone else who might be sane. They were often scolded together for farting in the same room at the same time. This formed in her mind a strong affinity with Toshi, although she had no way of knowing how he felt about her. A boy and his grandmother. The crazy and the senile. The lunatic and the hag. She did not understand much, but she understood poetry when it was present.

Hanako lifted her tired body from her chair and walked with him into her closet. She wasn't sure whether it was the floor or her joints she heard squeaking. The fragrance of ancient incense blended with mothballs. They sat on an old trunk she'd brought from Japan. It contained all that was important to her—old kimonos, photos of her and Taro looking as solemn as samurai, jewellery collected during their travels.

"Grandma," said Toshi. "You've got to help me write a letter."

"All right."

"We're going to write a love letter to Ma and pretend it's from Pa."

She gave him a look like she'd just swallowed a ball of barbed wire. Toshi explained how he couldn't write Japanese well enough to fool Mitsuyo. His parents only needed a gentle push into each other's arms, he said. They would drift apart hopelessly otherwise. Shoji and Mitsuyo's divorce could prove so traumatic that Toshi might even quit school to open a hot dog stand on Tongatapu if it came to that.

Hanako was only vaguely aware of Toshi's ramblings. She just wondered how things had ever got this absurd. Fighting the fires during the war. Her friends blown to tiny bits of flesh and fragments of bone. The hunger and thirst—the ungodly thirst—that followed. All those things had been absurd, but war was good enough reason for it. Now, they had everything they needed. Their bellies were full. There was a roof over their heads and clothes on their backs. There were no bombs raining around them. So why was everyone running around like decapitated chickens?

Still, there was not much else left for her to do. She could be a part of something, or be alone among her family, wandering around the neighbourhood, taking blame for everything for which they had no one else to accuse.

They were in the closet for a bit over two hours. At first, Hanako was hesitant. She imagined hearing Mitsuyo calling her for one thing or another. Later, around the time when they were halfway through their seventh draft, Hanako became impatient for Toshi to dictate something, anything.

It wasn't easy, as great art never was. Toshi would compose a piece of evocative, sensual poetry, only to realize that he'd ripped off Elvis Costello or the Talking Heads. He cried out and punched the wall, and they started all over again.

There were long spells when Hanako waited, calligraphy brush poised over fine rice paper. Toshi would sit quietly, waiting for his muse. When things seemed really hopeless, Toshi moaned, "Why?" He would think *Why?* which, as Shoji would later point out before he died, was precisely the wrong question to ask. They gave up after Toshi realized the poem he thought he'd just composed was "The Twelfth of Never," sung first by Johnny Mathis and later covered by Donny Osmond.

Muses were curious things, though. They struck at the most inopportune times. Toshi got up to go to the bathroom just past two in the morning, and the muses hit him right where he sat on the commode. The sentences flooded his sleepy mind, but he licked a finger and scribbled a few notes on the mirror so he wouldn't forget them. Then he ran to his room, his mind on fire, to gather a pen and some paper. He barely remembered to wipe down the mirror with his underwear before going to wake Hanako.

It was the time of night when everything was so still the hum of the earth roared in his ears. The grassy fields in his mind were ablaze. "Grandma," he whispered. It took a few tries, but she rose like a phoenix without the feathers. A few minutes later, Toshi and Hanako were sitting in her closet again, with only a candle for light. Its smoke stung their eyes. Toshi dictated the words that drifted across the shadows and onto the paper.

Dearest Mitsuyo,
What can I say about your eyes? Deep, yet shimmering, like
fine Russian caviar. You see right through me with those
eyes, don't you? See, that after all this time, the passion,
smouldering like charcoal half-smothered in chicken fat,
drives me, well, just a little bit crazy.
    We play the game, exchange fierce emotions volleyed
back and forth across the court of life. What is happening
to us, Mitsuyo? Is there any hope left for us? Or have you
grown too cynical for romance, living here in this strange
land, where men have hair on their backs and women have
breasts that put cows to shame? I think not. I know not.
I look at your skinny body and see a woman who longs to

be touched, to be kissed, to be "taken advantage of, good and hard," as the Americans might say.

Come to me, Mitsuyo. Come to me like an elephant might come to water after a week of stomping over the desert. Come and we'll make music that will make the baby birds swoon and fall out of their nests so rabid dogs can eat them up. Just like how I want to eat you up, Mitsuyo. Come to me.

Sincerely,
The Fireball of Love

"Perfect," Toshi murmured as he read it over.

"Can I go back to bed now?" Hanako asked. Her toothless, cavernous mouth opened wide as she yawned.

"Thanks, Grandma." Toshi considered giving her a hug and a kiss, just like he'd seen countless times on American television. The idea, however, was so absurd he went into a fugue state. The next thing he knew, Hanako was gone.

He thought about where to put the letter. Timing would be crucial. Life is timing. The letter needed to be conspicuous enough for Mitsuyo to notice, but Shoji had to be unaware until it was too late.

This plan exploited the Japanese tendency to not question anything so absurd. Someone in Japan once said making war with the most powerful nation in the world was a good idea, and everyone else pretended this made perfect sense. Someone else said Japan should scare the Americans by flying its own planes into their battleships, and everyone agreed again. If things went wrong, people cut their stomachs open. All these exquisitely demented ideas were forever unquestioned.

Toshi had little doubt that if his mother fell madly back in love with his father, the letter would be forgotten and ignored. The plan was flawless, and therefore all the more tragic.

Dawn was breaking. Nothing in the world moved, except for Toshi. He first went to the upstairs bathroom and thought about floating the letter in the commode, text up. Mitsuyo was sure to see it when she got up, but he only had one draft. There was leftover rice in the rice cooker, so he could not put it in there. Somehow the refrigerator seemed too cold. Under the dirty laundry in the hamper? In a shoe? None of these places seemed fitting. Besides, there was too much danger of Shoji seeing it first.

Running around the house in pyjamas on a cold December morning was trying. Toshi decided to hold on to the letter until after Shoji left for work. He walked along the dim hallway, back to his room to sleep.

When he awoke, sunlight was spilling into the room like violin music. The curtains moved lazily above the furnace grate. The days were shortest just before Christmas, so even though it looked late in the day, it was only just past noon. He opened the drapes and averted his eyes from the light that reflected off the snow on the front lawn. The trees cast a map of shadows on the frozen sidewalk. The cold muted everything but the incessant hum.

Shoji would be gone by now. Toshi grabbed the letter and ran downstairs, lumbering past Kei, who was sitting on the bottom steps practising scales on his Les Paul. A sound like a toad choking erupted from Toshi's stomach. Kei didn't look at him, but shook his head. Toshi went to the kitchen, where the floor was cold and made his toes stiffen.

Finding a place for the note could wait. He needed to eat something first. There was a tin of smoked oysters in the cupboard and some Ritz crackers. He found an avocado and some Swiss cheese in the fridge. He was looking for a knife when the phone rang.

"Motherfucker!" said the voice on the other end. It was Scotty. "Get your hairy ass over here! We scored us a fucking six-pack!"

Conflicting desires now grappled in Toshi's head. Beer. Marriage. Beer. The choice actually was not difficult at all. He forgot all about his note on the counter, illuminated by the after-noon sun in plain view, and ran upstairs to get dressed.

Shoji limped through the back door. He held on to the wall, pulling the wet boots off his frozen feet. Shoji leaned against the counter, massaged his deformed leg and sighed. He heard Kei play-ing guitar on the stairs. It sounded like a dentist's drill gone insane.

"Mitsuyo!" he called out, for no reason in particular. When there was no answer, he assumed she and Shima were out shopping again. He had left the car keys so Shima could use it.

He had taken a bus to the hospital to visit Chet. When Shoji walked into the room, Chet was sitting up in bed, wearing his thin blue hospital gown, sipping on pulp-free orange juice from a Tetra Pak. Scratching his half-shaven chin, he told Shoji that shit hap-pened in the bush. One had to expect it. "No big dog-doo," he said. Chet was already looking forward to Christmas next year. He only worried it might be difficult to operate a chainsaw while trying to balance on one leg. "I'll cut some poplar in November and stock up on firewood," he said, smiling. "Get some practice in."

Shoji noticed the cheese and the unopened tin of oysters. He saw the avocado and the crackers. Then there was the letter, lying lazily in the late-afternoon sun.

A broken heart does not necessarily crack down the middle. It sometimes just quits functioning, suddenly seizing up like an engine without oil. Shoji tried to recall when he had stopped lov-ing his wife. Or why he used to find her crassness charming. Now it seemed callous, and sometimes cruel. When did he tire of it, and of her? He'd buried himself, and his heart, in his work. It lay in the darkness, beneath the scholarly journals and the sigmas and lambdas.

As he read the note a second time, its words poured over his skin like acid. He was surprised now to feel anger. He didn't stop to consider how irrational this was. He saw irrationality everywhere except in himself.

Slowly his eyes fell on the car keys hanging by a hook on the wall. He went to the garage, where the car lay sleeping, content, without a care in the world.

"Mitsuyo!" he shouted.

He barely heard himself above Kei's guitar. "Turn that damn thing down!" he yelled as he climbed the stairs past his son, pulling his bad leg behind him.

When Toshi turned out the way he did, Shoji had felt betrayed. He felt betrayed when his mother died, so he was used to the feeling he felt now as he rushed down the hall as fast as he could. What he wasn't prepared for, though, was opening the door to his bedroom and finding Mitsuyo embracing Shima, her blouse half undone, lipstick smeared around swollen lips, wearing an expression that looked angry more than anything else.

HANAKO

"WHEN I LOOKED AND SAW YOU OUTSIDE MY WINDOW, Hanako, I almost choked on my wine and threw up on the frigging cat.

"You looked like a ghost, standing in the rain. The water seemed to fall right through you and your umbrella. Then my daughter and her husband and my three godforsaken excuses for grandchildren pulled up in the driveway and saw you. Jessica, my little four-year-old granddaughter, said that from behind you looked like a black mushroom. Heh-heh-heh. Your legs were so white.

"Why were you standing there like that? We brought you in and sat you by the fire, and you smiled like this was the most normal thing in the world. My family pointed to themselves and said their names, and pointed to me and said my name. It took you a while to understand, didn't it, old woman? Then you pointed to yourself and, in a voice as brittle as my bones, you said 'Hanako.'

"And I said, 'She lives with that Chinese family across the street with the funny kid,' and my daughter said Hanako was a Japanese name. Here all the while I was thinking you people were Chinese. There's a real fine Chinese restaurant on Oakland Avenue, you know. Nice sweet-and-sour chicken balls. You like sweet-and-sour chicken balls, Hanako?

"How long ago was that? Two months? Three? Time doesn't matter much when one day's just like the next. Now, everyone's Thanksgiving this and Thanksgiving that. More fuss than it's worth, if you ask me."

"Mr. Garber, your house smells. This cat smells. It rubs against my legs. It feels delicious, but then I have to clean the cat hair from my stockings when I get home. I know you're looking at my legs, you old pervert. I was raised more proper than you'll ever know. I would never allow any man other than my late husband—he's dead now—to even look at me that way. So turn away! Don't look!

"If you only knew how handsome my husband was. The day we met, he was in his student's uniform and cap. So refined. I almost ran into him on my bicycle. Did you know I could ride a bike? I used to wear *hakama*. Do you know what that is? Wide pants—looks more like a skirt. It was quite fashionable for us modern women to wear *hakama* back then.

"He came out suddenly from behind a cherry tree—it was March and the blossoms were dancing freely in the wind. I almost hit him. As it was, I fell into the gutter. My *hakama* were filthy, and he offered to have them cleaned. Then he smiled. I counted three cavities staring out at me."

"What the blazes are you nattering about, old woman?

"Just like Celia, God rest her soul. Nattering, nattering, all the time. Made me wonder when she ever took a breath. Can it really be thirteen years since she died? Thirteen years, I haven't known the love of a good woman. She was so beautiful. She was as refined as freshwater pearls. Her father owned a textile factory. My father was the finest tailor in Warsaw. I worked with him in his shop. Ah, Celia was exquisite.

"Of course, I was seeing another girl, a teacher at the local school, when we met. Helen was a fine woman also, but I could not marry her. How could Helen expect that I was going to marry her? Her family was educated but poor. They could not even afford a dowry.

"Celia said she saw Helen once during the occupation. She was walking and talking and laughing with two Gestapo officers. Celia was angry because she could not believe Helen was being so friendly with Germans! Only afterwards did she find out Helen had got hold of some false papers that would allow her to go to Germany to work as a non-Jew. Only she never made it because someone identified her, and she was shot.

"Ah, it was a shame, I feel so bad about it all now. How she was killed. How I had broke her heart."

"Taro had always wanted to see the world. And he did. He left us alone in a city that was about to go up in flames like dry cedar, but how could he have known? He was too busy working for the secret service of His Imperial Highness. He called himself a diplomat. Diplomat, indeed. He was a spy. A mouse. A rat. He spent most of his time in a place called . . . What was it called? Lithuania.

"You're a Jew, aren't you? He was always talking about Jews. He said a consul at the Japanese consulate in Lithuania was giving out exit visas to Jews even though it went against orders from the Ministry of Foreign Affairs. Can you imagine? I am so glad Taro was not so foolish as to risk his career for people he'd never met. I always say that if people feel there is a problem, they should try to fix it themselves before troubling others."

"Have some more tea. It will warm your bones, although I wish you wouldn't make so much noise when you drink. Don't they have any manners in Japan or China or wherever it is you are from? Someone as old as you should mind your manners, especially in front of young people. We have to set an example, you see?

"Back in the old country, my grandparents lived with us when I was a child. Then, even after I had my daughter, my parents still lived with us. We were happy to be together. We fought to stay together in spite of all the difficulties. We loved having them around us, at dinnertime, or listening to the radio in the living room.

"Even after the Germans entered Warsaw, we wanted to stay together. Ah, but how could we? In the early days of the occupation, they were taking Jewish men from their homes to clear the streets of rubble and repair the roads. We worked every day without food or drink, and naturally without pay, while my family waited at home, worrying and worrying.

"Because only Jewish men were being persecuted, my family convinced me to sneak out with a few other men to Soviet-occupied territories. We headed out early one morning on a truck to Lvov, but that didn't help matters much for anyone in the end.

"Back home, my parents did not survive the ghetto. Celia and our daughter were eventually taken to Auschwitz. My daughter perished there. Celia nearly went crazy after that, but somehow she managed to hang on until the liberation. We both came back to Warsaw around the same time, and were lucky to find each other through the Jewish Committee. My uncle helped to bring us here to America, where we had more children and where Celia now lies peacefully in the cemetery across town, while my grandchildren run around like it's their God-given right to have fun. And they forget about their grandfather. I'm lucky if they come visit and eat dinner with me once a month."

"There wasn't even drinking water in Tokyo. Fortunately, my daughters were evacuated to the countryside. I stayed, though, to do whatever I could to help. On some days, there were so many dead we had to pile them up in the middle of the street and burn them. Gasoline was precious, but the bodies would start to smell otherwise. The flames rose with our prayers to the sky that was grey,

I think, from all the ashes. Maybe it was just a cloudy day. The flag was so white, so red. So pure. The flames were impure, and burned with the stench of death. Mitsuyo and Tatsue never had to see that.

"Now we live here in America, where my grandchildren go to school with the sons and daughters of those who dropped the bombs.

"Remember the day when you gave me flowers from your garden? Mitsuyo thought I'd stolen them from someone's yard. She didn't even give me a chance to explain. She screamed at me while she mixed a raw egg in the fermented beans we were having for supper. At least the children still eat Japanese food. They look like they'd like to take me out with the next garbage if they could. Even Toshi. Did I mention Kei moved away to . . . Where was it again? Somewhere north, I think."

"Ah, the cat! Here it comes closer once again. My grandchildren named it Mongoose. I call it Piece of Shit. You know, I never wanted a cat. I always wanted fish. I told my children, I wanted something that wasn't much trouble. Like fish.

"For years, they never bought me anything. One day, I went to the pet store on Oakland Avenue and bought a goldfish and a small fish bowl. I didn't know if it was a boy fish or a girl fish, but I named it Eddie anyway. A week after I got Eddie, my children brought me this cat. What the hell were they thinking?

"If you understood what I was saying, you'd know that two days later Eddie was gone. And Piece of Shit pretended Eddie climbed out of his bowl and ran away from home. Mongoose. Piece of Shit. I cried that night. I only cried three times in my life. The first time was when Celia and I found each other after the war and she told me our daughter had not survived. The second time was when Celia died and left me all alone in this country. Then Eddie did the same thing and I found myself wailing like a baby in bed. That was the third time I cried, but also the first time I cried out loud. Maybe I'm just more tired now since living so long in America.

"That's when I started drinking, too. I keep the empty fish bowl in the living room to remind my children of their stupidity."

"Your cat is rubbing against my ankle again. It smells, but I have to admit that it's very loving. So affectionate. No one touches me like that any more. Don't get any ideas, you dirty old man. There is going to be only one man in my life, and he died working like a mule. There were times when he wouldn't come home from the office for days. When he would be filing reports through the night without sleeping. He did it all for me and our daughters. I'm just going to pretend I don't see you scratching your crotch."

"These polyester pants are hot and itchy. I ask my daughter for something that breathes, but what does she get me? Polyester! You want some more cookies? Help yourself. Eat all you want.

"All I'm saying is that people today don't understand what's important. That's why all the new things they have now don't make them happy. I look at my children and their children, and I tell you we were happier before the war. Of course, we had no television. We didn't walk around with these headsets connected to tape recorders. But this made us appreciate each other's company. I'm going to have some more wine. And hand me those cigarettes and matches, would you?"

As Old Man Garber drank himself to sleep in his chair with a cigarette still burning in his hand, Hanako left quietly, careful not to disturb him. She didn't go straight home. Wrapped in a fake fur coat Mitsuyo had bought for her last Christmas, she first went to the Silver Dollar Pizza Parlor to watch some bikers shoot pool. They all knew her name and loved to buy her beer. She drank a bit, which made her cheeks blossom.

Then Hanako walked over to Ronnie's Pawn Shop to see the latest acquisitions. Ronnie had a pot of coffee and some cookies waiting. In the glass case was an old radio, some rings, an oil paint set, brass knuckles and a Fender Stratocaster guitar. Ronnie shoved a box of cookies toward Hanako, motioning for her to take some home. Hanako refused, smiling. The last time she took anything home, her daughter had accused her of stealing.

On the way back home, she peeked into the window to O'Connor's basement bedroom. The former captain of any team that was important at Whitefish High School was taking a day off from selling aluminum siding. He was masturbating into an issue of *Cosmopolitan.*

The sun was falling fast. Shadows chilled the air. To the west, ribbons of rose-coloured clouds were wrapped around the sky. Shivering a bit, Hanako pulled her coat tighter around her hunched shoulders and turned toward home. Toshi would be home from work soon. Poor boy spent the day moving other people's furniture. His neck and shoulders would be tight as a drum. Maybe she could persuade him to let her give him a massage.

She needed a warm bath herself. Watching the bikers play pool under naked fluorescent lights had been hard on the eyes. Her temples throbbed in time with her heart. They'd also offered her a cigar, and she'd accepted. She saw a dying rose bush and wanted to vomit.

She shuffled her feet. Her legs were twisted and bowed, made that way from a lifetime of walking pigeon-toed in kimono. Hanako supposed it could have been worse. She could have been born Chinese; then her feet would have been bound and not allowed to grow bigger than a matchbox. Imagine! *Those Chinese!*

She'd made sure her daughters' legs were allowed to grow straight, not that Mistuyo showed any appreciation for this or anything else Hanako had done for her. *Let's face it,* she thought, *Mitsuyo is a bitch.* It had been almost a year since they found her with Shima, and she and Shoji were no closer to reconciliation. *Why did she do such a thing?* Mitsuyo had been angry at Shoji ever since he flew to his mother's funeral. Ryoko had been a bitch too, but what good would it have done for Shoji to miss her funeral?

Shoji slept in the den now. No wonder Kei needed to move away to Canada, wherever the hell that was. Canada. Somewhere beyond the horizon, anyway.

It wasn't until she turned the corner that she noticed the smell of the barbecue. This was a queer thing in November. Someone had piled the coals pretty high, she supposed, because it smelled like a whole house was burning. She saw it for the first time when she was just about home. Across the street, flames furled toward the sky from Mr. Garber's house like a proud flag. Only it was impure. It smelled of death.

She immediately wanted to run and hide, before Mitsuyo found her. But why? Hanako hadn't started the fire. But she knew she was not allowed to get away with anything. Before he moved away to Canada, Kei came home drunk one night and smashed Mitsuyo's favourite candy dish. The next morning, Mitsuyo blamed Hanako, screaming at her like a woman in labour.

Hanako hadn't even realized her daughter had been so attached to the dish, a gaudy, tasteless thing adorned with flowers and ducks. Kei looked on in silence, hollow eyes squinting at the noise. Hanako stared at the cracks in the floor tiles. She occasionally stole glances at her youngest grandson, the artist, the smart one, the musician.

She looked up at the burning house and noticed the cat through the second-floor window. It was not a particularly attractive cat. It smelled of stale rainwater. Charcoal-grey hair fell off in clumps whenever it rubbed against anything, and it was always coughing, just like her husband used to, before he died. More than once, Hanako had seen the cat after it had been in a fight. Fresh blood dried on matted fur, claws missing. It nonetheless carried on bravely like it was all so ordinary. This, too, reminded Hanako of Taro. And of herself after the firebombs had levelled the Tokyo she knew.

She didn't know the cat's name was Mongoose. She didn't know it was also called Piece of Shit. She only knew the cat was the only thing that had shown her any affection since Taro died.

She recalled how it came to her when she first saw it. The cat sniffed her hand to see if she had any food. When it saw that she had nothing, it still didn't run away. It purred and rubbed against her ankle. Hanako started bringing it food after that, but at first she always pretended that she had nothing. It never seemed to matter to the cat one way or another.

The cat seemed as aloof as always as the house burned around it. Hanako ran to the garden hose coiled at the side of the house. She was pleased to discover the old man had forgotten to shut the valves in preparation for the cold. She doused herself with water and shuffled as fast as her short, bent legs would carry her.

The sixteen-wheel Allied Movers truck came roaring around the corner just as Hanako disappeared into the burning house. Toshi saw his grandmother, her hair and dress dripping, throwing her shoulder lamely against the door and falling inside. Scotty and Horace Junior stared at the fire, wide-eyed and mouths agape, until Horace drove over a mailbox. "Who the fuck put that there!" Horace screamed. Still swearing, he threw the emergency brake on.

Toshi spilled onto the sidewalk. Horace stumbled from the other side of the cab, along with a few Baby Ruth wrappers. His sides jiggled like a waterbed as he fell onto the ground. Scotty stayed in the truck, still watching the fire as if it was the best television he'd ever seen. Toshi struggled to get up. The air was burning. Little orange fairies were flying about his face. Their kisses stung like tiny insects. Toshi ran toward Old Man Garber's house. That was when he saw Mitsuyo, standing in front of their house with a cast-iron skillet in one hand.

Sirens and screams cut through the smoke like flashes of lightning. When the world became this loud, Toshi felt he could actually make out some of the words it was crying out to him.

What's for supper? Why does everyone feel Curly was a better Stooge than Shemp? Toshi covered his ears and tried to concentrate on things that mattered. If only he could remember what they were. He stumbled toward his mother, squinting in the confusing duel between light and shadow. He wondered what his mother planned to grill for supper that night. Judging from the skillet, it may be either steak or pork chops. Could be fish, he supposed.

"Hey," Mitsuyo said when he walked up to her. "You look a total mess."

"Thanks. Grandma's in there."

"What?"

"Grandma's in there. I saw her running into the house as I pulled up."

Mitsuyo looked into her son's face, searching for signs of delusion as though she was checking his hair for lice. Toshi's eyes proved unusually lucid.

She gazed at the house and looked for some sign of Hanako in the smoke and flames. A couple of fire engines pulled up beside the Allied Movers van. A few firemen jumped off and barked like bloodhounds in all directions. Mitsuyo eyed them suspiciously.

Toshi looked at her, then said, "I'm going in after her."

"Have you gone completely mad?" yelled Mitsuyo, before remembering that Toshi, in fact, had. She looked at the house again.

Neither of them noticed Old Man Garber a few feet away, huddled with his family. He had woken in time to escape out a window before the flames surrounded him. When he looked at the fire, all he saw was his life in America burning away, turning to ash like his memories of war.

What he couldn't see was Hanako on the second floor, in the hallway, on her hands and knees, trying to duck beneath the smoke while holding Mongoose under one arm. It was hotter than Kyushu in August. She had to admit, though, that it was a dry heat. Every once in a while, she felt a piece of her hair turn to dust and fly away. It didn't matter. She was happy to have found the cat.

Her chest hurt, and she stopped frequently and tried to cough her intestines out. But the fire didn't scare her, not after living through the firebombs in Tokyo. Not after the entire city went up in smoke, like pieces of her scalp were doing now. That was what she called a real fire. The entire night sky turned red as though dawn had come early. Houses were collapsing all around her. Children, with faces burned to a crisp, limped toward her, begging for water that she did not have. Now, *that* was a fire.

Suddenly, Mongoose leapt from her hand, hopped among the flames and onto the windowsill. Hanako heard herself cry out involuntarily. From the window, Mongoose looked at her curiously, as if it were trying to understand some surreal painting of a woman crawling around like a dog in a fire. Hanako understood and nodded. They were splitting up. They had a better chance of survival separately than together. This would be especially true for the cat. *Good plan,* she simply thought, *for a dumb animal.*

Smoke was clouding her mind as well as her vision. She took a rest and thought back to the one night during the war when her best friend was killed.

Bombs were falling like bird droppings. Her friend's name was Mariko Tanuma, but everyone called her Tanuki, which meant raccoon, because there were always dark circles under her eyes.

Tanuki and Hanako were both in their mid-thirties, with their husbands gone. Tanuki's had been killed at Midway, and Taro was already in Lithuania by this time. Both of them had children evacuated to the country. Tanuki, who lived down the street from Hanako, always knew what to do when the sirens started up. She knew what to do as she and Hanako were running through the burning streets in their sandals and *yukata,* covering their heads with thick cotton hoods to protect them against fire and debris as the B-29s made another pass. The air screamed as the bombs fell. The ground shivered under their feet.

They reached the school where several trenches had been dug in the courtyard. The school itself had been burned to the ground the previous week. Its charcoal-black remains—bits of wooden beams, shingles and glass—were scattered about like the bones of another victim of war. The first trench they ran to was nearly overflowing. There was barely enough room for one more.

Tanuki removed the scorched hood, and her long hair burst forth like a black river. She told Hanako to climb in, because there was another just twenty yards away, and Tanuki could run faster. And she did. She ran like a cheetah. Hanako wondered how anybody who hadn't eaten properly for weeks could run so fast. She smiled in spite of everything when she saw Tanuki's figure drop into the trench and out of sight. *We both made it* was the thought than flickered in Hanako's mind just before she saw a bomb fall out of the sky and follow Tanuki into her trench.

It was amazing how protective a shelter can be, even if it was just a hole in the ground. The bomb burst just a short distance away, but the shock wave passed safely over Hanako's head as she crouched below the ground. But no bomb shelter was good for much when the bomb fell right into it.

A tidal wave of dirt and rocks and pebbles fell onto her and the others huddled in the trench. When she opened her eyes, Hanako saw a stub of flesh on the ground next to her that looked like a button mushroom. In a heartbeat, she recognized it as a big toe. Its nail needed to be clipped.

Hanako was too overwhelmed by the chaos to scream. All she could see was the sun shining through the black smoke, which was moving quickly, like wild horsemen. Red flames billowed like flower petals. She climbed out of the trench slowly. Her feet dragged, and she accidentally kicked a rock, turning it over to reveal a hand. As the dust and smoke cleared, she saw a leg, an arm and an eye.

The trench that was Tanuki's shelter was five times the size it used to be. Hanako spent two hours digging through the rubble, finding more body parts, none of which belonged to Tanuki. It was as though she'd never even existed.

After moving to Milwaukee, when Hanako watched American children hunt for eggs at Easter, she always thought of looking for body parts among the rubble after a bombing. But it wasn't Easter now. It was close to Thanksgiving.

Hanako looked at the cat still staring at her from the window. As she watched, it jumped out onto a nearby tree branch. The cat slipped easily among the knotted branches, themselves catching blossoms of fire. On the ground, it found Old Man Garber.

"Piece of Shit!" the old man screamed. "Oh, my God, Piece of Shit! Where did you come from?"

One of the firemen raised an eyebrow. Mitsuyo wasn't sure she understood the English correctly. Old Man Garber shoved his family aside and ran to the cat. The cat ran to him. To Toshi, everything shifted to slow motion and took on an otherworldly beauty. Old Man Garber scooped the cat into his arms, whispering its name over and over, lovers kissing in the rain.

"I'm going inside," Toshi said again to his mother.

"No!" Mitsuyo hissed. She whispered, though no one around them understood. "Let the firemen do their job. They'll find her if she's in there."

"But—"

"Just leave her!"

Mitsuyo would never know if her son ever heard those words, because in the next instant, Toshi was running like a pregnant cow. The burning house looked down upon him and laughed. "Buddah-buddah-buddah," he mumbled to himself, providing his own soundtrack to the drama that was unfolding. He could feel his life coming apart at the seams and relished the sensation of falling freely through air.

The firemen were too preoccupied to stop or even notice him as he lumbered up the front steps. His face was already red. He was breathing like a volcano. Hanako had left the door open for him, and the flames emerged and hid like a child playing hide and seek. The whole thing was somehow inviting. He stepped into the infernal hell on earth.

He thought it was hotter than a witch's tit that was drenched in gasoline and lit on fire. The walls and the floor roared at his intrusion. *What the fuck are you doing here? Go home, you goddamn Chink-shit motherfucker!* Toshi wished the voices in his head would keep his mother out of this. This was his last thought before Mitsuyo hit him from behind with the skillet. He fell to the floor like a cut tree.

A couple of bewildered firemen were looking in through the doorway. Mitsuyo yelled at them in Japanese. "Don't just stand there, shit-drippers! Help me get my son out of here!" They rushed in to take Toshi from her.

Upstairs, Hanako could no longer see anything through the smoke, so she closed her eyes tightly. So tightly that the only thing she saw was an occasional flicker of colour drifting in the black sea. She could feel her lungs turning to ash. The darkness expanded beyond the periphery of her vision, wrapping around her, shielding her from the pain.

The flames suddenly burst forth in front of her, the scarlet banners wild and beautiful. She realized the impurity of fire burning the dead was only a means to an end. The flames were impure only because the dead were still of this world. Once the body and the soul dissolved, the fire was purified, as it was intended.

Mitsuyo, on the street in front of the burning house, watched the roof give way. She cradled Toshi's head in her arms. Tears flowed like a river down her face, dragging mascara to her lips. She looked like a bad kabuki actor. The firemen around her were still running in circles, barking and swearing.

Toshi opened his eyes slowly. He looked up at his mother's face, still unsure where he was or what he was doing. He wasn't sure why his mother was crying. He opened his mouth to ask. Then he noticed his father's face peering down over her shoulder.

Shoji frowned, trolling for a rational, logical explanation as to why his son would be sprawled in front of a neighbour's house that was burning to the ground. Mitsuyo felt his presence, and turned. "Home so soon?" she asked, her voice cracking like misfired ceramic. "Think you might have some time to plan a funeral for *my* mother?"

Shoji didn't understand why Hanako would need a funeral. He didn't know his mother-in-law was burning to a crisp in the house. He didn't recognize the impurity of the flames. He took a few uncertain steps toward the fire. His bad leg pulled him back. He looked among the flames for an explanation of what was happening.

The first cancer cells were already starting to form in his chest that very moment. He would be dead in less than a year. Another catastrophe stalking him from around the corner. No one could have warned him. He watched, clueless, as the charred roof finally caved in. A fireman shouted commands across the lawn. Old Man Garber's family led him and the cat to a dilapidated station wagon.

Toshi closed his eyes. The light and the noise receded quickly. There were no voices yelling at him from inside his head. *Tomorrow,* he thought, *they'll all be back tomorrow.* Until then, he wanted desperately to sleep. His mother's lap smelled like a worn, comfortable blanket. Shoji placed a hand on Mitsuyo's shoulder. Her face collapsed like a castle of sand. Tears welled in her eyes for the first time since before she could remember. She turned her head and started crying into Shoji's hand.

"I'm sorry," she whispered. "I am so, so sorry . . ."

Shoji opened his mouth but said nothing. He watched as the columns of black smoke climbed to an empty, indifferent sky.

THE BOOK

CATASTROPHES WERE HAPPENING ALL THE TIME. That's what Yasujiro had told his son when Shoji was robbed of his mugworts and beaten up. Sometimes the catastrophes were so subtle they did not capture anyone's attention when they occurred. They were catastrophes, nonetheless. A small action, or even a lack of action, could often screw up someone's life more than the monumental events recorded in history.

No one would deny the Second World War had greatly affected Shoji's own life, but its influence on Toshi and Kei was not nearly as critical as that of a certain book, Kepler's *Harmonice Mundi*. To most people, the book was too esoteric to be anything more than a doorstop. Nonetheless, it extended a ripple across reality that left shattered spirits in its wake. It was the butterfly in Central America that caused the typhoon in Taiwan.

If Toshi could actually see the wall of mirrors that he imagined confronted Shoji after he died—if he could step outside time to see the infinite reflection of all reality—he would see how the book affected his life. He would see how it tugged at Kei as he slept with countless women while on the road with Head. How it pulled at Mitsuyo when Shima touched her hand for the first time. Still, there would be nothing Toshi could do to remove the book from the plane of existence. This was the irony of death. He would see everything but be able to do nothing, for he would lack time—any time to do anything—because he would be *outside* all time. Omniscience combined with impotence was death's cruellest joke.

Shoji told his sons that the most difficult thing about the war, after not having enough to eat, was not celebrating festivals. He said the only thing that might have been good about being dragged all over Japan by his father's work was the different regional festivals he may have been able to see. But the war had deprived him of that as well. In peaceful times, festivals meant food cooked out in the open, music and dancing. There were always drunks who liked to get into fights. Shoji detested them, but the crowd, the noise and the drums and conch shells more than made up for it. He never danced, but only watched and made mental notes.

Obon was the biggest celebration of the summer. When things were normal, Kitagawa, which melted in the sun in August, suddenly came to life during Obon. Sounds of hammers echoed from the temple down the path from Shoji's house. Men erected towers in the yard for the giant drums. Men and women in loose-fitting robes danced and eyed each other lustfully.

But this was wartime. There wasn't much to celebrate. There was no food to barbecue and sell. A big crowd dancing in the streets was not a celebration but a target. Lanterns at night were too conspicuous, and candles and oil were getting much too expensive anyway.

But Obon was more than just a party. It was a time when dead souls returned to look in on the living. Because there were even more dead people who needed prayer during the war, they could not cancel Obon completely. There were no dancing and feasting, but people in Kitagawa still went to the graveyard to pray. Rice-paper lanterns floated on the river, sending the nostalgic spirits back to the underworld, unlit because their family who were still among the living were too scared and too poor.

Shoji leafed through the book while sitting in his room. They lived close to the temple grounds. All day there had been crowds going back and forth outside their gate, sleepwalking in herds. The only ones showing any life were the drunks.

Ryoko went out to talk to some of the passersby. She came back in quickly when someone asked why they weren't going home to Tokyo for Obon. The souls of dead family must cry out to them, they said. Ryoko explained that Yasu was too busy, but she was lying. Even had they been in Tokyo, her husband would never pray to his ancestors. Prayer to him was either a grating chant or a chance to rest his eyes. He would not abandon his patients for it.

And Ryoko was kept from visiting her own home because Yasu and Shoji needed tending to. They were like small babies, loving but selfish. Yasu was out now seeing patients, who were also selfish. He would be coming home hungry.

The voices of the mourners washed across Shoji's room like a river. Prayer chants drifted from the temple grounds. The words on the page dodged his gaze, and he spent more time looking out the window as the sun fell westward. He thought about how difficult it had been to get hold of this book. This made him think about Kanako. Many things made him think of Kanako. Then he thought of how, because Obon was a Buddhist holiday, things would be pretty quiet at the Kaminohashi Jinja, the Shinto shrine run by Kanako's father. There were woods surrounding the shrine, and they were thick, silent. Shoji reasoned it might be less distracting to study there than at home, where there were too many people around him trying to wake the dead.

He crept downstairs. In the kitchen, Ryoko was preoccupied with yelling at Otama. Her voice spilt into the hallway. "Look,"

Ryoko said. "If you wanted to go home, you could have told me earlier in the year. With so many people coming and going, I can't possibly let you go now."

"But, ma'am," said Otama, who usually never talked back. "This is Obon. I should be with my mother. I thought you would know. . . ."

"I would think your mother should be able to accommodate our needs. She did get the ham I sent last month, didn't she? I certainly haven't heard back from her. And *please* stop fidgeting. Get a hold of yourself."

Colossal tears rolled from Otama's eyes, down her plump cheeks. As the war drew closer to its end, she had not shed an ounce of weight. She looked as healthy and robust as anyone did during peacetime. Her spirit, in contrast, was remarkably fragile.

Ryoko had in fact wondered whether her maid would want time off for Obon, but she'd been too busy to check. Since Otama herself hadn't asked, Ryoko reasoned that she could not be expected to read people's minds. How could she possibly know that Otama's mother, the senior maid on the Harada farm, had never received the ham? Had Otama actually delivered it, her mother would have immediately composed a long, maudlin letter of thanks to Ryoko and sent it back with some potatoes. She was simple, but keenly aware of custom. She would have told Otama to work through Obon, and maybe even the New Year.

Otama, too busy with catching up on laundry after three days of rain, was unable to visit her mother to deliver the ham on the day she received it from Ryoko. Later that night, after listening for hours to her stomach protesting the ever-present hunger, she allowed herself one slice to help her sleep. But hunger was the devil's laughter, and that one taste the devil's kiss. She suddenly found herself on the floor in the kitchen, her fingertips and lips covered with grease and salt. The ham had vanished from sight. Perhaps, she thought, Ryoko would give her another ham to take home on Obon. She had held on to that small fragment of hope like a jewel, until today.

Shoji walked out onto the street. Heat scattered in the breeze at twilight. All the stores were closed. Except for the mourners, the streets were empty. Shoji walked slowly, dragging his feet in the dirt. One star already hung in the sky, spinning by an invisible thread just above the dark mountains to the east. Shoji thought about how the light he saw was old light. Perhaps billions of years old. Old light coming to the end of an unimaginably long journey. The star may not even be there any more. Just light, lingering in the empty void like a ghost.

A dog barked in the distance. Shadows fell like sleep over the landscape. There were fewer people on the street as he walked across the twilight. Everything was still except for the river when he reached the wooden bridge. The water was below the darkness, but he could hear the turbulence.

The path leading to the Kaminohashi Shrine split from the road just around the bend from the bridge. The shrine stood behind a thick, lush forest. A narrow trail of stepping stones led through the trees. A few crows shrieked overhead, objecting to Shoji's presence. Their black forms lifted into the night like leaves caught in a storm. Shoji saw the main prayer hall, and suddenly found that he wanted to pray. He'd never prayed before, because Yasu had made it easy for him not to. Gods and ghosts had no place in a house of doctors and scientists. But at times like these, which were rare, Shoji found he needed to speak to something that would not immediately speak back.

Perhaps it was Obon. Perhaps it was just too quiet. Perhaps it was wartime, or all of these things. Darkness had completely swallowed the tops of the trees around the Kaminohashi Shrine. Shoji didn't think to go back to the Buddhist temple and pray properly. He simply stood at the front of the prayer hall, grabbed the thick rope hanging from the bell that was supposed to catch the attention of the spirits, and rang it as hard as he could. After he prayed, he threw a few coins in the large wooden alms box under the bell, then walked away.

He wasn't sure if he felt any better. At least he felt like he'd done *something*. He sat down at the foot of an aging pine and broke open his book. But the silence was as deafening as the muffled whispers of the mourners had been. The shadows spread faster than he'd expected. It was even harder to read here than it had been at home.

He looked up from his book often, because his gaze would not stay on the page. He glanced about, even when there was no movement around him. When he looked up enough times, he caught sight of Kanako standing a few feet away. She stood there like a pale ghost, fading like watercolour into the falling darkness. Shoji closed his book without thinking twice.

Her laughter made the silence shiver. "You're such a bookworm, Sho-chan," she said. "Don't you have any respect for the dead?"

"The time to work hardest is when everyone else isn't." Shoji repeated what Yasu always told him. Shoji thought it somehow didn't sound as clever when he said it. His face was hot. He hoped that if he were in fact blushing, the darkness would shelter him.

She laughed again. Shoji stood up slowly and dusted himself off deliberately. She waited for him, then started walking toward the bridge, toward town. Nothing but quiet, as if they were suddenly all that was left in the world. They both knew, though, that people were still wandering about the Fukanji temple grounds in the dark, in the graveyard, praying and mourning. "A lot of spirits to welcome home this year," she said without looking at him. "Everybody's gone now."

Shoji nodded. He pinched the fabric of his trousers.

"Where do you think our souls go when we die?"

Shoji sighed an impatient sigh. Had it been anyone but Kanako, he would not even consider a question that was so utterly fruitless.

"Well?"

Shoji thought about how energy could be neither created nor destroyed. It just changed form, like ice to water to steam. Did the soul behave in the same way? Was the soul a form of energy? He shook his head. Everything he saw and remembered was locked in his brain, perhaps chemically, or at a subatomic level as patterns of elementary particles. If the brain did not work, the patterns were not accessible. Shoji thought about radio. Alive or dead, with a turn of a switch. This was also what happened when plants weren't watered, when captive birds weren't fed, when people went off to war. Nothing more than the turn of a switch.

"Nowhere," he answered. "When a flame dies, it doesn't go anywhere. It just ceases to exist." He threw his fingers open in the air, like he was setting something free.

"That's not too comforting."

"No, it's not, but that's why we go out of our way to stay busy at Obon, right? To comfort ourselves by pretending souls are back from wherever they go when we die. Keeps our minds off oblivion. Keeps us from seeing the obvious truth."

"I don't think it's obvious at all."

Shoji didn't want to talk, but his mouth moved anyway. A cloud cast over the moon and the darkness grew opaque. He knew he was coming up to the bridge because of the sound of rushing water below. There would be no light back in town either. In wartime, night was absolute. The town was dead. *See?* he thought. *This is what death is like.*

Yet, in the dark, there was movement. Not just the animals and insects that lived for the night. The darkness itself moved, like a living, breathing thing. The night allowed him to see what it wanted him to see, and hid other things. Kanako's face had become a shadow. Shoji could still make out her eyes, her thin jaw, her breasts, but he could not tell if she was still smiling. "I wanted to thank you for helping us out the other day," he offered. "For buying the book, and for getting Kono off our backs."

"You're welcome."

"He didn't hurt you or anything, did he?"

"Or anything."

As they reached the middle of the bridge, the air turned cold. Shoji shivered a bit. He leaned onto the railing and found it moist, sandy. He rubbed the grit between his fingers. Everything was always damp in Japan. "Why do you hang out with such a jerk, anyway?"

He heard her laugh, saw her finally smiling. "Kono-chan is okay, Sho-chan. He just likes getting his way, that's all. He calls the shots and does as he pleases. I like that."

"Are you *mad?* Listen, Kono might do whatever he pleases now, but in a few weeks, he'll be drafted and he'll have to fall in line then. And if he survives the war, he'll be good for nothing but laying roads or maybe becoming a yakuza. Either way, he won't be calling any shots then."

"If any of us live that long, Sho-chan," said Kanako. Suddenly, her voice was angry, too. "Besides," she went on. "who are you to talk? There's something about you, like how you insist on getting beat up all the time instead of letting Kono-chan just have his way. You're okay, too. I told him that, you know."

Shoji felt himself blush again. He was certain Kanako saw this time. He felt as if he was glowing like the sun.

"You're probably right," she said. "You'll grow up to be some great scientist, and you'll travel and see faraway places. Kono-chan might be working for some construction foreman, but I've got a feeling he won't live that long. Why not let him have his freedom now? Now, someone like Shima-san, he won't be straying far from home."

"Shima?" Shoji's eyes widened a bit. "But . . . but he's just like me."

Kanako laughed harder. The river seemed to laugh with her. "Are you kidding? You might have the same taste for boring books, but he's not like you at all. More to the point," she said, drawing closer, "you're nothing like him, or most people we go to school with. Except maybe Kono-chan."

The moon emerged from behind the clouds. Its silver haze masked the small, insignificant stars. As it came overhead, its light poured onto Kanako's face from behind the mountain peaks. Shoji saw she was looking at him, unwavering. Her eyes, like deep pools of *sumi*, perfect black ink. Shoji thought of the wet, sweaty blouse she wore on the day she'd bought the book for him. That was the day she disappeared with Kono. And it was around this time that he realized why he'd decided to come here instead of studying in his room. When he noticed she wasn't turning away, he also became aware of his erection.

One morning, about a week earlier, Shoji had awoken to find his father rummaging through his closet. "I need some extra pillows for the clinic," Yasu said. The previous night had been sweltering. Shoji had kicked off his summer futon. His penis was standing at attention, like a proud soldier. As he fumbled for cover, Yasu laughed. "Sho!" he cried. "Savour your erections. Remember these moments when all you can think about is sticking your prick in a jar of warm honey, because they aren't going to last forever." Shoji was too busy adjusting his robe to say that he'd never given any thought to jars of honey, never mind sticking his dick in one.

Shoji reached out and touched Kanako's face. He pulled her closer. Faltering, he leaned forward, treading on the newness of the experience. Minuscule beads of water flew upward from the river below, falling on their faces. She smelled like cherries. For all his understanding of time and space, Shoji at that moment wished for something utterly childish. He wished for time to stop. He wished he and Kanako could be framed in the moment, with the singing fountain of emotions, absolutely happy, forever and ever. Their lips pushed against each other, crushed repeatedly, before he felt Kanako pulling away. "See," she whispered, "you're just like Kono-chan."

There was movement in the direction of the shrine. "Kanako!" a stern voice called out from the dark. "Are you there?"

Kanako pushed Shoji so hard he almost fell off the bridge. "I have to go!" she whispered. "My father's already in a bad mood because everyone ignores the shrine during Obon."

"Wait!" Shoji called out as loudly as he would dare, but Kanako was already gone. She was off the bridge and disappearing into the dark woods.

The taste of her lips lingered. The clean, fresh smell of her hair. The hardness between his legs. The ache in his arms. When the moon hid behind a cloud again, Shoji was left in the dark with only his desires. Licking his lips, rubbing his penis through his trousers, he knew he was a pathetic sight. So out of control. So irrational. He left quickly, feeling at once guilty, bewildered, elated and, for the first time, conspiratorial. The image of his best friend crying and striking at the ground on that summer day slipped in and out his thoughts. He recalled the heat as they both watched Kanako and Kono disappear down the road. He could hear Shima's anguished voice. It did not leave him alone. Yet, neither did the taste of her lips.

As he turned around to take his first step homeward, he did not notice the subtle quake in reality. The quiet detail that later ate up his being—just like the cancer that would eventually kill him.

When he eventually died on that rainy day in Milwaukee with his family watching over his last breath, he would recall this moment. If Toshi was right—if Shoji's spirit drifted out of his body after he died, to the wall of mirrors framing all of time in all of reality—

then Shoji would be witness to this moment forever. He would watch for all of eternity, and relive the kiss, the erection and the guilt. He would witness his younger self, in all the confusion and all the darkness, forgetting the book at the foot of a tree, back by the shrine.

HOT POT

WHEN TOSHI STARTED WORKING FOR SCREECH MOVERS
Limited in Toronto, he noticed that people were moving from
neighbourhoods where all the houses looked different from each
other to suburbs where they looked exactly the same.

It seemed to Toshi that people were moving away from the city
in hordes. This was because the houses in the city were eating them
alive, according to Mildred's new lover. "You hammer down a new
floor, and the ceiling falls on you," said Rosanne, who had the eyes
of a panther. She was strumming her guitar on the lawn of her new
duplex as they hauled the furniture inside.

Toshi nodded. When he wasn't working, it seemed he spent
most of his time readjusting the doors in the old Victorian town-
house, retiling the bathroom, touching up cracks in the ceiling. As
he hauled the easy chair from the truck, Millie ran back and forth
across the lawn, fussing about which crate should go where. Rosie
was calmer, as if the music anchored her.

Mildred and Rosie had been friends for a while but became
close when Rosie started taking Mildred to AA meetings. Everyone
was talking about this new band in town called Head as if they'd

appeared in the sky overnight instead of drifting among the streets of Toronto for seven years. Kei and Telly were constantly touring. Back in the old apartment, there had always been girls calling for Telly. Mildred screamed about "the sluts and the whores," then crashed in her bedroom with some vodka.

"Sluts and whores," Mr. Man would repeat over and over in her doorway as she spun into oblivion. Her translucent skin turned pink when she became angry. Otherwise, she was as pale as vague memories.

Rosie was hanging around the apartment then, because Kei had included a couple of her songs in the sets and, later, on Head's first CD. Later still, another local band that had already made it onto the American charts picked one of Rosie's songs up, and she became a rich woman. She was in truth ready to leave Head behind her, but before she did, she confessed her feelings for Millie.

Millie waited until Kei and Telly found their Victorian row-house to announce she wouldn't be moving with them. She moved first to Rosie's crumbling bungalow in Cabbagetown, an area known for its churches and vagrants. A couple of months after Toshi and Mitsuyo moved up from Milwaukee, just after Head started its tour of northern Ontario, Millie asked Toshi if the new moving company he was working for could help them move to Mississauga.

Toshi and Kenny, his boss from Newfoundland, along with Max, Kenny's brother-in-law, moved Mildred and Rosanne to a street on which it was impossible to tell one house from the next. Still, they seemed happy. Millie and Rosie took Tai Chi and pottery together at the local community centre. Rosie even taught guitar and songwriting classes there, even though she could afford to just sit at home and write music. Mildred gained some weight, and there was even colour in her cheeks. They went for walks down the treeless streets, often holding hands. On their block, one family was shocked, while the rest either didn't know or didn't care.

The president of Screech Movers Limited was rugged, square-jawed and smart. Kenny and Max swapped a lot of Newfie jokes. Listening to them made Toshi shiver. He could not imagine telling Jap jokes and laughing. Kenny looked like nothing could hurt him, not even being a Newfie in the big city.

For the most part, Toshi was glad to have moved to Toronto. Other than Kenny and Max, he didn't know many people yet, but he knew himself well enough to know that this could be a blessing. He had always lived on the periphery of any crowd, and that's where he was most comfortable. He had often been the centre of attention while growing up, for all the wrong reasons, and that was never fun. And he liked Kenny and Max.

He often went for walks, alone or with Angie, on Queen Street or on the beach, watching the sailboats and seagulls. People with skins of all different hues came to the lakefront for picnics. On a sunny day, there was nowhere better to be despite the smell of the dead, polluted waters.

The shelves were overflowing with rice cookies, instant noodles, dried kelp and bonito stock. Packages wearing bright colours and often a cute cartoon animal lined both sides of the aisles. There was Japanese-style curry as well as instant custard mix. There were pickled cabbage, meat-filled dumplings and fish cakes in the refrigerator. And there was rice.

Mitsuyo wished someone from the house would come with her when she shopped for Japanese food. Then she could buy one of the large, heavy bags of rice, rather than a small one that never lasted long. Kei, Toshi and Telly seemed interested only in eating the food she cooked, not in helping her shop for it. Angie was obviously avoiding her as much as possible. And bringing Mr. Man was out of the question.

"Hayakawa-san!" shouted the shop owner from behind the counter. His wife stuck her head out from the back room where she

233

was wrapping the daikon in plastic. The husband pulled a page of the *Toronto Star* lining one of the crates. It was the entertainment section. "This is your son, isn't it, Hayakawa-san?" he asked eagerly, pointing to a photograph among the newsprint. "You must be very proud."

His wife came out of the back to join them, wiping her hands on her apron, smiling and nodding. "Yes, it's that Kei-san," she chimed in. "It's always nice to see Japanese succeeding, isn't it? It makes us proud, too." A few white people in grey and black clothes peered from behind the counter, wondering what was being said in Japanese. Maybe something about new and exciting things to eat raw.

Mitsuyo found she could only smile and nod. She remembered that before she moved to Toronto, she had in fact been proud of Kei. He had not followed through on her plans to make him a concert pianist, but at least he was making money as a musician. Even when he seemed to be languishing in those awful apartments, she believed it would be just a matter of time before success found him. She of course would never tell him that.

But now she was living with him and Telly in Toronto. Now she saw how Kei's band was actually being mentioned in the newspapers. When she saw how they were always away, playing, and how they had even cut a CD, and when she saw how they still lived in a rundown rowhouse, empty of any furniture except the things she'd brought from Milwaukee, she wondered what it had all been for. She thought about Carnegie Hall as she filled her basket with packages of ramen.

When she got home, she put away the groceries and brewed some tea. Warming her hands with the cup, she stepped out onto the veranda and breathed in the sunshine. She looked across the tops of parked cars and saw her neighbour, a stout woman with white hair whose name she never remembered, sweeping her porch across the street. Mitsuyo waved. The woman saw her, and smiled a smile brighter than the floral patterns on her dress before turning away and going into her house.

Mitsuyo's smile fell back into the solemn frown that seemed engraved on her face now. When she wasn't thinking of Kei, she thought of Toshi, who was out either moving furniture or flirting with Angie. Mitsuyo knew. Oh, she knew. They weren't fooling anyone. Mitsuyo could feel her mind going brittle. Her knees and spine rattled when she walked. She felt too tired most days even to change out of her nightgown. She felt utterly alone, even though she wasn't. Telly and Mr. Man were always home.

Mitsuyo never knew what to do with them. It was like having pets that were simply unlovable. Telly had become unbearably sullen, but even she could not blame him, seeing the kind of week he'd been having. Head was back in Toronto for a while, playing local gigs for a few weeks before going on the road again. As soon as he got home, Telly learned that Millie and Rosie were moving into a house in the suburbs. Then Kei fired him from the band.

The evening had started out pleasantly enough. Even Mitsuyo was in a cheery mood with both her sons close by. They were sitting in the living room, sipping wine on the couch that was as warm and cozy as mashed potatoes. Mitsuyo had got used to the water pipe that was always present. Then Kei announced that the band had found a new bassist, not even taking Telly aside to give him the news. Mitsuyo often marvelled at how much Kei could be like his father. Kei was more emotional than Shoji, though, and making announcements like this did not come easily to him.

"It wasn't my decision," Kei muttered. And of this, Mitsuyo had no doubt. She knew that if nothing else, Telly's presence was comforting to Kei. Telly was familiarity, and Kei had so few things in his life that were familiar. Still, he was sounding more defensive than he should have. "Everyone in the band feels you're holding us back. It's nothing personal, for fuck's sake. We just need a stronger bass line, and you're not showing up for enough rehearsals to give us one."

The wineglass was half full when it shattered against the wall. The glass sounded like chimes as fragments fell onto the hardwood floor. The beige wall bled. Mitsuyo ran to the kitchen for a rag. Angie rushed to Telly and held him by the shoulders. She could not bring herself to look at Kei, who was already on his way to the bedroom. Angie shielded her eyes from most things unpleasant. Mitsuyo watched Kei disappear around the corner. Kei looked so much like Shoji from behind.

Since then, Telly spent most his time drinking and taking sedatives. He appeared from his room only once or twice a day, stumbling off to the kitchen in dishevelled jeans and a T-shirt to eat anything that didn't require cooking. Whatever he chose would be all over the floor by the time he went back up to his bedroom. Mitsuyo would have to clean everything, because she knew Angie would never get around to it. Mr. Man sometimes helped by filling a plastic pail with Pine-Sol and carrying it around while Mitsuyo mopped.

Mitsuyo tried her best to be patient with Telly. She recalled how Telly was such a little boy when Kei first brought him to the house. Bigger than Kei, but certainly smaller than Toshi. She could clearly see Telly's soup-bowl bangs, freckles and buckteeth. He seemed awed by everything Japanese in the house, from the calligraphy scrolls hanging on the living-room wall, to the Ultraman bust on the piano. He could never bring himself to eat sashimi, but loved tempura, especially the sweet potato. He had been Kei's first and only friend for a very long time.

Whenever she saw him sitting alone, she offered to make him some tempura, making it a point to mention the sweet potato. Whether he understood her or not was never clear, even the one time he flipped her the finger before curling up to sleep. Oprah was on, and Mitsuyo watched for a while before turning it off. Telly was snoring before the first commercial.

Summer was yielding to autumn, and there was an edge to the wind. Kei said he would be off on another tour soon, so Mitsuyo made one last attempt at reconciling her son with his friend by making *chanko-nabe*. Any of the Mongolian-style hot pot dishes adopted by the Japanese would have sufficed, but *chanko-nabe* was the most lavish. She asked Toshi to run to both the butcher and the fish market and buy sliced beef, chicken, shrimp, scallops, mussels and clams. She went to the Japanese grocer herself for some tofu, napa, fresh shiitake mushrooms and clear noodles. Then she made a broth from bonito flakes and threw everything in to stew.

The soup bubbled noisily in the large chrome pot at the middle of the table. *Chanko-nabe* was favoured by sumo wrestlers, as the high-calorie dish ensured weight gain. It also promoted camaraderie among the fighters. It was hard not to get close to someone with whom you were sharing food from the same pot simmering in front of you, the wet aroma of steam wrapping itself around everyone like a mother's hug.

At dusk, just around the time when the streetlights began to flicker, Hawke appeared at the door with a case of Sleeman's. He came over often on nights when he wasn't working at the Twisted Neon, and he seemed earnestly to treasure every moment he spent with Kei.

Mitsuyo poked at the hot pot under the kitchen's naked light-bulb. She was disappointed that Telly had not come down for dinner. Even as the food disappeared quickly, she kept throwing glances toward the stairs. She looked occasionally at Kei also, but he seemed oblivious and was stuffing his cheeks like a hamster. Everyone was feeding hungrily. Hawke could not refill his bowl fast enough, and made frequent trips to the refrigerator for beer. Mr. Man offered a rare smile. Even Angie was enthusiastically picking at the tofu and greens while Mitsuyo made clucking sounds with her tongue.

When the pot was nearly empty, Mitsuyo threw in some rice to make *ojiya*. The rice softened, absorbing flavours from the meat, seafood, and vegetables they had devoured earlier. Eventually the soup began percolating, singing happily that the best was yet to come.

Mitsuyo seasoned the mixture with some salt and soy sauce, then ladled it into individual rice bowls. She smiled as she handed a bowl to Hawke, and kindly told him to eat because an extra few pounds could mean the difference between life and death for a bouncer. Hawke snorted when Toshi translated. Fragments of leftover meat and vegetables dotted the gruel. Everyone attacked their bowls as if they were having their first meal in weeks. Mr. Man alone sat unmoving and not eating, staring at the ceiling as if he couldn't believe that it wouldn't come crashing down on all of them.

"What's the matter with *him?*" Mitsuyo asked Kei.

Hawke took Mr. Man's bowl and waved it under the old man's deformed nose. Mr. Man suddenly gave a painful yell and fell back in his chair. He scrambled to his feet like a marionette jerked up on its strings. His eyes were wide with horror. He opened his mouth as if to speak. Nothing emerged from the dark cavern of rotting teeth but a scream so loud and a whistle so terrible that it haunted Mitsuyo for the rest of her life.

"Japs!" he cried out. "You're fucking Japs!" A trail of spittle unfurled from his trembling lips. Kei rolled his eyes and sighed. "Japs!" Mr. Man kept screaming. "I am not an animal (*tweet!*), you goddam *bastards!*" Stumbling, he locked his gaze on each of them for a fraction of a breath. Hawke reached for him, but Mr. Man waved the hand away. Then he bolted out of the kitchen and ran to the front door, which he swung open so hard its loose hinges nearly gave way. Barefoot, Mr. Man faded into the last remaining twilight.

They all stood at the front entrance, bewildered. The evening breeze coming in from the lake was too cold to be comfortable. A car drove by, spilling rap music as it went. The stairs creaked, and a familiar voice called down from above. "What the fuck's going on? Can't a guy get any fucking sleep around here?" Telly came down the stairs, scratching his belly under a wrinkled black T-shirt.

Hawke had his napkin stuffed down the collar of his shirt like a bib. Grains of rice were stuck in his thick moustache. He held a pair of chopsticks in one hand as he looked up at Telly. "Mr. Man's gone crazy," he said.

Telly squinted as he looked out the door. "I got news for you, fat boy," he said. "Mr. Man's always been crazy." Then he looked at Kei as if everything was his fault. They held each other's gaze for a while before Telly chuckled and sat down to put his shoes on. "Well, I guess we all better go looking for him now, right?"

They ran into the street and split up. Mitsuyo decided to stay home in case Mr. Man came back, and was irritated when she realized Angie wasn't doing the same. As if she didn't need any help cleaning up after supper. And Toshi looked on as Angie followed Kei toward Queen Street, two steps behind him like a pale shadow. Telly and Hawke went toward the lake, so Toshi decided to walk toward downtown. The sky was indigo and empty. The CN Tower and the SkyDome, the stadium that resembled nothing more than a giant white conch shell, stood illuminated a short distance from the high-rises in the city's banking sector. Toshi stepped onto an overpass crossing the Gardiner Expressway and watched as galaxies of headlights and taillights flowed in both directions with him standing at the centre of the universe.

So many lights, so many souls, so many stories. Over there on a high-rise, in a point of light no larger than a pinhead, he thought, if he tried hard, he could see a mother breastfeeding a newborn. Farther away, he thought he could make out a lawyer going over his depositions in an otherwise dark, abandoned law office. He imagined inside one car was a family of noisy children and weary parents going out to a downtown restaurant. He could very easily have forgotten about Mr. Man had he allowed himself. The sights and sounds of the countless separate lives surrounding him merged into a familiar, melancholy hum.

JEALOUSY

ANGIE CALLED KEI FROM TORONTO EVERY NIGHT WITH some news about Mr. Man. He had regained much of his memory, but none of his sanity. Mr. Man's real name, as it turned out, was John Banker. His son flew up from Boise as soon as he learned his father was still alive and was living in Canada.

Kei and Angie had found Mr. Man in an alley off Queen Street, curled up next to a Dumpster. The broken glass strewn on the ground had shredded his bare feet. He flinched when he saw Kei, but did not resist when they put him in the back seat of a cab. He was still mumbling, peppering his gibberish with the word "Jap." Angie watched Kei's back as he sat in the front of the taxi with the driver. The familiar storefronts now seemed to fascinate him.

They went to St. Joseph's Hospital, where a doctor sewed Mr. Man's feet with twenty-seven stitches and gave him a sedative that made him calm enough to remember his real name.

John Banker was a veteran of the Second World War, a survivor of the Bataan Death March. The march was not the kind of thing that Mr. Man could fold up neatly like a blanket and put away after a good night's sleep. The experience had stuck to his ribs. His malnourished, pale skin had stretched across the same ribs while the Japanese were starving John Banker in Siberian POW camps.

December 7 was a date forever etched into Toshi and Kei's consciousness. On Pearl Harbor Day, every year, taunts from O'Connor and the others rained on them like bombs from B-29s. Because of the international dateline, the war began on December 8 for everyone on the Asian side of the Pacific Ocean, including John Banker, who was stationed at Nichols Field in the Philippines. Bataan was five hundred square miles of peninsula surrounded by waters bluer than the eyes of American movie stars. The fish was good, and the people were friendly, although the jungle was full of stomach-churning diseases. Still, John considered it an okay post. Until the Japanese came along.

On a painfully bright day when the sun burned the sands on the deserted beach and bare skin roasted like a pig on a spit, John looked up just before noon at the infinite, empty sky. He saw planes like black fish swimming in clear water, coming toward them with the rising-sun insignia on their glimmering scales. The American planes were lined up neatly, like bowling pins. The destruction was fiery, fast and loud. The fuel dump took a direct hit.

The fighting lasted until April. The Japanese infantry landed, and John knew things were going to get difficult when he saw a few Japs impaling themselves on the barbed wire so others could use their bodies to climb over the American defence perimeter. The impaled were screaming and shouting in Japanese. John always assumed they were glorifying the emperor or Buddha or something. Had he comprehended Japanese, he would have understood they were letting everyone know how it *really, really* hurt to sacrifice one's body this way. A couple of them were crying for their mothers.

There was a lot of walking after the U.S. surrender. History remembered it as the Death March, but the American soldiers, already malnourished from months of low rations, staggered more than marched. Wobbled in the insane tropical heat with no food or water. They dared not crawl, because an overly enthusiastic Jap bayonetted anyone who fell.

The sun was blistering the back of his neck when John noticed a few Japs emerging from the bushes up ahead of him, slapping each other on the back, giggling and zipping up their flies. They looked as if they were coming home after bowling. When he got closer, he noticed the body of a young Filipina woman lying on the ground on her back. Her torn clothes were gathered around her thin neck. She lay still, a trickle of blood tracing a thin path from her lips to the back of her neck. Her small breasts were rising and falling, riding a wave.

Japs were pushing a few American men off cliffs, just for laughs. Anyone who collapsed from exhaustion, or was walking too slowly, wound up on the wrong end of a rifle. Some begged for their lives, but seldom were any spared. John was amazed he could listen to so much screaming and still not go crazy. But if he did, could he tell? The majestic mountain peaks on the island looked strangely warped. He never knew there was such burning hunger outside of hell. But then he realized, who was to say he wasn't there already?

From the day they first put on their uniform, soldiers were taught to be proud, of their uniform, of their country, of themselves. But it was hard for John to be proud while watching his buddies speared and shot, left by the roadside to be run over by a truck. It was hard to be proud while watching other guys vomiting on their shoes because they drank filthy water from a swamp. But it was harder *not* to drink. It had been the first water made available to them after two days of marching.

John Banker marched for four days and was stuffed into a boxcar on the morning of the fifth. Heat swelled in his head like a bright red balloon. His knees gave away in the crowded steel oven, and once he sat on the floor, there was no room to stand up again. It was a couple of degrees cooler below anyway. A warm rain was falling inside the train, and it took a minute for John to realize someone was vomiting on his head. Guys with dysentery were shitting themselves all over the place.

It was around this time that John Banker's memories started to fragment. He had no idea how many were dying around him. He barely recalled his name. He could remember, though, the taste of a rare steak washed down with a cold Miller. Memories of good times were like remembering the scent of flowers. They were all John would have over the next one thousand days. After a few days at a camp near Baguio, he was shipped through the Korean peninsula to Manchuria.

In northeastern China, John Banker no longer feared the heat. Now he dreaded the cold. The draft coming through the barracks cut through flesh, of which there was less and less on his bones anyway. All he and the others were given to eat was watered-down gruel, sometimes made from rice but more often from millet. Men were still falling from starvation and overwork. The men who died in winter, when the ground was frozen, didn't get a burial until spring.

The land was barren, as were his spirit and the spirit of everyone around him, the prisoners and the guards. Beyond the tall barbed-wire fences, all they could see was the windswept earth. In the fall, dust flew everywhere, homeless. In the winter it clung to the ground, refusing to yield. John walked around in a stupor until the guards yelled at him to do something. Whenever he didn't react fast enough, they beat him, their laughter ringing through his skull like church bells. One guard hit John's mouth with a rifle butt, and his front teeth went flying. That was when he started whistling as he talked.

On a day as cold as his spirit was dead, he was carting some coal across the compound when the rope around his waist came loose and his filthy, torn pants fell around his ankles. He tripped and fell flat, skinning his lips. A young captain named Sakamoto started laughing so hard he almost gagged while John stood up, spitting blood. The captain stopped laughing only when he saw John's big dick billowing in the breeze.

The Jap was still grinning, though, as he ran to John, who was pulling up his pants and licking his swollen lips. Sakamoto pulled his wallet from his breast. From it appeared a photograph of a pretty blond girl, sitting on a stool and smiling a stilted, awkward smile. John was sure the captain had stolen the picture from a care package sent to some prisoner. Maybe it was the prisoner's girlfriend. Maybe it was his sister. Sakamoto obviously didn't care who she was, just that she was blond.

"You have blond girlfriend?" Sakamoto asked John. It was the first time any Jap expressed any interest in hearing what he had to say.

Eyes twinkling like fairy dust, John smiled. "Sure (*tweet!*)," he said.

Sakamoto was not a bad-looking guy, except for his tight, thin lips. "Tell me," he said, leaning closer, pointing to his crotch. "When American girl is blond, hair down there is blond also?"

John couldn't remember the last time he laughed so loudly. "Not always," he answered, blinking. "Sometimes they shave it all off."

The captain could not have looked as shocked or delighted if he had heard Japan had won the war. He looked at the girl's picture in his hand, and swallowed, hard. "That is . . . very, very good," he finally said.

Since that day, Sakamoto hunted John around the camp to ask him about his girlfriend. John had to make up the answers. Her name was Lorelei, John told him. Sakamoto worked for weeks to put his mouth around that one.

"Wauwewai?"

"No, sir. Lorelei."

"How you spell?"

"L-O-R-E-L-E-I."

"Oh. . . . Wauwewai?"

According to John, Lorelei was blond, had breasts like water-melons, legs like bean sprouts, eyes like glass and lips like strawber-ries. She said little, ate less and fucked like a rabbit. She shaved her cunt, and when her pubic hair grew back, she dyed it a rainbow of colours. She gave blow jobs, rim jobs and was especially fond of bondage. John had to keep her locked up because otherwise she would be sleeping with all the neighbourhood boys. And their dogs. John and Lorelei did it everywhere: in the bathroom, the kitchen, the car, the park, public washrooms, the graveyard, church.

Sometimes Lorelei invited her friend, Rosalinda. She was a redhead, but otherwise, she and Lorelei could be twins. The three of them would do it at the local nursing home, kicking old men and women out of their beds, unless, of course, they wanted to join in. When they finished, they usually relaxed with a bottle of cham-pagne. Lorelei didn't smoke, but carried around a lighter and always lit John's cigarettes.

Sakamoto flared his nostrils like a bull and beads of sweat trickled down to his thin lips whenever John related these stories. He and Sakamoto sat down two or three times a week over the next few months, sharing a pot of hot tea in the office, across a deli-ciously warm stove. The frost on the window hid some truths that were too obvious. Sometimes, John would forget whether the lat-est details were consistent with earlier versions, but Sakamoto didn't seem to care.

John owed Lorelei a lot. Thanks to her, Sakamoto gave him canned meat, vegetables, fruit and cigarettes, usually stolen from American care packages. Unlike some of the other prisoners, John received his mail. More importantly, John's mail made it out of the camp. He asked his family back in Boise to send any pictures of blond women they could get their hands on—movie stars, calendar girls, John's cousin Patty. It didn't matter who it was as long as she had lots of cleavage. Cleavage could be the difference between a rotting carrot and a can of Spam.

Sometimes the photos made it through to John. Other times, they were mysteriously missing from the envelope. It didn't matter. They mostly wound up with Captain Sakamoto in the end anyway. If they did make it to John, though, he gave only half to Sakamoto and bartered the rest with other prisoners, usually for cigarettes.

On an especially cold day in November, a Jap colonel touring the area stopped at John's camp for inspection. Most days, there generally wasn't much for guards—especially the officers—to do except to kick and yell and spit at the prisoners. Sakamoto as usual was jerking off in his office. Pictures of blonds from Boise, Idaho, were scattered across his desk.

A framed work of calligraphy hung above the door. It read *Hissho*, which meant "certain victory." Sakamoto was very close to his own little certain victory, as the colonel's jeep pulled up to the gate. The snow scattered like frightened children.

John was on burial duty. He was in a hurry because the ground was starting to harden. Two of his friends had died in the past week. The extra rations John had shared with them couldn't hold back the tide of malnutrition. Despite all the extras he was getting from the captain, John also looked like a twig. The hunger still burned like acid. He watched the colonel go into the captain's barracks.

Sakamoto's hand was a blur over his crotch. "Wauwewai!" he called out to the photos on his desk. "Wauwewaaaaai!"

The Jap colonel's favourite pastime was polishing the samurai sword that he always carried tied to his belt. His second favourite was polishing his boots. His third was dusting. He was already in a bad mood that morning because of having to endure the smells of a POW camp, which never went away, even in winter. He especially hated the latrines. Having to shit outside was cold, but infinitely better than sharing the toilet with another human being. The thought of bare asses and naked dicks spreading germs through the air made him queasy. The sight of Captain Sakamoto whipping his dick around, casting bacteria in all directions, was the last thing the colonel wanted to see that morning.

He also didn't find the pictures of blond American cows arousing, or amusing. "Where did you get your hands on such filth?" he sputtered, foam shooting from his mouth. Sakamoto ran around with his pants down at his ankles, looking for a cloth with which to wipe his hands. For reasons the colonel himself did not quite understand—almost an instinctive reaction to anything threatening—he drew his blade. Having nothing else to do with it, he punctuated his curses by jabbing the air with his sword.

John Banker never got any Spam after that day.

Instead, Sakamoto, who after the colonel's visit wore a conspicuous scar across his thin lips, gave John all the most unpleasant chores. John had to clean the latrines, bury the dead, collect horse manure for fertilizer and do the guards' laundry. Instead of more rations for extra work, all John got were beatings. Sakamoto never said another word to John, even as he whipped the prisoner's backside himself.

No one was getting care packages from home any more, because the Japs were keeping them. The captain especially seemed intent on making sure no more smutty pictures of American women made it among his guards, much less the prisoners.

John Banker ate nothing but lifeless, thin gruel. People who fast for pleasure claim that when they stop eating completely, the hunger lasts only a few days, after which there is a period of sublime satisfaction. The prisoners in John's camp were fed just enough to keep the flames of hunger burning. The desire to eat became as urgent as the need to piss or crap. At every meal John looked for bits of meat or vegetables among his tepid gruel. He was always disappointed. He was hungry in his sleep.

He grew even thinner, and so did his mind, as if there wasn't enough skin and bone to contain his soul.

John Banker was sent home at the end of the war. Back among his family in Boise, he was a hero. He was also a lunatic who didn't know his own name. He disappeared one Easter weekend, around the time his son, Bruce, turned twelve years old.

"They're saying that he's well enough to go back to Boise."

Kei stared at the can of Molson Export in his hand and tried to remember where it came from.

"Kei, when are *you* coming home?" Angie's voice was fragmented. There was static on the line.

Shadows moved in the dimly lit motel room. The woman who had passed out in the van was coming to on the couch. She wore a sparkling blue tank top with painted jeans and had a mouth that was big and full and lined with perfect teeth. She looked at Kei like she really needed something to eat. He smiled at her tenderly, though his eyes remained hard. She sashayed over to him. "I'll call you tomorrow, baby," Kei remembered to say into the phone before hanging up. He hardly saw the girl's face before her tongue dove into his mouth.

Just as the girl's bony hands reached Kei's belt buckle, a familiar melody came floating over the din of the crowd. Someone had slipped Head's first album into the CD player, someone who didn't know that Kei could not stand to hear himself sing. He listened to music by others to allow a bit of their beauty to grace his soul, but listening to his own songs was like swallowing his own vomit. The guitar swelled and drilled into his ears.

Sanctuary in my own mind as I lie broken on the sidewalk.

The girl was still fumbling with his pants. He shoved her aside and strode over to the boom box sitting on the kitchen counter. The crowd was like a dark cloud, shapeless, shifting. Every night on tour it was the same. Like a tape looped onto itself, parallel events played out time and again. He turned the stereo off to a chorus of boos. Wiping his nose, he looked through a handful of CDs to find something, anything that might make him feel better.

"Kei?" It was Rodney, Head's new bassist. When Kei didn't respond, Rodney went on shyly. "Listen, man, I've never really had a chance to thank you properly for bringing me into the band. I mean, it's everything I ever wanted." Rodney hadn't shaved in days, but his whiskers were growing in patches. Kei tried to guess how old he was.

Everything he ever wanted? Kei stared at Rodney until he shifted uneasily on his feet. Looking around at the crowd, lost in a fog of cigarette and pot fumes, Kei wondered why this would be everything anyone would want. He looked at the girl he'd left behind by the wall. Her attention had turned elsewhere. Someone had spread a few lines of coke on the coffee table. Did it get better than this? The room spun like a carousel. He wanted to get off because he was getting sick.

Someone had turned the stereo back on, and he winced as "Sanctuary" started up again. He closed his eyes and saw Angie sitting on the bed in the old apartment. He could hear her voice, singing the song in a way he never could. When he opened his eyes again, the walls were collapsing around him. Jaime Saunders, too, had sung one of his songs. She also had changed the song simply by singing it with her own voice. He could hear her guitar, chords like river water running, running to nowhere. Such a long time ago.

"No, no, no, no," he mumbled, putting his hand on the CD r and dragging it off the counter. Rodney watched, wide-eyed outh agape. The music stopped with a crash.

e slid into Kei's nostrils and started poking around, making er. "Shit," he said, taking the cigarette from his mouth. He flung it over the railing and adjusted the guitar straps across his bare shoulders. The day was clear and warm. A couple of kids were playing hopscotch across the street, their blond hair shimmering in the sunshine. Angie sat at the corner of the veranda, laughing.

"When are you going to give up?" she asked, still smiling as she walked toward him. She caressed his back. "For God's sake, you've been trying for years. I mean, you have a CD out now. You're going to be a big star. It seems like such a little thing."

Kei wrinkled his nose. "Yeah, I suppose," he said, clasping the pick between his fingers. He strummed his guitar. The gentle chords flowed like sugar water from the amp behind him.

He switched to a minor key, which he preferred anyway. His fingers ran across the frets as if they feared for their lives. The sound broke the air into jagged pieces. But as grating as the scales were, they were like swan feathers compared with the chords that followed. Loud and dissonant, they protested against the blue lake-water and the bright clouds drifting by lazily. From the corner of his eye, he could see the kids across the street cover their ears and run into the house.

He layered a crystalline melody over the chords, hammering down on the strings, bouncing notes in every direction. He played through the progressions a few more times before finishing with a harmonic that flew away toward the horizon.

Angie kissed him on the cheek and whispered, "There, that's more impressive than being able to play guitar and smoke a cigarette at the same time."

Kei made a face. "But I've always wanted to be able to do that."

"Then you'd better keep practising," she said. And then added, as if she'd just remembered, "I love you." He pretended not to hear. There was no one left on the street.

That could not have been more than a few months ago, thought Angie, but at some moment between now and then, time had started to fold over onto itself. A day could seem like a year. She sat in the dim kitchen, sipping barley tea. Her flannel nightgown was warm, but her feet were bare. Her toes could feel winter coming.

It was already past one in the morning. It used to be that if she couldn't sleep, she could at least count on company from Mr. Man, who would be up until early morning. No one seemed to miss him, except maybe Toshi. Angie heard the floor groan behind her. When she turned, she saw Toshi standing in the doorway.

"Telly's gone," he said.

"I know," Angie replied.

"He said he was taking the train back to Milwaukee. I guess he wants to see his family."

Angie nodded. There was no family here for Telly any more.

"Was that Kei on the phone?"

The melody in her head was fading away.

"He sleeps with other girls when he's on tour, you know," he said, not quite looking at her. Angie's eyes grew wider. She hadn't realized Toshi thought of such things. What he was saying, though, was also old news.

"Don't you care?"

"It's not as if we're married, Toshi."

"Why do you stay with him?" Toshi recalled how Telly used to cheat on Millie, too. He sometimes wondered if Millie became a lesbian because Telly was hurting her so much. Angie said nothing.

"What do you mean, you're moving out?" her mother had asked.

"What do you think it means?" She wanted to pack as little as possible. She did remember to grab a couple of her vegetarian cookbooks from the kitchen that smelled of rotting meat.

"Alex called. He said you could have your job back."

"I don't want it back, Mom." The Plymouth outside honked. The neighbours would not be pleased. Why the hell did it take so long to pack so little?

"Please don't leave me here alone with him," her mother implored. "I don't think I could handle things without you."

A fragment of hope made Angie arch her eyebrow. She reached for her mother's hand. "You could come with me, Mom. Right now. While he's away."

"How can I let him come back and find the house empty?" Big beads of tears were falling freely down her mother's face. "If I could at least let him know I'm leaving. He didn't even leave a number where I could call him."

"He never does."

Her mother smiled at Angie, like some terminally ill patient who'd stopped asking why. "I can't go with you, dear." And the perfect lie fell into place between them, like it always did. "He's all I have."

Angie flew out to the street, where Kei's car was parked with the engine running. She threw her bag onto the back seat and climbed in. Kei flicked his cigarette out the window and drew Angie closer. His kiss was bittersweet, smoky chocolate. He drew back after a long time. "Ready to go?" he asked.

"Oh, yeah!" She laughed.

"I was looking at some beds for us," Kei said as he pulled the car away from the curb. "They have some cheap ones at the mattress store across from the Twisted Neon. We're not going to have much else in the house to start, though."

"It doesn't matter," Angie said. Nothing mattered any more—except Kei and his music. She looked back at the house where she grew up. She was startled to see her mother standing at the doorway, waving goodbye.

Angie had been thinking about her mother a lot lately. She tried to recall when she, too, became too lazy to confront truths. Sighing, she shook her head free of Toshi's question. She had often considered having her mother come and live with them, but there was Kei and Mitsuyo. She thought of how the only person who would be welcoming was Toshi. Angie thought about calling Kei again, even if it meant having to talk to some incoherent, drunk groupie. Toshi was still staring at her like a helpless puppy.

Toshi had played this scene out in his mind countless times—confronting her with the truth about his brother, seeing the knowledge free her. As usual, things were more complicated than he'd expected. And he was much clumsier than he'd imagined himself to be. The change from friendship to something more was not unexpected, but it was abrupt and awkward nonetheless. With nothing clever left to say, he reached out and grabbed her hand roughly.

Angie closed her eyes. Toshi was kind to her, and yet so trying. She never understood why she needed him to be trying. She desperately wanted her burdens, and Toshi could be a comfort and a burden at the same time. Still, she wished she could turn back. She wanted to pretend she never yearned for Toshi this way, but her life had become so cold, so hollow, she thought anything to help her forget might be a good thing. She had tried to forget her parents. Now she was trying to forget Kei.

Toshi was breathing harder as he pulled her toward him. They were like two long freight trains rolling at a snail's pace toward one another, unable to avoid the catastrophe they knew lay ahead. When they kissed, Angie noticed for the first time how similar Kei and Toshi were in their features, except that Toshi's jowls spilled over his collar. He scooped her into his arms. She was as light as a whisper. It was nothing carrying her up the stairs. The whole house seemed to shake with each step. The floorboards cried out loudly as he took her down the short corridor to the master bedroom. She lay in his arms, unmoving.

He was surprised by how calm he felt. The hum in his head softened, like the rush of the ocean when the wind dies. He lowered her onto the bed, and pulled her flannel nightgown over her head. Her naked beauty was ghostly white, immediate yet distant, like the works of art they saw together in the gallery. For the next while, Toshi saw himself as lean as Michelangelo's David, or, he remembered, Bruce Lee. Her soft wetness swallowed him whole, and he hung in the tension between yearning and gratification that seemed to stretch on forever.

They lay together afterward, tracing unintelligible images on each other's skin with their fingertips. Toshi wrapped his arms around her shoulders and squeezed. He could not believe how quiet everything had become.

Down the hall, the door to the bedroom Toshi shared with Mitsuyo was open. With only the harshness of the bedside lamp to illuminate the darkness, Mitsuyo lay in bed, staring at the ceiling, her eyes open wide, angry and afraid.

THE RAID

THERE WERE NO AIR RAIDS ON THE NIGHT OF OBON. The following evening, the planes appeared shortly after dinnertime.

Just before the sirens began to howl, Shoji had been at his desk, touching himself, thinking of Kanako kissing him in the woods. Wisps of air caressed his sweating forehead. He did not often think of women before books. What was happening to him?

Beneath his window, Yasu was standing at the front gate, trying to keep cool. Just the previous night, the street had been full of people on their way to the temple grounds. Yasu waved at his face with an intricately decorated fan. It was scented with the ethereal fragrance of sandalwood. He fanned the back of his neck, then spread his *yukata* open to fan his chest. Beads of sweat traced a path across his abdomen. He opened the bottom half of his robe and waved at his legs and what hung in between. He was about to remove his loincloth to gain better access, when a familiar voice called out from the gate.

"Hello? Good evening. Terrible heat, isn't it?" It was the same voice that had called out from the woods to Kanako and Shoji on the bridge. The voice that had interrupted that delicious mid-summer night's wet dream.

Shoji could hear Yasu reply, "Ah, Joko-san, it's been a while. Hello, Kanako-chan."

Hearing Kanako's name made Shoji stand up hastily, a cold fist gripping his belly. *Why was Joko here?* he thought. Had he seen him with Kanako the previous night? Could she have given him away? He didn't dare show himself at the window. He stopped breathing as if he might hear better. He wished the crickets weren't so noisy. What made insects call out in the darkness anyway?

Joko had inherited Kaminohashi Shrine from his father just two years before Japan invaded China. He had been fat all his life and wasn't about to let a little thing like war change him. There were ways of getting by. Kono used the money he extorted from Shoji and Shima for extra potatoes. Otama lived on stolen ham and rice dumplings. And Joko was never short of food. Yasu once told Shoji that anything to do with prayer and fortune was lucrative when souls were flying out of bodies at an alarming rate.

"Is there any of that delicious ham still available?" Joko asked, smiling. He wore a white shirt with grey slacks, both spotted with perspiration. Out of his ceremonial robe, he looked like he had little to do with the divine. He often bartered rice and fish for Ryoko's smoked meat. She was getting less ham and bacon delivered now that the enemy had blown up the roads and bridges, but he was unable to comprehend this.

"You'd better ask my wife," said Yasu, who looked like he was still considering removing his loincloth and fanning his crotch. "Though I think we gave the last bit away to that Nozaki boy. I treated him the day before yesterday for malnourishment. He was getting so skinny he couldn't piss without falling over backward."

Joko sucked air between his teeth loudly. "Ah, yes. Life is difficult for us all right now. And people can hardly pay alms when they don't have enough to eat."

"You don't say?" said Yasu, expertly feigning surprise. "I'd have thought people around here would rather starve than anger a god. Every time some kid is tricked into flying a plane into the side of a ship, his family is paying you what little they have for a good luck charm made of paper. What does good luck on a suicide mission mean, exactly?"

Joko sniffed the air. "It's true, Doctor, we've been busy at the shrine, but at the same time, people seem to consider war and hard times as excuses to steal. I can't tell you how many times thieves have pilfered our alms box."

"Only a lowlife would steal from a shrine," added Kanako. "Isn't that right, Father?"

Hearing her voice made something slam shut in Shoji's head. He knocked over his chair when he stood up. The wooden steps felt warm beneath his feet as he went down the staircase. He moved gingerly. The smell of a burning mosquito coil stung his nostrils as he stepped outside into the fetid summer air. He saw Kanako, standing in a blouse and skirt, almost translucent in the lantern's pale orange hue. He saw from how the light moved in her eyes that she had not given them away after all.

Yasu ignored his son and kept his gaze on Joko. "Surely, it must be a good time for you," he said. "Everyone is going on about this Divine Wind nonsense and acting so crazy, I'm starting to think I'm only the only sane person left in the village." He grabbed at his crotch and scratched vigorously.

"Dr. Hayakawa!" Joko seemed unsure whether he was offended more by Yasu's words or his actions. "Are you saying I do not suffer? Much of what I do is solely intended to give comfort to members of our community during these difficult times. If families are unable to pay, I often give my services for free. This in spite of the fact that I haven't even been able to afford paying Kanako an allowance since the war started."

Shoji blinked. He looked at Kanako, who looked back at him and smiled.

Shoji would never know whether the Americans were aware of Obon and, if they were, whether they cared. They came the next night, though, as Yasu and Joko argued in the street, oblivious to Shoji and Kanako and how they looked at each other. The air-raid sirens wailed, sounding as if the spirits of the dead were lamenting their return to the underworld. But if the dead could not return to the living, war could always send the living to the dead. Suddenly the darkness was alive with people shouting and screaming.

"Shit!" Yasu shouted. "We've got to get to the backyard!" No one noticed that the crickets had fallen silent.

Ryoko and Otama met them out back, where they all filed into the unusually large and well-furnished air-raid shelter. "What is this?" asked Kanako, feeling the wood panelling on the wall. "A cellar?"

Shoji looked at his sandals.

"A cellar?" said Yasu. His eyes bulged, and he scratched his crotch more vigorously. "Why, Kanako-chan, this is our air-raid shelter!" He seemed offended that the shelter that looked nothing like a shelter was not recognized as such.

"It's a bit small, don't you think?" Ryoko said, smiling. There was no door. Cries of panic were still drifting in from outside.

"Here," said Ryoko. "Put these on." She passed out hoods made of thick cotton that supposedly provided some protection from sparks and falling debris. She was glad she always kept a few extras in the bomb shelter in case of guests. They all put the hoods on. Otama had fashioned some of them from discarded kimono and floor cushions. These were decorated with a bright floral pattern.

"We don't have anything like this at the shrine," said Kanako, still feeling the walls.

"We can't afford to build one," said Joko, looking at Shoji's father.

The sirens were slowly drowned out by the sound of hot engines cutting through the sky and the horrible, deathly whistles of large masses falling through the air. Space seemed to shatter when the first few bombs hit. Even in the shelter, the air began to smell of fire. Shouts for water could be heard in the distance. Yasujiro barked at Otama to extinguish the lantern. Tremors ran through the earth, and the wood panels in the shelter shook. The screams grew louder and more numerous.

Yasu muttered, "We could use some real divine wind right now."

Shaking, screaming, breathing and his own heartbeat was all Shoji could hear in the dark. A few more explosions jiggled his bladder and cut through his skull like an axe. The air stilled, like a sudden, hushed gasp.

"Dr. Hayakawa, your front gate is on fire!" someone shouted from the street.

Ryoko rushed out before her husband could stop her. Shoji and Kanako also jumped out from the security of the shelter, because they were young and believed they were going to live forever. The men, who were left abandoned in safety, looked at each other for the first time with a kind of understanding, almost affection. It wasn't easy being men, working their entire lives building sanctuaries for their families, surrounding it with a fortress of high walls. Their wives and children still danced gaily into the perils at every opportunity. Yasu and Joko sighed and dragged their feet up the steps.

Smoke immediately smothered their breathing. The sky was lit by a fire that was almost festive were it not for the frightful prayers for mercy. Hurried excitement nonetheless filled the air, making some giddy.

"*Kuso!*" Shoji yelled when he reached the front of his house and saw people running in every direction with buckets. Sandbags travelled from one pair of hands to another, piled around fires that had grown too large to extinguish and could only be contained. Shoji was relieved to find that only the front gate of his house was burning. The house itself was still untouched, but the wind was rising, bringing the sparks dangerously close.

Otama ran to the water reserve at the side of the house. Filling wooden pails, she handed them to Shoji and Yasu, who ran back to the front and hurled the water at the gate. It took a few trips back and forth. Yasu fell once, and his robe fell open, billowing like ghosts. He yelled at Shoji to keep going. "Just leave me!" he cried, as if they were trying to run from an enemy's hail of bullets. The fire died before long, gasping for air.

Yasu shouted at Shoji to get some blankets. "We have to get on the roof and smother any sparks that might land there!"

Joko felt faint. He looked like a fish sucking water, but at the same time the excitement was intoxicating. He stood rocking back and forth, with a profoundly stupid smile on his face, as if the innocent, angelic child trapped in the fat, ugly toad was emerging in the firelight. But when Kanako took his hand, the toad regained some control. "The shrine," Joko gurgled between gasps. "Kanako, go see if the shrine is all right."

Without answering, only throwing a quick glance in Shoji's direction, Kanako bolted through the gate and faded into the smoky darkness. Her look was enough for Shoji to get another erection in spite of everything.

Shoji looked up at the roof, where Yasu, stripped down to his loincloth, scurried over the tiles like a skinny spider. He was still wearing his floral cotton hood. "Sho!" he cried down, swooping about with a blanket, chasing away the sparks that drifted on the wind like hungry moths. "Get your bony ass up here!"

Either the screams died down or were drowned in the resuming rumble of B-29 engines. The sound seemed to come from the direction of the Maruyama Chemical Plant, just beyond the shrine.

Yasujiro looked like he might slip and fall at any time. More sparks were riding the smoke, drifting toward the house. The shouting grew louder again. Countless catastrophes were occurring simultaneously. All Shoji could do was choose which to deal with first. And for Shoji, there really was no choice at all. "Sorry, Father!" he shouted up to the roof. He started running, past Ryoko, who stood crying with one hand over her mouth, trying to maintain some fragment of civility under very uncivilized circumstances. Shoji ran out the gate and followed Kanako toward the Kaminohashi Shrine.

Chaos swelled around him as he ran, arms tightly by his sides. The flames grew bigger and more vicious, the cries more desperate. Heat cut into his exposed skin and left scars, but he was barely aware. The air was heavy, and the smoke felt like sandpaper in his chest, but he hardly noticed this either. He ran past houses that had collapsed, and past people who were trying to drag a woman out from under a fallen beam. As he ran with his upper torso at stiff attention, the thought that he might stop and help never crossed his mind. And memories are funny things, because he later would not even remember seeing that house.

He was fast, but she was surprisingly fast also. He panicked when he couldn't see her ahead of him. Hungry hands reached out for him as he ran, some bloody, all covered in dirt, everyone pleading. He saw a woman burning. Her cotton hood had caught fire. Shoji removed his and threw it aside. Slowly, his stiff arms began to move, propelling him forward as he ran, faster and faster, but not fast enough.

He finally caught sight of her just as the sound of the crowd receded behind him. The night was clear, and the wind was high above the river. Moonlight fell upon her figure running away from him across the bridge. She had removed her hood as well, and the wind combed her hair. She shimmered, like water in sunshine. A shaft of fire suddenly rose on the mountainside, then another, and another. The thunder followed two heartbeats behind. Shoji knew the Maruyama Chemical Plant was gone. In the end, it hadn't mattered how much mugwort had been collected.

The fire on the mountain was breathing loudly. The roar of engines fell onto them from overhead. Kanako stopped, about three-quarters of the way across the bridge. She looked up to the dark sky from which rained a loud, piercing whistle. Shoji watched her, and all he could think of was how she always stood with her back perfectly straight. She never seemed ashamed of anything. At a time when Japan was feeding its young to the war, when good people stole scraps of food, when countless people's lives were being wasted with everyone passively riding the currents of time, Kanako seemed so unaffected, so pure.

The first bomb fell about twenty yards upstream, sending a pillar of water into the air. Mist flew in every direction, blooming like flower petals. The shock wave was enough to shake a few beams loose on the bridge, and Shoji saw Kanako struggling for balance. He stopped running.

Another bomb was falling, falling as though it could fall forever. Half the bridge blew up along with Kanako, sending shrapnel and wood splinters everywhere. The wall of air hit Shoji's face hard, sending him flying backwards. A sharp pain shot up his leg. The earth gave way and he fell flat on his back. He smelled fire and water, and the bridge and the trees burning. Above him, small, billowing flames—fragments of burning wood—rode the wind. Before passing out, he saw an ancient cedar tree toppling over, its branches alive with fire, falling onto him like a soldier whose bravery wasn't enough to stop the madness.

The river swallowed Kanako's body hungrily, as if it, too, hadn't eaten much during the war. Her eyes were wide open as she hit the water. She tried to swim, but discovered that both her arms and one leg were useless, broken in the fall. Pain cut through her limbs, her spine and back teeth. The water doused her screams.

She discovered then that a lot of things go through a person's mind when drowning, whether in a river or a burning house. As Kanako's lungs filled with water, her mind's eye was watching her father count the money from the alms box. She was young, then, had just started school and wouldn't even consider stealing from the collection. The water swirled around her swollen legs, but in her memories she was laughing and running across the schoolyard on a sunny autumn day. She held up the rice cake she'd taken from Kono-chan, just because boys in the second grade were unbelievably easy to upset.

Her chest heaved. Muscles contracted so hard she thought her ribs might break. The images swept past her like a summer rainstorm. She was in the woods, allowing Kono a touch of her small breasts. It was also in the woods that she found Shoji, pretending to be reading. Always in the woods, where so many secrets live in the shadows.

The dead were counted the next day and stacked into a small pile on a grassy field just outside Kitagawa, on the opposite side of the Kaminohashi Shrine and what had been the Maruyama Chemical Plant. Several people had to do the counting, each more than once, because the number never added up the same twice. Many people were missing, and their absence seemed as odd as houses without roofs, or dogs without tails.

Kanako's body had washed ashore at the next town down the river. Joko was lucky they were able to return her body in time for the memorial service. They hadn't known who she was; just that she was carrying a good luck charm from the Kaminohashi Shrine. Her body arrived at the field where they were about to begin the cremation. She and a couple others, all dead, lay on the back of a cart drawn by an emaciated old horse.

The sun was high in the sky. It was close to lunchtime. The men helping to dig the pit and to gather hay to burn were looking at the horse with starving eyes. The horse, too, was too hungry to care. Joko was busy preparing for the service. There was no one else, because the abbot from the Fukanji temple was killed when the roof collapsed in the prayer hall. They had found him and the acolyte, burned to a crisp, clinging to each other like frightened birds.

In better times, money was gathered in the community to donate to the bereaved families for incense and to pay for the labour of digging the graves. After a bombing, though, no one knew when the planes would come next, so everyone helped to get rid of the dead in a hurry. The ditch diggers were volunteers. People brought their own incense. Straw and kindling were laid at the bottom of the pit, and over them the bodies were laid to rest for the last time.

Joko was falling into madness, unable even to get through the prayers. His white ceremonial robe evoked both mourning and surrender. He fell silent in the middle of a particularly whiny chant. He looked with bulging eyes at the pit containing the dozen or more bodies and seemed to recognize Kanako for the first time. A scream bubbled up his flabby throat. No one could tell whether he was flailing his arms out of despair as he leapt into the ditch or if his lumpy body simply lost its balance. He looked like a flag billowing crazily in a high wind. He fell out of their sight for just a second, then they heard a large animal's wail erupt from the pit. When some of them dared look inside, they saw Joko crawling over bodies to reach his daughter.

Yasujiro turned his head away. He hadn't slept since the bombing, tending to the injured at the hospital. He had treated Shoji after they found him on the ground near where the bridge used to be, his leg crushed under a tall, charred cedar. Ugly patches of purple and green mottled Shoji's face. Yasu knew his son would be sleeping for a long, long time—maybe forever.

He tried not to think about it now, as he inspected some of the unidentified dead bodies, many burned to cinder. An old man, bandages hiding half his face, approached Yasu. He bowed, crying out of his good eye, and thanked the bewildered doctor for saving his life when an oil lantern exploded in his face during the bombing. Yasu blinked. He could not remember ever seeing the man before.

He waved the man away. Yasu had always criticized the war, but it had never been so immediate, actually touching his skin as it was now. The stench of rotting bodies floated in a film in the air, falling onto him.

Among them lay the Nozaki boy, whom he had treated a few days earlier. He had given him Ryoko's ham. Burns covered most of his thin body, leaving him unable to breathe through his skin. He died alone among the confusion. Yasu noticed the boy was covered, too, with bandages, expertly tied. Yasujiro recalled vaguely that he'd seen the boy shortly after the bombs fell. He could not remember anything more specific about what he might have done or said. He remembered only the fatigue, and the cries that never stopped. He'd just kept working, not bothering to comfort the desperate, or to say goodbye to the hopeless.

The old man with the burned face would not stop bowing. He blubbered something incoherent through his swollen lips. Yasu was about to excuse himself to go home. His eyelids were as heavy as sacks of rice. He wanted only to crawl into his futon, let free a big fart and take a nap.

Kono suddenly appeared from the growing shadows. He took the old man by the shoulders, whispering into his ear the way people talk to runaway horses. It took a breath for Yasu to realize the old man was Kono's grandfather. Then Yasu noticed what young Kono was wearing—a formal Imperial Armed Forces uniform as stiff as the limbs on the dead in the ditch.

Kono saw Yasu staring with his mouth open. The young soldier grinned and saluted the crazy old doctor. Then, suddenly unsure of himself as only a boy his age can be, he also hastily bowed. "I wanted to come pay my respects before I left, Doctor. But then the bombers came, and . . ."

Pay his respects? To whom? To a crazy old man who believes the world in which he lives is the only thing more insane than he? Or to his son who lies alone in the hospital while he tends to the already dead? And how long until the young soldier, now impetuous and proud, joins the pathetic poor souls in the ditch?

Kono stared, eyes wide and bloodshot, at Yasu, who realized he'd been thinking aloud. But he didn't care. "Kono-kun," he added. "You should reconsider."

"I beg your pardon?"

"Don't go. Your ass will be blown into mincemeat."

Kono looked around him and saw the crowd staring. Then he looked back at Yasu. "But my orders . . ."

"Run," Yasu insisted. His voice grew more urgent, like an anxious lover's. "Run like the wind. I can help you."

"My God, will you be quiet?"

Ryoko rushed to her husband's side. Her hand floated in the air, uncertain. She wanted more than anything to cover her husband's mouth to keep him from saying more. But there were so many people around them, staring, whispering. She took the crook of his arm as forcefully as she could. There were a few more bodies to be thrown into the pit, but everyone had stopped working. This gave Joko time to climb out. Yasu looked at his wife's face, and fell silent.

Tamura, the *kempeitai* captain, materialized out of the air, as obtrusive as an uninvited dinner guest. Through grinding teeth, he muttered, "Dr. Hayakawa, I'll thank you not to distract this young man who has chosen to serve His Imperial Highness."

Who was this man? What gave him pleasure? What dreams did he dream? What was his favourite food? Yasu knew such specifics about the man were irrelevant. Tamura was the personification of all the evils of the Pacific War—of Japanese imperialism, of fascism, of prejudice, of stupidity. His was the face that was everywhere during the war but which no one would claim afterwards. He appeared out of nowhere and would disappear into thin air. For the time being, though, he was real, and apparently very upset. As always, he was carrying his sword.

Yasu was too tired to fight the tide that was pushing him out to a sea boiling over with anger. "The emperor is an inbred fool," he muttered, gently pushing Ryoko aside. Her knees gave way and she fell to the ground, cowering under her kimono sleeve. Yasu looked at her blankly.

There were many things that could not be said aloud during the war, and claiming the emperor was an inbred fool was definitely one of them. Tamura blinked, unsure of what he'd heard. Only a fraction of a breath later, his eyes settled. His face flushed.

"You people are mad," Yasu whispered. He turned to Kono, who was standing to the side, fiddling with his belt. "Be smart for once in your life," said Yasu. "Go home!"

"I beg your pardon!" Joko cried. He stood between Yasu and the pit, teetering as if the earth was moving beneath him. Dirt and blood stained his robe. He stood with his arms open, the wide sleeves swinging loosely. His eyes demanded vengeance, and it would be extracted, if not from the enemy, then from whoever was convenient.

"Dr. Hayakawa, there was a matter I wished to discuss at your home last night." Misguided satisfaction twisted Joko's face. "Rumour has it that you had an opportunity to capture that enemy pilot who got away a few weeks ago. That you were actually hiding him in your backyard in that monstrosity you call a shelter."

"Is this true?" Tamura asked, smiling. It was not as if he hadn't heard the rumour himself.

Yasu looked at the sky. There was no hope. He floated alone on a sea of mistrust and anger and fear. Whatever he said was lost among the waves.

Tamura fumbled with his sword handle. "Dr. Hayakawa, you will immediately withdraw your comments about the emperor."

He may as well have tried to stop a typhoon from forming. "As soon as that bastard emperor withdraws our troops!" Yasu heard himself shout. "That's when I'll retract my words, you pompous shit-for-brains bastard! I know where you shove that goddamn imitation antique sword handle when you're horny!"

Was madness saying just what was needed, or was it refraining from saying anything at all? The question ran through Yasu's mind like quicksilver.

Tamura took a firm grasp of his sword and drew it from its scabbard in one flawless motion. He'd always loved *kendo*, Japanese fencing, but could not stake claim to a samurai heritage. His name was Tamura, which meant rice paddy village. This was wartime, though, when anyone could become a *true* samurai. He had been practising his swordsmanship with even greater fervour, and it showed. In an uninterrupted arc, the blade rose, then fell onto Yasu's shoulder, slicing his upper torso diagonally across his heart and down to his opposite hip. The blood sprayed upward. Scarlet rain fell onto Tamura's face.

"No!" Ryoko rushed and held her husband by the shoulders. After a precarious struggle, she was dragged down by his falling body. When he fell over, it escaped no one's attention that he wasn't wearing a loincloth. Ryoko wailed, blood spreading across her robe, for once not caring what anyone around her saw. She lay crying for a long time. No one was able to sedate her, because the only doctor in town had just been chopped in two.

The town, for lack of a better solution, decided to cremate Yasu's mutilated body along with the rest of the dead. Because there was some confusion caused by the cold-blooded murder occurring in the light of day, they did not get around to the mass cremation until evening. A layer of the dead, including Yasu and

Kanako, hid the straw and kindling at the bottom of the pit, and another layer of straw covered the corpses.

Finally, it was time to light the fire, but like many things about the war, there was nothing glorious or dramatic about the ceremony. Joko muttered on in a painful monotone as he waved a wand with a banner of folded paper on its tip. The hay and the kindling smouldered. There was smoke everywhere but no fire. Tamura barked an order, and some gasoline was poured onto the dead. A shaft of flame billowed from within the pit.

By now, the moon floated above the mountain peaks. Tamura assigned Kono to stand guard, making sure the fire did not die until the dead had turned to ash. As the gases inside the bodies expanded from the heat, many of them burst. Usually, it was the belly that exploded, sending methane gas into the flames, which ignited into a mesmerizing blue ball of light. Watching these flares shoot upward and fade made Kono shiver. Dying did not scare him. A fear of ghosts, on the other hand, was different.

The next day it rained. All Otama could hear through the half-open window was the sound of water beating the ground like a *taiko* festival drum. Shoji lay before her, still unconscious on the cot. Ryoko was at home. She hadn't stopped crying since yesterday. She did not stop sobbing even for the short time sleep and fatigue claimed her.

Otama thought maybe she should look for a kettle and boil some water for tea. A guest always meant tea, even when everything else in the world had gone stark raving mad. The only other thing she could hear in Yasu's office, barely audible beneath the relentless beating of the rain, was Shoji's deep, regular breathing. Shima sat on a chair, watching his friend's chest rise and fall underneath a blanket. He sat perfectly still. A tiny pearl of water fell every once in a while from his face onto his lap. His clothes were drenched. Otama was shocked to see he hadn't bothered to bring an umbrella. But this made it easier to hide the fact that sometimes you can do nothing to hold back the tears.

On his lap lay the book, also wet and worn, the cheap paper soaked in rain and tears. It was the *Harmonice Mundi*. The book that Shoji had forgotten at the foot of the tree, the one that never ceased to cause Shima anguish for the rest of his life. He curled his hand into a fist and ground his teeth together. Suddenly he brought his hand down on the book's cover. Then he did the same with the other hand, then the other.

He had gone the previous day to the Kaminohashi Shrine to deliver some fish he had caught in the Kita River. Their silver bodies hung from a strand of rope. He had little else to offer. He imagined Kanako's surprise when he handed them to her.

It was another hot day. The air was wet and heavy. Rocks were scattered across the path winding through the woods, and lost in his daydream he tripped over one. It was as he was getting up that he saw the book at the foot of a tree. He noticed the smell of the fish that were scattered on the ground. The light somehow no longer looked the same.

"Shoji forgot it when he came to visit me last night," Kanako said as he bent over to pick it up. He hadn't noticed her standing there. She gathered up the fish, and gave them back to him. He'd forgotten he'd brought them for her.

Kanako smiled, like everyone smiled before telling secrets. "Shoji and Kono-chan are just the same, Shima-chan. Did you know that? They're just the same."

Shima's fists were starting to bleed. Crimson blotches mottled the wet paper. The pounding frightened Otama so much that she left the room to find the kettle. Tea always calmed things down, she told herself. Brew some tea, and everything will be fine. Shima kept hitting the book, over and over, as though it would eventually give forth something in response. He was no longer sure where the nightmares began or ended.

THE TRUTH

"THE WORLD CRIES OUT ITS DESPAIR!" SHOUTED THE
holy man outside Terminal 3 at Pearson Airport. He was chasing
tourists away with a Bible in one hand and a rolled-up newspaper
in the other. Bloodstains that looked like bursts of fireworks were
splattered around the headline about the war in Bosnia. The newspaper really was black and white and red all over.

He wore a white dog collar, and a tattered shirt over suit pants
that looked like they'd been dragged through the sewer. His eyes
said they saw the devil everywhere he turned. Kei didn't notice him
until he got too close.

Hawke suddenly appeared, and shoved the holy man aside as
though waving away a fly. The holy man flew onto the mountain
of suitcases. An old, rusted Ford Bronco was parked at the curb.
Hawke opened the passenger door as quickly as he had dealt with
the holy man. "Fuck you!" the holy man yelled, struggling to get
up. "God fuck you to hell!"

"How was your flight?" Hawke asked, shoving Kei into the truck.

The bright afternoon sun's glare across the windshield made
everything beyond a ghost world. As Kei settled into his seat, the

engine turned over loudly and the truck started to glide forward. The engine was deafening.

"Thanks for coming to get me," Kei said above the din. Hawke waved the formality away with an open bag of plain Doritos.

Feeling the steady rhythm of the lampposts passing by, Kei thought about Telly. All the years they had spent together, yet he was gone now nonetheless. So were Mildred and Rosie. Mr. Man, too. And now, Toshi and Angie might be deserting him as well. He wasn't sure how he felt about that. Hawke was finished with the Doritos, so he threw the empty bag out the window. The headwind whipped it out of his hands. Kei wanted to think about what he would do now, but his eyes drifted to the side mirror. He saw the Doritos bag in the distance.

Hawke offered him a beer from a cooler behind the seat, but Kei shook his head. He was too tired. Not enough sleep lately. Mitsuyo would not have reached him last night at all had he been drinking as usual instead of going to bed early. He'd absent-mindedly picked up the phone when it pulled him roughly from a reverie of melodies and colour. He often played a familiar piece of music in his head to lull himself to sleep. At times, some Dvorak. Bach's fifth Brandenburg was also nice. Just never one of his own songs.

In the stark darkness of a nameless motel, he had finally settled on "Summer Song" by Louis Armstrong. The melody sung by the raspy, dark-chocolate voice was turning over slowly behind his closed eyelids, like the sun shifting the shadows of trees on a playground full of kids. Then the phone rang. What Mitsuyo had to say was not unexpected. He was surprised, though, that she would be so eager to play snitch.

"Rodney called," Hawke remarked. "He said everyone freaked when they found out you were gone. He sounded pretty fucked up." Hawke chuckled. Kei knew Hawke had never approved of Telly being replaced. "Anyway, I told him I didn't know where you were."

Kei only nodded, though Hawke was driving and was not looking at him.

"Don't fucking worry about it, Kei. Just do whatever it is you have to do."

Kei was mildly amused at how Hawke had become the only remaining person he trusted. At the Twisted Neon, there were countless times when Hawke put himself between Kei and some abusive drunk without a moment's hesitation. "I've got this thing where I compulsively step in front of belligerent people," he once explained. "I think it's an attention thing. I was a middle child, you know."

After they became friends, Hawke told Kei once that he used to be a defensive lineman on his high-school football team. He wasn't half bad, he said, until his knees blew out in grade twelve. Any talk of football made Kei think of the Whitefish Gumbos and O'Connor. Yet Hawke and Head had been together for a long time, and Kei had become accustomed to Hawke's adoration. Hawke never seemed to grow tired of his music and the band.

The Bronco pulled off the expressway. It passed by a schoolyard, where white kids, black kids, kids in turbans as well as yellow kids tumbled over one another like a fruit basket falling over. Kei watched them wistfully as they ran, climbed and laughed together. Still, he suspected that even now Pearl Harbor must come up once in a while in schoolyards, and some Japanese kids were running home every day after school.

The Bronco drove by three hot dog carts sitting in a row. Behind each sat a vendor, a tired-looking woman and two weary men. None of them seemed interested in selling anyone a dog. A few feet away, a little girl stood with skinned knees, crying, while her mother ignored her. Catastrophes were happening all the time, beyond anyone's control. The most anyone could do was try to manage the manner in which they reacted to the catastrophes. Their reactions defined them. Kei recalled that the way Shoji had reacted to finding Mitsuyo in Shima's arms was to do absolutely nothing.

The street in front of the house was empty when the truck pulled up to the curb. Just as time could stretch and shrink like a neurotic inchworm, so could space. Picasso knew this. So did the Japanese *ukiyo-e* printmakers. Walking up the steps to the front porch, Kei had time to notice the discarded paper coffee cups and the cracks in the concrete. He walked slowly because he could tell, though there was no movement inside, that someone was home. The steps went on endlessly. So did the porch with all its rotting wood. Then, abruptly, Kei found that his hand had reached the doorknob.

The door opened without a sound onto the living room, dimly lit in the late afternoon. Kei could see through to the back of the house, where Toshi and Angie sat side by side at the large kitchen table. As he drew near, he saw a plate of doughnuts and two mugs of coffee on the table in front of them. A long-forgotten image flashed past Kei's eyes. It was of the Japanese doll festival and the emperor and empress figurines, perched on their platform like an elderly couple in love with each other all their lives. Hawke shook his head and sighed. He removed his glasses and rubbed his eyes. Some things you could see coming a mile away. Kei felt the anger rising even before Angie said anything.

"Kei," she said, standing up. "You're home." Kei found it hard to tell whether she was smiling. A walking, breathing Mona Lisa. Her flaming hair fell across the front of her sweater.

"Home," said Kei softly, "is where you get screwed up the ass."

"What are you doing here?" Toshi asked. The normally docile eyes were challenging, defiant. "I thought you weren't coming back for a couple more weeks."

Music flowed from the stereo in the living room—Pavarotti

singing "Nessun dorma." Despite himself, Kei couldn't help closing his eyes and listening. Such wondrous passion. Opera was a world of extremes, and that was why he adored it. He opened his eyes and saw Angie looking at him. Even in the dim light, he could see her skin was perfect, but perfection did not deserve to last. It existed to be ruined. He heard himself laughing softly as he reached out to take a handful of her hair.

He pulled hard, and she fell to the floor. "Get out." He spoke softly, but the words that fell from his mouth were scalding. "Get the fuck out of here, and don't ever come back."

Toshi hesitated. Raising a hand against Kei did not come naturally to him. Still, he saw Angie crumpled on the floor. Her feet were bare and her toenails painted bright red, and he remembered how he loved her. Then the anger came easy.

"Don't touch her!" he yelled, and lunged at his brother for the first time in his life. Rage painted everything in front of him a bright white, and for a fleeting but luxurious moment, he felt indestructible. But a massive shadow moved across his path, and a sudden, sharp pain ran from his wrist to his shoulder. He screamed and threw his body against Hawke, who'd taken hold of his hand. Toshi saw the ceiling flip, and then there was nothing in front of his face but the floor.

Toshi propped himself against the wall, his shoulders quaking. "Fuck you!" he cried out. Hawke was grinning, wordlessly daring him to come at him again. Kei stood behind Hawke's broad shoulders, watching the floor. "Fuck you, Kei!" Toshi said again.

"Kei, will you listen to me?" Angie was still on her knees. Her hands covered her eyes and were wet with tears. "My God, please just listen to me. I'm so lonely. You never talk to me any more. You're away for weeks at a time, and when you do come home, it's still like you're not here. What the hell am I supposed to do?"

"Fuck you!" Toshi tried one last time, but the only one who was looking at him was Hawke. Kei, and even Angie, didn't seem to hear him.

Moving slowly, he started for the front door. The air felt like an anvil on his shoulders. The voices emanating from the walls and the floor were deafening. Walking through the living room, he vaguely noticed movement at the top of the stairs. He saw Mitsuyo looking down at him. She was wearing a wig that didn't fit her, in size or colour. He also noticed for the first time how she looked so much older than she was. Since when had she grown so thin? How sallow her skin? How hollow her eyes? She wore a pink Sailor Moon smock, stained with what looked like shit but in fact was miso. Greasy strands of greying hair sprouted from beneath the wig. Toshi was afraid that if he blinked, Mitsuyo would wither to dust and leftover hair.

From somewhere beyond the crowd of voices in his head, he could barely hear Angie calling his name. He had no idea where he was going, just like he had no idea what Angie really wanted. Why was she looking at Kei as though he still mattered to her? He stumbled out onto the deserted street. The day filled his ears with the ocean's rush. The autumn sun toasted the pavement, which hummed its approval seductively. Blades of dying grass celebrated their demise with impassioned songs. At first he thought about heading toward Queen Street, but then he looked beyond the cars crawling on the expressway and saw the blue waters moving languidly in Lake Ontario.

The sun in May was warm and nurturing. Their spirits soared on the breeze as they rode their Schwinn Stingrays. Telly and Toshi had the larger bikes, so they rode ahead, slowing down every few blocks for Scotty and Kei to catch up. There was little talking. Telly was Kei's friend and Scotty was Toshi's. There were private jokes and secrets that could not be betrayed. Only the sun looking down on them saw everything.

In their knapsacks, they carried the sandwiches Mitsuyo had made. Ham, with mustard, on white bread, potato chips and Coke. There were also those mysterious Twinkies and Ding Dongs, which never grew stale. They were like vampires.

The waves from Lake Michigan lapped at the rocks. Small dead shiners were scattered about the water and the sand. Toshi thought the thin, layered clouds above the horizon looked like shiny fish scales. The lake looked like an ocean, and the air smelled like the sea.

The beach was private, owned by whoever lived in the immense houses sleeping on the cliffs overhead. The boys didn't care. The lake drew them forth from their awkwardness. They laughed loudly and swore with abandon. For a moment, they forgot about the differences in their ages and trampled the grey water's edge, giggling. They splashed water at each other, screamed, fell a few times, and laughed some more.

Toshi lost his balance and fell into the water. The hum of the earth was a deafening roar underwater. But was it noise or music? When his head surfaced, he could hear only the weak chirping of birds. He dove again beneath his own reflection to listen to the earth some more. His lungs protested when they were forced to breathe Lake Michigan. He resisted the urge to stand up. He truly wanted to understand whether what he heard was noise or music, the latter being some sort of expression. He wanted to understand what the world was trying to tell him.

He was about to black out when Telly grabbed him by the back of his neck and dragged him to shore, where he promptly threw up. There was a lot of swearing and laughing around him. He looked at the water wistfully, but knew he lacked the courage to try again.

But he had been a kid, then, and the shouting and the screaming in his head now were becoming unbearably painful. He needed to silence them, or drown them with something else. He walked weakly, struggling for balance, following the highway along its side until he came to an underpass that opened out onto the lakeshore. As he walked under the bridge, the cars passing on the Gardiner Expressway above him seemed to be calling down to him in anger. *Where the fuck do you think you're going, Chink?* He waved his middle finger above his head. Only some pigeons and a couple of seagulls saw him, and they paid him no mind.

Traffic was moving fast on Lakeshore Boulevard, beyond which lay the park and the beach. The afternoon reflected off cars running hurriedly off to who knew where. An undercurrent of anxious anger flowed under the tires, though there was nothing apparent to be angry about. The boulevard was six lanes wide, not counting the turning and merging lanes.

Toshi looked across the street, past joggers and cyclists and couples lounging on park benches, to the glimmering lights on the surface of the lake, shifting and changing with the hum in his head. He started laughing when he saw how close he was now. Maybe things were finally going to start making sense. He was so pleased he did not notice that he was walking against a red light. No one could blame the driver of the van that hit him as he stepped off the curb.

Toshi heard the van's horn blaring. He felt his ribs break and his stomach explode. There was surprisingly little pain, although his breath filled with a warmth that made him gag. He landed, hard, and heard braking tires and desperate, frantic voices dancing in the air above him. He wanted to turn his head to see what was going on, but nothing moved. When he opened his eyes, he could only see the asphalt beneath his face, but shadows rushed past at the periphery of his vision. He closed his eyes again, and smiled.

He felt warm and lazy, and he began to swim in the vast, black ocean that spread behind his eyelids.

When Shoji died, Toshi had imagined his father was confronted by a wall of mirrors. Because each mirror contained all the light from every moment in time, the wall became a curtain of luminosity that was brighter than the brightest star. Toshi understood now for the first time that the unceasing hum that he'd heard all his life was coming from this light. He choked again on his breath. He supposed correctly that he was now dead or dying.

He felt naked, but was beyond caring. His thoughts were calm and coherent for the first time that he could remember. He saw the blanket of light folding outward into a quantum field. He felt the vibrations of shimmering strings that seemed to keep the whole thing together.

Toshi could see amoebas forming back when life on Earth was in its infancy. He saw the glaciers moving through the valleys among the Rocky Mountains. He thought he saw Adam and Eve, and aliens coming to Earth, making a few pyramids and leaving, never to return. He saw Chinese contractors swearing like the devil when first presented with the plans of the Great Wall. Toshi saw the first Thanksgiving feast, at which someone complained the turkey was too dry.

Some things he saw pained his heart. Poor souls, frayed by human cruelty, wandered the spiritual wasteland that was Hiroshima, Auschwitz, Nanjing and countless other places in other times. There were also smaller catastrophes that he could not bear to watch. As many birds as there were stars died among Toronto high-rises and in the silence of pine forests. Children dropped their ice cream cones, over and over and over again.

We made it, Toshi! We made it!

Toshi's awareness, coloured with the hues across the spectrum, folded outward like inverse origami. He heard Shoji's voice and felt his presence. He also heard and felt his grandparents, and even Kei and Angie and Mitsuyo, who, he knew, weren't dead yet. The idea twisted his mind into a pretzel, and yet he felt a sublime joy. Outside time, everything that *will* happen *has* happened. Just as much as Toshi could see all of the past, he could see all of the future. He saw how his mother would die one day, and Kei and Angie and Telly and Hawke, each in their own time. He saw the death of every living thing that ever occupied, or would occupy, a part of reality.

Around him were countless souls. They were separate, yet united in this awareness of each other. Like water molecules in a vast ocean. He felt his father's spirit, still characterized by a physicist's curiosity, confronted by this same vast understanding of time and space that could only be seen from this place. He was aware of his grandmothers, whose souls were free of all the pettiness of having to treat their children as adults. He was also surrounded by those who were to die at some time in the future. He was apart from Mitsuyo, and yet was with her. He had left Angie behind, and yet they were reunited in this place that was at once a part of life yet distant.

He saw all these things—and infinitely more—at once. It did not even take an instant, because he was now outside time, where words like "instant" and "moment" were without meaning. And the light he saw was not light as it existed physically—light implied the movement of photons and movement implied time. The light Toshi saw was more an awareness that contrasted itself with darkness. The hues of this light characterized the moment. Some moments were coloured by jealousy and pettiness. Others by benevolence and charity.

Surely nothing—no words, no symbols, no vestiges of human spirit—can hold meaning over eternity, when even mountains erode and the seas evaporate. Toshi saw his father writing these words in a letter to Kei. Toshi now knew Shoji had been wrong.

There was indeed something that held meaning across all these catastrophes. A truth linked a microscopic virus on a planet in a faraway solar system with grass that grew on Earth. It coloured the moment when a mother got up at night to nurse her baby. Its hue permeated through every dawn. It was especially bright in spring. It shaded letters from a lost love, and the face of a son who looked up from his mother's grave. Most important to Toshi, it filled the moment his father died in the hospital room one rainy day in Milwaukee.

It was a kind of love, a state of attraction, though not just that. It was also selflessness, which was best manifest in the most difficult task any living thing undertakes—forgiveness. It was easy to desire another. It was even easy to sacrifice everything for a love that was reciprocated. To forgive a trespass, though—to love even when it meant being humiliated, hated or forgotten—required something more.

Kei would never be certain what it was, exactly, that made him follow Toshi out of the house. There just didn't seem to be anything more to say—to Angie, to anyone. Nor did he really understand how he knew his brother had headed for the lake. Maybe he knew Toshi better than he cared to admit. He thought about this as he, too, started to make his way toward the expressway. At first he walked, then his steps turned into a light jog. "Toshi!" he yelled. He shouted his brother's name, over and over, as if nothing but the name mattered. Funnily enough, for a brief time, nothing else did.

He crossed underneath the Gardiner Expressway onto the Lakeshore, and knew the moment he saw the crowd who would be lying at its centre. He elbowed through the circle of people. Kei shouted things he would not be able to recall later, but stopped abruptly when he saw his brother. Toshi looked like a giant tabby cat lying on its side. Blood poured from his nose and mouth, and his shoulders were twisted in a strange way. "Don't move him!"

someone shrieked, but Kei could not hear. Nor could he resist kneeling down and cradling Toshi's head, which seemed to carry all the weight of the past.

When his father died, it seemed fitting to Kei that his family alone had gathered in the sterile hospital room. Ever since they left Japan, all they had were each other, so it was only appropriate that they be together by themselves for the last few moments before everything would irrevocably change. Now, too, when he understood his brother was dying in his arms, Kei could not imagine Toshi's death coming to pass any other way. Kei, who would run home ahead of Toshi, embarrassed to be seen with him—who used to kick Toshi as he lay in the school hallway with his forehead against the floor. All his life, Toshi had been nothing more to Kei than an irritating presence, a grating noise. Kei alone would bear witness to his brother's demise because there was no one else more apt, nor more obligated.

Toshi opened his eyes slowly and saw Kei's face contorted in pain as if he was the one who'd just been run over. Toshi smiled, enjoying the warmth of toasted asphalt beneath his back. There were voices around them, shouting something about how Toshi had just stepped in front of the moving van, and how an accident victim shouldn't be tampered with. None of this seemed to matter very much. Someone said to Kei that an ambulance was on its way. That wasn't going to be necessary either, Toshi knew. He wasn't staying. He could tell from the cold in his hands and feet, the warmth oozing around his throat.

He couldn't breathe without inhaling his own blood. There was something he had to say, though, because he would not have another chance. Toshi looked into the deep, rich pool in Kei's eyes and reached up to touch his brother's face. Kei looked down, and Toshi saw him crying for the first time in a long time. Toshi tried to say, "I forgive you," but wound up gurgling, "Gai gorgiive gyuuu."

Kei must have understood somehow, because his eyes were cloudy, even as he tried his best to smile. He tried to say something but choked, and only nodded in reply.

Still grinning, Toshi fainted and Kei buried his face in his brother's bloodied shirt. Traffic had come to a standstill in both directions, though the sun never stopped shining.

WATER

ON THE MORNING OF SHOJI'S FUNERAL, TOSHI HELD tightly on to his sweet-and-sour-smelling sheets, as if he would fly away otherwise. His dreams were dark and shapeless, but when he opened his eyes, he saw the sun was shining through the trees outside his window. He coughed a few times and lit a cigarette.

Kei was still snoring in the next room. He'd been sleeping a lot since he got home. It was as if he was trying to get away, not back to Toronto, where he lived in that dilapidated apartment with Angie, Telly, Millie and Mr. Man, but to another time when the room was truly his. Angie had flown in last night, barely in time for today's service, because all she and Kei could afford were stand-by tickets. Mitsuyo wasn't about to pay for anybody who wasn't family. Toshi knew Angie was probably already up and out on her daily walk.

He listened. It was hard to tell whether or not Mitsuyo was awake. The only time he was sure was when he heard her sobbing. It wasn't long before he heard her yelling downstairs. "Get down here for breakfast! We've got a lot to do today, you idiots!"

The memorial service took place in a chapel in a funeral home not far from the university campus. Shoji had been cremated a few days earlier. His body had been moved there the morning after he died. They had gone to fill out documents that said Shoji had indeed died, and that it was in fact Shoji who had died. Someone, Toshi realized, had to keep track of the comings and goings of people.

Mitsuyo spent an hour deciding on the casket. She chose one of the most expensive, because of the ornate gold handles that lined its sides. The majestic coffin, it turned out, contrasted awkwardly with the cremator, a furnace that looked much like any other oven, except it was much bigger. The control knobs were on the wall of the room. The paint on the ceiling was cracked. No prayer. No music. Kei knew his father would have liked that.

There were prayer and music, though, at the memorial service that was Buddhist, as arranged by Mitsuyo. It was not unlike the funeral held for her father, so many years ago, except Shoji had no choice but to be at this one. He sat smugly in an urnful of his ashes on a table at the front of the room.

The weather that day in Milwaukee was cloudy with sunny breaks, with ten per cent chance of rain. There was a cool breeze, so all of the aging professors wore trench coats. Inside the chapel, they filed into rows of grey and greying hair. With eyes trying to focus behind wire-rimmed glasses, they sat waiting for the service to begin with the patience of those who had glimpsed the physical intricacies of the universe. There were three Protestants, one Catholic, another Hindu, four Muslims, a couple of Catholics turned Buddhists, but mostly they were atheists, as Shoji himself had been. They saw an empty void beyond the workings of a particle accelerator or the alphanumeric equations scattered across the blackboard.

The Buddhist priest was chatting up a Methodist minister who'd just ended her service and was hanging around with time to kill. They sat and talked under the bare wooden cross that cut into the pillar of light descending from the skylight. The shadow of the cross fell on the empty bench in front of the pipe organ.

The priest replaced his smile with solemn reverence just before he stepped up to the lectern.

"Within a system, a change in one component affects all others—a change such as death, for example. No one is feeling the effects of death today as much as the family of the deceased, but even the most distant planet in our solar system has been affected in some small way by the departure from this world of a single soul."

There were lesser truths. Toshi felt warm knowing that the effects of his father dying would ripple across space and be felt in galaxies on the other side of the universe. The priest rambled on for a few minutes, then chanted a guttural prayer. Mitsuyo pursed her lips.

Kei scanned the room. His fingers curled into fists when he found he could not spot Shima. There had been no fax, no telegram, nor anything else to indicate that he'd once been Shoji's best friend, and his wife's lover. Kei just moments earlier had learned that a woman from Greece who never even knew his father but simply admired his work had flown in for the service.

Although he wasn't terribly successful yet, Kei was aware already just how much his music could move people. He simply didn't realize science could affect people the same way. Chet Wilkins hobbled up to the lectern on one foot to say how much he missed Shoji on campus. How brilliant was Shoji's mind. How much he enjoyed showing Shoji's family the American ways. Then he cautioned everyone on the perils of using household hardware. "It only takes a moment," he said, and the priest nodded gravely.

Then Kei stood up and sang, accompanying himself on an acoustic guitar. It was a song he'd written himself, but one that Angie had presented to him as if it were a stranger on the night they met.

"Falling through starlight down to a sea of mist,
You take me under to a colder place."

With nothing to take away from his melody and lyrics, the song became as spiritual and haunting as any traditional folk ballad. By the time he strummed the last chord, countless eyes were shimmering among the pews, like stars revolving in some tragic constellation. Even Mitsuyo's lips were trembling. Angie smiled. This was what Kei did best.

The priest closed the service by inviting everyone, on behalf of the family, to a buffet at Mr. Lee's restaurant. Mr. Lee, who had been crying even before Kei played his guitar, suddenly straightened up, as if he'd remembered the last obligation he had to his oldest and best customer. Dinner would begin in two hours, the priest said. The family had something to which they had to attend first.

They drove to the beach on the shore of Lake Michigan, where, a lifetime ago, Toshi and Kei came for picnics with Scotty and Telly. The sun burst forth from among the clouds as Angie slipped off her shoes and stockings, squeezing the sand between her toes. Mitsuyo looked at her blankly, then did the same. Kei left his shoes on, and Toshi did whatever Kei did. The wind was strong, but not unpleasant. It capped the waves with shimmering white tiaras. They stood watching the lake breathing for a while. Toshi nervously held on to the urn containing Shoji's ashes. They could see a couple pushing a stroller in the distance down the beach.

Although no one said anything, each could feel everyone else's discomfort. How did Shoji come up with this bright idea anyway? Did he see it in a movie? Why were they all there? Kei squinted into the horizon, shading his eyes with his hand. He imagined the water flowing from the St. Lawrence through the other Great Lakes. He felt time floating away, into the Mississippi to the Gulf of Mexico. He thought about the priest's sermon. He motioned for his brother to give him the urn.

Toshi looked at Mitsuyo, who didn't move. Kei motioned again. Toshi placed his father's remains in his brother's arms, glad to be relieved of the responsibility. With his shoes still on, Kei walked down to the water's edge, and didn't hesitate at all before stepping in. He struggled for balance among the waves, which were higher than they seemed from shore. They churned the water and lifted the sand from the lake's floor. He removed the lid from the urn, which glittered gold in the afternoon sun. The wind shouted into his ears.

"God speed, old man!" he cried out, as he turned the urn upside down. "We'll see you on the other side!" The ashes disappeared as soon as they mingled with the grains of sand waiting in the water, drifting underneath the reflection of the sky.

The couple with the stroller came up to Mitsuyo and Angie as they stood a few feet apart from each other, fidgeting and sobbing. The man and the woman, confident, young, tanned and well-dressed in expensive casuals, looked at Kei, hip-deep in Lake Michigan in his suit. They turned to each other, puzzled. Wearing their brightly coloured sweatshirts and designer jeans, they weren't used to uncertainty. They didn't like it.

Their baby was bald, blue-eyed and beautiful. He smiled at the sky, the sun, the sand and the waves like they were the most entertaining things in the world. He turned to Toshi, and for a moment, their eyes met. The baby choked back a giggle when Toshi waved, a wave too small to be threatening. They held each other's gaze, each slightly puzzled by the other's familiarity. Toshi listened to the sound of waves growing louder. The rush of wind fell into harmony. The combined roar became a wall of sound. Nervousness lifted like a bad dream.

Toshi glanced at Kei thrashing about in the lake. He'd dropped the urn. He was swearing like a sailor looking for it, his hands invisible beneath the lake's surface, groping in the murky waters. A few times, he thrust his head underwater, as if this might clarify things he could not comprehend.

When Toshi turned back around, the parents were wheeling the stroller toward the parking lot. From behind, all Toshi could see of the baby were the tiny hands and the chubby fingers clawing at the air. Toshi grinned, and noticed for the first time that there wasn't a cloud in the sky. The wind and the water were already washing away the stroller's tracks.

Acknowledgements

My heartfelt thanks go to:

My dear friend and editor, Meg Taylor, who makes my wishes come true; my tag-team agents, Suzanne Brandreth and Dean Cooke; Maya Mavjee and the tireless troops at Doubleday Canada; Ted Goossen (the empanadas and beer were delicious); Malcolm Lester; Shaun Oakey; Don Christie; Keiko Tanaka; Noriko, Hisako and Toku Yabuki; and my parents for the stories.

And to my children, Aria, Kai and Koji, for all the joy; and my wife, Linda, without whom none of this would be possible or worthwhile.

About the Author

Rui Umezawa was born in Tokyo and spent his childhood in Italy, the United States, and Canada. His short stories have been published in *Descant* magazine, and he is included in *AWOL: Tales for Travel-Inspired Minds* (Vintage Canada). He has a black belt in karate and performs as a storyteller, drawing on traditional Japanese folk tales. Rui Umezawa lives in Toronto with his wife and their three children.